HIS
FACE
IS THE
SUN

MICHELLE JABÈS CORPORA

HIS FACE IS THE SUN

HODDER CHILDREN'S BOOKS

First published in Great Britain in 2025 by Hodder & Stoughton Limited
This paperback edition published in Great Britain in 2026 by
Hodder & Stoughton Limited
First published in the United States in 2025 by Sourcebooks

1 3 5 7 9 10 8 6 4 2

Text copyright © Michelle Jabès Corpora, 2025

Cover Illustration copyright © Micaela Alcaino, 2025
Map and chapter header art by Gerralt Landman

The moral right of the author has been asserted.

*All characters and events in this publication, other than those clearly
in the public domain, are fictitious and any resemblance to
real persons, living or dead, is purely coincidental.*

All rights reserved.
No part of this publication may be reproduced, stored in
a retrieval system, or transmitted, in any form or by any means, without
the prior permission in writing of the publisher, nor be otherwise circulated
in any form of binding or cover other than that in which it is published
and without a similar condition including this condition being
imposed on the subsequent purchaser.

A CIP catalogue record for this book
is available from the British Library.

ISBN 978 1 444 97740 0
WTS ISBN 978 1 444 98679 2

Printed and bound in Great Britain by Clays Ltd, Elcograf S.p.A.

The paper and board used in this book
are made from wood from responsible sources.

Hodder Children's Books
An imprint of
Hachette Children's Group
Part of Hodder & Stoughton Limited
Carmelite House
50 Victoria Embankment
London EC4Y 0DZ

The authorised representative in the EEA is Hachette Ireland,
8 Castlecourt Centre, Dublin 15, D15 XTP3, Ireland (email: info@hbgi.ie)

An Hachette UK Company
www.hachette.co.uk

www.hachettechildrens.co.uk

TO MY FATHER:
*Whose stories of his life in Egypt
are the reason this book exists*

AND TO THOTH:
*Thank you for the words
Thank you for the wisdom
Thank you for the magic*

PROLOGUE
PAWS

The cat's belly was heavy with the night's kill. She padded across the palace's polished floor, wet paw prints shining in her wake. Her tail flicked irritably. She'd been hunting in the garden when the storm hit, sudden and fierce, catching her just as she'd pounced on her prey. True, the mouse had satisfied her appetite, but her fur was soaked. Aside from falling into the river or having her tail pulled by one of the toddling palace nunus, it was the worst thing that had ever happened to her.

Outside, the storm continued to batter the palace walls, the sound not unlike the *shhh* of the khamasin wind blowing through papyrus reeds. For the third time, the cat stopped to shake herself from nose to tail, annoyed to be subjected to such discomfort. Damp air flowed through the corridor, and the torchlight danced. It illuminated scenes pictured on the walls, giving the impression that the kings painted there moved of their own volition—hunting and worshipping in colors bright with yellow ochre, umber, and malachite.

The cat remembered several of the painted pharaohs—the scowling one with the big ears, who'd had a voice like a guinea fowl; the one crowned as a boy, who'd never lived to become a man. She'd known them both, flattening her ears against the squawking commands of the former, taking bits of meat under the table from the fingers of the latter.

After that came the previous king, pictured with his weapon arm raised to smite the enemy kneeling at his feet. The palace had been loud and crowded during his reign. Her tail had been trod upon by pounding feet more than once, and everyone was too preoccupied to pay her any heed. But then he, too, was gone.

The new king hadn't been around for very long, but the cat already liked him better than his predecessor. He'd bent to pet her once, and often left out half-eaten plates of food for others to clean up behind him.

The cat was only too happy to oblige.

Sometimes, she wondered if she'd lived too long. Every time the palace filled with a new king and his servants and family, she stopped to wonder if, in all the excitement, she'd forgotten to die. Then again, no one seemed to have a problem with her continued presence. On the contrary, they treated the cat as if she were a god. The people even threw a special festival every year in her honor. There was music and dancing in the streets, and servants brought great steaming platters of meat for her to sample.

It was really quite nice.

One day, she'd sniffed at the garland of fresh flowers a priest had placed around her neck and thought: *Maybe I am a god*. After so many years of worship, it was easy to believe it was true.

In the corridor, she paused at her own image on the wall. The cat knew it was her because they'd painted her wearing her favorite gold-beaded collar. In the portrait, she was frozen in the act of catching a bird in the marshes, rearing up on her hind legs, her mouth open to catch and to bite.

It's a fine likeness, she thought. *Noble. Impressive. But are my stripes still so black? My teeth so sharp?*

Perhaps time had caught up with her, after all.

The cat sighed. She was wet, cold, and tired. The mice, it seemed, got faster with every passing season. And hadn't the multiplicity of kings already given her all this place had to offer? What good was it to be a weary god in a tedious world?

Feeling sorry for herself, she continued on her way, off to find a soft place to lick the rain from her body.

She was turning toward the servants' quarters when a high, primal keening echoed through the corridor. The sound stopped for a moment, as if to breathe, and then began again, the same as before.

The cat's ears swiveled, listening. She desperately longed for the warm crook of a maidservant's legs, her preferred resting place for the night. But that sound...it called to her. Finally succumbing to her curious nature, she crept on silent paws toward the fearsome lamentation.

She followed the shrieks to a portal covered with a blousy curtain, firelight leaking through the thin fabric. Within, other voices, hushed with worry, joined the keening cry. The cat slipped through, barely disturbing the curtain as she went.

The heat inside the chamber was oppressive, the air salty with sweat. There was a table, and a low bed painted in gold. In the center of the chamber, a naked woman squatted on two large bricks placed hip's width apart on the tile floor. Her copper skin glistened. Attendants in white sheath dresses flanked her on either side, mopping her brow as she cried out with that unearthly noise. Her belly hung between her legs, as large and round as the moon.

One of the attendants nodded rhythmically, murmuring, "Make strong her heart, and keep safe the child. Make strong her heart, and keep safe the child…"

The other attendant was silent, her eyes flicking back and forth between her lady and the door. She was a solid girl, her thick, calloused hands supporting the woman's body with unwavering strength.

As the naked woman's cry faded to silence, the attendant took a deep breath. "Your vapors have gone cold, my queen," she said, indicating the dish of water positioned between the birthing bricks. "Shall I fetch you more hot water? Perhaps it will ease your suffering."

The queen panted, a single bead of sweat clinging to the tip of her nose. "The only thing that will ease my suffering," she growled, "is the arrival of my nurse. Where is she, Nebet? Where are the priests? It's an ill omen for a child to be born without the gods' words in his ears, but I cannot wait much longer."

Nebet looked desperate. "I don't know, my queen. This storm is unlike anything I've experienced before. Even for the growing season. Perhaps the nurse and the others are caught in its grip and have been delayed—"

"Delayed?" the queen moaned as her labor pains intensified. "For the birth of a king? They had better be *dead*!" Her face twisted in agony, and she began to wail once more. Nebet and the other attendant winced and held the queen's arms tighter as the pain crested, then ebbed.

Once she could speak again, the queen gasped, "Open the curtain! I cannot breathe!"

"But the storm!" the other attendant protested.

"Curse the storm," the queen spat. "Open it now!"

"Yes, Queen Bintanath."

The girl scurried to the window, leaving Nebet to support

the queen alone. The attendant threw the window curtain aside, allowing a humid breeze to blow through the chamber. The queen sighed with relief, her body sagging heavily against Nebet, who struggled to hold her weight until the other girl resumed her post.

"Ah… that feels good," the queen muttered.

Near the bed, the cat raised her pink nose to the air. She smelled something strange. Something beyond the scents of sand and stone, of green things pushing through the black earth. It was a smoky, burning smell, laden with honey and wine, juniper and myrrh. It rode the western wind, its origins unknown.

"Queen Bintanath…" Nebet said warily, after kneeling to peer between the woman's legs.

"What? What is it?" the queen asked. Her eyelids drooped with exhaustion.

"I'm afraid I can see the baby's head. There is no more time."

The queen gritted her teeth. "No," she said, a note of despair in her voice. "It can't happen this way. It's not right… A king needs his blessings—he needs his gods-given name! Where *are* they, Nebet?"

Nebet turned to look at the door once more, her eyes narrow, beseeching, as if she were manifesting a savior to walk through it by sheer force of will.

Another strong breeze blew into the chamber. It lifted the door curtain, sending it billowing into the corridor beyond. At the same moment, three women entered the room. Two were tall and willowy—one dark, one fair—their hair fashionably dyed deep blue. The third was short and sun-weathered, her mottled skin covered in warts. All three women wore long white gowns, belts of turquoise and lapis, and beaded headdresses over their plaited hair.

Queen Bintanath jerked up her head to look at them, her expression first of relief, then of confusion. "Who are you?" she demanded. "How dare you enter this chamber without my leave!"

"Calm yourself, dear lady," the short one said, her voice low and graveled. Her right breast hung over the scoop of her gown and swung gently as she approached the queen. "We are here to help."

The queen's confusion only deepened. "Help? Did Nurse send you?"

The fair one smiled, her blue lotus–colored eyes crinkling. "We were sent, yes," she said.

The queen looked from one woman to the other, still suspicious. "You don't *look* like nurses…"

"My sister and I are mother to many children," the dark one added softly. Despite the difference in their eyes—hers were obsidian black—the two women looked quite similar. "And our companion has attended innumerable births. We are but simple dancers, my lady, visiting from afar—but if you trust us, we will help you welcome your children to this world."

"Children?" the queen asked, puzzled by the plurality.

The short one nodded. "Not one, but three."

The queen opened her mouth, perhaps to deny this, but what came out instead was a deep moan. "It's coming again," she cried, "It's happening too fast." The pain drove whatever protest she might have made from her mind. "Yes, help me," she begged them. "By the gods, help me!"

Without a word, the three women moved with graceful, practiced movements—the fair one before the queen, the dark one behind, like a shadow, and the short one positioned low, her leathery hands reaching between the laboring woman's legs. Nebet and the other attendant backed away, wide-eyed and awed by the three strange dancers.

As waves of agony crashed over the queen, unrelenting now, the short woman croaked a command:

"Push!"

The queen gripped the fair one's arms, squeezed her eyes shut, and screamed.

Before and behind her, the sisters held her and swayed, whispering words unknowable.

"Push!"

The queen took a ragged breath and screamed again. Moments later, a small, fleshy bundle dropped into the short woman's hands and let out a lusty cry. Taking a piece of sharpened flint from her belt, she cut the cord and handed the wet, squalling infant to the dark one.

"A boy," the dark one said, gazing at the child with those flashing midnight eyes. "Meryamun—He Whose Face Is the Sun."

The attendants gaped at each other in shock. To not only deliver the new king, but to name him? Everyone knew that honor was reserved for the high priest of Amun. Who were these women to demonstrate such brazen heresy?

But the queen, still in the throes of labor, gave no protest. "The pain, why has it not ceased?" she cried out instead.

The short one reached once more between the queen's legs. "Because you are not done, my lady. Now, again—push!"

The queen roared and bore down, her toes curling into the bricks beneath her feet. Within moments, another baby was delivered into the short woman's speckled hands. Cutting the cord, she handed the second child to the fair sister.

"A girl," the fair one said, smiling as the baby cooed. "Sitamun, She Who Knows All the Names."

The queen's body went slack, and she crumpled. The two attendants rushed to her side, grasping her by the shoulders. They made to carry her toward the bed, but the short woman stopped them. "Not yet," she said huskily. "There is one more."

Queen Bintanath looked up and shook her head. "The pain is gone now. How can there be another?"

The short one shrugged. "Perhaps this one takes the pain onto himself." Reluctantly, the queen stepped back onto the birthing bricks and resumed her position. "Please, my lady. Push."

Still perplexed, Queen Bintanath closed her eyes and tensed.

The short one reached out just as a child, smaller than the first two, fell into her open palms. The infant was silent as she cut the cord.

"Is he all right?" the queen asked, peering down anxiously.

The short one gathered the small child into her own arms, giving him her finger to suckle. He gazed up at her with a tiny serious face. "He is fine. Another healthy boy. Bakenamun, He Whose Heart Is Hidden."

The queen gave a deep sigh and smiled, contented. Outside, the driving rain washed the world clean and made it quiet with a mother's hush.

When the nurse and priests—dripping and disheveled—came crashing into the chamber a little while later, primed with apologies, they found the queen tucked in bed with a babe nursing at each breast. Meryamun suckled hungrily, while Sitamun reached her tiny hands toward the flickering torchlight as she drank. The third child, Bakenamun, watched from the attendant's arms, waiting patiently for his turn. Each child wore a necklace of twisted linen, strung with beads of carnelian and gold.

Nebet was busy gathering up the soiled cloth and closing the curtains against the rain, which had slowed to a diaphanous mist. Her eyes were wide and haunted, as if she'd witnessed something holy and inexplicable.

The dancers had vanished into the night.

The long-awaited nurse stood before the bed, penitent, her expression that of a dog expecting to be whipped.

"My queen," she stammered, "We tried to reach the palace sooner, I swear to you. The temple road was flooded, and I—"

"Those women you sent me, the dancers," the queen broke in, her voice unusually placid. "They were very good. Strange… but good."

The nurse, who had sent no such dancers, blinked. Then, without missing a beat, she bowed her head. "I'm pleased you liked them, Queen Bintanath." Something had diverted the queen's wrath. It would not do to question it.

"Tell the king to come greet his sons and daughter," Queen Bintanath commanded. "Surely he will be delighted to find them so numerous. The gods have blessed us today."

"They certainly have, my queen," the nurse agreed, and with a parting bow, she hurried through the corridor with the wind at her back.

The cat watched it all with interest, her golden eyes unblinking. She was warm and dry, and enlivened by the activity around her. *Perhaps there is more to see here before I die*, she thought. *Perhaps I shall remain a while longer*.

Winding delicately around the birthing blood still pooled on the tiles, she found her way to a pile of discarded linens, pawed it into a satisfactory shape, and began licking herself with a rough pink tongue.

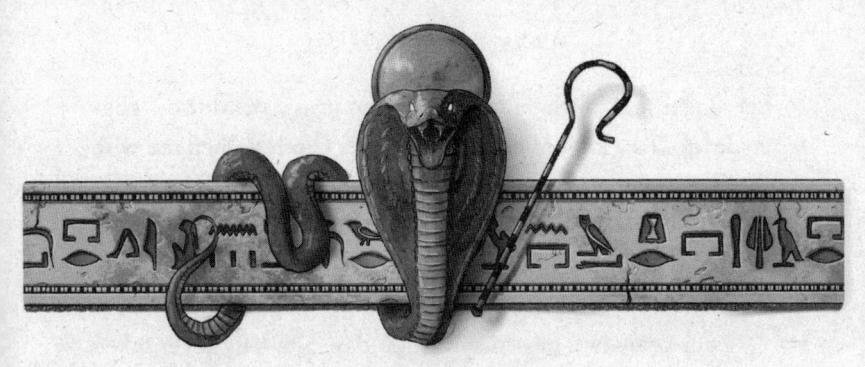

1
SITA

Sitamun lay on her stomach by the edge of the pond, watching the fish. There were about a dozen of them, ranging from the size of her hand to the length of her arm, and they floated lazily in the crystalline blue-green pool. Sita dragged the tips of her fingers across the surface of the water, and the fish came to suckle at them with their round, hungry mouths. Whether they'd come to know her after years of daily visits to the pleasure garden, or whether they thought she was food, it didn't matter much. Spending time there—her body nestled among the fragrant lotus, mandrake, and poppy flowers, her bare legs and shoulders baked by the midday sun—was one of Sita's favorite things to do. At that time of day, it was a place of quiet contemplation, an escape from the clamorous crush of palace life.

Sita's carnelian amulet, carved in the shape of an Isis knot, dangled from her neck, nearly touching the water. When the head priestess visited from Bubas and gave it to her on her thirteenth birthday, Sita thought it was an ankh, but the woman had clicked her tongue and told her no. "You see the arms?" she'd said. "They go down. It's a knot of cloth, not a cross. Cloth stained red with the first blood of womanhood—a threshold you shall soon pass over, little princess. With this amulet, the blood of Isis, the spells of Isis, and the magic words of Isis shall protect you from those who would do you harm. Wear it always."

Four years had passed since that day. Sita had never taken it off.

Likely thinking it was a bit of juicy flesh, one of the fish nibbled at the amulet until Sita tucked it into the folds of her dress. Having lost interest in the taste of her fingertips, the fish slowly drifted away. When their wake stilled, Sita saw herself reflected in the water's glassy surface. The warm breeze had blown her hair into a tangle, so she raised a hand to smooth it.

Her long black hair was her pride—thick enough that she could refuse extensions and her mother wouldn't make a fuss. It hung in the traditional style for girls her age, with two tresses falling over her shoulders, and the rest gathered into a golden ring to trail down her back. One of the attendants had woven golden thread and red carnelian beads into it, which made a gentle ringing sound whenever she moved. She'd complained about the noise at first, saying she felt like one of the palace cats, who could be tracked by the sound of their beaded collars tinkling as they walked. Seeing it now, though, with the sunlight glinting off her bejeweled hair, Sita had to admit it was very pretty indeed.

She became aware of her unique looks at a young age, more from the way others treated her than from noticing it herself. In her eyes, she was no lovelier than any of the young servants in the palace. Any one of them, treated to fine oils for their skin and clothed in linen and jewels, would have been equally appealing. Sometimes she lamented the aggressiveness of her face, her aquiline nose, her thick brows, her strong chin. Her perspective on the matter changed over the past few seasons, however, when she noticed a shift in the way young men reacted to her presence.

As before, there was respect, deference. But there was something else too. Something new. It was the same look the striped palace cat gave the plump little birds as they flitted about in the garden.

Hunger.

At first, the change had startled Sita. It forced her to see those men—some of whom she'd known since they were boys—in a whole new light. Forced her to see herself in a new light too. Perhaps her striking appearance wasn't a disadvantage at all, but a strength. After that realization, she'd quickly developed a hunger of her own, and longed to satiate it.

Unfortunately, doing so was no easy feat. Sita rarely left the palace aside from official functions, and none of the men within its walls were available for a tryst, even a playful one, without serious political consequences.

None of them, that is, except for the servants.

And the guards.

One of the ducks on the pond squawked and flapped its wings, sending a ripple across the water. Sita held her breath and remained perfectly still, listening.

A woman's quiet giggle reached her ears.

Sita slithered her body lower to the ground, her heart racing. She wasn't the only one who knew the garden offered privacy at this time of day. And although she enjoyed watching the fish, they weren't the real reason she came.

She peered through an opening between the rosebushes that lined the opposite side of the pond, which gave her a clear view of the sycamore tree that stood nearest the garden wall. Two figures appeared—a maidservant and a guard—each scanning the garden to ensure they were alone.

Sita smiled, invisible among the lotus flowers.

Satisfied, the maidservant turned back to her companion and threw her arms around his neck. "I've missed you," the girl said. She was slight and narrow-waisted, her arms and shoulders muscled from carrying trays of food and drink for the king's meals.

The man grinned with a voracious look that Sita recognized at once. He was bare-chested and wore a schenti, a white pleated skirt that ended just above the knee. The curved blade of a khopesh was tucked into its scabbard at his side, and a collar bearing the Eye of Horus encircled his neck. "What did you miss?" he murmured, his eyes drinking her in.

"Your touch," she said, coy.

"What else?" he asked, his mouth at the hollow of her throat.

"Your lips." Her eyes closed, her face upturned.

"I'm so sorry to have kept you waiting," he said huskily. With one hand he reached through the fold of her dress, searching for what lay beneath.

Sita watched, her lips slightly parted, a delicious warmth blooming in her belly. Above, in the branches of the sycamore tree, two long-tailed monkeys seemed to be watching too.

"Quickly," the girl said. "We don't have much time."

"As you wish," the guard replied, pressing the woman's back against the tree's rough bark. The monkeys chittered, but neither of the lovers seemed to notice.

Sita's cheeks reddened. She knew she should look away, but she couldn't. Her gaze was fixed on them, hypnotized by the sway of his hips, the arch of his back, and the way the woman had to cover her mouth to keep from crying out. She stared, her whole body leaning forward. A soft moan escaped her lips, floating into the air like a wisp of smoke.

Sita clapped a hand over her own mouth. *Fool!* she scolded herself. *Have you no sense at all?* She studied the couple intently, praying to the gods that they hadn't heard her.

To her horror, the maidservant and the guard had stopped.

"Did you hear something?" the girl whispered.

Sita's insides turned to water at the thought of being caught spying. True, she was the king's daughter, and they were mere servants—but she knew the ways of the palace. That girl need only whisper the story to one of her kitchen friends, and soon the attendants would know, and then the lesser wives and their hangers-on would know, and before the sun set, her mother would know too. Queen Bintanath would not look kindly on her daughter having such an unseemly hobby.

It was the monkeys, she thought, setting the idea into the breeze in hopes that one of the lovers would catch it. *Just the monkeys, nothing more.*

"Someone's coming," the guard said urgently. "Go out the gardener's entrance. I'll make sure they don't see you."

Sita was confused. If they didn't hear her, what *did* they hear? She watched the girl place a hurried kiss on the guard's cheek before disappearing behind the rosebushes. She was about to slip away herself when she heard footsteps on the stone path, followed by a familiar voice.

"Femi! Enjoying the pleasures of the garden, are you?"

The guard cleared his throat. "Indeed, I am, my queen," he replied.

Sita felt the blood drain from her face.

Of all the people in the palace, she thought, *it has to be my mother!*

She peered over the tops of the flowers to see Queen Bintanath, blazing like a poppy in a long red dress that was belted with gold. Two wide straps loosely covered her breasts, and over that, she wore a wide lapis and obsidian collar in the shape of a vulture, its wings stretching over her broad shoulders. A delicate lattice covered her mother's favorite wig, which had been a gift from a visiting emissary many years before. Sita only remembered him because he'd brought the first pomegranates to the kingdom—fruits now cultivated freely in Thonis and in the gardens at the Temple of Amun. Sita had been a child when she'd first tried one, and she still thought they were the most delicious things she'd ever tasted.

The emissary, like so many others, had commented that Sita and her brother must have gotten their good looks from their mother. Seeing her now, Sita had to agree—although she hoped that time would be kinder to her than it had been to the queen. Her mother's face and body, long and elegant as they were, looked as if life had whittled her into a collection of flint-sharp edges.

The two monkeys chose that moment to dash down from their perch and skitter across the queen's path. She startled slightly, her ochre-stained lips curling, before recovering her composure. Sighing, she brushed an invisible mote of dirt from her dress and refocused on Femi. His wiry black hair, cut short like most of the palace guard, shone with sweat.

"I'm looking for the princess," the queen told him. "I know she likes to come here in the afternoons. She should be preparing herself for the festival tonight, not lounging in the dirt with monkeys."

Femi shook his head. "My apologies, Queen Bintanath, but I haven't seen her." He stood awkwardly, with one leg half-crossed in front of the other. He looked as if he wished the ground would open and swallow him whole.

The queen huffed with irritation. "I've looked everywhere else. She must be here. *Sitaaa!*" The last was shouted at a pitch that sent the long-tailed monkeys scampering back into their tree.

Sita's mind whirled, knowing she had only moments before it was too late to act. What was she supposed to do now? Without more than a few seconds consideration, she flipped onto her back, grasped her amulet in her hand, sent a quick prayer to Isis, and sat up.

Both Femi and the queen noticed her immediately.

"There you are!" the queen said, exasperated.

Femi stared at her with a mortified expression. "Princess Sitamun..." he said weakly, dropping his head in deference to her.

"Oh, hello, Mother, Femi," Sita said, making a big show of yawning and stretching before rising to her feet. "I was in the seventh sleep. My tutor had me reciting passages from the Tale of Sinuhe today, and all that reading made me tired."

Queen Bintanath rolled her eyes. "I'm going to have to speak to that man. I don't know why he insists on wasting your time with silly stories when you should be focusing on politics and taxes. A king's daughter should know those things."

But I love the stories, Sita thought. *They're certainly more entertaining than taxes.* But she knew better than to argue. "Yes, Mother," she said instead.

The queen waved her closer. "Now come along, your attendants are waiting. I thought you were excited about the Bast Festival—and yet here you are, sleeping instead of getting ready."

"I *am* excited!" Sita retorted.

"The palace cats are more prepared than you!" Her mother went on as if Sita hadn't spoken. "Ugh, you smell like fish. Tell your attendants to add some cyprinum oil to your bath, and your hair..."

Sita started to follow her mother out of the garden but was arrested by Femi's searching gaze. "Do you often... ah, nap in the pleasure garden, princess?" he asked carefully.

"Oh yes, all the time," Sita replied, feeling mischievous. "I always have such vivid dreams." She shot him a provocative glance.

The guard's throat bobbed. He opened his mouth as if to ask

something more, but then he glanced toward Queen Bintanath's receding figure and closed it.

Sita suppressed a smile, delighted at her reversal of fortunes. Just a moment ago she'd been panicked about her reputation, but now poor Femi was worried about his own. This was the perfect opportunity to reassure him that she was on his side, that his secrets were safe with her, that she could be *trusted*…

"Are you attending the Bast Festival tonight?" She tried very hard to sound casual.

"I am," Femi replied. "All the guards will be on hand to ensure the safety of the revelers."

"So, you must have gone to the last festival," Sita said, eyeing her mother. She'd been waylaid by one of the lesser wives, who appeared to be plying her with questions. "And two others before that, since you joined the guard four seasons ago." She said that last part without thinking and regretted it immediately. *Why should you know how long he's been here? He's going to think you've been counting!*

Femi smiled, as if he knew he now had the upper hand. "Why yes, I did," he said. "How good of you to remember."

Sita licked her lips. Why was she being so stupid over this man? He was nothing, just a servant. A weapon to wield. She could have him if she wanted. All she had to do was say the word…

But you don't want him that way. You want him to come to you. You want to play the game, just like everyone else does.

"What was it like?" she asked.

"The Bast Festival?"

"Yes."

Femi chuckled and shook his head. Then he regarded her with his green hooded eyes. "Like a dream you don't want to wake from."

Sita blinked, her cheeks hot.

Was he winning, or was she? Sita wasn't sure she knew—or cared.

"*Sitaaa!*" her mother called.

"I-I must go," Sita stammered.

"You must, indeed, my princess." Femi bowed his head.

"Perhaps," she said, moving toward the queen but still looking at Femi, "I'll see you there?"

"Perhaps you will," he replied. His head was still bowed, so she couldn't see his face, but Sita swore she could hear the smile in his voice.

She walked out of the walled garden, half-listening to her mother launch into another list of preparations. The fluttery feeling in her belly had returned. She'd overheard enough whispered conversations between the maidservants to know that Femi was a favorite among them. He'd enjoyed the occasional dalliance with several women, but he was honorable enough to keep the details to himself.

She'd started paying more attention to him after that, catching glimpses of him on duty, laughing with the other guards. One day, while she was walking from her bedchamber to meet her tutor, she caught him gazing at her with that familiar, hungry expression.

That was how the game started.

It wasn't long after that she'd discovered his habit of bringing girls to the pleasure garden in the afternoons. In addition to the maidservant she'd just seen, there were two other girls Sita had witnessed enjoying Femi's company—surprisingly the girls seemed to know this and were perfectly fine with the arrangement. Perhaps they had multiple partners themselves. It was a kind of freedom that a princess could never have, and Sita envied them for it. She too, wanted to drink from Femi's cup, but for nearly a season, she hadn't mustered the courage to make the next move.

Until today.

She giggled, and before stepping into the cool dimness of the palace, stole one last glance behind her. But Femi had already gone. The garden lay empty and yellow-bright. Left to their own devices, the two monkeys chased each other across the stone tiles while a falcon circled slowly above them in the cloudless blue sky.

"Be sure to keep your wits about you tonight," Queen Bintanath said as she hurried Sita through the palace's main hall toward the women's quarters. Shafts of sunlight arced in through high square windows, illuminating the richly painted walls, columns, and broad-leafed palm trees planted in the center of the hall. Around them, servants and nobles went about their business, nodding respectfully as they passed.

One of the palace cats sauntered by, a black-striped one that reminded her of a female tabby she'd had as a baby. It couldn't have been the same one, though—that was so long ago. The cat wore a jeweled collar and looked sleepy and well-fed. Like all the other cats, she was probably getting special treatment on Bast's special day.

"People come from all over Khetara for the festival," the queen went on, "And not all of them share our values. They'll take you to the sea and bring you back thirsty if you let them—princess or no."

"Uh-huh," Sita said, noncommittal. The queen had many skills, the foremost of which was sucking the pleasure out of almost anything.

"I've tasked Mery with keeping an eye on you," Queen Bintanath said. "He attended the last festival, so you should be fine if you remain together."

Sita grumbled under her breath. She was still annoyed that her brother had been allowed to attend last year's festival and she hadn't, despite them being the exact same age. It wasn't surprising, though—what with him being a boy and Mother's favorite.

Mery the beautiful.
Mery the brilliant.
Mery the future king.

Still, she wasn't going to let her brother's watchful eye prevent her from having a good time.

"What about Kenna?" she asked.

The queen sighed. "Bakenamun wishes to spend the evening at the temple, alone with his scrolls."

"Truly?" Sita couldn't hide the note of disappointment in her voice. Her other brother had always been a studious, dour boy, but she still wished he would share in the celebrations. Studying with the Sem priests seemed to be the only thing he was interested in of late.

"I tried to convince him, but he claims to be 'busy.' Too busy to live, it seems!" The queen sucked her teeth. "Calling himself a 'Man of Anubis.' There are families suited to that"—she grimaced—"position... but ours is *not* one of them! I'll never understand why your father puts up with it."

Sita looked away. She felt sorry for Kenna. As the only daughter, she was granted a slice of the queen's favor, even if Mery had the lion's share. But their small quiet brother had never felt the warmth of their mother's light shine on him, not ever. It was no wonder he preferred the shadows of the temple.

Just then, the hustle and bustle of the main hall seemed to slow. Queen Bintanath stopped, and Sita nearly ran into her.

"Well," the queen said, "You bring up the cat and it comes jumping. Here's your father now."

Sita peered around her mother's shoulder as the king's palanquin approached. It was one of her father's everyday palanquins—carried by four servants instead of the standard twelve he used for festival days—but it was still a chair fit for a pharaoh. Bedecked in gold, the sides of the throne were engraved with a parade of supplicants kneeling before Amun, and the armrests were the heads of two rearing cobras. King Amunmose reclined in the throne, his head resting on one fist. He wore a green pleated schenti and gold sandals, and had a leopard-skin pelt tossed over one shoulder. Sita saw that the leopard's fur was patchy in places, and that the king's clothes, which once stretched over a thick, well-fed body, now draped loosely over him. A simple gold circlet, embellished with a jeweled serpent's head, fit over the green-and-gold-striped headdress that hung down either side of his face. His vivid garments were in sharp contrast to his sallow face, which the dark lines of kohl and green eye paint did little to improve.

He looked hollowed out, like a skin without a snake.

The change had happened gradually, and at first, she hadn't noticed it. No one had. But soon it became more and more apparent, not only to her, but to everyone who laid eyes on him. Her father—who had last season been his portly, gregarious, and famously inappropriate self—was not well.

Despite his attempts to keep the illness a secret, whispers had spread through the palace corridors, growing louder and more numerous with each passing day. It was impossible to ignore his repeated absences from meals and social gatherings, the frequent visits from the physician-priests, or the increasing number of healing amulets strung around the king's neck.

Just that morning, Sita had overheard her attendants talking quietly as they swept the floors of her bedchamber. "I heard Pharaoh is in the grip of a demon," the girl had said. "I heard the priests have tried everything, and still, he gets worse and worse."

Sita dismissed their idle talk. The servants loved nothing more than a good bit of gossip, though such blasphemy would have brought a whip to their backs if anyone besides Sita had overheard it. She saw no reason to report it herself, though. After all, the attendants were simply concerned.

Sita thought perhaps she should be worried too, but then again, she had no reason to doubt the power of the priests. They were the best in the world. Besides, it was ridiculous to think that her father, the god-king of Khetara, would ever allow such a paltry thing as disease—demonic or not—to keep him from the throne.

So, Sita tried to ignore the way he looked, just as she tried to ignore the way he treated her, because that was what a good daughter was supposed to do.

Queen Bintanath leaned close to her husband. "Aren't you meant to be meeting with the viziers about the grain tax?" She spoke quietly enough to keep the conversation private.

King Amunmose swatted at the half-moon-shaped fan that a servant was waving at him and looked at her with disinterest. "Greetings to you too, wife of mine. As a matter of fact, I just came from that meeting. It was very short. The viziers said, 'My king, there is not enough grain,' and I, in my great wisdom, told them—'Then grow more.'" He glanced at a passing maidservant and winked.

Sita saw the muscles in Queen Bintanath's jaw twitch. "Now, imi-ib," the queen said sweetly. It was a term of endearment her mother often used when she was furious. "Far be it from me to contradict your judgment, but I have heard that the situation in Low Khetara grows more dire by the day. And things here in the north are hardly any better. My messengers tell me the village markets in Per-Amun and Menef are struggling, and Bubas follows right behind them. You should have seen the scant supplies

I received from my last shipment coming downriver. Skinny cattle, uninspiring produce, and barely a dozen pots of ochre and bottles of oils to go around."

The king's eyebrow arched. "You're telling me some limp lettuce is cause for alarm? My dear, I'm sorry the delicacies and eye makeup you ordered were not to your liking, but I'm not going to start a war over it."

The queen closed her eyes, as if to summon the necessary strength to continue. "I am not suggesting you start a *war*, my king," she said, with exaggerated patience. "What I fear is that these issues are symptoms of a larger problem, a problem that could grow if left untreated. I am merely suggesting that, perhaps, a bit more consideration might be appropriate? After all, without the word of the pharaoh, the viziers are but legs without a head to lead them."

"*Perhaps*," the king replied, mimicking Queen Bintanath's tone, "your ears should choose what they consume more carefully." There was an edge to his voice. "The viziers are frightened of their own shadows. Low Khetara is under control. It has been so since the beginning of my reign, and it shall remain so until the end." He spoke the last word with finality.

Then his expression softened, and he smiled. "Really, Binta, on the night of the Bast, this is your concern? Today is a day of worship! Of celebration!" He nudged one of the litter bearers with an elbow. "And for raising the skirts up! Isn't that right, Tabu?"

The litter bearer smirked. "Yes, Pharaoh."

"You see?" King Amunmose said heartily, slapping the man on the back. "Even Tabu knows what's really important in life. And it's *not* the viziers and their cursed grain tax."

Queen Bintanath closed her eyes, her lips pressed into a thin line. "As you say, my king."

Her father's gaze flicked to Sita. "I bet you're looking forward to the day you'll go to the festival. Isn't that right, Sitamun?"

Sita blinked. "But I am attending the festival tonight, Father," she said. "It will be my first time."

The king stared back at her strangely, as if seeing her anew. "No," he balked. "Is it possible so much time has passed already?" The words were nostalgic in meaning, but the tone behind them held something akin to dread. Sita had the feeling that her father wasn't really thinking of Sita's growth, but of the passage of his own life.

The king had never paid much attention to his children. He was usually too busy seeking out life's various pleasures—food, drink, sport, women. Queen Bintanath was his Great Wife, it was true, but the palace was teeming with lesser wives, concubines, and the issues that came from his coupling with them all. He clearly enjoyed the women's company, but dealing with their complaints was a task the king felt was better left to other people. So although Sita had the honor of being the single most important woman in the palace—the woman with the purest royal blood—even she rarely attracted her father's interest.

"Yes, my brothers and I turned seventeen during Peret," Sita said, before adding, "I pray that tonight I may honor the goddess and earn her favor." She could at least put on the appearance of a proper daughter, even if her mind was busy with her own life's pleasures—particularly those found in the garden.

The king eyes grew soft as he gazed into the past. "Ah, yes," he mused. "I remember well the night you three were born. 'And the storm turned the dry land into a sea, and the priests and nurse went through the flood on foot, and when they arrived at the palace, they rejoiced in what they found there: not one child, but three, delivered to the kingdom from the hands of the gods.'"

Sita smiled at the familiar words of their birth story. Ever since she was a little girl, Nebet had regaled her with the tale of that night, when Khetara was struck by a storm unlike any other before or since. They'd come into the world at the beginning of her father's reign, and the story had taken on a legendary quality—many believing the three dancers who'd helped their laboring mother were goddesses themselves. The whole kingdom fell in love with the triplets and their seemingly divine birth, which in turn, helped her father's credibility considerably.

He'd needed it too. The previous king, the Great Sematawy, had united the Two Lands and died in battle—a hero with no living heirs. Her father had been Sematawy's chief vizier, and although it made sense for him to take the throne, he had no royal blood. To follow a legend, Amunmose had needed a legend of his own.

The triplets gave him one.

King Amunmose shook his head and chuckled. "How much of it is memory, I wonder, and how much is simply the story we've always told ourselves? Maybe it doesn't matter. We say something often enough, it eventually becomes the truth." He paused, contemplative. "It reminds me of something that happened many years ago, just after you were born. A desert priest requested an audience with me. He went on and on about some ancient oracle, and how it was related to your birth. None of the priests of Amun had ever heard of him or his family name, just some pretender looking for an avenue to power. We threw him out, of course. But he didn't stop raving about death and destruction until he was outside the palace gates. He really believed that nonsense." The king leaned down from his palanquin and grabbed Sita by the shoulder, pulling her close. The smell of his breath made her nose wrinkle. It was heavy with wine, and something else. She recognized it from when one of the lesser wives had died in her quarters overnight, only to be discovered, stiff and cold, the next morning. It was a sour smell, the smell of rot.

"Those are the most dangerous sorts of people, Sitamun. Remember that. The people whose belief is so great that it blocks their mind from reason." He pulled one of the amulets from his neck and pushed it into her palm. "Here, take this," he said. "You need it more than I do."

Sita looked at the carved piece of malachite in her hand. It was a scarab beetle, no different than the thousands she'd seen people wearing all her life. Why was he giving this to her now?

"Do you know what the scarab means, daughter?" he asked.

Sita thought back to what she'd learned from her tutor, who had spent years teaching her how to read and write the gods' words, about Khetaran history and its stories and gods. Memorizing kings' names and coronation dates bored her to tears, but she enjoyed the rest, even if her mother thought her mind was better filled with other things.

"It's a symbol of transformation and rebirth," she said. "The scarab beetle rolls her ball of dung and lays her eggs within, just as Khepra rolls the morning sun across the horizon, creating life anew each day."

The king wagged his head, as if he was only partially satisfied with this answer. "Yes, yes, that is true. But what I want you to remember about the beetle is this: When you're in *really* deep shit, you must seek something unexpected inside you. Only there will you find an answer." He narrowed his eyes. "Do you understand me, Sitamun?"

Sita could feel her eyebrows arching. "Um…"

Her father's solemn face broke into a grin. He laughed until he was seized with a coughing fit, and sat back in his throne, taking a long drink from the cup of wine at his side. "Did you like that, Tabu? 'Deep shit.' Pharaoh is a man of a thousand talents, is he not?"

"Talents immeasurable, my king," Tabu agreed.

Queen Bintanath squinted at the angle of sun outside the windows and tapped her foot on the ground. "I'm sure Sitamun appreciates your gifts of wisdom, imi-ib," she said. "But she really must get dressed for the festival."

Ignoring this, the king craned his neck as a pretty little girl ran through the hall with a young woman at her heels.

"Is that Maet?" he called. "Is that my little plum?"

The little girl squealed and dashed toward the palanquin, her sidelock bouncing. She was quickly scooped up by one of the litter bearers and placed on the king's lap. Maet was the daughter of one of his lesser wives, and a personal favorite.

Sita tried not to be jealous. After all, Maet was only six.

Maet took the king's face into her tiny hands and stared at him very seriously. "You look funny, Yati," she pronounced.

The king stuck out his tongue and crossed his eyes. Maet giggled. "Come now, kitten," he said. "Let's find something delicious to eat, shall we?" He turned back to Sita. "Enjoy the festival tonight, Sitamun," he said, then spared a glance for his wife. "Binta," he said, and then promptly gestured for his servants to proceed.

Sita watched as her father's palanquin continued its slow journey through the hall, feeling slightly disquieted by his ramblings. *He's ill and probably drunk*, she reasoned. What kind of medicines were the priests giving him, anyway? Were they to credit for his strange talk?

"Come along now," Queen Bintanath said, pulling her away. "We've wasted too much time already."

"Sita? Sitamun!"

Sita sat up abruptly, sloshing floral-scented bathwater over the edge of the alabaster basin. "What?"

Her middle-aged attendant sat by the edge of the water, wearing an indulgent smile. "If you're finished, you should get out. The water is getting cold."

"Oh. Yes. Sorry, Nebet." Sita rose from the water, her copper skin coated with a glossy sheen of olive oil.

"Careful now." Nebet offered her hand to help her out of the bath, taking care that Sita didn't slip on the tiled floor.

The woman's hand was strong and familiar, more so even than her own mother's. Nebet had been with Sita—nursing her, watching over her, and tucking her into bed—ever since she was born. Her once dark hair had turned gray, and no matter how many times Sita said she could dye it brown again with juniper berries, Nebet always refused. For all the time and effort Nebet spent on Sita's appearance, she spent none on her own. Whenever Sita brought up the topic, Nebet liked to pronounce that she had "earned" her gray hairs, and no one was going to take them from her.

Nebet picked up a soft linen cloth from the stool where she'd been sitting and used it to pat Sita's body dry. "Daydreaming about tonight?" she asked.

"I was," she said, though exactly what she was imagining was far too embarrassing to admit to Nebet. It involved Femi, and activities similar to the ones she'd witnessed in the pleasure garden.

After calling the other attendants to clean up the bath and prepare Sita's attire, Nebet sat the girl down in front of a brass mirror that hung on the wall of her chambers. In its reflection, Sita watched Nebet begin to weave her wet hair into plaits, lacing thin golden cylinders onto each one.

"You should enjoy yourself at the festival," Nebet said after a while, her voice thoughtful. "But don't forget its true purpose, for it is not for your pleasure alone."

Sita blushed at the word *pleasure*, as if Nebet had somehow seen the images of Femi floating through her mind. "But Bast is the goddess of pleasure," she replied, recalling the lithe cat-headed woman she'd seen on scrolls and palace walls. "The more we celebrate, the more we honor her, isn't that right?"

"It is," Nebet agreed. "She sees our music, our dancing, and our celebrations as a testament to life, and she rewards us with her protection. But has your tutor not taught you Bast's other name?"

Sita's brow furrowed. Nebet was a very devout woman. Sita's bedtime stories, in addition to the one about her birth, had always been about the gods and their adventures, and Nebet never once forgot to make her daily offerings. So Sita wasn't surprised by the question, but she was a little embarrassed that she didn't know the answer.

"I guess he hasn't," she admitted.

Nebet sucked her teeth. "We insult Bast with this harmless vision of her power. Imagine, a cat with no claws! You cannot shine a light on one side of something without casting darkness on the other."

Sita was taken aback by the sudden the passion in the woman's voice. Nebet was usually so soft-spoken, so tender. "What do you mean? What is Bast's other name?"

Nebet stopped her braiding and glanced up, meeting Sita's eyes in the mirror. "She is the Lady of slaughter. Defender of the innocent, avenger of the wronged."

Sita swallowed.

"It is she who protects a home from evil spirits," Nebet went on, pulling the brush through Sita's hair a little too roughly. "Spirits like the one that sickens your father. You would do well, my girl, as you dance and drink tonight, to pray to the goddess to deliver him from that demon, before... before..."

"Before what?"

Nebet was silent for several moments. Her face had gone pale.

"I apologize, Princess," she said, laying a hand on Sita's shoulder. "I don't know what came over me. I've been overcome by this terrible feeling lately… this dread. But it's no excuse. I've overstepped my bounds. If you want to dismiss me, I'd understand."

"No, no, it's all right," Sita quickly replied, putting her hand over Nebet's. She didn't like the deference in her attendant's voice. "You're only trying to help. I would never send you away, not for anything. I promise to do my best to honor the goddess, for Father's sake."

"And for yours," Nebet added quietly. "It's you I care about the most."

Just then, the other attendants returned. "Your dress, Princess Sitamun," one of them said.

Sita stood, wearing nothing except the Isis knot and scarab amulets, while the girls draped a sheath of gossamer white linen over her head. The fabric was so thin that the shadow of her naked body was still visible beneath it. Over that, the girls slipped an elaborate bead-net dress that reached all the way to her ankles, made up of thousands of red, blue, and black ceramic beads arranged in a diamond pattern. Next, they latched a wide beaded collar, featuring a golden scarab, around her neck—along with a golden cuff for each wrist. While one of the girls fitted two golden hoops into her ears, the other painted her eyes with kohl and her lips and cheeks with red ochre.

Nebet stood back from the flurry of activity, her arms crossed over her chest, only stepping in to adjust a plait here, a fold there.

"You're sure this is what you want to wear tonight, Sitamun?" Nebet asked. "It is lovely, but a bit…"

"I'm seventeen now, Nebet," Sita replied, tilting up her chin. "I shall dress as the woman I am."

"As you wish," Nebet replied softly.

She was touching Sita's temples and the hollow of her throat with rose petal oil when the blade of a shadow sliced across the floor from the direction of the corridor.

Sita turned to see a man leaning against the doorway, the blaze of the setting sun at his back. He wore a white knee-length schenti, belted with an ornamental pendant that hung between his legs. The finely crafted pendant was made from the same obsidian and ostrich-shell beads that decorated his collar, which he wore over a sheer, loose-fitting blouse that revealed his bare chest underneath. His hair, like Sita's own, was thick and black, and fell to his shoulders in shining waves. He regarded her with eyes not unlike the ones she'd been staring at in the mirror a moment before. Eyes full of fire and mischief, just as they had been since they were both babes in arms.

"Greetings, sister," Meryamun said, his voice honey smooth and honey sweet. "Are you ready to go?"

Sita stood, her golden plaits tinkling like bells. Her attendants moved away, their heads bowed. Sita stole a look back at Nebet. The older woman returned it with a small smile, but it didn't reach her eyes.

"The goddess awaits us," the prince said.

Sita grinned, her excitement overtaking her annoyance at having a guardian, and the wary feeling that clung to her since the strange encounter with her father. Was she ready to leap into the night? Into whatever wild and delicious wonders the festival might bring? Was she ready to drink this life until it ran over her lips and down her throat and spread like fire across her skin? Was she ready to abandon herself? To forget her manners, to fall into the arms of a lover, to scream into the sky, to dance until dawn?

"Yes!" she exclaimed.

"Well then…" Mery crooked his arm toward her.

Sita stepped into her golden sandals and out the door.

2
NEFF

She was alone in the desert on a moonless night.

The air was still and unbroken by the breath of any other living thing. There was only the dunes, stretching into eternity like the primeval waters that covered the earth when the world was new.

A fresh set of tracks disturbed the ground up ahead. They were small and cloven, and she followed them, her feet sinking deep into the sand with each labored step.

The lamb lay in a patch of light, and because there was no moon, she knew that the light came from the creature itself. Blood flowed from a grievous wound in its side, staining its white wool crimson. Despite this, the lamb made no sound. It turned its strange horizontal eyes toward her.

"Beware."

The lamb's mouth did not move, yet she knew it was the lamb's voice that spoke. It was a doleful sound, the sound of unwanted news, of nightmares come alive.

"Beware, for soon the Great River of Khetara will turn to blood."

She took a step back and pressed her hands against her ears to block out the voice, but it continued.

"Lies will grow fruitful as wheat in the fields, and where once there was order, chaos will reign. A secret shall rise from beneath the earth, and the Red and the White Crowns will be forever broken."

"Stop," she said, but the voice did not quaver or cease, even as blood pooled around the lamb and spilled out in impossible torrents, soaking into the desert and spreading across the whole of the land.

"Take heed, Thonis, Great House of Amun! Beware of what is unseen among you!" The lamb roared, and the desert became a chaotic red sea of gruesome, viscous dunes.

"Take heed, Sakesh, Great House of Ra! Beware of what burns and destroys you!"

She felt herself sinking. The lamb floated above the surface of the new sea, its gaze never wavering, its unearthly eyes focused solely on her. She screamed, thrashing in the thick waters until the copper tang of blood filled her mouth.

"Beware! Sorrow and ruin to the Children of the Two Lands!"

Nefermaat woke with a gasp.

She sat up from the reed mat where she slept and looked around her family's humble home, bleary-eyed and panting. Morning light leaked in through the small square windows on each side, and next to her, her mother and father's sleeping mats were vacant. She grasped at the threads of the dream, desperately trying to hold on to the words, the images, before—

"Oh, good! You're up," her mother said, coming up the mudbrick stairs from the ground floor below. She was carrying a jar of beer under one arm and a cloth-wrapped loaf of bread in the other. She moved briskly. "We're about to eat. Hurry up and get ready, Neff. You know how your father hates being late to market."

Neff rubbed her eyes. Whatever tenuous hold she'd had on her dream had vanished, leaving her with a cold, uneasy feeling that she'd forgotten something terribly important.

"I'm coming, Mamet, I'm coming," she mumbled, and slipped into the woven papyrus sandals at the foot of her sleeping mat. She smoothed out the wrinkles in her white kalasiris dress and adjusted the straps over her shoulders. After washing her face in the basin and combing her fingers through her chin-length curly brown hair, she made her way up the stairs to the roof.

It was still early, so the sun was pleasant and not too hot. Neff took a deep breath of fresh air and gazed around her. Mud-brick homes similar to theirs crowded around them in even lines leading south, punctuated by the great Temple of Bast standing at Bubas's southern border. Beyond that, Neff knew, lay the lands of Low Khetara—Hurwar, Per-Abu, and Sakesh. They were names she'd heard in stories told across firelight, about a Great War that happened years before she was born. Stories of might and glory, and of King Sematawy's legendary victory over the southern pretender. To the west was the wide blue finger of the Iteru, and due north on the banks of the river delta lay Thonis, home of the pharaoh and the capital city of the kingdom.

Everything west of the Iteru was the Red Lands. Bearded tribesmen in dark voluminous robes would sometimes venture into the village from across the river to trade with the Khetaran merchants, but they never stayed long. Her father, along with everyone else she knew, didn't really trust them.

"I'm happy to do a trade," Neff remembered hearing one of the vegetable merchants say, "But I'm not inviting them to stay for supper!" Neff had never actually met a desert tribesman herself. They usually came to trade for food, tools, and fabric, and weren't often in the market for the magic scrolls her father sold. *They probably don't believe in that sort of thing*, she thought. For a moment, she stared at the golden rolling desert, which seemed to stretch all the way to the horizon, the ghost of that dream still hovering at the edges of her memory.

"Stop wasting time, Neff!" her father called, waving her over with impatience. "Sit and eat!"

He was seated beneath the large woven canopy that took up one corner of the roof, already tucking into the beer and bread her mother had brought up for them from the cellar.

He was bald-headed, with a round face and prominent nose, and wore a crisp linen tunic that Neff's mother hung on a line every night to keep it from wrinkling. It was tied at the waist with a fine well-stitched belt, a luxury he'd purchased months ago after a week of haggling with the leather merchant. "We're moving up in the world, Ahura," he'd told her mother when she balked at the price. "I must look the part. If you want people to respect you, you must command respect! That's what I always say."

Neff went to sit underneath the canopy, taking a chunk of bread and cup of beer for her own breakfast.

"It goes without saying that the prosperity scrolls are our most popular items," her father said through a mouthful of food, continuing a conversation that must have started before Neff joined them. "But you'd be surprised how many love and beauty scrolls I'm selling. Can you believe it? They're starving to death, but still they come, trading their last onion to look plump and pretty for a lover. Pah! Well, a fool's trade is as good a trade as any, that's what I always say…"

Neff's mother shook her head. She was small and delicate, her hair and skin the soft brown color of a mourning dove. "It's getting worse every day. There's hardly anything to trade, and even less to trade for! Do you know how much I had to hand over for a few days' worth of beans and vegetables?"

"That's why we need to think *bigger*. Do you see? To keep up with the changing market. Imeny tells me they do a brisk business in the Thonis market selling curses."

"*Curses?*" Neff's mother exclaimed. The broom she'd been using to sweep the dusty roof stilled in midair. "Pepi. You wouldn't."

"I would if they sold, Ahura, yes, indeed. You can't be squeamish about these things, especially not at a time like this. If we want to keep our heads above water, my dear, we have to give the people what they want, whether it's good for them or not."

Neff's mother scowled but resumed her sweeping with a sigh of resignation. "If you say so, imi-ib. Who's Imeny again?"

"The *jeweler*. You know the one. His wife has that mole. Here." Her father pointed to the side of his face.

"Oh, yes. Yes, of course. The one who oversalts her fish."

Her father chuckled. "We'll never share a meal with *them* again, will we?"

Neff chewed her bread, half listening to her parents' prattle. Her father's spell scrolls hadn't always been so popular, but over the past year, he'd built up a reputation as a merchant of good fortune in Bubas. This had been accomplished through a combination of luck and cunning. Luck because two village women had found husbands shortly after using his love scrolls, and cunning because Pepi made sure that they told everyone in the village all about it. By spending time listening to people at the market every day, her father had grown to understand their fears and desires, and used that information to sell, sell, sell. If the spell worked, the customers always came back for more. If it didn't, and they returned to her family's stall to complain, her father merely came up with a logical reason—invariably one that could be blamed on the customer themselves.

Pepi wrote the spells in the common script, a highly simplified version of the "gods' words" that the merchant class used to do business—but a large portion of the population couldn't even read that. Writing was considered a magic all its own, and most Khetarans viewed anyone who could do it with a sense of awe. Which made it easy for Neff's father to tell the disgruntled customers that they didn't say the words right. "If you don't say them in the right way," he'd proclaim, "the magic doesn't work!"

So they'd buy another scroll, desperately attempt to memorize his instructions, and try again.

He'd send them off with a smile and resume bellowing his famous phrase to anyone in the market who might listen. He'd said it so often, Neff often heard her father muttering it in his sleep.

"Spell scrolls! Very effective! They've worked a thousand times!"

The business's success had allowed them to build the two-story house that her mother so lovingly swept and tidied every morning. Her father was rarely at home. He was always the first vendor at the market every morning, and the last to leave. After their evening meal, he wrote new scrolls until all the light faded from the sky.

When Neff turned six, her father began teaching her to write the common too, so that one day she could help him run the business. At thirteen, she was nearly old enough to work the stall herself, but her father wasn't convinced that she'd mastered the necessary attitude to be a good salesman. "You give up too easily," he'd said the day before, when she'd allowed a woman to walk away empty-handed. "All that customer needed was a little more convincing!"

"She said no," Neff had argued. "What was I supposed to do?"

Pepi shook a finger at her. "The mouth says no, but the heart shouts yes! Couldn't you hear it? Your problem, my girl, is that you don't believe in the product."

Neff had looked down at the scrolls, arranged in neat piles. Cures for headaches, infertility, broken hearts. "But the scrolls don't *really* work, do they?"

Her father sucked his teeth. "Hold your tongue, Nefermaat. Have you learned nothing from me? Haven't I taught you that words have power?" He shook his head. "You're not just selling a scroll, child. You're selling hope. Now, I can't guarantee that my customers will always receive what they desire, but if you make them *believe*... well, they certainly have a better chance."

"I'm sorry, Yati," she'd said. "I'll do better next time."

There on the roof, Neff remembered the exchange as her mother ruffled her hair and planted a loving kiss on her head. *If the magic works*, she thought, *why couldn't it give Mamet the big family she wanted?* The concentration of her mother's devotion, which could have been more comfortably spread across three or four additional children, was sometimes difficult for Neff to bear alone.

"Are you all right, Neff?" her mother asked. "You look a bit pale this morning."

"Bad dreams again," Neff replied, taking a drink of the thick, sweet beer.

"Really?" Her mother frowned. "Do you remember what they're about?"

Neff sighed. "No. As soon as I wake, they fade away."

"I used to have one about a date palm tree," her mother said dreamily, leaning on her broom. "I picked the fruit and ate and ate, but my belly was never full. Your father had some ideas about what it meant, but he's no Hour priest. I think I was just hungry."

Even if I could afford to visit an Hour priest to interpret my dream, Neff thought, *I wouldn't know what to tell him!* She'd only had the dream occasionally at first, but now it came nearly every night. And although she couldn't remember anything about it, she somehow knew that it was always the same dream, over and over again.

She'd begun to dread going to sleep.

Neff knew that dreams, like words, were powerful. They were messages from the gods. And some nagging, relentless urge kept telling her that she shouldn't ignore this one. If she didn't figure out what it meant, she was certain the dream would never let her go.

Her father smacked his lips as he finished up his beer. "Perhaps your dream is telling you to wake up earlier, like your yati, so we aren't late to market!" he said. He stood up from the table and clapped the crumbs from his hands. "Come on, it's time to go!"

Neff shoved the rest of the bread into her mouth and washed it down with the dregs of her beer. She was brushing her dress clean when she suddenly remembered what day it was. "Wait!" she exclaimed. "We can't go to market now. Bast is coming through the village this morning."

Every year, the village of Bubas had the honor of watching Bast, their patron goddess, be taken from her shrine and brought downriver to Thonis, where the Festival of Bast took place. Neff had never been to Khetara's capital city, but her friends had said that the streets were lined with gold and precious stones of many colors. She hoped to see it one day, but until then, she and everyone else in Bubas took pleasure in the goddess's annual visit, when a lucky few would have the opportunity to address her with a question or a prayer.

A question... Neff thought suddenly, an idea germinating in her mind.

Of course! Why hadn't she thought of it before?

Because you'll get in trouble!

Then again, how much trouble could it possibly cause?

Neff ran to her father and gripped his arm. "Please, Yati, we must see Bast! We've never missed her, and all my friends will be there. No one will be shopping at the market anyway! Everyone in the village will be waiting for the goddess too!"

Neff's father rubbed his temples. "Ach… we only sold five scrolls yesterday," he grumbled. "I was hoping to make up for that this morning."

"We can rush to the stall as soon as she's passed," Neff cajoled him. "We'll stay until nightfall. We'll stay until midnight! We'll sell more scrolls, because of everyone visiting from other villages." *Please*, she thought. *Please let me go.*

Her father dropped his head back and stared at the cloudless sky. "Do you hear this, Ahura? I've taught her too well." Then he nodded. "You drive a hard bargain, my girl. Fine, we'll go. It would probably look bad if we didn't. But we won't stay for a moment longer than we have to!"

Neff grinned and craned her neck to plant a kiss on her father's shining bald head. "Thank you, Yati! Thank you so much!"

Neff helped her mother quickly finish the chores. The goddess would leave her temple soon, and they needed to get a good spot on the street before the crowd grew too thick. Because for the first time in her life, Neff planned to approach Bast with a question of her own.

If anyone could help her remember her dream, it was the goddess herself.

The main street of Bubas was already buzzing with villagers by the time Neff and her parents arrived. It took them a little longer than usual because her father kept stopping to chat with everyone he saw, fishing for information about their lives so he could sell them a spell scroll.

"You and Khabak have been married for what, two seasons

now?" he asked a young woman waiting with her husband on the street corner. "Don't you think it's time to think about starting a family? I've got a scroll for that, you know. You'll be with child within the month!"

Neff rolled her eyes. *Come on*, she thought. *Not now!*

Finally, they managed to find a perfect spot to see Bast. It was near the edge of town, where the road started to curve toward the Iteru River. At the end of that road, a boat waited to carry Bast to the capital.

Neff saw a couple of her friends in the crowd—Henhen, the baker's daughter, and Istara, the papyrus merchant's girl. She'd known them both forever, and often visited them in their family's market stalls whenever Yati let her have a break. She waved. They waved back, beaming with excitement.

"Neff!" Henhen called out. "Will you be at the festival tonight?"

Neff remembered her promise to stay at the market until midnight and bit her lip. "I hope so!" she shouted back.

Bast only visited once a year, and that night, the village would be alive with celebrations. There'd be singing and dancing, and perhaps even some tiger nut sweets. Neff's mouth watered at the thought of the little balls of nuts and dates and honey. Her mother wasn't the only one with a sweet tooth.

"My father got permission to ask the goddess a question!" Istara added. "Isn't that amazing? He's been waiting for the nomarch to choose him for two years! He's going to ask her to give us another brother! Not that I want one." She laughed.

Neff ignored the sting of envy. "Amazing!" Turning away, she felt a thorn of doubt creep into her heart. Even if she didn't get into terrible trouble for addressing the goddess without permission, who was to say that the goddess would answer her question?

Don't think of that, she scolded herself. Standing on the tips of her toes, she strained to see over the crowd to where Bast and her retinue would process. *She'll be here any minute!*

Then, a ripple of excitement passed through the gathered villagers.

"She's coming!" someone shouted.

A moment later, Neff saw it: a beautifully crafted wooden palanquin, held aloft by four bald-headed men in white loincloths, carrying a sacred boat. It was about five cubits long, with cat heads carved into its bow and stern. A canopy covered the center of the boat, and behind its blowsy, translucent curtains, Neff caught her first glimpse of the goddess.

Bast was beautiful. An exquisitely carved statue, the goddess was a cat-headed woman in an intricate striped-pattern dress, made from dark smooth bronze. She held a basket in the crook of one arm and a sistrum in the other. At her feet sat four bronze kittens—three large and one small.

A tall, sharp-eyed woman with deep-brown skin walked at the front of the procession. Like the litter bearers, she was bald too. A black tattoo drawn in the shape of the widget eye adorned each of her shoulders. Over her simple white dress hung a large golden necklace—a broad collar in the shape of a half-moon, adorned with the head of a cat.

The high priestess of Bast. Neff wondered how old the woman was. No matter how many times she'd seen her at the annual festival, she never seemed to age.

As the priestess walked with Bast's boat sailing through the crowd behind her, she shook a sistrum, and the rhythmic, jangling sound of its copper rings silenced the crowd as she came. Neff watched the palanquin stop at intervals, allowing the villagers who stepped forward to petition the goddess.

"Will my father be healed from his sickness?"

"Should I take revenge on those who have wronged me?"

"Will I ever find love?"

With each question, the palanquin paused for a moment before leaning forward for yes, or backward for no. After receiving their answer, the petitioners bowed their heads in thanks and retreated back into the crowd.

The questions seemed endless, despite the limited number of people with permission to ask them. It wasn't surprising, given that poverty and hunger loomed over Bubas like a shadow, but it took what felt like an eternity for the goddess to make her way down the street to where Neff and her parents were waiting. Her father watched the position of the sun, growing increasingly impatient.

Finally, he said, "We've seen the goddess. People up the road are starting to leave. We should get to our stall before we lose the whole morning."

"Not yet," Neff pleaded. "Just a bit longer."

Her father huffed in exasperation but blessedly said no more.

Neff turned back to the street—and just in time. Bast's retinue was right on top of them. She'd been so eager for this moment, but now that it was upon her, Neff felt a sudden terror at stepping out into the street.

It was just a dream.

The procession passed in front of her, the sound of the high priestess's sistrum clanging in her ears.

It was just a dream.

A moment more, and her opportunity would be lost.

Neff had all but decided to abandon her plan when a breeze ruffled her hair, carrying the smell of honey, smoke, and wine. Neff closed her eyes, intoxicated, and when she opened them again—

She gasped. She had stepped out right in front of the high priestess.

The woman regarded her with dark imperious eyes.

All around her, the crowd murmured in surprise.

"Sweetheart?" she heard her mother say, quiet and afraid. "What are you doing?"

"Get back here!" her father barked, and Neff felt his hand on her arm. But before he could pull her back, the high priestess spoke.

"You have a question for the goddess, child?" Her voice was velvet soft, like a purr.

Neff swallowed. "Yes, High Priestess. I didn't get permission to ask, but…" She caught a glimpse of Henhen and Istara watching her, open-mouthed. Gathering her courage, Neff balled her hands into fists. "But I think it's important."

After a moment of consideration, the priestess nodded and swept an arm toward the palanquin. "You may approach the sacred boat."

Neff almost collapsed with relief.

She stood before the goddess, her body covered in a cold sweat. She could feel the weight of the crowd's stare.

"My petition is not a yes or no question," she said. "Is that all right?"

The high priestess cocked her head, curious. "You may ask whatever you want, child. Whether you are given an answer?" She shrugged. "That is up to Bast to decide."

Neff nodded and turned to face the canopy. She clasped her hands in supplication, both out of respect and to stop them from shaking. She began to speak.

"Praise to you…" She paused, ashamed of the weakness in her voice. "Praise to you," she began again, a little stronger. "O Bast, Great Lady of Bubas, beloved mistress of pleasure and secrets. Please hear my prayer. Every night, I have a dream. The same dream. I know it's important, but I can never recall what it's about. I'm sorry if it's too much to ask, but I thought maybe you could help me remember." Her whole body tensed as she waited for an answer.

Nothing happened.

People in the crowd shifted uncomfortably. Out of the corner of her eye, Neff saw her father's face, pink with anger and embarrassment.

Neff felt the sting of humiliation deep in her chest. *Fool*, she thought bitterly. *What made you think the goddess would speak to you?*

Then, all at once, a fierce wind began to blow, like whispers through papyrus reeds. It carried the same intoxicating smell as before, but stronger. Many in the crowd cried out and covered their faces as the khamasin lifted whorls of sand, sending pricking clouds into their eyes. Neff braced herself and squinted at the palanquin. Unlike everyone else, the litter bearers stood resolute as the sand struck their bodies. The wind lifted the canopy's filmy curtains in a slow, undulating dance, removing the only barrier between Neff and the goddess. Neff stared, her eyes locking on Bast's dark face.

Behind her, the priestess began to shake her sistrum once more, the percussive sound growing louder and more ominous with every passing second.

The goddess's feline face loomed large above her, one moment the tranquil, gentle face of a mother looking down upon one of its children, and the next—

The cat became a lioness.

And she roared.

Neff screamed as her mind was suddenly battered with images. Visions of darkness and desolation and blood. So much blood.

The lamb.

The lamb.

The lamb.

The images were unrelenting.

She knew at once that she'd seen them before, but not like this, never like this, not with her fragile waking mind. Neff tried to close her eyes, but her body wouldn't respond. She felt as if an invisible hand had reached out from beyond the veil and held her fast. Her screams turned to sobs of terror.

The lamb.

The lamb.

The lamb.

She saw it all. The desert. The grievous wound and the crimson wool. The sea of blood. Seared into her mind like a sizzling brand. And the words of the lamb. She heard those, too.

Then, as if someone had yanked her up from the bottom of the sea—it was over. The images stopped, the sistrum quieted, the wind eased. And as it did, the blowsy curtains fell back in place, shielding the goddess from sight.

Neff gasped like a drowning girl coming up for air.

She blinked, dizzy and confused. Her face was damp with tears. She wavered, unsteady on her feet, her mind caught between dreaming and waking. A small frightened moan passed through her lips, and she collapsed onto the dusty road.

The high priestess was the first to reach her as the crowd erupted in confusion.

"What happened, child?" the woman asked, kneeling by her side.

Neff curled into a fetal position, her palms pressed against her eyes. "I remember… I remember…" she cried over and over again. "The lamb…"

Half a dozen people, including Neff's parents, pressed closer, all of them trying to see for themselves what had happened.

"Move away!" the priestess shouted in irritation. "Give her some air."

The people took a couple steps back.

"Come," the priestess urged, gently pulling Neff's hands from her eyes to help her to her feet. "Get up if you can. We can't have you lying in the middle of the—"

The priestess stopped abruptly, her jaw slack. Behind her, the crowd fell silent.

Neff blinked into the blazing sunlight, bewildered by the wide-eyed faces encircling her.

Why do they look so scared?

Suddenly self-conscious, she sat up, wiping at her tears. It was only then that she noticed the red smears on her fingers. The sight of it sent her head spinning—had she cut her palms in the fall? But no, her hands were uninjured. Where was the blood coming from?

Shaking, she touched a finger to her face, to the track of tears she could feel still falling from her eyes. It came away shining, bright as carnelian.

Neff's heart was in her throat as someone shouted, "Gods preserve us! The girl cries tears of blood!"

News of Neff's encounter with Bast swept through the assembled crowd, and people closed in so that they, too, could catch a glimpse of her. The noise and press of bodies was terrifying, and Neff clutched at the high priestess for protection.

Raising the sistrum high in the air, the priestess shouted, *"Enough!"*

Cowed by her fury, the crowd fell back and quieted.

"You dare disrespect the goddess on her day of worship? Go back to your homes and places of work. Speak not of this, lest you are willing to bear divine judgment for the carelessness of your words." There was a pause as she turned in a circle, as if to encompass every soul within her sight. "Do you heed me? Now, go!"

With a low murmur, the crowd dispersed. After sharing a word with the litter bearers, the high priestess turned back to Neff, who still sat on the dusty road. Her face, which had been imperious a moment before, softened. "Come with me, child," she said, reaching out to Neff.

Hesitant, Neff took her hand, and the priestess pulled her to her feet.

The high priestess turned to Neff's pale-faced parents, who huddled nearby, and said, "You will accompany me to the river."

It was not a request, but a command.

Neff's mother and father nodded, and followed them to the riverbank without saying a word.

There was a large boat and crew waiting there, ready to carry Bast and her protectors north to Thonis for the festival that night.

"Go and cleanse yourself in the river," the high priestess told Neff. "I must speak to your parents."

Why? The word sat on Neff's tongue like a small stone. She'd wanted to ask it, but it remained heavy behind her lips, held there by the high priestess's imposing gaze. Obediently, she knelt at the edge of the riverbank.

She felt strangely numb as she dipped her hands into the cold water and watched the blood swirl away. When she was done, she cupped her hands and splashed water against her face. She gasped as the cold drove the cloudy feeling from her mind. Suddenly, she became very aware of what had just happened—aware and afraid.

What if Bast took offense to my question? she wondered. *Has the goddess cursed me? Perhaps the high priestess is telling Mamet and Yati of my fate. What if I have doomed them as well?*

Tears began to well in her eyes and she quickly wiped them

away, terrified she would find more blood. But they were clear, normal tears. Whatever had happened to her before was finished. It felt unreal, like a dream. Yet unlike her other dreams, the images the goddess showed her hadn't faded. Every time she closed her eyes, she saw the lamb, and heard its ominous voice.

I remember now, Neff realized. For better or for worse, the goddess had answered her prayer.

Neff glanced back at her parents. She couldn't hear what the high priestess was saying to them, but she could see its effect on their faces. Her mother's eyes were wide, and she had both hands pressed to her mouth. After a moment, she dropped them into a pose of supplication.

"Please," her mother said, loud enough for Neff to hear. "I'm begging you. You can't. She's our only child."

"Ahura! Control yourself, woman," her father scolded.

He took her mother's hands in his and quietly apologized to the high priestess. His expression was stony, serious—totally unlike the smile he always wore for his customers. But he didn't look horrified. In fact, he seemed… excited?

With a curt nod to Pepi and Ahura, the high priestess concluded her discussion. She turned from them and met Neff's gaze. "You may join us now."

Neff rose on wobbly legs and approached them. Her eyes darted from one person to another, trying to anticipate what was about to happen. The pride in her father's expression confused her, and the sorrow in her mother's filled her with dread. The high priestess's face was unreadable. When she spoke, it was without preamble.

"You have been touched by the goddess, Nefermaat," she said, and Neff's name had never carried such weight. "Your life now belongs to Bast and the gods of this land. I have spoken to your mother and father, and it is agreed that you will accompany me downriver to Thonis, where you shall be prepared for the priesthood." She paused to allow her words to sink in.

Neff stared at her, speechless. "B-but," she stammered, "I'm not—"

"It is not an easy life," the high priestess continued. "Not for a girl, not for anyone. But it is the life chosen for you by the divine. Obey their decree, or suffer the consequences of their displeasure. Do you understand?"

Neff swallowed, trying and failing to catch hold of the thoughts and questions that whirled through her mind.

"What about my things?" she blurted. "I have nothing but the clothes on my back." She looked down at her white dress and was mortified to see bloodstains down the front of it.

"You need take nothing but your immortal soul," the high priestess replied. "All else will be provided for you at the Great Temple. Now come. I have already tarried too long. The goddess awaits."

Neff shook her head. It was all happening too fast. Her house, her sleeping mat, the little paddle doll she kept from when she'd been a baby... would she see any of them again? And what about Henhen and Istara? The stall at the market? Who would help her father run it? When she'd left home this morning, she never thought it would be for the last time.

She turned to her mother. "Mamet?" she said, a quaver in her voice.

"Oh, my sweet girl." Her mother gathered Neff into her arms. "You must take care of yourself, all right? Always wear your sandals outside, and watch for snakes, and remember how I taught you to keep your hair shiny, yes?" Her eyes brimmed with tears.

"Mamet." Neff hugged her mother's small body against her own. "I'm scared. I don't want to leave you."

Neff felt her father's hand against her head.

"Don't you see?" he said as she turned to him. "This is wonderful news, my girl. Wonderful! I was angry when you stepped out of the crowd, but now I see you were led by a divine hand! Now when the people come to our stall in the market, I will tell them all about you. My Neff, chosen by the goddess to do great things. I've always known it. Always. When you were born, I told your mother. Didn't I, Ahura?" He turned to his wife, and she nodded, too overwhelmed to speak. "I told her: 'Name her Nefermaat.' *Beautiful truth*. That's you. You're going to make us proud. Do you hear? They'll come to see me from all over Bubas, from all over the kingdom, just to hear your story."

"But—"

"Go on now," he broke in. "Can't keep the goddess waiting, can we?"

But I thought you were already proud, Neff wanted to say. Instead, she took a deep breath, pressed her lips into a thin line, and said, "No, Yati, we can't." She turned to face the high priestess.

"Are you ready?" the woman asked, gesturing toward the sleek vessel that rocked gently in the current.

"No," Neff whispered, her lip trembling. "I'm not."

She stepped onto the boat.

3
RAE

"Two!" an old man shouted, thrusting two fingers into the air. Raetawy pressed up onto her palms and spit a mouthful of bloody dust onto the ground. Panting, she leveled a gaze at her opponent. He was circling her, smiling for the crowd who had assembled to watch—and wager—on the matches of the day. He was tall and fast, his long arms allowing for a strong reach. But he was scrawny too, and his arrogant swagger made him careless.

"That's one throw for Rae, and two for Buto!" the old man announced. His face had a lumpy quality, his nose crooked from being broken too many times. He clutched a sweaty scrap of papyrus with dozens of bets marked down in a hurried scrawl. "First to three wins!"

Get up, Rae told herself, ignoring the pain in her foot where it had twisted beneath her. *Give them nothing.*

Rising to her feet, Rae adjusted her belted tunic and smoothed her shoulder-length black hair, which had come loose from the simple linen strip she'd used to tie it back. The crowd quieted when they saw her move into a fighting stance and wait for the next round to begin.

"You want more?" Buto said. A couple of his friends in the crowd jeered. "I'll give you as much as you want."

Rae narrowed her eyes. "Oh," she growled, "I don't think you have that much in you."

The crowd *ooh*ed at that, and Buto scowled. "In a minute I'll have you on your back again, where you belong." He lunged.

Rae ducked under his arm, sliding on one knee and grasping her opponent around his legs. With a shove of her head against his hip, she cinched his knees together and drove him to the ground.

The crowd whooped in surprise.

"Two for Rae!" the old man shouted over the din. "The score is tied!"

Buto was up on his feet in an instant, red-faced. "Does your father know you come here, eh, Rae? Does he know that his daughter rolls on the ground with every man in the city, like a whore?"

Rae's face flushed with sudden heat. "Watch your mouth."

Buto smirked. "You'd think he'd try to put a stop to that. Or did they cut off his *balls* too?"

With a roar of fury, Rae barreled toward Buto, ready to knock the smile off his face. But instead, Buto grabbed her by the arm and wrist, turned his back, and flipped her over his shoulder. Her stomach churned as the world turned upside down with a sickening lurch. She landed hard on her back, and every bone in her body sang with the impact.

"Buto wins!" the old man announced.

Her opponent thrust his fist into the air. "Ha!"

The spectators cheered in reply before crowding the old man for the spoils of their bets.

Rae lay on the ground, staring at a sky crisscrossed with clotheslines that reached between the low mud-brick buildings of Sakesh. Two mourning doves peered down at her from their perch on one of the lines, their heads cocked in curiosity.

A familiar shadow fell over her, nearly blocking out the noonday sun. Blood still pounded in her ears as the bullish, swarthy young man pulled her to her feet. "Come on," her friend Omari said. "Up."

"Better luck next time, eh, sweet lips?" Buto said with a wink, before turning to join his friends. They laughed and clapped him on the back before walking away.

Rae nearly chased after them, but Omari took ahold of her shoulder.

"Rae," he warned.

"Curse that son of a dog!" Rae sent a piece of pottery flying with the tip of her sandal. The small pot sailed into a wall and shattered into a thousand pieces. Startled, the two mourning doves flew off in a flurry of feathers, followed closely by the remaining onlookers, who eyed her balefully before shuffling out of the wide alleyway. Rae and Omari were left alone, staring at the sad remnants of a pot that had never done anything to anyone.

"Are you finished?" Omari asked after a few moments of silence.

Rae swallowed, her fury finally drained. "Yes," she said dully.

"Good. Can we go now?"

She glared up at him. Despite her own impressive height, Omari towered over her. His square face and wide nose made him look like he should be the one brawling instead of her. They were neighbors and had grown up together, having both been born during the Great War—though Rae was a season older and never let him forget it.

"Fine," she said with a sigh, grabbing her pack from where she'd discarded it before the fights. They made their way back to the street, walking side by side. "Just don't say it," she added.

"Say what?" he asked amiably. "That you would have seen that throw coming had you not been blinded by rage?"

"Lions fetch you, Omari…" Rae said, shoving him. "I told you not to say it."

"Oh, I'm sorry," Omari replied, his tone mocking. "I forgot that you'd rather fill your ears with dirt than wisdom." He grinned. "You know Buto only baits you because you always bite."

"But Omari," Rae argued, "He so deserves to be bitten."

She followed him onto the crowded, noisy street, which was filled with merchants hollering about their meager wares, women with skinny babies balanced on their hips, and men leading oxen laden with cargo. The air was thick with the smells of roasting meat, animal dung, and sweat.

Omari said nothing for a few minutes, his eyebrows raised in that how-many-times-have-I-told-you expression that infuriated her.

"Oh fine, fine!" Rae finally said, throwing her hands up in defeat. "I was wrong. You were right. Is that what you want to hear?"

Omari closed his eyes, blissful. "Say it again… slower this time."

"Ugh," Rae said with disgust. "The point is, next time, I won't take the bait. Happy?"

Omari chuckled. "Next time…" He shook his head. "You're really going to keep doing this, Ay?"

Rae smiled at the nickname he'd used for her since childhood. *Donkey*. She'd always been stubborn—butting heads with the bigger boys even then.

"Why shouldn't I? It helps calm my savage mind. Imagine what I'd be like if I stopped?"

"You'd be unbearable, I'm sure. Still, there are other ways of channeling your fury." Omari looked pointedly at her fat lip.

Rae licked her mouth and tasted blood. She swiped it away. "What other ways?"

Omari was thoughtful as they walked. Then he said, "I need to stop at the weavers' workshop before we go back home."

He didn't answer my question, Rae noticed, but let it go. She glanced up at the position of the sun and sucked her teeth. "Not for too long, I hope. I have to help Father finish harvesting before sunset. He'll soon be wondering about me."

"I'll be quick," Omari assured her, and turned into a street lined with single-story mud-brick workshops. "You don't even need to come in. Actually, it might be better if you don't."

Rae glared at the back of Omari's big head. *Now I'm definitely going in. The nerve of that ox! Telling me what to do...* Anyway, there was someone in there she wanted to see.

The two wove through the throng toward the artisans' quarter. The buildings, whose windows and doors had once been lined with colored tile, were faded and crumbling at the edges. Rae cast her eyes over them and sighed. The days when Sakesh had been the jewel of Low Khetara were gone—artifacts of her youth and the end of the Great War. It had been nineteen years, but the city had never recovered from the wounds of its defeat. Low Khetara hadn't simply lost their king to Sematawy and his army; they'd lost their way too.

A ragged man, his face lined with scars, hunched near the corner of a bakery, a walking stick gripped in his gnarled hand. The city was abundant with men like him—old soldiers who'd been left with no land and no purpose after the High Khetarans took away their weapons and station. Rae had only been a baby when King Rahotep fell to the northern scourge. But she'd grown up hearing stories of her father's life in the king's palace, where he'd worked as a royal scribe. When she was little, the stories had delighted her. They were so full of sound and color—of wonders that she could only dream about. But as she got older and came to understand what they'd lost, the stories only made her angry.

Eventually, her father stopped telling them.

But he never stopped trying to teach her what he knew, and over the years, he had given her the kind of education that had become so rare in Low Khetara that even most men never received it. By the time she turned ten, she already had a basic knowledge of Khetaran history and religion, and she could read and write the common script fairly well—more than well enough to keep the records for the farm. Thanks to the High Khetarans, her father couldn't really write anymore himself, but through his painstaking descriptions of how to form the letters and words, they'd made it work.

The one thing her father never taught her was the gods' words, the true language of the scribes. The gods' words were the origin of all Khetaran writing, the sacred birds, snakes, cups, eyes, and hands from which the common script had been derived. Perhaps Father never taught her how to read or write them because he never had the time, or didn't see a need, but Rae suspected it was more than that. Her father wasn't broken like the ragged man on the street, but the fissures in his spirit were still there, hidden under the surface. Rae got the sense that he thought there was no point to writing in the sacred word, because the gods were no longer listening.

Rae passed close to the old soldier as she followed Omari into the weavers' workshop. The beggar was nodding rhythmically, staring ahead with cloudy, unseeing eyes.

"The lamb," he muttered, his face creased with agitation.

Taking pity on him, Rae reached into her pack and pulled out half a loaf of bread. She pressed the food into the soldier's empty hand.

If he noticed her charity, he didn't let on. He gripped the

bread until the crust crackled under the pressure. "The lamb, the lamb," he chanted under his breath.

Rae shook her head grimly and stepped into the workshop.

She immediately blundered into a woman carrying an armful of spindles loaded with fine white thread. The woman cursed and said, "Watch where you're going!"

"Sorry, sorry, sorry!" Rae snatched a fallen spindle from the floor and placed it on top of the teetering pile. The weaver tutted at her before flouncing back to her station.

The workshop was a frenzy of activity, filled with women spinning flaxen thread or weaving fabric on long wooden looms. Everything was so white and pristine that Rae felt embarrassed by the state of her dress. Her tunic was spattered with abstract patterns of dirt and blood—and her sandals? She grimaced. They didn't bear examination. Clearing her throat, she attempted to smooth the flyaway strands of her hair, but probably only made it worse.

Omari was already speaking with one of the weavers—an expansive older woman with wrinkled light-brown skin and hair that had gone gray at the temples. Mamet Mut. The two spoke as she passed the weft beam between the taut warp threads in a steady rhythm, while a smaller woman used another wooden beam to bang the threads tightly against one another. The movements filled the workshop with sound—*Shh, clack! Shh, clack! Shh, clack!* Rae tried to hear to what Omari and Mamet Mut were saying, but between the looms and many voices, she could only make out a few words at a time.

"... meet tonight..."

"No, the Medjay won't find..."

"But Asim said..."

Rae's brow furrowed. *The Medjay?* Omari was a carpenter's son. What business did he have with the pharaoh's lawmen?

She was about to march over and ask just what in Ra's name

he was up to when her gaze fell upon a young woman spinning thread on the other side of the room.

Omari and his secrets were instantly forgotten.

The girl was a cascade of soft curves, from her tightly curled hair down to the roundness of her figure. A small clay pot sat at her feet, filled with a mass of wet flax fibers. The girl coaxed a single rough fiber from the mass, holding it aloft in one hand, while in the other she held a wooden spindle that she rolled along her bare thigh, spinning the fiber into fine thread. The movement was like a slow, undulating dance, and Rae couldn't help but stare.

The girl caught Rae watching her and smiled. "Hi, Rae."

Rae's cheeks grew hot. "Tam."

"What brings you?"

"I… Omari needed…" She coughed. Her throat was suddenly dry. She'd only known Tamerit for a season—the girl's family had moved from Per-Abu to live with their cousins, and Tam had joined the weavers shortly after. They'd met in the market when they'd both reached for the same basket of figs. Their fingers touched, their eyes met, and Rae felt her body become liquid. Since that day, Rae had taken every opportunity to drop in on the weavers to see her again.

"Oh," Tam replied, sticking out her lower lip. "Omari needed something, eh? Are you sure you don't need anything?"

"I do need something," Rae replied, teasing.

"I agree," Tam replied. "A bath."

Rae laughed, and then covered her mouth with one hand.

"Maybe *after* you've cleaned yourself up," Tam went on, "we could—"

Suddenly, Mamet Mut stepped between them, eyeing Rae with disapproval.

"Omari!" she bellowed. "You didn't tell me you brought your friend! So, are you two finally getting married?"

Rae looked over at Omari and blanched. He stared back at her with a strange expression, then hurried over, his palms raised in protest.

"No, no, not today, Mamet Mut."

She wasn't Omari's mother—she had no children, in fact—but Mamet Mut acted like she was everyone's mother. She claimed to know every single soul living in Sakesh, and more than that, knew what was best for them. Mut wasn't her real name, but everyone called her that because, like the great sky goddess, Mamet Mut seemed to see everything that happened in the city and was never afraid to share her opinion about it.

"Ta-ta, ta-ta," Mamet Mut complained. "So slow, Omari. You've had your whole life to ask her and still you wait. For what? Ra only knows. Do the weavers a favor and give us a little excitement one of these days, won't you?"

Rae couldn't help but laugh at her friend's embarrassment. "Yes, Omari," she said, elbowing him. "Why can't you be more exciting, like your friend, the fighting donkey?"

Omari rubbed the back of his head with one hand, unable to meet her gaze.

What's wrong with him? Rae wondered. *This isn't the first time Mamet Mut has badgered him like this. Why is he acting so weird?*

Omari turned back to the big woman and gave her a little bow. "I'll do my best, Mamet," he said. "But for now, we must get back home. Our work awaits us."

Mamet Mut waved him off, laughing with the other women.

Rae looked back toward Tamerit, desperate for the girl to finish her thought, but the young weaver had gone back to her own work, rolling the thread onto her spindle. Rae finally caught her eye and mouthed *sorry*. Tam shrugged one shoulder lightly, her every movement an invitation.

Rae bit her lip and groaned softly. *I'll be back*, she promised herself as she followed Omari out the door. As soon as the harvest was done, she'd return to reap what that unfinished moment had sown.

They left the artisans' quarter behind and took the river road out of town. Soon, the crowds thinned, leaving Rae and Omari side by side in awkward silence. For as long as she could remember, everyone in Rae's life had loved to talk about how she and Omari would be married one day. It had been funny when they still wore the sidelock of youth, naked and carefree, spending their days wrestling with the other children and swimming in the Iteru until the sun went down. It was only when they got older, and the talk grew more serious, that it became a problem.

Rae loved Omari, but she didn't want to marry him.

It took meeting Tamerit to really understand why. Not that she'd tell Omari that. She wasn't sure he'd understand.

Besides, Rae was fairly certain that Omari didn't want to marry her either. After all, Rae didn't think she was what most Khetaran men wanted in a wife. She was tall and thick-bodied, her shoulders broad from a lifetime of farmwork. She didn't oil or style her hair, her hands were rough and her knuckles calloused, and in her free time, she fought men in alleyways and used the spoils to trade for beer.

Not that it mattered if the men liked it or not. Rae wasn't going to change for anyone.

Omari was like a brother to her. Romance, she was sure, was far from his mind, at least when it came to his stubborn old friend. There were plenty of other girls who would be better suited to him, and Rae often pointed them out in the street. He'd dutifully look them over, but as far as she knew, he'd never pursued any of them. If he had, he would have told her about it. They told each other everything.

Speaking of secrets…

Rae cleared her throat. "So… what was that all about?"

"What do you mean?"

Rae swore. "Don't play games. What were you talking about with Mamet Mut? Something about the Medjay? What are you up to?"

Omari frowned, his eyes on the road before them. The sun had sunk past its zenith, casting long shadows on the dusty ground as they walked. To the west, the River Iteru snaked in both directions, as far as the eye could see. Trading ships and small fishing skiffs crowded its waters, some riding the current north to High Khetara, others catching the wind in their sails and sailing south to the cataract, where the waters turned wild and game was bountiful. Green fields stretched across both sides of the great river, her gifts transforming the desert into the rich black loam from which everything grew. Already Rae could smell it in the air, that earthy perfume that was a welcome respite from the heavy stink of the city. That and the gentle sound of the Iteru's flowing water was usually enough to raise her spirits, but her friend's strange behavior made her uneasy.

"Omari," she said, her voice low. "No secrets, remember?"

It was a promise they'd made to each other when they were small, after Rae's mother died. She'd been sick for a while, but her parents had kept the knowledge of her illness secret from their young daughter. They'd believed they were doing her a kindness, but Rae was devastated by what seemed to her like a sudden, unexpected loss. She hardly spoke to her father during that first lonely season. Her mind was filled with thoughts of what she would have done differently if she had known, how she would have spent those last days holding her mother a little bit longer, would have said the things she never got to, would have better prepared herself for that final goodbye. Omari had come to her on one of those dark days and sat by her side, watching the boats float by on the river. "I'll never keep secrets from you," he'd said. "I promise."

Rae had leaned her head on his shoulder and whispered, "Me too."

She looked at him, still seeing that little boy from so long ago. She felt a pang of guilt, thinking of Tamerit and what she herself was keeping from him, but quickly pushed it from her mind.

Omari rubbed the back of his head, as he always did when he was nervous, but said nothing.

"Well?" she prodded.

Omari's jaw clenched. "You must keep this to yourself, do you understand?" He scanned the area around them. Other than two farmers and a donkey carrying sacks of grain far up ahead, they were alone on the road.

Rae's pulse quickened. "Yes, of course," she said. "I swear it."

Omari stopped walking and turned to face her. They'd reached the edge of his family's land, where their mud-brick home and carpentry workshop stood. "There is a group of like-minded men who want to liberate Low Khetara from the pharaoh's oppressive rule. They have been meeting at night, in various secret locations, to make a plan of action that begins here, in Sakesh. The weavers have been passing messages along to the men so that they can avoid being seen together on the street. Not all of the weavers know, mind you, but Mamet Mut and a few others do. The Medjay don't like it when Sakeshis assemble in groups of any number, so…" He faltered.

"Wait… *you're* one of these 'like-minded men'?" Rae asked.

Omari squared his shoulders. "I am."

Rae felt a chill, despite the blazing heat of the sun on her skin. "I don't understand. Since when are you so interested in politics?"

"Since my eyes were opened to injustices I can no longer tolerate."

"Omari," Rae scoffed. "I know things in Sakesh are bad, but what—?"

"Look around you," Omari broke in. "Our city is falling to ruin. Once proud men beg on the streets, dressed in rags, while High Khetarans live in luxury, wearing robes threaded with gold they stole from our land. Don't you ever think about it, Rae? Don't you ever wonder why you're so angry?"

Rae was taken aback. It felt as if she were talking with a stranger. Omari had always been so soft-spoken and easygoing, in many ways her opposite. Looking at him now, she had to wonder what depths lay beneath his placid surface—what she'd been too busy to notice while focused on her own problems.

"Of course, I think about it," she said, sullen. "But I'm too busy keeping food on my father's table to have secret meetings with strange men." When Omari didn't reply, she asked, "What is it that you plan to do, anyway?"

Omari shook his head. "I've said too much already. I don't want you and Ankhu involved if something goes wrong."

"Wrong?" Rae asked, alarmed. "Omari, what are you planning? How do you know you can trust these men? Who are they? If you go and get yourself killed, I swear I'll—"

"Keep your voice down!"

Rae was shocked by the force in his voice. He grabbed her, squeezing her wrist in his work-roughened hand. Rae's instinct was to pull him toward her and throw him onto his back, just like she did to Buto—but she didn't. Omari must have sensed the tension in her, though, because he quickly released his grip.

"I'm sorry," Omari said, his voice quiet once more. "But these are dangerous times, Rae. I recommend you keep your unbridled stupidity to a minimum."

Omari's gentle jabs typically made her laugh, but this time, a rush of rage flooded her body. "You're calling *me* stupid? I'm not the one sneaking out in the middle of the night searching for a fire to burn in!"

Omari glared at her, a similar fury reflected on his face. Then it dissipated, and he sighed. "Look, I didn't mean to—"

But Rae was too angry and hurt to listen. "Don't worry," she broke in. "Even a fool like me knows how to keep her mouth shut." And with that, she strode past him toward home.

"Rae, wait," Omari called after her. She didn't look back. "Rae!"

After that, he must have given up and gone inside, because only the sounds of the river followed her home.

Soon, the slender palms lining the edge of Omari's family land were behind her, and the familiar fields of golden wheat began. The feathery stalks were nearly chest-high, and Rae stretched her hand out to let them tickle her palm. She pushed the fight with Omari from her mind. *You've got too much going on to worry about him.*

Rae's back ached thinking about all the work that needed to be done on the farm. She and her father had already harvested the southern field—but it was the smaller of the two, and besides that, the year's crop, much like everyone else's, had been middling at best, so they'd have to make sure to harvest every stalk to have enough wheat cut and bundled to pay the king's tax. If the northern field took extra time, so be it. She began to plan out the rest of that day, and the next, and the next. The orderly, ordinary thoughts soothed her.

She caught her father as he was leading one of the humpbacked brown zebu back to its pen. He was her equal in almost every respect—from his broad muscled frame to his large knob-knuckled hands, and the sun-bronzed color of his skin. Only his frizzy halo of graying hair—which made him look far older than his years—separated them.

"You see?" he said to the cow when he spied Rae coming up the path. "I told you she'd be back. And in one piece too." His gaze fell upon her face, and he cocked his head. "Well, mostly."

Rae raised a hand, wincing when she touched a puffy welt under her eye. *Add that to the fat lip, I guess.* Had she landed on her face one of the times Buto threw her? She couldn't really remember. Shrugging, she gave her father a sheepish grin. "Tripped over a rock in the road. You know me."

"Clumsiest girl in all Khetara—yes, I know you." Her father chuckled, giving the zebu a pat on the rump and closing the narrow wooden gate behind her. He fumbled with the latch, cursing, and Rae hurried forward to help him.

"I got you more salve from the market," she said, pulling a small clay pot from her pack after securing the gate. She opened the plug to show him the white ointment that smelled of beeswax and olive oil.

"It certainly took you long enough," he said, giving the salve a cursory glance. "It seems like every week it takes you longer."

"The market is... ah... busy this time of day," she lied, poking at the ointment with her finger. Her father had a way of seeing straight through her, and she couldn't bring herself to meet his gaze. "Why don't I put some of this on your arm before we get started? It will keep your skin from chafing."

"Later," her father said, waving away the pot. "I've already got it secured."

Rae looked down at his right arm, where a curved wooden sickle had been fitted onto the stump where his right hand had once been. Years ago, after he'd expressed his frustration about reaping wheat one-handed, Omari's father had fashioned the special tool for just that purpose, and her father had been using it ever since.

"I'll say this about you, Ankhu," the carpenter had said the first time they'd tied it to his arm, "You're as stubborn as your zebu."

It was true. After the end of the Great War, Father could have easily become one of those broken men, like the one she'd seen on the street. He'd lost so much in the aftermath—his lofty position as a palace scribe, his home in the city, and his right hand at the wrist. He hadn't written a single word since—the High Khetaran soldiers had made sure of that.

As a rule, Khetarans often collected the hands of their enemies as a way to account for the number slain, but for some reason, they'd allowed Ankhu to live. Perhaps the soldier who'd done it thought it a mercy, but Rae knew that although he'd escaped with his life, a part of her father had still died that day.

Several years after that, he'd lost his wife too.

He was left with two things, and two things only: a bit of land outside the city and a motherless little girl. So instead of losing himself at the bottom of a jug of beer, her father had tied a sickle to his arm and nurtured them both.

Rae loved him for that. Of all the suns in her sky, he shined the brightest.

"Come now, Rae," her father said. "The day grows short, and we have much to do."

Sighing, Rae took up a length of rope and followed her father to the northern field. "I wish you would let me help with the reaping." She slapped at a mosquito on her neck. "It would go so much faster…"

"No, it wouldn't," her father replied impatiently, as he did every time they had this argument. "Someone would still need to gather and bundle the wheat, and you know I can't. Besides, reaping is a man's job. Let me have my pride, won't you, woman?"

Rae rolled her eyes. She knew he was right about the gathering, but she also knew it would feel good to wield a sickle, to cut the stalks with sweeping strokes and watch them fall at her feet. Maybe, if she could do that, she wouldn't feel the need to pick fights in the street.

Don't you ever wonder why you're so angry?

Omari's words nagged at her like an itch she had to scratch.

Don't you ever think about it, Rae?

It was a stupid question. She thought about it every day. Everyone did. Sakesh was falling to ruin, more rapidly than ever before. But what could she do? What could anyone do? She might as well have tried to stop the wind from blowing.

Omari was wasting his time. Worse, he was endangering his family. Rae glanced over at her father, already glistening with sweat as he swung his sickle across the wheat. Despite her weekly treatment with the salve, she could see that the skin around the rope harness was raw and weeping. She hated to see him struggle, but she couldn't see that there was an alternative. Her father had nearly lost his life in the war with High Khetara. What could possibly be worth risking it again?

The sun was low on the horizon, a golden disk burning in a pool of bloodred light. From the middle of the northern field, Rae and her father saw a large sailboat coming up the river. Its white sail was taut with a bellyful of wind and boasted the sigil of a ram's head painted in black and red ochre. The boat sliced swiftly through the water, nearing the edge of their land.

Rae's father shielded his eyes to squint at the approaching craft. "It's the nomarch."

Rae dropped the wheat she'd just finished bundling on top of the pile and stood panting, her arms akimbo. "But he's not due to visit for ten days. We're not ready!"

"I'll handle it," her father muttered, and began walking to meet the boat.

Rae followed close on his heels, wiping the sweat from her brow.

The nomarch and his retinue of soldiers and scribes were already disembarking when Rae and her father reached the river road. Sakesh's representative to the crown was a short, stooped man with chin-length black hair—probably a wig—and a bulbous, florid nose. He wore a long robe made of fabric so fine and so white that it made Rae and her father's clothes look gray. He stopped in front of them, his men assembling themselves in formation behind him.

"Ankhu," the man said by way of greeting. He chewed a glob of mastic, his lips making a smacking sound.

"Nomarch," Rae's father replied, bowing his head.

"We've come to collect the king's tax," the man went on, still chewing. "Please show my men to your store."

Rae saw her father's jaw tense. But when he spoke, his voice was calm. "I would be most pleased to do so, except that we have only eighty hekats of wheat ready today. We can have the other twenty in ten days' time, if that suits you."

The nomarch stopped chewing and was silent for a moment. "What suits me," he said with casual malice, "is getting what I ask when I ask for it."

"With all due respect," Rae's father replied, "You're ten days early—"

The nomarch continued as if Rae's father hadn't spoken at all. "Furthermore, the tax is now one hundred *and fifty* hekats. By decree of King Amunmose."

Rae felt the blood drain from her face. *A hundred and fifty hekats*, she thought. *But that's… We couldn't possibly…*

As if sharing her thoughts, her father scoffed. "You can't be serious. That would take out more than half of our harvest. The king must know that the crops have been poor this year. What are we to live on?"

The nomarch's eyes narrowed. "I'm sure I don't care, Ankhu. But if you would like to keep your other hand, you'll produce the remaining seventy hekats and have it ready in four days. I'd much rather have it now, but what can I say? I'm feeling generous." He spat the mastic gum onto the ground at her father's feet. "And if you don't have enough wheat, perhaps I'll take your daughter as payment instead." He sauntered over to Rae, his heavy-lidded eyes roving up and down her body. When he leaned in close, his breath bitter and hot, it took all her willpower not to lace her arm around his neck and squeeze. "She's an able-bodied girl," the nomarch mused. "I'd be happy to put her to work at my estate."

Rae looked over at her father. His face was a mask of studied passivity. "You'll have your seventy hekats."

It was only after the nomarch's soldiers had carried the prepared wheat onto the boat and the king's scribes had marked the number on their scrolls and sailed on; after her father, silent and brooding, had returned to the house; after she had stowed their tools and made sure the zebu were settled in their pen for the night; it was only then that Rae walked out through the fields to the desert, fell to her knees, and screamed her rage into the night.

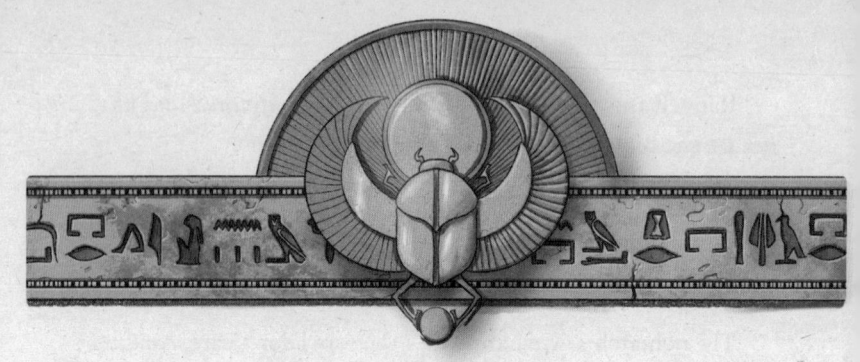

4
KARIM

A bouquet of dry flowers tied with strips of cloth.

An animal bone blackened by fire.

A still-sharp flint with a carved wooden handle.

A shard of pottery the color of the sky.

Karim laid these items in a row on the sandy ground and stared at them, hoping that if he looked at them long enough, they might reveal their secrets. So far, they were silent on the matter. Kneeling on the valley floor, golden cliffs rising on either side, he ran his hands through the sand, searching, sifting, letting the grains run through his fingers.

"How long we will sit in this heat, hey?" Hager muttered, dragging the back of his hand across his brow. "I'm roasting." He perched on a nearby boulder like a spider—all skinny limbs and sharp angles. Like the other Jackals, Hager wore a dark coarse robe, open at the chest, with wide sleeves that he'd rolled up to his elbows. A cloth of similar style draped over his head, shielding his long, narrow face from the blazing sun.

"Until I am filled," Karim replied as he stood, brushing the sand from his palms. He rubbed the dark stubble of his chin thoughtfully. "Something is here. I know it."

"Aha, he *knows* it," Babu jeered. "Just as he knew it yesterday. And the day before that. And yet, our hands remain empty! We waste our time, Karim. Here is nothing but rocks!"

"Yes, there are many rocks," Karim agreed. "Some on the ground, others in your head. But there is more than that, Babu."

Babu shook his head. "You tell him it's a bull, and he tells you to milk it," he said to Hager. "Why don't we leave him here, hey? He can sleep with his trash and be happy."

"Because without me you're lost, Babu-sen," Karim said warmly. "You couldn't find an oasis if one bit you on the ass."

Babu had twenty-one years—only two seasons more than Karim—but he was at least a double handsbreadth taller and built like a hippopotamus. Even so, Karim couldn't resist baiting him. When it came to finding tombs in the desert, he was very good. Keeping his mouth shut? Not so much.

"Pah!" Babu grumbled, then spat on the ground. "You best watch where your words will lead you, sen—or you might find yourself at the end of my dagger. A Jackal you may be, but my patience has limits. When the sun passes its zenith—we go."

Karim bit back a retort and nodded. "Fine."

"You really think there's something out there, hey?" Djet asked, sidling up to Karim as he surveyed the valley for the hundredth time.

Djet was plump and smooth-faced, barely out of boyhood. He'd begged Babu to let him join the Jackals, despite his age. After losing both his parents in a raid on their people's camp a season ago, he was left with nothing and no skills to speak of, aside from his curious mind. *Never too young for tragedy*, Karim had thought at the time. At Karim's urging, Babu had relented, allowing Djet preliminary membership to their esteemed company, who were renowned across the Red Lands for relieving the Khetarans of their buried treasures.

"I do think there's something, yes," Karim replied. How could he explain to the boy, or to any of the Jackals, that it was more feeling than thought? That whenever he searched for a tomb, something tugged at him, like a rope around his chest, pulling him in the right direction?

Better not to explain. Better to trust his instincts. They had never failed him—so why was this day any different? He'd found the objects, and searched all the obvious places, but so far, no luck. The Jackals had already uncovered half a dozen other hidden tombs in the valley, although they'd all been plundered before their arrival. Still, they'd managed to find a few choice baubles, and that kept them looking for more. They'd scoured the area from back to front though, and Babu was convinced there was nothing more to find.

Karim disagreed.

He squinted at the sky. He was running out of time.

"I'm going to scout up that way," Karim told the others. "You stay here, hey?"

"Fine with me," Hager said with a yawn.

"I'm coming with you!" Djet exclaimed.

"Too bad," Babu sighed, gripping the haft of his spear. "I was going to use the boy for target practice."

Djet paled, which made the other Jackals laugh.

"Come on, sen," Karim said, ruffling the boy's dark hair. "Help me get the tools together."

After gathering up his talismans and slinging his pack over one shoulder, Karim made his way toward the valley wall. Djet scampered by his side like an enthusiastic puppy.

"If anyone can find it, you can," he said, beaming. "Of that, I am sure."

Karim grinned and touched a knuckle to his nose in thanks. Tomb robbery may not have been the noblest of occupations, but for him, it was the best in a series of unpleasant options. Men of the Anen tribe either tended to the flocks, which were the lifeblood of their people, or they took up spears and fought to defend them. Karim had resisted choosing a path during his youth, despite his father's urging, but his indecision came to a head several years ago when a pack of Shass raiders had come upon their camp in the middle of the night, made off with a dozen sheep, and killed three of their men.

One of those men had been Karim's father.

He'd been left to care for his mother and three younger siblings, with no trade to speak of. His brother, several years younger than Karim, swiftly dedicated himself to the blade—hungry to avenge their father's death if the Shass tried to plunder them again. Although Karim understood his desire, he didn't share it. Neither leading warriors into battle nor sheep into pasture sounded particularly appealing. Either way, the job always ended in slaughter.

His little sisters, who were only ten and eleven years old, had seemed to age overnight. The last vestiges of their childhood had died along with their father.

Soon after the raid, the tribe moved camp. After several days' travel, Karim had been sitting by the fire at dusk, feeling adrift, listening to the swish of his brother's practice spear and the crackle of the flames. Gazing at his new surroundings, he'd fixated on the shape of a distant pyramid. The sight reminded him of the stories his father had told him about the Khetarans, the river kingdom that shunned the tribes of the Red Lands.

"Their river—they think it gives them supremacy, hey?" his father used to say. "To them we are like vermin, but when the time comes to bury their sacred dead, where do they bring them?

To *our* home. *Our* land. They think that whatever the sun touches belongs to them."

It was because of the Khetarans that the lives of his people were so full of hardship, Karim's father had said. They were pompous and greedy, spoiled by the riches the river had brought them—completely unlike the rugged Anen, who had no time for superstition and frippery. Worse, the Khetarans had the audacity to use the Red Lands as their personal graveyard and build massive monuments and underground tombs there, but offer no respect to its people.

By the fire, Karim left his own sorrow—the loss of his father, and the suffering of his family in the wake of his death—at the Khetarans' feet as well.

Perhaps he was too much of a coward to fight and too capricious to tend a herd, but Karim knew one thing. He was clever enough to find a few Khetaran tombs and take back some of what they owed him—what they owed all his people. A little gold to balance out the blood piled up on their ledger. Besides, Karim enjoyed a bit of excitement, and grave robbing beat wading through hordes of sheep any day.

That was the real reason Karim had spoken up for Djet when the boy's own tragedy struck. In Djet's plight he'd seen a mirror of his own.

"So, what are we looking for?" Djet asked as they ascended a rocky hill at the foot of the valley. A cloud of dust rose around their feet as they climbed.

"Something that doesn't belong," Karim said, squinting at the cliffside ahead.

They stood together, scanning the area. Then Djet spoke. "Everything looks the same."

"Look closer," Karim replied, a hint of a smile in his voice, "and tell me all that you see."

Djet straightened, his round face suddenly serious as he studied the landscape before him. If this was a test, he clearly wanted to pass.

"I see a bit of lovegrass. There and there," he began, slowly. "A pile of stones. An old acacia tree. A small hole—perhaps a snake burrow? And... and..." He struggled to continue, then sighed in frustration. "I see nothing, Karim-sen. I am sorry."

"You see more than you think." Karim pointed to the pile of stones Djet had mentioned. "How do you imagine those came to be there?"

Djet looked at him and shrugged.

Karim waved him closer, and together they approached the pile. He bent and took up a handful of the stones, smelling them and rolling them between his fingers. Standing again, he ran a hand along the valley wall, thoughtful.

"Nature alone gathers no mounds, not the size of this one," Karim said. "This is the work of man. These stones are different from the others around them, which means they must have been dug from within the cliffside..." He walked forward a few feet, then stopped. Kneeling, he called Djet to his side, pointing at a thin stream of sand pouring from a crack in the wall.

"Tell me. Does this belong?"

Djet's brow furrowed in concentration. "Sand can't flow through solid rock. Which means—"

"Which means," Karim broke in, standing back to survey the wall before them, "It's not a wall. It's a door."

Time passed, and the shadows grew long.

The sun was past its zenith, and Karim knew that Hager and Babu would be growing increasingly impatient with their delay.

It will be worth the wait, Karim thought, and put his worries about the other Jackals out of his mind.

He and Djet worked tirelessly, using copper chisels to carve out the edges of a door, which had been packed tightly with dirt to appear flush with the cliffside. That done, they concentrated on widening the gap on one side. When it was large enough, they wedged two sturdy tree branches into the opening and began working together, heaving at the levers with all their might, trying to shift the massive stone slab away from the valley wall.

"Push!" Karim grunted as he strained against the branch for what felt like the hundredth time. Djet threw his whole body into it, sweat streaming down his face. "Now, pull!"

They shifted their feet forward, leaning their bodies away from the poles in unison. Finally, Karim felt the slab move, grinding a fingerbreadth across the ground.

"Again!" Karim shouted. The two of them pushed and pulled with renewed vigor. The slab moved slowly, but it moved.

"Enough, enough," Karim said after a while, removing his branch from the crevice and leaning against it for support. His muscles throbbed with pain. He rotated his arm in its socket, trying to loosen the tightness there.

Djet dropped his branch and stepped toward the narrow opening in the valley wall. "What do you think is in there, hey?"

Karim pulled the covering back from his head and wiped his brow with the back of his hand. Scrabbling in his pack for his bow drill, he knelt and spun the drill until he got a spark to light the candle he'd brought. Once the wick was burning, he placed a palm on the stone slab and poked his head into the mouth of the cave, holding the candle out in front of him. Turning his body sideways, Karim held his breath and squeezed through the crevice, taking a single experimental step inside. As he did, a burst of wind blew through the opening and into the tunnel beyond, ruffling his curly brown hair and nearly extinguishing the candle.

It sounded like whispers. There was a smell too. It was faint, but it reminded him of a fire long turned to ash, and something sweet and intoxicating.

Karim swept the candle around him, beating back the thick darkness. He couldn't see much at first, just more piled rocks and walls stippled with axe strikes. But then the light illuminated something on the ground. He bent to pick it up.

"Well?" Djet called impatiently. "What do you see?"

Karim held the object close to the flame. It was a ring, its band wrapped in fine gold wire, and its two arms holding a block of gold with engravings on each of its four sides.

A cobra.

A feather.

An eye.

A scarab.

Karim slipped the ring over his knuckle and smiled.

"Something wonderful," he murmured. "Bring the torch."

A moment later, Djet squeezed through the narrow opening, pulling their packs through after him. From one he removed a long clay object with a cup at the top, into which he'd stuffed several handfuls of dry scrub. Karim took it from him and used the candle to ignite the kindling. When it was bright and crackling, he handed the candle to Djet, and directed the flaming torch into the corridor ahead.

"There are steps, heading down," Karim said, a tingle of excitement growing in his belly. "Stay close."

The air was cool and still as they descended the rough stone stairs, and there was no sound except the ones they made themselves. It was the kind of ambient silence that Karim never got used to, no matter how many times he found himself scavenging inside some dark tomb. His breath seemed unnaturally loud, and the pulse of his heart made him uncomfortably aware of the flow of his own blood. It was difficult to forget his delicate hold on life when stealing into the home of the dead.

Still, it wouldn't do to reveal any of his morbid thoughts to the impressionable young Djet.

"So," Karim said brightly, his voice echoing through the tunnel. They'd reached the bottom of the steps and now progressed down a sloping hallway leading deeper underground. "What will you do with your share of the riches, hey?"

Djet chuckled nervously. "Oh, well… there is this girl…"

Karim laughed. "Isn't there always?"

He could nearly hear Djet blush. "I was thinking I could trade for a bottle of jasmine oil, or maybe some fine fabric for a new dress…"

"Luxuries that would delight any child of the desert," Karim mused. They'd reached the bottom of the hallway, which ended in a portal to some kind of large antechamber. His torch held aloft, Karim took one step through the doorway and stopped, his heart thudding heavily in his chest in reaction to what he saw there.

"Djet-sen," he said softly, "You will have those things and more for your lady love. Much, much more."

Djet came up next to him, peered into the antechamber, and gasped.

There was so much packed into the chamber, the eye was challenged to remain on any one item. They took it all in like starving men at an endless feast. There were golden chariots, golden couches and beds—their feet carved in the shape of lion's paws—a golden chair, golden chests engraved with birds and lotus flowers, statues, weapons, fans made of ostrich feathers with jewel-encrusted poles…

Gold, gold, everything was gold.

The sight of it filled Karim with an indescribable hunger that bordered on lust. He wanted to touch the gold, to feel its smoothness under his fingers and know these riches belonged to him.

And Djet, and Babu, and Hager, an irritating voice reminded him. He waved away the thought. There was no reason for squabbling among the Jackals. Here, there was more than enough treasure to go around. The tombs he'd found in the past had conceded a few choice items, but this... this was the kind of discovery that changed a man's life forever.

Djet whooped with excitement and slipped into the antechamber, rushing from one wonder to the next, exclaiming in rising volume and pitch about everything he saw.

"Look at *this*, Karim-sen! There's more than furniture! Bottles of fragrant oils! Jewelry, beads... and fabric unlike I've ever seen! There's food too. And jars of wine!"

Karim wandered through the room in Djet's wake, letting his free hand caress the back of a chair here, the top of a chest there. He picked up a goosenecked jar of wine, tore out the stopper with his teeth, and spat it onto the floor.

"Still good," he said after giving the jar a sniff. Tipping it back, he took a long thirsty swig.

"There are dead birds wrapped in cloth, sen," Djet called from the other side of the chamber. "Lots of them! And—a horse too! Karim-sen, even the dead horse wears gold!"

Still nursing the wine, Karim took a closer look at the golden chair, illuminating the exquisite artwork engraved and painted along its surfaces with his torch. It was brightly colored, as all the other paintings he'd seen in Khetaran tombs, but the style was different. Unlike the rigid, staid figures he was used to, the figures were curved, their heads and limbs overlong. They seemed to vibrate with activity, as if in defiance of the stillness forced upon them.

His curiosity piqued, Karim set down the wine jar and knelt

to take a closer look. The scene on the back of the chair was one he'd observed before. He didn't know what it meant, but usually it depicted a man or woman facing a falcon-headed god, who offered them a looped cross. This painting was the same, save for one aspect.

Instead of the falcon-headed god, the figure holding up the cross had the head of a bizarre creature. It was black and looked almost like a dog with its long, downturned snout and tall, blunt-ended ears. Something about the dark figure made the wine turn sour in Karim's stomach.

"This tomb," he whispered, more to himself than to Djet, who was off exploring. "Something about it is... odd."

The man in the painting was pictured wearing a striped head-dress, which was common too. What was unusual were the two animal heads peering out from his brow—a vulture and a cobra. Karim didn't know much about Khetaran art, but he knew what those animals meant when they appeared attached to a crown.

Given its location in the valley, Karim had expected the tomb of a nobleman, or maybe a nobleman's wife at best. But this was something more.

He'd found the tomb of a king.

Karim's head spun, and not from the wine.

"Hey!" Djet called, a note of fear in his voice. "Karim-sen! Come here!"

Getting to his feet, Karim picked his way through the piled-up treasures, following the sound of Djet's voice. He found a portal to another, smaller chamber and Djet standing inside, his body partially lit by candlelight. Raising his torch high over his head, Karim saw that the chamber walls were alive with pictures carved in relief, just as incredible and just as strange as the ones on the golden chair. There were scenes of hunts on the river and great festivals, and lines upon lines of the Khetarans' mystifying writing—hands, lions, crooks, birds, open mouths—their meanings unknown. But again, they were all painted in that odd style, the figures curved and distorted, making them look… Well, there was no other word for it.

Wrong. They looked wrong.

Unlike the antechamber, this room was empty but for a massive stone box in the center.

Djet stared at it.

"The dead man. He is inside?"

Karim nodded. He walked up to the waist-high black granite box, marveling at the intricate cross-hatched engravings that covered every fingerbreadth of its surface. The Khetarans certainly went to a lot of trouble for their dead. The people of the Red Lands simply buried them where they lay, under a pile of stones—giving their bodies back to the desert from which they came. It seemed more natural to Karim, and quite a bit easier too. Still, without the Khetarans' eccentric customs, Karim would have been left without a job.

"Hold this," he told Djet, handing him the torch.

"W-what are you going to do?" Djet stammered, his eyes wide and flashing in the firelight.

"What we Jackals are meant to, hey?" Karim gripped the corners of the box's lid. "Now move aside."

He took a deep breath and threw all his weight into it with a grunt. The lid moved with a harsh grinding noise that reverberated through the dark space. Karim heaved again and again, until the huge stone lid toppled to the floor with a deafening crash. One of the corners cracked and crumbled, but it otherwise remained intact.

Panting, his brow beaded with sweat, Karim took the torch back from Djet and shone it into the box. Inside, carved in the shape of a man, was a wooden coffin painted almost entirely in red. Its golden face stared back at Karim with piercing eyes, its expression inscrutable. Golden hands were crossed over its chest, holding a crook and flail dotted with black and blue. Between these, inlaid approximately where his heart might be, was a large blue amulet made of lapis lazuli. It was cut in the shape of a scarab beetle, with more Khetaran writing engraved on its surface.

"It could be his name," Djet whispered, leaning over to look. "You think?"

"You might be right." Karim pulled a copper chisel from his pack. He wedged it under the edge of the amulet and began prying it loose. The chisel slipped in his sweaty palm, and the blade raked across his finger.

"Ach!" Karim hissed, pulling his hand back.

"Are you well, sen?" Djet asked.

"Fine, fine," Karim said. The cut wasn't deep, but it was bleeding, splashing red droplets across the top of the coffin. He sucked his finger, then wrapped a rag from his pack around it. He picked up the chisel to try again. He squinted. The blood splatters had vanished. Maybe his eyes were playing tricks in the dark?

He wielded the tool more carefully now, and after inserting the chisel with greater precision, the amulet finally came free from the coffin.

"There we are," Karim said with a smile. He held the blue stone to the firelight. It felt heavy and warm.

Then came a sigh. Like a released breath, right next to his ear.

Karim jumped. He took a step back from the box and glanced at Djet. The boy stood a few feet away, the stub of candle in his hand. "Was that you?"

"Was what me?" Djet cocked his head in confusion.

Karim blinked and shook himself. "Nothing," he muttered, and turned his attention back to the amulet. It was the largest piece of lapis he'd ever laid eyes on by at least tenfold—it alone was worth a fortune. He laughed in disbelief. "What a day this has been."

Djet's eyes were hungry at the sight of the stone in Karim's hand. "We are rich, then, hey? Rich as kings!"

"We're getting there." Karim agreed. He glanced up at the torch. Like the candle, it would burn out soon without more kindling. But he had to know what else there was to find, what else he might want to tuck into his pack, before going back to tell the others.

He thought about the other Jackals, reconsidering his earlier plan to share everything equally. It wasn't that he didn't trust Babu—

No, that was just it. He *didn't* trust Babu. The man was a snake, and as likely to slit Karim's throat in the night as share the spoils of this place.

Perhaps Babu would surprise him and dole out the treasures fairly, but in case he didn't...

I have to look out for myself.

"Go back to the first room," he told Djet in a rush. "Gather up whatever you can fit inside your pack. Jewelry, gold, anything valuable. I'm going to search the next chamber. When I'm finished, we leave. We must return to the others and tell them what we've found."

Djet nodded and was about to take flight when Karim gripped his shoulder. "We tell them about the tomb, yes. But we don't tell them about the contents of our packs, hey? That we keep to ourselves."

Djet grinned, an impish glint in his eye. "I take your meaning very well, sen," he said and disappeared back the way they'd come.

Slipping the scarab amulet into his pack with the other treasures he'd already picked up, Karim turned toward the last door.

His mouth was suddenly dry despite the wine. It looked darker than the others had, somehow filled with a deeper, thicker blackness.

Your eyes play tricks on you, he thought. Spending too long in utter darkness can make a man go mad. *Hurry, else you begin to act the fool.*

He stepped through the portal and a wave of confusion washed over him. The innermost chamber usually held the treasury—the most valuable items in the entire tomb. But there was no more treasure to be found. No precious jewelry, no fine cloth, no solid gold baubles of any kind. The room was smaller than the other two and looked almost empty save for a large statue dominating the space.

Karim took another step forward and stumbled over something on the floor. He knelt and found a tiny wooden man, one of its legs now splintered in two. The floor was covered with them. Hundreds of tiny wooden men, each one the same as the last, were arranged in orderly lines throughout the room. They all faced the far wall and the statue of the strange animal-headed god he'd seen painted on the back of the chair, its long ponderous snout and tall ears carved from the same black granite as the stone box outside. It held a gold looped cross in one hand and reached out to the army of tiny men with the other, its open palm extended in welcome.

There's nothing here worth taking. But something compelled Karim to look further. That invisible rope around his chest pulled him in.

Tucking the damaged figurine into his pack, he tiptoed through the army of wooden men and approached the statue. An engraving of a long oval with writing inside decorated the statue's open palm. At a glance, Karim guessed they were the same symbols as the ones on the amulet. The name, perhaps, of the man whose tomb they were robbing.

Not man, he corrected himself, *king*.

Satisfied that there was nothing more of value in the room, he turned to go. Something wet seeped through his sandal. "Ech," he grunted, lifting his foot. A bit of water from an underground spring, probably. He wiped it with his hand, but stopped when he saw the red, sticky smudge it left behind.

Karim directed the torch at the floor where he'd been standing near the base of the statue. Oozing from beneath the pedestal was a thick pool of what looked like—

"*Karim!*"

Karim's heart jolted as Djet's cry shattered the silence. "What?" he shouted, stepping back from the statue and nearly tripping over a hundred tiny soldiers.

"Did you hear it?" Djet's voice was shrill with terror.

"Hear what?"

And then he heard it.

Knock.

Knock.

Knock.

Karim sighed. "Stop fooling, you goose. We don't have time for it." He tried to keep his tone light, but the crimson pool had unnerved him. What was Djet playing at?

"I'm not doing it." Djet's voice was quieter now, more a sob than actual words. "It's... it's coming from the coffin."

"It's *what?*"

Knock.

Knock.

Knock.

A chill shot down Karim's spine. No, it was impossible. It couldn't—

A breeze scented with wine and honey blew across his face. His torch guttered and went out.

In the suffocating darkness, Karim heard wood cracking and splintering, and then something heavy crashing to the ground.

Karim stood rigid in the darkness, not moving, not breathing.

Then came a gentle rustling, so soft Karim could barely hear it over the thundering of his heart.

Another sound exploded so loud and searing that Karim couldn't believe it didn't light up the entire tomb with its brilliance.

It was the sound of Djet screaming.

5
NEFF

The sun had passed its zenith by the time Bast's boat reached the outskirts of Thonis. The current carried it swiftly downriver with no need for oars or sails—as if the Iteru itself knew the goddess had an important appointment to keep.

Neff had washed the blood from her dress in the river, and it had already dried in the afternoon heat. It wasn't clean, really, but it would have to do. She leaned against the side of the boat, watching the capital grow from a distant smudge to a sprawling, vibrant city, spread out on land so flat that her view of it was unbroken.

First there were the green fields and the farms, crawling with workers and long-horned cattle, then came the flat-roofed mud-brick houses, not much different from her own. But there were so *many* of them. Most were shabby and poorly constructed, but as they drifted deeper into Thonis, the houses grew in size and quality. Instead of the standard brown mud brick, the fine houses boasted white limestone walls that seemed to glow under the desert sun. Ornamental paintings decorated the doorways with geometric patterns in red and yellow ochre and malachite, and flowering bushes and trees grew everywhere, adding pastel patterns of pink and orange and cream. The roads were not lined with gold as her friends had claimed, but the city was wondrous nonetheless.

They passed huge trading ships unloading cargo from distant kingdoms—ostrich feathers and animal pelts and fragrant spices whose scents were carried on the wind. Neff sniffed the air, and the smoky, intoxicating smell of whatever emerged from that ship reminded her of magic.

And that reminded her of home.

She squeezed her eyes shut, willing herself not to cry. Not only because she worried that blood would leak from her eyes, but because she didn't want to show weakness in the presence of the goddess. The vision Bast had shown her—the vision from her dream—may have been terrifying, but she had been given it for a reason. Neff didn't want to be snatched from her life in Bubas, but if she wished to understand the meaning behind the vision, the temple was the best place to do it. She didn't know much about the Temple of Amun, but she knew all the greatest wisdom of Khetara lay within its walls.

They passed a busy marketplace crowded with vendors shouting about their wares, an artisans' quarter, and several grand homes that were at least three times the size of the largest house she'd ever seen. She saw expansive private gardens, with date palms and fruit trees growing around them, and even a house with a miniature temple built beside it. She watched an older man head toward it with a tray of sacred offerings. There was nothing like that in Bubas. Nothing even close. Although Neff knew she had only traveled several hours downriver, she felt as if she'd entered another world.

As they drew closer to the city center, crowds began to form on the riverbanks, craning for a glimpse of the goddess before she reached the temple. There was already a palpable energy in the air, though the Festival of Bast wouldn't start until sundown. People cheered and waved, and children ran into the water, deeper and deeper until their mothers shouted at them to stop. Most had their eyes on the goddess, but others stared at Neff with curiosity.

One of the little boys who waded in the water called out to her. "Who are you?"

Neff opened her mouth to answer but reconsidered. Instead, she shook her head and looked away as the boy's mother released a string of threats until he swam back to shore.

Names had power in Khetara. Her father—despite the dubious quality of his spells—had taught her that much. In this new place, among strangers, she would be wise to take care to whom she entrusted hers. Besides, the question seemed complicated.

Who are you?

Neff thought she had known when she'd woken up at home with her family that morning. But now, on Bast's boat, with her old life vanishing into the horizon like a mirage, she was no longer sure.

Unsteady, Neff grabbed hold of the side of the boat as it steered toward the riverbank. The bald priests who had accompanied them from Bubas leaped nimbly onto land and tethered the boat with ropes. The head priestess emerged from her cabin at the prow, squinting into the sunlight. She stretched her arms, nodded respectfully toward the goddess, and held out a hand to Neff.

"Come child," she said. "We have arrived."

Neff forced herself to walk a short distance from the high priestess as they followed Bast and her retinue up the temple road. She didn't know what waited for her at the end of this journey, and the last thing she wanted was to cling to the priestess like a babe still wearing the sidelock of youth. She walked straight as a rod, eyes forward, trying to mimic the other woman's austere bearing. Even so, she couldn't prevent her eyes from drifting, eager to drink in the incredible sights all around her. The road was lined with ram-headed lion statues, at least a dozen crouching on each side. The statues studied her as she passed, their curling silver horns glinting in the sunlight, their eyes so lifelike that she shivered under their gaze.

Between and beyond the statues, a large crowd had formed to watch Bast's entry into the temple. Many of them carried palm branches, jewel-green and fresh, which they waved at the procession, back and forth, the leaves slowly crossing and uncrossing in a mesmerizing rhythm. Others clapped their hands and sang songs Neff didn't recognize, all in time with the high priestess's sistrum, which she'd begun shaking the moment the procession had begun. It was all sound and movement and color, so dizzying that Neff had to stop looking and stare straight ahead once more. Only, what lay in front of her wasn't any less overwhelming.

The temple gate was flanked by two enormous pylons—square, flat-topped towers that were engraved from top to bottom with sacred writing and images of warrior kings and gods. On either side of the stone gate, on pink granite thrones, sat enormous twin statues of Amun.

Like every other child of Khetara, Neff knew his name and his titles. The King of All. Protector of the Pharaoh. The Hidden One. The Invisible. She knew him, too, by his blue skin, his plumed crown. In High Khetara, there was no greater god than he, whose intangible form represented all that was mysterious in the world. As Neff passed close to the statues, she felt once more that the answers she sought would be hidden within Amun's great house.

She wasn't sure why she felt so certain. In fact, the certainty of her thoughts frightened her. She'd never been a particularly strong-willed girl, always doing whatever her father and mother asked of her. Even Henhen and Istara would comment on how easygoing Neff was. Henhen was loud and boisterous and loved to race, so when they were together, Neff raced with her. Istara was quieter and preferred board games like Mehen and senet, so when Neff spent time with her, she became quiet too, adjusting herself to compliment whoever she was with, as mutable as water.

But then the dreams had come, along with the first blood of womanhood, and she'd felt the change almost overnight. Like a soft clay figure left to bake in the sun, she hardened into a shape she hardly recognized. *But who am I becoming?* Neff had wondered, frightened by the powerful new sensations that filled her mind and body, and by the knowledge that a strange wind was blowing her in a new direction.

As she approached the gate, she studied the blue-skinned face of Amun. She, too, was hidden and obscure. Not only from the world, but from herself. Perhaps her time at the temple would bring things to light.

Before Neff and the high priestess could pass through the gate, a barrel-chested man with a leopard skin slung over his tunic marched out to stop them. He was completely hairless, and his skin looked as if it had been polished to a high shine.

"What is the meaning of this?" he demanded of the priestess. "This child cannot enter here!"

"Master Montuhotep, I apologize," the high priestess said. "This girl is with me." She placed one hand on Neff's shoulder, like a blessing.

Master Montuhotep didn't look impressed. With his burnished skin and eyes heavily outlined in black kohl, he seemed ageless, almost inhuman. "Then I'm sure you realize, Mistress Karo," he replied, as if to a naughty child, "only those of the priesthood or the royal line may pass through this gate."

The high priestess leveled the man with a challenging gaze, but her voice remained formal and polite. "Of course, High Priest. I was planning to discuss the matter with you after the girl has completed the cleansing ritual. She has been chosen by Bast to enter the priesthood, and as this is the goddess's festival day, I thought it most auspicious. I'm sure you agree." She spoke the last with the same condescension that he'd used moments before.

Master Montuhotep's nostrils flared. "Chosen?" He glanced at Neff doubtfully. "She is nothing but a girl. A common girl, at that. How did you determine this?"

"She asked the goddess to interpret her dream and received a vision."

"And?"

"And she cried tears of blood."

Master Montuhotep's eyebrow quirked. "Blood, you say?"

"If you don't believe me, you can ask anyone in the village of Bubas," the high priestess Karo added. "They all saw it happen."

Master Montuhotep swallowed and looked at Neff with new eyes. His gaze strayed down to her body, and Neff was dismayed to see shadows of blood still remained on her dress. Instinctively, she wrapped her arms around herself, shielding the stains from view.

"I see," the high priest said. "And I expect you brought her here to train under my tutelage?"

The high priestess bowed her head. "As the preeminent Hour priest of Khetara, I thought it best, Master. Perhaps if you teach her, she will be able to interpret the goddess's message."

Neff was amazed. She'd never be able to afford the services of an Hour priest to understand her dreams, and now she was meant to become one? For all her fear, the idea filled her with excitement.

Master Montuhotep crossed his arms over his chest and shook his head. "I don't know. A common girl…"

"Not the first," High Priestess Karo said. "There are records of other children exhibiting a special connection to the gods, speaking their will unto man." She paused, then added, "You forget that I was once a common girl as well. Unless you also doubt my right to the priesthood?"

The Master scoffed. "Of course not. But you know as well as I that the honor is most often passed from father to son. This is… highly irregular."

The high priestess smiled and opened both her palms to the sky. "The gods work in mysterious ways."

Master Montuhotep looked as if he had tasted something bitter and nodded. "Very well. I will do… what I can."

High Priestess Karo bowed her head. "The goddess expects nothing less." Neff could have sworn there was a threat laced between those words.

Master Montuhotep turned to Neff, his lip curled slightly in distaste. "You will come with me. These walls are sacred, and one must be cleansed of the… *taint* of the outside world in order to remain within them. Do you understand?"

"Yes, um, Master," Neff replied, and started to follow.

"Just a moment, please," the high priestess said. She put an arm around Neff's shoulder and pulled her aside, into Amun's shadow. "Now listen to me, child," she said in a low, furtive voice. "The priests here are holy men, yes, but they are men still. The master will keep his word, but he and the others will not appreciate your presence in their domain. Just because you are allowed inside the temple does not mean you are welcome there. Take care in what you do. Watch. Listen. Do not disclose anything you don't have to. And above all—choose your friends carefully. A good friend is a gift, but a bad one can lead to ruin."

Neff's pulse raced as she listened. The high priestess's words reminded her too much of her mother's. But the Mistress Karo wasn't her mother. In fact, they'd only met that morning.

"Why are you helping me like this?" Neff asked.

The high priestess considered the question. "Because I was once like you. I thought perhaps I could save you from some of my mistakes." A sad smile graced her face. "But it is really more for me than for you. You must make your own mistakes, Nefermaat. We all must. Just remember: you may doubt yourself, but never doubt the goddess. You are on this path because she deemed it so. Stay on it, no matter where it leads."

Neff had been on the edge of tears all day, and once again they threatened to overflow. "I will," she said, tremulous. "I promise."

"May Bast be with you, wherever you go," the high priestess Karo intoned, touching Neff lightly on the forehead, the throat, and on each shoulder. "Defender of the innocent. Avenger of the wronged. Lady of slaughter. Mistress of secrets."

Neff watched the high priestess depart through the gate and follow Bast's retinue, where the goddess would remain and receive blessings and gifts until she returned to her boat for the festival that night.

Master Montuhotep waited just beyond the gate, his expression grim. He watched the goddess pass by and then turned to Neff, who stood on the boundary between the outside world and the world of the gods.

She took a step, crossing under the winged scarab painted on the archway above her. One more step in shadow, and another into the light.

Neff followed Master Montuhotep through a large open courtyard and into a hallway lined with thick columns carved and painted to look like bundles of green papyrus. Together with the ceiling high above—purple-black and decorated with a thousand stars—the hallway gave her the sensation of walking through a great stone forest. He then led her to a small chamber off to the left, where half a dozen women clad in white linen dresses glanced up to see them. Like Master Montuhotep, they too were bald, their eyes lined with black kohl. But they also wore blue-green eyeshadow and rouge on their lips. The women all stood at attention. The room smelled like a bittersweet mixture of honey and salt.

"The high priestess of Bast has brought us this girl to educate in the ways of the priesthood," Master Montuhotep said, irritation clear in his voice. "You will put her through the purification rituals."

Several of the women cast pitying glances at Neff, and for the first time, she began to understand what these rituals would likely entail. She put a protective hand over her soft curly hair. Suddenly it became hard to breathe.

Master Montuhotep must have caught one of those glances. "I do not care that she is young," he added forcefully. "If she is to be a member of the king's temple, then she is subject to the same customs as the rest of us. Besides, she is absolutely filthy. I will not have lice in my house of worship."

Lice? Neff thought, offended. *Just because I live in a village doesn't mean I have lice!*

One of the women bowed her head. "Yes, Master. Leave her to us."

"I'll be back for her shortly," Master Montuhotep said, and turned from the room.

It was only then that Neff took stock of her new surroundings.

The long low table in the middle of the room, covered in little pots and strips of cloth, the line of copper blades mounted on wooden handles, the pool of dark water in the far corner.

"We are Wabet." The woman's voice was kind but serious. "Novice priestesses in the House of Amun. You will remove your dress, please."

Neff hugged herself, her heart racing. She shook her head slowly from side to side.

"You must be brave now, child," the priestess said, walking forward to lead her by the shoulder to the long table. "For you to be welcome in this temple, it is necessary to remove the impurities of the world from your body. But I will not lie to you. It is going to hurt."

She stayed still the first time they slathered her in the warm honey and patted cloths onto her skin. But after they ripped it off, taking every hair on her arm with it—they had to hold her down.

Hot tears flowed down Neff's face as they did it again and again, the pain leaving her skin red and raw. She cried out as they ripped the soft fuzz from her belly and the hair between her legs. But it wasn't until they brought out the copper blades and began cutting off fistfuls of her curly hair that she really began to weep.

For their part, the Wabet said nothing. They did not scold her for her anguish, nor did they offer any comfort. They were like one creature with many arms, each working in union with the others to complete the ritual as quickly and efficiently as possible. Neff didn't bother begging them to stop. One look at their faces told her it wouldn't have made a difference. If she was looking for a friend in this place, she doubted she would find one among them.

When they were finished, they sat her up and led her to the pool in the corner. The smell of salt emanating from it stung her eyes, and as soon as she stepped into the water, it lit her already inflamed skin on fire. She shrieked in pain, and tried to scramble back, but the Wabet gently, firmly forced her back in.

"You will be cleansed," the priestess said. "You will be pure. And the gods will welcome you."

"Please," Neff sobbed. She couldn't help herself now. She felt desperate, like a cornered animal. "Please don't make me."

"You will be cleansed," the priestess said again. "The word is the deed."

"The word is the deed," the other Wabet intoned, and the priestess pushed her head under the water.

Neff made no sound while the Wabet rubbed her with rough black pumice stones, ensuring that no trace of hair was left on her body. She stared straight at the wall and a large painting of the great mother, Isis. The goddess knelt on a dais, crowned with the sun disc, and spread her golden wings as if about to take flight.

Neff had never seen such a painting up close, and its brilliance and detail mesmerized her, and helped her ignore her body as it cried out for relief. She licked her lips, tasting salt, and didn't know whether it was from the pool water or from her tears.

Isis, she thought. *Queen of the throne. Goddess of magic. She Who Knows All the Names.*

She gazed longingly at the painting and wished that she too, could spread her wings and fly away. That flicker of hope she'd felt on the boat was threatening to go out. Was this new life always going to be full of such pain and suffering?

Finally, the Wabet completed their task and guided Neff out of the water, patted her dry with linen towels, and dressed her in a simple gown exactly like theirs. They applied black kohl and green powder to her eyes, and red ochre to her lips. That done, they checked her head to foot and declared her ready to be welcomed into the temple.

"You will await Master Montuhotep's return," the priestess said. "He will show you to our quarters and explain what is expected."

Neff nodded, numb, and began to follow the priestess to the door, recoiling from the soft pile of her hair on the ground. It reminded her of a dead animal. On the way, she caught a glimpse of herself in the brass mirror hanging on the wall.

She stopped. The person staring back at her was a stranger.

She was completely bald, her skin glistening, her face outlined in color like one of the wall paintings. But it was her eyes that struck her most. They were huge and dark and haunted, no longer her own. They had seen things, wonderful and terrible things. In the matter of a single day, she had lost everything about her life that was familiar, including her own reflection.

From the wall, Isis watched her with eyes not unlike her own.

Who am I, now? she asked the goddess. *If you know all the names, can you tell me mine?*

It was too much. Too much for a young girl who'd only that morning been at home with her mother and father, waking to another day at the market. It was too much for anyone, really. She took a step back from the mirror, and then another, and then pushed through the gaggle of unwitting priestesses and ran.

Neff dashed through the corridor, her breath coming in shuddering gasps. She had no plan and no idea where she was going. She passed other small chambers and ran past several young priests who shouted at her when she nearly upset the armfuls of papyri they were carrying.

She didn't stop.

She was tired and scared, and wanted nothing more than her mother's arms and the comfort of home. Bast was a mother herself—wouldn't she understand?

She turned right, then left, then right again, eventually losing track of where she'd been and uncertain she'd be able to find her way back. The corridor sloped downward, and Neff realized it was leading her into an underground tunnel beneath the temple. She hesitated, her eyes unaccustomed to the sudden murk. Thankfully, there was no one else around.

As Neff's heart slowed, regret set in. *This is hopeless. I can't go home. I have to go back. When Master Montuhotep finds out I ran away, I'll be in terrible trouble...* The thought ignited a whole new fear in her belly as she imagined the high priest's punishment. She was about to turn around when a low, monotonous chanting reached her ears. It was coming from a chamber at the end of the hallway. Flickering torchlight spilled from the portal, creating dancing shapes on the floor and walls beyond.

Curiosity and fear battled within her as she stood there, listening.

"Heka," the voices said. "Open to us the words and ways of magic. Open our eyes, bless us with your wisdom, and we shall be your humble vessels upon this earth."

Curiosity won.

Neff crept toward the firelight, her bare feet silent on the smooth stone floor. She pressed herself against the edge of the doorway, taking several deep, steadying breaths before peering into the room.

The underground chamber was shadowy, lit only by two torches on the far wall. Even still, Neff could see that the walls were covered in the gods' words, the black writing crawling from floor to ceiling like an army of spiders. In the middle of the room, surrounding a table covered with a variety of strange objects that

Neff couldn't identify, two masked priests stood facing each other with their arms raised to the heavens. A third priest stood with his back to them as they continued to chant—now quietly enough that Neff couldn't make out the words.

They wore half masks with animal faces: an ibis bird with a long beak like Thoth, the god of writing, and a falcon with piercing eyes and a sharp beak like the sky-god Horus. They looked frightening, there in the firelight, but at the same time, Neff was entranced. Her father had taught her about the many different types of priests in Khetara, and so she knew at once who these men must be and what it was they were doing.

Heka priests.

"Magic," Neff whispered to herself. *"Real magic."*

She watched, transfixed, as the third man turned around to face the others. He too wore a mask, but his was in the shape of a ram. In one hand, he held what looked like a hippopotamus tusk, rounded at the edges, and covered in delicate engravings. As she watched, the words carved into the tusk seemed to move and glow with an unnatural light.

Am I imagining it? Neff wondered, thinking perhaps it was another vision. No, there was none of the surreal quality of a dream. She could feel the roughness of the wall on her fingers, the coolness of the floor beneath her feet.

"Open to me, Isis," the priest intoned, "And blow the breath of life where there is none."

"The word is the deed," the other two priests chanted.

Neff's eyes widened as the light brightened, illuminating what he held in his other hand: a long serpent-headed staff. The priest brought the staff close to his mouth and spat on it.

But wait—was it a staff? How could a wooden staff move as this one did? Undulating, curling upon itself like something made of flesh and blood?

Neff gasped.

The priests froze. All three of the animal faces, grotesque in the firelight, turned toward her.

"Who's there?"

Neff jerked back from the door and pressed herself against the wall. *If they catch me here, I'll be in even more trouble!* She tried to slip back the way she came and made it halfway there before a hand fell upon her shoulder. Instinctively, she tried to pull away, but the hand only gripped her harder.

Neff turned to see one of the Heka priests, his eyes glinting from beneath the ram-faced mask.

"What do you think you're doing?" he demanded. "You dare spy on a sacred ritual?"

Neff felt the bones of her shoulder grinding together under the man's grip, and she whimpered, knowing there was no one, not in the temple, nor even the city beyond, who could help her. She was absolutely, completely alone.

"I'm sorry." She closed her eyes, waiting for the blow. The angry words. The promise of punishment.

"Ah, Herihor!" said a new voice, clipped and somewhat raspy. "I see you've found my assistant."

Neff opened her eyes. The voice had come from a doorway at the end of the corridor, where a young man stood in shadow, holding a roll of white cloth in the crook of his arm. He was small and slight, only a handsbreadth taller than Neff herself. By his face she could see he was older than she—seventeen or eighteen, perhaps. He had a beakish nose and eyes so large that they reminded Neff of a creature who'd lived in the dark too long. But despite his gaunt aspect, there was kindness in the curve of his lips.

He also sported a nest of dark unkempt hair, which Neff later realized should have tipped her off that there was something very different about him. After all, why—among a sea of hairless priests—was this strange little man allowed to keep his own?

"Assistant?" the priest Herihor asked, his grip on Neff's shoulder loosening slightly.

"Yes, I've been overwhelmed with work lately," the small man said, walking toward them with an odd, sloping gait. "And it isn't easy for an embalmer to find good help. Isn't that right, Mistress… ?" He eyed her meaningfully.

"Nefermaat," Neff blurted.

"Indeed," the small man went on smoothly. "Mistress Nefermaat and I just came by to collect some fresh wrappings. She must have gotten turned around while I was in the storage chamber."

"Y-yes," Neff added, playing along. "I'm afraid I got lost. I'm new."

Her rescuer bobbed his head. "The temple does take some getting used to!"

Herihor lifted his mask, revealing a narrow, pinched face. He regarded the small man with more deference than Neff would have expected. "Your… assistant," he repeated, as if the words were foreign to his tongue.

"Indeed!" the small man said with an air of finality. "Now, I must beg forgiveness for interrupting your…" He craned his neck to peer inside the chamber, and Neff followed suit. The two other priests stood ramrod straight and silent. The serpent staff was nowhere to be seen. "Communion with Heka. Amun knows how important it is to get everything exactly right. It won't happen again."

Herihor's gaze flicked from the small man to Neff and back. Finally, he nodded and released his grip.

The small man bowed his head, and Neff followed suit.

"We'll be on our way, then," he said, and handed her the bundle of wrappings. "Good day to you, Herihor."

The priest bowed his head in return. "And to you, Prince Bakenamun."

Neff's eyes widened, but she said nothing, then hurried to follow the small man up the corridor and back into the temple proper.

Like everyone in Khetara, she knew of the king's triplets. The tale of their divine birth, attended by the gods themselves, was one told to many children by their mothers as they lay down to sleep. Prince Mery and Princess Sita were more well-known, as they were the ones sent to greet the people during holy days and festivals, but Prince Kenna, their estranged brother, was more of a mystery. Neff had once heard the papyrus seller at the Bubas market say that Bakenamun had rejected palace life in favor of serving the gods as a Sem priest—not a high priest, but an embalmer. Her father had rejected the gossip as ridiculous.

I guess the papyrus seller was right.

Even still, the small man didn't seem like a prince. It was as if he tried to take up as little space as possible and was accustomed to going unnoticed. But whether or not he looked or behaved like a prince, he *was* a prince. If he had been anyone else, Neff had a feeling that the Heka priest wouldn't have let her go unpunished.

"Thank you, m-my prince," she mumbled, suddenly uncertain how to behave. "I'm very grateful for your help."

Prince Kenna shrugged. "I have a soft spot for misfits, considering I am one myself. You're Montuhotep's new novice, are you not?" He scoffed. "Someone in your position needs all the help she can get."

"How did you know?" Neff asked, taken aback. "I only just arrived."

"Oh, it's simple, really. Very simple. First, I saw one of Montuhotep's servants running to his quarters with a jug of wine, and the high priest only drinks when he's upset. Second, it's clear from the state of your skin that you have just come from the Wabet, which means you're newly arrived. Third, you have freckles—leading me to believe you spend a lot of time in the sun. Probably not an upper-class girl. Daughter of an artisan? Or a merchant, perhaps? Quite an unusual choice for the priesthood. So, a common girl is initiated into the priesthood at the same time that Montuhotep—who does not like children—is driven to drink." He shrugged. "I put two and two together."

He must have noticed the apprehension on Neff's face, because he continued. "Montuhotep is more bark than bite, and most of the other priests are too busy with their work to give you a hard time. Still, you must be more careful in the future." He waggled a long, skinny finger at her. "I won't always be around to get you out of trouble."

Neff nodded, amazed at the prince's powers of deduction. He didn't seem to fit with the priests she'd seen so far, so serious, elegant, and pure. He was a vulture among herons, a bit off-putting, but probably just misunderstood.

Also, unlike the other priests she'd met, Prince Kenna made her feel safe.

When they reached a fork in the corridor, the prince stopped. "You can hand back those wrappings now. Head over there and make a left. You should get back to Montuhotep before he works up too much of a temper."

Neff looked down at the wrappings and found that she didn't want to give them back. Doing so would mean her business with the prince would be finished.

"Do you… really need an assistant?"

The prince blinked. "That was a bit of a fabrication," he said, apologetic. "I do most of my work alone. Most people find it… unpleasant."

Neff imagined sharpened blades and dead bodies and swallowed, feeling a little sick. Yet anything was better than being alone.

"I could help with that," she offered, trying not to sound forced.

"I don't know," the prince said. "Montuhotep will need you for lessons, and he'll surely send you all over the temple running errands for him. He does that with the novices. You won't have much free time. I doubt you'll want to spend it with me."

He started to turn away, and Neff's heart sank. Then she remembered her father's words. *You give up too easily. All that customer needed was a little more convincing!*

Don't let him go, Neff thought to herself. *His mouth is saying no, but his heart is shouting yes!*

"I like keeping busy," she blurted. "Whenever I'm not with Montuhotep, I could come and help you, fetch you things. Whatever you need!"

Prince Kenna stopped midturn and regarded her with interest. "And what would you ask of me in return?"

Neff hesitated. She couldn't ask him to be her friend, but she could ask for information. "If I have questions about life here at the temple, would you answer them?"

"Why wouldn't you ask the master such questions?"

Neff decided to be honest. "Because the master frightens me. And you don't."

Prince Kenna's eyebrows shot up, and he chuckled. "I cannot argue with that logic. As you wish. You may assist me by accompanying me back to my chamber and carrying the wrappings. But we should hurry."

Neff squeezed the wrappings, elated, and began walking next to him again. He gave her a sidelong glance. "Why do I get the feeling you already have a question?"

"'The word is the deed,'" she said, recalling the phrase she'd already heard more than once. "What does it mean?"

"Ah, yes," he said. "That is the central tenet of Khetaran magic. It refers to the idea that words alone have great power—when we speak something into the world, in many ways we make those words true. It is at the heart of every curse, every blessing, every prayer. What we say makes the world."

Again, this reminded her of something her father had told her. *You have to believe in the product.* Maybe her father knew more about magic than she realized.

"Heka is created by the combination of objects, words, and actions," the prince went on. "How one combines them to create a specific effect is known only to those granted access to the secret knowledge housed in this temple. The papyri here contain something like cooking recipes—take this item, move this way, say these words, and aha! The gods approve your request. If you know how to do it, it is as simple as breathing. If you don't, it's like someone asking you to turn day into night."

He thought for a moment and added, "Although I suppose you can make an exception for royalty. It is said that unlike priests, who must study papyri to do magic, those of royal blood are born with Heka within them." He snorted. "Although as yet, I have no access to such powers."

Neff was fascinated and wished she had time to hear more. "How do you know so much about magic if you're not a Heka priest?"

"When I first came to the priesthood, I wasn't sure where I wanted to focus my studies. So I learned all of them."

"All?!" Neff exclaimed.

"Of course. How was I to make an informed decision if I didn't have all the facts?"

Neff had no answer to that.

"You are a curious girl in many ways, Nefermaat," Prince Kenna mused, stopping at a portal which must have led to his work area. "As I mentioned before, it isn't every day that someone such as yourself would be attached to Master Montuhotep, to be taught in the ways of the Hour priest. Something quite extraordinary would have to happen to bring you to him." The unasked question hung in the air between them.

"I had... a vision," Neff offered.

The prince's eyes sparkled with curiosity. "Of what?"

There was a pause. In the silence, images of blood and violence flashed through Neff's mind.

Again, the prince seemed to read her expressions as if they were one of his papyri. "I'm asking too much. You're tired. You've had a long day."

The longest, Neff thought.

"Perhaps you can tell me about it tomorrow. I'm certain to have some mundane tasks for you to complete, once the master has finished with you."

"I would like that," Neff said, relieved.

The prince bobbed his head. "Good." He held out his hands.

It took a second before Neff understood. As soon as she placed the roll of wrappings into his hands, the prince turned on his heels and disappeared through the portal.

Neff was elated, her earlier anguish temporarily forgotten. She had done the first important thing! She'd found someone in the temple who she could look to for help. For guidance. Someone that someday, she might be able to trust. And not just anyone—a prince!

The master's booming voice thundered down the corridor. "Nefermaat! Where are you? It's festival day, girl! I don't have time for this!"

Neff stopped, the urge to run threatening to overcome her once more.

No. You were brought here for a reason. You promised the high priestess you would stay on the path. And now you've promised a prince of Khetara that you'd be his assistant.

Her father's last words to her echoed through her mind. *Can't keep the goddess waiting.*

Gingerly, she touched her head. It was smooth and warm. It didn't feel quite like part of her yet, but maybe someday it would.

Then she took a deep breath and called, "I'm here!"

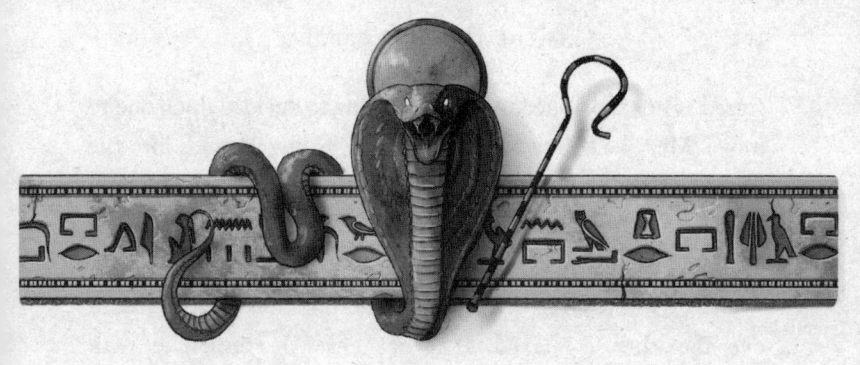

6
SITA

"Is it time?" Sita asked anxiously.

"Patience, sister," Mery said. "Ripe fruit is sweeter, you know."

They sat opposite each other at a small table near the front of the palace, waiting for the signal to begin the procession to the Temple of Amun. Sita and her brother were to offer their greetings to Bast as representatives of the king before joining the festival celebrations themselves. She could hear the crowds outside the gates—a constant murmuration of excited voices and beating drums—and longed to be among them, to throw herself into the blaze and burn, and burn, and burn.

The waiting was torture.

She stared at the ivory gaming board on the table between them, trying and failing to concentrate on her next move. They were playing Hounds and Jackals, which had been—along with Mehen and senet—one of their favorite games since childhood. She tossed the four throw sticks, counted up the black sides, and stared at her jackal-headed pieces, trying to decide which one to move. Mery had already gotten four of his five hounds into the protective shen hole at the top of the board, whereas Sita only had three. After a minute, she threw her hands up in defeat. "I give up! I can't win."

Mery was leaning back in his chair, one shapely leg crossed over the other, as relaxed as she was tense. He studied her with affectionate amusement. "Sitamun, Sitamun," he tutted. "You look at the board, but somehow you don't see it." With that, he picked up one of her pieces and moved it across the board into the shen.

Sita studied the new configuration and huffed in irritation. With that one move, Mery had cleared the path for her victory.

"Don't be so hard on yourself, sister," Mery said with a wink. "What you lack in strategic brilliance, you make up for in charm and wit."

Sita stuck out her tongue at him, but it was impossible to stay mad at Mery. Ever since they were children, her brother had been the one person who was always there for her. When, at the age of seven, she was ill from a snakebite and their father didn't even come to visit, Mery had been there to hold her hand. When Sita couldn't sleep, she knew she could always sneak into Mery's bed, where they'd curl up together like a pair of kittens. It was Mery who shared her love of stories, Mery who helped her choose what dresses to wear to the banquets, Mery who was always up for a game, no matter the hour—as long as he was playing with her.

He stuck out his tongue back at her, and they sat like that, laughing, their bodies mirrors of each other. They'd always been this way, matching each other's expressions and movements without trying. It often annoyed her that, despite their similarities, Mery was the one people worshipped. In general, Sita did what she was told. Mery, on the other hand, could be extremely demanding—he'd been known to fly into rages if his needs weren't met, or if anyone dared contradict him—but when things went well, there was nothing more wonderful than his praise. He was, in every respect, a prince destined for the throne, and everyone in the palace basked in his light.

Sita did too.

Mery grinned. His features were like masculine versions of her own—though Sita always thought they looked better on him. "Keep in mind, dear sister, things get a little wild at this festival. As soon as we leave the temple—"

She interrupted him. "I know, all right? *I know*. Mother already gave me the lecture. 'People come from all over... Not all of them share our values...'" She rolled her eyes. "I don't need a lecture from you too."

"Fine, fine," Mery said. "Just don't do anything I wouldn't do!"

Sita snorted. "That isn't saying much."

One of the guards approached. "Excuse me, prince, princess." He bowed his head. "The palanquins are ready to take you to the temple."

Fifteen minutes later, after a twilight ride down a private temple road, Sita and Mery stood shoulder to shoulder in the open courtyard of the Temple of Amun. All around them, assembled under a purpling sky, priests and other servants awaited the goddess. Since her arrival from Bubas earlier that day, Bast had been kept in Amun's sanctuary, the Holy of Holies, until her festival night began.

Sita squirmed, working hard to keep a noble expression on her face while her belly fluttered with anticipation. She felt shy and exposed in her filmy gown and bead-net dress, but at the same time, she was excited too. Her sheltered life in the palace had kept her more girl than woman, but that night, everything was going to change.

Scanning the gathered throng, she spied Kenna standing with some dour Sem priests who looked as if they hadn't seen the sun in several seasons. Other than his messy thatch of black hair, her brother looked exactly like them. Gaunt, unsmiling, strange.

How could he have shared the womb with me and Mery, and yet share so little else?

He caught her looking at him and nodded in silent greeting. Sita nodded back, stifling the irritation she often felt when he refused to take part in his royal duties.

It's fine if he wants to hide away here in the temple. But on days like this, the least he could do is stand with us as our brother. She closed her eyes and gently pushed her annoyance aside. *Not worth it. Not tonight.*

The crowd rippled with low chatter. Something was happening. One of the lowly Wab priests ran up to Master Montuhotep and whispered in his ear. The high priest nodded and waved the younger man away.

Sita scowled. She'd never liked Montuhotep. He was so… *clean*. Sure, all the priests maintained similar standards, but the high priest was different somehow. Every time she saw him, with his shiny skin and his crisp white robes, she had a sudden desire to throw mud at him.

Despite her feelings, Montuhotep was her father's right hand. The viziers were meant to be the king's most valuable advisers, but everyone knew that role belonged to Montuhotep alone. His interpretations of her father's dreams, as well as his portents of the future, were sacrosanct. No one could speak against the high priest's word without earning themselves painful—and often permanent—consequences.

Montuhotep turned toward the sanctuary, and everyone else followed suit. Sita's pulse quickened. The goddess was on her way.

Only one person wasn't turned toward the Holy of Holies. A bald young girl, no more than thirteen years old, her neck long and birdlike, dressed in the standard garb of a priestess. She stood rigid at Montuhotep's side, as if on the edge of flight.

She was staring at Sita.

Their eyes met, and Sita was surprised when the girl didn't lower her gaze in deference. Sita found herself unable to look away, despite the goddess's imminent approach.

"*Sitamun,*" Mery whispered in her ear.

There was something deep and treacherous about the girl's eyes. They made Sita feel exposed, as if all her secrets were laid bare. *Who is she?* she thought, still staring.

"*Sitamun…*"

Sita felt herself falling, as if into a deep well. She heard a roar, and a rhythmic, percussive sound, like a heartbeat.

The lamb…

"*Sita!*" Mery elbowed her in the side.

Sita blinked. "What?"

Mery pointed toward the center of the courtyard, where the high priestess of Bast and her retinue stood with the goddess, awaiting greetings from the prince and princess.

"Oh," Sita breathed, her cheeks reddening. She could have sworn she'd only looked at the girl for a moment, but it must have been longer. *Perhaps I spent too much time in the sun today*, she thought. When she glanced back at the young priestess, the girl was watching the goddess like everyone else.

"Focus, please," Mery muttered through a smile. He bowed his head, and the high priestess returned the gesture.

Sita cleared her throat and bowed her own. Mery had probably seen the high priestess before, when he'd attended the previous Bast Festival, but this was Sita's first time. High Priestess Karo was an imposing woman, tall and broad with a roughly hewn, chiseled face and glossy deep-brown skin. But what was most striking were the tattoos on her shoulders.

They were wedjat—Eyes of Horus.

High-ranking priestesses were rare in Khetara, but the ones Sita had seen had all shared those particular markings. Her tutor told her that priestesses usually had a pair of wedjat on their lower backs as well.

"Those women are divine vessels," her tutor had said, "not to be sullied by the acts of man. The eyes remind all who see them that the gods are watching."

High Priestess Karo saw Sita peeking up from her bowed position and studied her with interest. As if she and her many eyes could see right through her.

"Rise, Princess Sitamun," the high priestess said. "You may both approach the goddess."

Sita and Mery walked forward and knelt before the statue of Bast, who was barely visible behind her gauzy curtains. Sita thought of Nebet's words back in the dressing chamber.

She said I should pray to the goddess to deliver my father from evil.

Taking a deep breath, Sita closed her eyes.

She tried to pray for him. She really did. But like a drop of ink in water, another thought pervaded all others, coloring her mind with one, singular desire.

I wish to be free.

She immediately wanted to take it back.

No, no, no, she thought, desperate. *Do as Nebet told you to. Don't pray for that. Why did you pray for that? That's stupid, and selfish, and—*

But the moment was over. The high priestess laid a hand on Sita's shoulder, and she opened her eyes.

"Women of Khetara!" the high priestess announced, raising

her arms high. "Tonight we honor the birth of our goddess! We honor her by laying down our burdens and our silence and filling the sky with a glorious noise! The greater our rapture, the greater praise we give to our divine mistress!" She paused and gazed out at the throng with a catlike smile. "Let the Festival of Bast begin!"

A deafening, ecstatic roar erupted from the crowd beyond the gate, and Mery turned to lead the procession. Sita followed him between the massive pylons and under the shadow of Amun's gate, her heart thrumming. When she stepped out into the open, her blunder with the goddess was forgotten. She stopped, so overwhelmed by what she saw that it took her brother's prodding to get her going again.

There were so many people.

Beyond the road lined with ram-headed sphinx, the crowd was like a rolling ocean reaching as far as the eye could see. As the king's daughter, she had gone to other well-attended festivals and sailing days. But this... this was different. Holy days were formal, serious affairs, with a lot of prayers and rituals and standing very still. Yet there were no serious faces in the crowd before her, no stillness. Everything was sound and movement, from the drumbeats that echoed from every corner of the city to the dancing women who waved to her as she passed by.

Beside her, Mery glowed in the dying light, imperishable as a star. Nothing ever seemed to rattle him—not the pressure of his position nor the thousand eyes upon him as he faced the endless throng. He fed on their adoration, suckling at it like mother's milk. Sita walked one step behind him, attempting to mirror his confidence by keeping her shoulders back and her head held high.

They processed slowly down the main temple road toward the river. Palace guards flanked them on each side, protecting Sita and Mery from the crush of people. Still, the crowd pressed close, the heat of them stirring something passionate in Sita's soul, tugging at the door where she kept her desire locked away, willing her to set it free.

With every step, the crowd's energy grew. Women—both young and old—tossed their hair to the rhythm of the music, lifting their skirts to reveal all that lay beneath.

There was a reason that only people of a certain age were allowed to participate in the Festival of Bast.

The half-clothed women danced with each other, with the wide-eyed, delighted men, and screamed their joy into the night. Sita felt herself blush, but she could not look away from the flesh around her, the curves of those bodies, the intoxicating way their movements cast shadows. She thought of her own body, separated from the night air by that thin layer of cloth, and had the urge to rip her gown away. To throw herself into that sea of noise and skin and ecstasy.

She must have veered toward the crowd because suddenly a guard's hand was at her elbow, guiding her back to the center of the road.

"I'm all right—" She stopped short when she saw the guard's face.

Femi.

He met her eyes. Like the other guards, he wore only a short black schenti, its cinched waist and elegant pleats accentuating the sleek animal quality of his body. Her frustration gave way to desire.

He must have sensed it. In the turn of his mouth, the widening of his pupils, the new tension in the muscles of his neck, he seemed to say, *I want you too.*

She edged closer to him, so that the curve of her hip just barely brushed against his as they walked. The contact, light as it was, sent shivers up her spine.

They soon reached the riverbank, where the pharaoh's ship

waited to follow Bast's boat to the edge of Thonis as the goddess slowly made her way back to her temple at Bubas. Dozens of people were already on board. Several of the king's lesser wives and concubines were there, as well as a few of the younger up-and-coming palace officials, and of course—more guards. They cheered as one as she and Mery approached, raising their cups in greeting as Femi helped her up the ramp to join them.

Someone handed her a rattle, and someone else gave her a cup filled with wine. It was sky blue, shaped like a lotus flower, and fit perfectly into her palm. Hands touched her back, her shoulders, her arms. She was in among them now, their smiling faces flashing in and out of the firelight as her name echoed around her.

"Sitamun!"

"Sitamun!"

"Sitamun!"

The voices were all young and sparkling and beautiful.

Then she felt lips at her ear.

"Drink deep, sister," Mery whispered. "This is your night."

She smiled and took a sip of wine. It was thick and honey-sweet. She licked her lips. Normally, a sip was all the wine she was given—usually as part of ceremonies at the palace.

Tonight, I can have as much as I like, she thought, and drank the rest. It slipped down her throat and filled her with a slow, satisfying heat. When the cup was empty, she held it out, and someone filled it to the brim.

By the time the boat was floating down the river, its banks overflowing with revelers, Sita had begun to float too.

Time fell away. The singing, talking, and music became an amalgamated hum of joy. She was unsteady on her feet—either from the rocking of the boat or the drink, or both. There were bowls of roasted tiger nuts and platters of fresh plums, and when Sita pierced the skin of the fruit with her teeth, the sweet juices dribbled down her chin. Her body tingled with every casual touch, every brush of fabric against her nakedness, every cool breeze through her hair. She sang and laughed, shaking her rattle high in the air, her voice joining the great cacophony and getting lost among many.

It felt so, so *good*.

Sita looked for Femi but couldn't find him, and she worried that he might have stayed behind on the riverbank. But then, all at once, he was in front of her, not dancing, not drinking, simply watching her with those hungry eyes. She grinned, delighted, and fell into him. Her inhibitions long since drowned in wine, she pulled Femi into the shadows of the ship's empty cabin.

It was cool and quiet inside, and they were blissfully alone with the jars of wine and baskets of uneaten fruit.

Great goddess, she thought as she touched him in the dark. *I honor you tonight.*

She pushed him against the wall, her hands caressing the slick muscles of his chest.

I open my heart to you, Bast, and celebrate you.

She pressed herself against him, feeling his hot breath on her lips.

I honor you with my body.

"Sitamun," Femi murmured.

In the thousands and thousands of times someone had spoken her name, no one had ever said it quite like that.

I honor you with pleasure.

She slid her fingers across his jawbone, through his short-cropped hair, around to the nape of his neck. And then she kissed him. He lingered there, tasting her and rumbling with approval.

"So sweet," he murmured, and pulled her toward him once more.

She smiled into his mouth and breathed him in, all salt and heat and longing.

I honor you with my whole self.

I honor you.

I—

An amused chuckle severed the moment like a blade. Sita jerked back from the embrace.

"Mery!" she gasped. "What are you doing?"

Her brother leaned in the cabin door, his face half-cloaked in shadow, a lotus cup in his hand. He took a long drink from it and smiled innocently. "What? You're not the only one who likes to watch."

Sita felt the blood drain from her face. She swallowed, feeling naked again and not in a good way.

Femi had taken several steps from her and glanced between them, his face filled with barely disguised terror.

"I apologize, my prince," he said to Mery, bowing his head. "Forgive me, I—"

Mery waved a hand at him dismissively. "I don't concern myself with my sister's toys. Particularly when I have so many of my own. You don't think me greedy, do you, soldier?"

"Of course not, my prince."

Mery strolled past Sita toward the guard. "I am, in fact, immeasurably generous, am I not?" He trailed one elegant finger along Femi's bare shoulder.

The guard stood rigid, his eyes downcast. "Yes, my prince." A bead of sweat trickled down his temple to his throat.

"Mm," Mery said, as if he were tasting a sweet and deciding whether it was worth eating. "Good. Now get out of my sight."

It was almost imperceptible, but Sita saw Femi's body sag with relief. He chanced one last look at her—half regret, half apology—before hurrying out of the cabin and back into the crowd.

Sita wrapped her arms around herself, embarrassed and shaking with anger.

"How could you?" she demanded. "Humiliating me like that? You *know* how much tonight meant to me, and you *still* thought it funny to—"

Mery scoffed. "You humiliate *yourself*, chasing common beasts. Not that I don't see the appeal of him." He stepped close to her, his fingers twisting in her hair. "In fact, I quite enjoyed seeing you get what you wanted. In a way, it's almost like watching myself." He tucked a stray lock of hair behind her ear. "You know how much I love getting what I want."

Sita recoiled, swatting his hand away. "You're drunk."

"So. Are. You." Mery tapped her on the nose to punctuate each word. "Why else would you throw yourself at one of the guards?"

"I don't interfere in your dalliances," Sita shot back, trying to keep her feet under her as the boat swayed in the water. Or was it her head that was swaying? "What gives you the right to meddle in mine?"

She'd intended to be imperious, but instead sounded like a petulant child.

"Fine, fine," he said with a laugh. "I'm sorry for ruining your fun."

Sita crossed her arms and turned away. She heard him sigh. When he spoke again, the teasing tone had gone, and he sounded apologetic.

"What was I to do?" he asked. "Mother told me to watch over you."

She turned to look at him, and he pouted. Sita's heart softened.

"You didn't have to frighten Femi like that," she said, determined to remain annoyed at him. "He wasn't doing anything wrong."

"Oh, but I had to frighten him. Can't you see that?" Mery asked, putting his arm around her and leading her to the door of the cabin.

"No, I can't."

Mery shook his head. "One day soon, I will be pharaoh. Not only will I be his commander, but I will command the entire Khetaran army. It would not do for him to think me soft. Thoughts like that are locusts—they multiply, destroying everything in their path. That guard and all the others must believe, with their whole hearts, that they live only through my benevolence."

Sita glanced at him. The wine had certainly loosened Mery's tongue. Everyone in the kingdom knew that he was their father's successor to the throne, but she'd never heard him speak of it with such seriousness before, and the words somehow didn't sound like his own.

"Where is this coming from? Father?"

"Not him," Mery said with a snort. "Sematawy." An expression of reverence passed over his face. "I've had his complete letters brought over from the House of Life. Our tutor taught us about him, of course, but it's different to read of his exploits in his own words. 'If it can be done, it will be done.' That was one of his favorite pronouncements. When he set his mind to something, he made it happen—no matter the cost. Because of that, Khetara saw greatness during his reign, as it will see again in mine."

King Sematawy. The name swept her back to her tutor's chambers, where she'd spent so many sweaty afternoons poring over dusty papyri. Sematawy was the king that preceded her father. He was the Great Uniter who slaughtered the unholy king of Low Khetara and joined the two lands as one. His exploits were legendary, and everyone in High Khetara—from pauper to prince—considered him their hero.

Mery was no different, of course, and he'd taken an interest in the old king from a young age. It made sense, given his own path to succession. Still, the immediacy in his voice, the fervor, was new. She'd have thought—despite the lack of intimacy between them, that Mery would have turned to their father for guidance about becoming pharaoh. After all, Sematawy was a wartime king, and Khetara had enjoyed peace throughout their father's reign.

Thoughtful, Sita gazed upon the boat and jubilant masses in the moonlight. "Look at the people, how they celebrate. Is Khetara not already great?"

Mery chuckled without humor. "Again, sister. You look, but you do not *see*. These festivals give the people relief, but it is fleeting. Tonight they celebrate, tomorrow they return to their barren fields and hungry children. It's a bandage over a festering wound, one that has been eating away at this kingdom since the first years of Father's reign. Just because you choose to ignore it, whiling away your days in the pleasure garden, doesn't mean it isn't there."

Stung, Sita's cheeks grew hot.

Suddenly, she felt awful. Where before it had been joyful, the noise of the festival had begun to make her eyes ache. The drumbeats pulsed in time with the pounding in her head.

The festivities were winding down. Out on the deck, some still sang and danced to the music, but many revelers had stretched out together in the shadows on soft furs. A huge crescent moon hung over them, its mirror image reflected in the river.

She stubbornly finished her wine, though her stomach rebelled against it. She was irritated at Mery, both for wrecking her time with Femi and for forcing her to think about matters of state on a night that was supposed to be fun. There might be truth to what he said, but in that instant, she didn't care. She wanted to say something to hurt him back, to ruin his evening as he had ruined hers.

"You fancy yourself a king, but Father is still very much alive. I doubt he would appreciate talk of his death before its time, even from Mother's favorite son. He will be well soon, and you'll have a long wait to follow in Sematawy's footsteps."

Mery smiled widely and leaned his head against hers, as if to impart a secret. "No," he whispered. "I don't think I will."

Sita squinted at him. "What do you mean? The priests are healing him. They've been conducting daily rituals. I saw the amulets."

Mery yawned and stretched himself like a cat. "The priests may as well stop up the river's flow as heal what ails our father, Sitamun."

"I don't understand." Sita shook her head. "How do you know what ails him?"

The moon went behind a cloud, and the boat was thrown into darkness, lit only by firelight.

"I know, sweet sister," Mery replied, his face in shadow, "because I have been poisoning him."

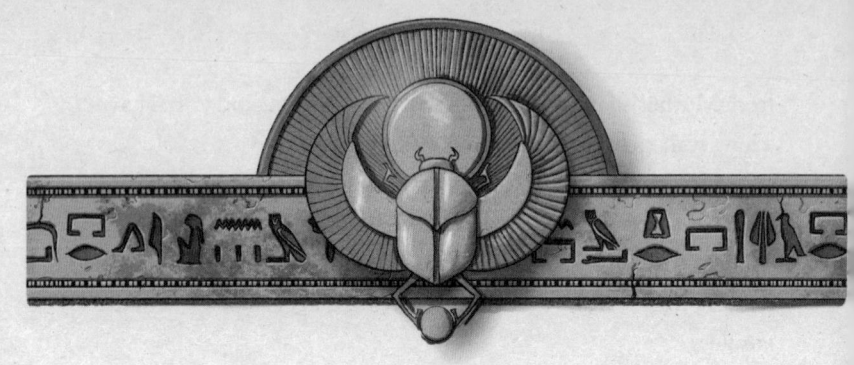

7
KARIM

He never forgave himself for what happened next.

Karim stood in the dark tomb, his breath coming in short gasps. Djet's scream still reverberated in the stale air.

Did you hear it?

Djet's last words echoed in his mind.

It's coming from the coffin.

Karim held the guttering torch aloft, but the light barely reached the threshold. He'd left Djet in the burial chamber. There had been knocking, then splintering wood, and then—

Stop it, Karim scolded himself. *Stop being a fool and go to him. Quickly. The boy could be hurt.*

He took a deep, steadying breath, and lowered his free hand to the knife on his belt. Perhaps an animal had attacked the boy—a snake, or some other underground creature.

That doesn't explain the knocking.

Karim picked his way back through the maze of little soldiers. Perhaps some part of the tomb had come loose and fallen on Djet.

You know it didn't.

Karim gritted his teeth, willing his mind to be quiet. He was a practical man, but there in the dark, he could feel a kind of madness creeping in.

"Djet?" he whispered, taking another cautious step forward. He hated how small his voice sounded, how fragile and weak. "Djet?"

There was no response.

Karim crossed back into the burial chamber. The sting of smoke and something metallic filled his nostrils. Bile pushed up into his throat as he tried to control his breathing. Djet was nowhere to be seen. *Where could he have gone?* If something scared him, perhaps he ran out. Karim took two more steps, and his torch illuminated the black granite box and the coffin within. The corner of its lid was just visible on the floor nearby. Trembling, Karim peered inside.

The coffin was empty.

He recoiled from the box, nearly dropping the torch on the ground.

It's a trick, he thought, his mind reeling. *A Khetaran trap. It has to be.*

A whimper, soft and wet, sounded to his side. Slowly, he lowered the torch, illuminating a bundle of rags on the ground.

He drew closer.

"No..."

The rags were the remains of familiar clothing, sodden with blood and still hanging from a small shivering body.

Karim fell to his knees next to the boy, frantic, but terrified to touch him. He couldn't identify any one wound—the blood seemed to come from everywhere at once. Djet's eyes were closed, and his lips moved, long red trails sliding out from between them.

"It's going to be all right, hey?" Karim said gently, not believing the words as he said them. "Come on, I have to get you out of here." Tentatively, he reached out for the boy's arm.

At his touch, Djet's eyes flew open. They first focused on Karim, kneeling there in a pool of light, then slid to gaze over Karim's shoulder.

Karim had witnessed horror in his life. He had heard the cries of sheep as they were eaten alive by lions. He knew the screams of mothers after they'd been told their sons had been killed in battle. But never in his life had he heard a sound as harrowing, as bone-chilling, as the one that escaped the boy's throat.

Karim shot to his feet, humming with fear. Then, though the torch burned a mere handsbreadth from his face, Karim felt a chill on the back of his neck.

It's right behind you. It's right behind you. It's right—
He ran.

Images of strange painted men and golden treasures flashed before him as he dashed headlong through the darkness, the torch spilling red-hot embers into his wake as it died. He discarded it on the ground and immediately tripped over something in the crowded first chamber, landing hard in the dirt. In an instant he was up again, groping for the door, led only by the finger of sunlight reaching through the crevice they'd opened in the cliffside. He scrambled through the passageway, squeezed his body into the opening, and collapsed under the blinding sun, elbows on knees, sucking in lungfuls of fresh air. After he caught his breath, he squinted at the horizon. The sun sat lower in the sky than he expected. *How long were we in there?* It felt like only minutes but—

Djet.

The name nearly stopped his heart.

You left him to die.

He leaned against the sunbaked rock face, the heavy pack

slipping off his shoulder. He hugged it to his chest, panting, the guilt like a blade in his gut.

I had no choice, he told himself. *The kid was going to die either way*.

Still, he'd left him to die down there in the dark. Alone.

He shivered.

No, not alone.

Karim had heard rumors about Khetaran magic, of curses that protected their dead from thieves. But he'd never given them a second thought. The Khetarans were an arrogant people, but they weren't stupid. What better way to prevent the plunder of their tombs than with stories of torment and damnation?

It was a ruse.

Or at least, that's what Karim had believed.

After what he'd seen in that tomb, he wasn't so sure. Something had wakened down there. Something... evil. And none of it would have happened if they'd gone home when the other Jackals wanted to. But Karim had felt the tug, had sniffed treasure on the breeze, and like a dog with a bone, he couldn't let it go. Worse still, he'd brought Djet down with him.

He stared at the stone door, his dread returning in full force. If the thing had strength enough to kill, surely it could escape the tomb. Which meant Karim was still in danger—and so was everyone else.

What have I done?

He threw his shoulder against the door, desperate to shove it back into place. If he could seal the entrance again, the thing would be trapped inside and couldn't hurt anyone else.

Yet no matter how hard he tried, the door wouldn't budge. Opening it with levers—and Djet's help—was one thing, but closing it again proved impossible.

I need to get the others.

Karim stumbled down the cliffside, sending a shower of small stones with him, and ran as fast as he could toward where he'd left the other Jackals.

Babu and Hager were lounging about, eating dried dates and taking long swallows from their waterskins. Their packs lay in a pile, Babu's spear stuck into the sand nearby. When they heard Karim approaching, they stood, consternation clear on their faces.

"Where were you?" Babu grunted in annoyance. "The sun nearly sets! You want to be food for the lions? We have to hurry back if we're going to get home in time for supper."

"Please, Babu," Karim said, panting. "Just listen."

"No, *you* listen, you son of a dog. You'd better have something to show for wasting my time or I'll—"

"Shut up, Babu!" Karim snarled. "I found something."

Babu's cruel, sharp eyes darted to Karim's bulging pack, to the glint of gold peeking through the mouth of the fabric.

"Found what exactly?" he asked, his interest clearly piqued.

Given the space to speak, Karim hardly knew where to start. "I found a tomb unlike any other I've seen. And... there was something down there."

"If you found a tomb," Babu broke in, his eyes narrowed. "Why didn't you come for us sooner?"

"It doesn't matter," he said, urgently. "I'll show you where it is. You have to help me, please."

"Hey," Hager said. "Where's Djet?"

Karim swallowed his next words. A falcon cackled somewhere in the distance.

"Yes," Babu said, low and dangerous. "Where is Djet, eh, Karim-sen?"

Karim's pulse quickened. *Those eyes. That scream.* He started to answer, then faltered. How could he possibly explain?

Karim saw Babu staring at the red stain on his hand. It wasn't

Djet's blood, but what was he supposed to say? That it came from underneath a statue? Babu would never believe it. Karim swallowed, taking a step back as the reality of the situation began to dawn on him.

Babu's expression shifted from irritation to distrust the longer it took Karim to reply.

"He's dead, isn't he?" Babu demanded.

Karim put his hands out in front of him. "Yes—but I can explain."

"Oh, I'm sure you can," Babu said, closing the distance between them. "You found something in that valley. Something so good, you wanted to keep it all to yourself. So you killed the boy, and now you come here to trick us, to lead us into a trap so you can kill us too. You may think you're smart, Karim-sen, but your act doesn't fool me."

"It's not an act! There's a monster down there, and it killed Djet. I know you don't trust me, but I'm telling you the truth!"

Babu barked a laugh. "A monster! All right, sen, here's what you're going to do," the big man said, reaching for the dagger at his belt. "First, you're going to hand over that pack. Then you're going to lead us to the tomb. And after that, if you do exactly as I say, I promise to kill you quickly."

Karim backed away, his heart racing. "You're making a mistake," he said, his eyes flicking to Hager, who'd pulled the spear from the sand and was advancing toward them, cutting off Karim's escape. Babu loomed over him like a monolith, casting a long shadow across the sand. "I swear to you! The Khetaran curses, they're real! You need to help me reseal the tomb, before that creature gets out and kills us all!"

Babu scoffed. "Seal it? What, with the treasure still inside? How stupid do you think I am? Now, either you give me that pack or I cut you down and take it. Hager and I can follow your tracks and find the tomb ourselves. It's really up to you, sen. Whether you die now or later makes no difference to me."

Karim set his jaw, his hand tightening on the pack's strap.

Babu shrugged. "As you wish." He unsheathed the knife.

For such a large man, Babu moved incredibly fast.

He lunged with a guttural cry, slashing out with the dagger. Karim scurried backward, but it was like trying to evade a hippopotamus at close range. The first attack bit through the fabric of his robe, but the second found the flesh beneath, cutting a deep furrow across Karim's chest. He doubled over, hissing with pain as blood began to seep from the wound. But he had no time to worry about that. A moment later, Babu kicked him in the gut, and Karim dropped to the ground like a stone.

He lay there writhing, his wound forgotten in the struggle to breathe. He rolled onto his back, gasping, his mind working furiously. The pain, like the blazing sun, was nearly blinding. He tried to speak, to stall for time, but all that came out was a shuddering moan. Karim dug his fingers deep into the sand.

Babu stood over him and sheathed his knife. "Not so clever now, are you?" the big man said with a sneer and kicked him again.

Karim cried out as stars exploded before his eyes. He tried to curl his body into a ball to protect himself from the blows, but Babu put his foot on Karim's chest, pinning him in place. He felt his ribs buckle under the weight.

Babu chuckled. "Always lording it over us with your talent for sniffing out treasure. Well, we don't need you anymore, do we? This haul of yours should keep us comfortable for quite a while."

Removing his foot, he knelt beside Karim, groping for the pack that was half-trapped underneath Karim's limp body.

"Knee-deep in woman flesh too." Babu's breath was hot and sour on Karim's face. "Perhaps I'll snap up one of your little sisters, hey? They're nearly ripe for the picking."

At that, Karim forgot his pain. With a cry of fury, he threw a fistful of sand into Babu's face.

Babu shrieked in surprise, clambering to his feet to wipe the stinging sand from his eyes.

"I'll kill you, you—!"

Karim sat up and buried the blade of his own knife into Babu's thigh, straight up to the hilt.

The unfinished curse transformed into a scream. Karim jerked the knife out again, and the big man crashed to the ground, clutching at his leg and its growing red stain. Karim got up, one arm wrapped protectively around his bruised ribs. The sudden movement sharpened the pain—but the will to stay alive had sharpened his mind.

With Babu out of commission, Hager advanced with the spear, aiming it directly at Karim's heart.

"Drop the knife or I'll run you through where you stand!" he shouted, his voice barely audible over Babu's howls of agony. "Don't think I won't!"

Karim licked his lips. Hager was a coward, and if he was going to murder him, he'd probably have done it by now. Still, Karim wasn't eager to test him. He dropped his bloody knife.

"Now give me your pack!" Hager demanded.

"Kill him, you fool!" Babu roared from where he lay, spit flying from his lips. "What are you waiting for?"

Karim's gaze flicked from Babu's bloody leg to the glittering spearhead hovering a handsbreadth away. It was trembling, just slightly.

"All right, easy, easy," he said. He allowed the strap of his pack to slip from his shoulder, and took the heavy bundle in his hands. Babu watched him suspiciously, hate burning in his eyes. Hager nodded, urging him to hand it over.

"Catch." Karim threw the pack at Hager. Startled, the thin

man dropped the spear to pluck it from the air. In the same instant, Karim sprung forward, bringing his fist around in an arc and connecting with Hager's left temple.

He crumpled like a pile of sticks.

Karim was running before Hager hit the ground, grabbing up his pack and knife and stumbling through the sand as quickly as his injured body would allow. Babu screamed curses at his back, calling him every bad name Karim had ever heard—and some he hadn't. The big man was so mad that he managed to get to his feet and give chase for a short distance, which was impressive given the amount of blood pouring out of his leg.

"You can never come back!" Babu shouted, his voice growing more and more distant. "I will tell everyone what you've done. You step foot into any tribe, *anywhere*, and I will know it! And when I find you, and I will slit your throat from ear to ear like the dog you are!"

Karim kept running.

"You are a dead man, do you hear me?" Babu yelled, barely audible. "You are nothing and no one!"

The next time Karim chanced a look back, Babu was nowhere to be seen.

When Karim could no longer run, he walked. And when he couldn't walk, he continued anyway. If he didn't keep going, there was still a chance that the others could catch up to him. From the position of the sun, he knew he was moving toward the river and the outskirts of the Khetaran kingdom. He wasn't welcome there either, but finding some kind of sanctuary was his only chance of survival.

The evening fell quiet after that. The desert rolled in great, unbroken waves in every direction, and although Karim had lived his entire life in the Red Lands, without the comfort of his people close by, it quickly became a forbidding place.

The pain in his ribs was bad, and the heat was worse, but neither compared to the torment of his shame. Karim shifted his pack, the weight of its treasures reminding him of what they'd cost.

What will you do with your share of the riches?

As Karim walked, he imagined the Jackals making their way back to camp, where a girl would be waiting for Djet. He imagined Babu telling her that the boy she cared for was never coming home. Djet would never bring her a bottle of jasmine oil or a lovely new dress. And as he imagined the girl's grief, Karim felt the weight of the riches in his pack become heavier with every step.

Keeping the setting sun at his back, Karim walked east toward the Khetaran border. Babu had made it clear that going back to camp wasn't an option, so his only choice was to find someone willing to take him in. He thought of his mother and his siblings. What would the Jackals say about him to the rest of the Anen?

They'll say that I betrayed them.

That I abandoned my family.

That I'm a murderer.

His mother wouldn't believe them, but what would it matter? Not only would his family be forced to live in disgrace, but they will have suffered another loss.

He thought of his brother's anger, his sisters' sorrow, his mother's stoic fortitude. *She's endured so much already, now she'll have to endure this too.*

Thoughts of Djet haunted him as well. There were moments, as he trudged up one side of a sand dune and half fell down the other, when he felt that the boy still walked at his side. It was comforting, until he remembered Djet wasn't really there.

But the worst thoughts were of that distant cliffside and the door, left open just enough to allow whatever lurked within to get out.

It had all gone so wrong, so quickly.

A gust of sand blew into his face and he coughed. The pain was searing.

He used his head covering to shield his face from the elements, leaving only his eyes to bear the stinging wind. His body felt like a bag of loose bones, and he was certain he had at least one broken rib. The knife wound had stopped bleeding, but the fabric of his robes stuck to it. At some point, he'd have to pull it free to bind the wound. The thought made him swoon, forcing him to stop a moment to rest.

The truth was, he had no idea how far it might be to the nearest village. It could be one hour, or it could be seven. The first would mean his salvation. The second...

If anyone can do it—you can!

It was almost as if Djet were right there, whispering into his ear.

"Are you sure about that?" Karim croaked in reply. "Because right now, things don't look so good, sen." He had no food, no water, and very, very little hope.

More time passed, and the sun dropped to the horizon, melting into a mirage that stretched across the landscape. Karim licked his dry, cracked lips. The illusion reminded him of a glittering riverbank. But he'd lived in the Red Lands long enough to know it was a cruel trick the desert played on dying men.

Karim reached the top of a dune and was about to make his way down the other side when his legs gave out from beneath him. He cried out, toppling forward, and rolled end over end to the bottom, where he landed flat on his back.

He almost didn't get up. It would have been so easy to lie

there. To give up and sleep. His body certainly wanted him to. Sure, he might get eaten by lions, but was that so bad? He was about to doze off when Djet's voice seemed to call to him again.

Look, Karim-sen!

"Leave me alone, boy," Karim muttered, spitting out a mouthful of sand. "Can't you see I'm trying to die?"

What do you see?

Even in death, Djet wouldn't let him be. Karim grunted as he struggled to his feet, a mad kind of laughter bubbling up in his throat. He looked around.

"I see nothing!" he cried into the vast emptiness. "Do you hear me? Nothing behind me, nothing ahead, just a useless expanse of…"

That's when he saw it, as clear as day on the shifting horizon. A small stone structure, half-ruined, with several broken columns like jagged teeth.

"It can't be," he whispered, and stumbled toward the edifice with renewed vigor. As he got closer, he almost expected the structure to vanish—another trick of the light—but it didn't. And before too long, he found himself standing right in front of it.

Though crumbling, the structure had once been grand, with gray limestone blocks that were beautifully cut and stacked with precision. The exterior walls were engraved with wondrous images: lotus flowers, rearing lions, great animal-headed figures, and the strange Khetaran writing.

Best of all, though, was the well.

It was perhaps only a few handsbreadth in diameter, but Karim had the feeling there was water to be found at the bottom.

He put his hand on the wall, still not quite believing that it was real. The abandoned building was the perfect shelter for the night. He could rest, fill his waterskin from the well, then continue his journey in the morning before it got too hot.

He was so overcome with relief that he didn't notice the footprints in the sand. The pile of burnt animal bones. The smell of smoke in the air.

So, he was really quite surprised when he heard a soft canine growl and something sharp poked him in the back.

"Make one wrong move," a gruff voice said, "and I'll run you through."

Karim sighed and put his hands up in surrender. "Would you believe you're the second person to make me that offer today?"

"Turn around. Slowly."

Karim did. Standing before him was a black dog with a long snout and pointed ears, and a grizzled old man who may as well have been built from the same stone as the building behind him. He had a square, chiseled face, wide nose, and a thick coat of wiry white hair covering his entire body. Karim might have mistaken him for one of his fellow tribesmen, except for the Khetaran lilt in his voice. Khetarans were known for keeping their bodies smooth and hairless, but it appeared as if this man had long given up the practice.

"I'm not armed, hey?" Karim said. "Just a traveler seeking refuge."

"Don't get many travelers up this way. Criminals mostly," the man growled. He studied Karim with suspicion, his eyes stuck in a permanent squint.

The dog sniffed at the bloodstains on Karim's clothes.

"I realize how bad this looks," Karim said, pulling his hand away when the dog began licking it.

"Do you now?" The man snapped his fingers at his canine companion. "Behkai, heel." The dog whined but returned to his side.

"I do. I promise, I mean you no—"

The pack slipped from his shoulder, and the large scarab-shaped amulet he'd pried from the king's coffin slipped out. It landed on its side, rolling in a slow circle before coming to rest between them.

Karim swallowed. "I can explain."

The man didn't reply. He stared at the blue stone on the ground, like it was a piece of sky that had fallen to earth.

"You see," Karim went on, "I was walking along, and wouldn't you know it, that stone was just lying there…"

The man bent to pick up the amulet, his spear all but forgotten. He ran his fingers over the engravings, his brow furrowed in confusion.

"You dare lie to a priest?"

Karim blinked at the brawny, hairy old man. "You're a priest?"

The man tore his gaze from the amulet to give Karim a withering look. "Yes, and you're a tomb robber." He stepped forward, shaking the stone in Karim's face. "And if you tell me where you *really* got this, I'll let you live. Tell it well, and I might throw in a meal and a place to sleep."

In the west, the sun finally dipped under the horizon, throwing the desert into almost instantaneous darkness—like someone blowing out a candle.

What are you going to do? Djet's voice whispered.

Karim nodded to the priest. "You've got yourself a deal."

What Jackals are meant to do, *sen*, he thought. *Survive*.

That evening, Karim sat with the priest by a crackling fire in the open courtyard of the building, underneath a roof of stars. The priest had given him water from his well, both to drink and to clean his wounds. The cool night air was a balm, soothing his burnt skin and aching muscles. He'd explained his injuries by telling the old man he'd gotten into a "disagreement" with a friend, and thankfully, the priest hadn't pressed him for more details.

From a series of chambers that Karim assumed formed the priest's living quarters, the man had brought hunks of rough bread, a bunch of white onions, and a jar of beer. Karim hadn't wasted a moment digging in. He was ravenous. It was a simple meal, and it was exactly what he needed. As soon as the sweet beer and nourishing bread hit his stomach, he felt more like himself again. The dog, Behkai, had made himself comfortable by his side, staring at the food in Karim's lap and licking his lips. The giddy madness that had been creeping over Karim receded, leaving his mind blissfully clear.

And with that clarity, came questions.

"So, Pasenhor," he began, struggling to pronounce the strange name the priest had offered him. "This is your home, this place?"

"Call me Pa," the priest rumbled. "And yes, it is. Although more importantly, it is a temple. A House of Khnum—though I'm sure that means very little to you." He scoffed. "Very little to most of Khetara, I'm sorry to say."

"Khnum," Karim mused. It was a round word, rolling like a ball in his mouth. "He is one of your gods, hey?"

Pa nodded. "One of our oldest." He gestured toward a faded painting of a ram-headed figure. The figure held a jar from which water flowed into a river below. "God of the Iteru, the Divine Potter—he who sits at the Great Wheel and forms man out of clay, placing him in the wombs of our mothers and onto Fate's path."

He paused, gazing into the shadows of the sanctuary beyond the courtyard. "This temple guards an oracle Khnum gave to our people long, long ago. An old king placed it here for safekeeping, so that when the time came, the word of Khnum would be remembered and the people of Khetara would take heed." He huffed and spat a piece of grit into the fire.

"If this Khnum is so great, why don't your people worship him anymore? Why does his House sit forgotten by all except you?"

Pa stopped chewing and gave him a look. "Time, for one. Khnum is one of the old gods, and people are fickle. Gods fall in and out of fashion like women's dresses, and traditions are forgotten. Over the past few generations, Amun has taken precedence in the north, and Ra in the south. Amun can also take the form of a ram, but Khnum is the original ram-headed god. The one true lamb."

Karim didn't comment in hopes that Pa would continue. Despite his feelings about the Khetarans, he was fascinated by the priest's story. Sure enough, the old man had more to say.

"The current king hasn't helped. Under Amunmose, the kingdom slips ever further into perdition. Do you know the last time someone from the surrounding villages came here to pay their respects? At least a season—perhaps two!" He shook his head. "The king thinks his three children and their fortuitous birth legitimized his rule, but there are many Khetarans who still believe—"

Pa stopped himself and chuckled, before shaking a gnarled finger at Karim. "You're very clever, aren't you, boy? Trying to get me riled up, talking all night. You're probably waiting for me to tell you where you can find more Khetaran treasures. No, no. The deal was—I ask the questions, *you* answer. If you don't like it, I have a very sharp spear to reintroduce you to."

As before, Karim held up both hands in surrender and said nothing.

Pa refilled his cup of beer. After a moment's consideration, he refilled Karim's cup too.

"Now, tell me how you came upon this scarab." He held the lapis amulet in his palm.

Karim shivered, a finger of cold night air slithering across his neck. "I discovered an old tomb in a valley west of here. It was hidden in the cliffside, untouched for hundreds of years, maybe more. I don't know a lot about Khetarans, but I've seen enough tombs to know that this one was ancient, and not only that, it was the tomb of a king."

He expected the priest to be surprised by this revelation, but Pa expressed only confusion. "It is… troubling," he said, studying the stone.

"What is?"

"I have been a priest for many years—since Sematawy's reign. But before Unification, I studied to be a scribe. It served me well, not only to be skilled in reading and writing the gods' words, but also to be educated in Khetara's long history. One of the first documents I produced during my tutelage was a complete list of Khetaran pharaohs. As you can imagine, it is a long list and good practice for any scribe. I wrote the name of each and every pharaoh and memorized them all.

"This here," he said, pointing to the oval shape carved into the stone, "is a shenu. It is a circle of protection we draw around the names of our kings. Names are powerful, you know, and must be protected at all cost. If evil comes to know your true name, they can harm you gravely."

Karim leaned over to see the stone better in the firelight. There were four symbols: what looked like a folded cloth, a loaf of bread, a jagged line, and a vulture. "So the word inside the circle is the name of the king who was buried in that tomb? I'd wondered."

"It is," Pa agreed. "His name was Setnakht." He pursed his lips. "There's only one problem."

"What's that?"

"There has never been a king by that name."

It was Karim's turn to look confused. "There must be some mistake."

"There is no mistake. Khetarans are famed for our record-keeping abilities. We know how much grain was grown fifty seasons ago and how many lions the pharaoh killed on his nineteenth birthday. You think we would forget a king's entire reign? Not possible." He hesitated, his face thoughtful. "Unless…"

"Unless what?"

"Unless it was erased from history on purpose."

"Why would anyone do that?"

Pa shrugged. "I've heard rumors of pharaohs being struck from the records, but I never thought it could be done. A king would have to do something truly vile to earn such a punishment…" He turned over the stone and squinted at it, brushing at the dust with his hand. "There's something else here. Faint, but still legible."

Karim felt a chill. "What does it say?"

"'This is the heart of a king,'" Pa replied. He looked up at Karim. "This is strange magic, thief. I must know more. If I were a younger man, I would travel to the Great Temple of Amun for answers. The oldest records in Khetara are kept there. If there remains any evidence of your missing pharaoh, that's where to find it." He sighed. "But a young man I am not. The journey is long and arduous—I'm not sure I'm up to the task anymore. So, for now, I'll have to appease my curiosity with whatever it is that you know. Tell me: What else did you see down in that tomb?"

Karim thought of the bleeding statue, of the strange god on the tomb walls, and of the creature he'd awoken. If he told Pa what happened, maybe he would understand. Maybe he'd know what to do.

Are you really so quick to trust a Khetaran?

Karim had never broken bread with one before, no less confessed such a secret. Pa seemed to be a good man, a man of honor, but he was still one of the river people, and Karim knew better than to let his guard down so easily. What would the priest think, if he told him about the monster he'd awoken? Would he believe him? Or would he, like Babu, simply think that Karim was merely covering up his own murderous acts?

No, he thought. *I think I've confessed enough for one night.*

"I'm very tired," Karim demurred. "Maybe I can answer your questions tomorrow, after a bit of rest?"

Pa grumbled. "Isn't it a bit early for a young pup like yourself?"

"Well, I lost a lot of blood. Then I nearly died in the desert, so—"

"Pah!" the priest barked, swatting away his words. "Fine. Sleep. Behkai will keep the snakes at bay—won't you, boy?"

Behkai's tongue lolled from his open mouth, showing many bright teeth.

"Well, the beast likes you," Pa said, crossing his arms. "That's saying something."

"Will you go inside now?" Karim asked, settling on the ground with his pack for a pillow.

Pa poked at the fire with the tip of his spear, causing the embers to flicker and glow. "Eh, I'll stay here a while to make sure you don't try anything stupid."

"Are you sure it's not because you enjoy my company?"

The priest snorted. "Don't push your luck, thief. I'd be just as happy to gut you and let Behkai have you for his dinner."

Karim closed his eyes and smiled. He thought sleep would come quickly, what with the warm fire and his full belly, but he found himself awake long after both Pa and Behkai were snoring. He turned to look at the amulet, sitting nearby on a piece of cloth that Pa had brought to clean it. It made him think of that lonely, desolate valley, and of that tomb's open door.

"Setnakht," Karim whispered and immediately regretted saying it. It sounded less like a name, and more like a curse.

8
RAE

Rae woke the following morning with an itch to fight. Her father was already up, having eaten his morning meal and cared for the zebu while she was still asleep.

"We have much to do," he said when Rae emerged, rumpled and blinking into the sunlight streaming through their front window. "If we have any hope to harvest enough grain for the king's tax, we must work from dawn until dusk."

Rae groaned, imagining all Buto's boasts when she failed to show up. She longed to introduce his smug face to the dirt, to stand over him in front of all his arrogant friends and—

She clenched her fists.

Not today.

Her father thrust a hunk of bread at her and got to work attaching the sickle to the raw stump of his arm.

Rae grunted and took a bite of the stale bread. "Ugh," she said, choking down the food and reaching for the water jug. "Do I at least have time to get some fresh loaves from the baker?"

"Fine," her father said irritably, "but don't be long. We have no time to waste."

His face was deeply lined, and there were dark rings under his eyes. He was far from an old man, but the past two seasons had aged him considerably. They'd been hard days, and it seemed that they were only going to get harder. Rae felt a twinge of dread.

She washed with cold water from the basin, tied her hair up with a strip of linen, and shouldered past her father out the door.

"Don't start without me," she warned him. "I don't want you hurting yourself trying to do too much."

Her father gave her a look of contempt. "I'm not the one going into town and challenging every man in sight, now am I?"

Rae froze, a blush rising to her cheeks. "You *know* about that?"

Her father laughed. "They took my hand, daughter of mine, not my eyes and ears. I'd have to be a fool not to see what's really been going on. How many times can one person possibly trip over a rock and fall on her face?"

"Oh." Rae could hardly meet his eyes. "Are you… are you angry?"

Her father sighed. "Your mother—may she live forever in the West—was a gentle woman. You didn't inherit your belligerence from *her*."

Rae's gaze flicked over her father's shoulder to the small shrine in the corner of their house. There was a low offering table before a mud-brick pedestal, on which stood the small limestone bust of her mother. Her father had traded away a fine silver ring he'd gotten from King Rahotep to have her likeness made after she died.

"You have her eyes, and her smile," her father went on. "But I'm sorry to say that the rest you get from me. I may not seem like much these days, but there was a time when I, too, had fire in my belly. When war had me longing for a blade in my hand and an enemy before me." He adjusted the sickle on his arm with a grimace. "But that fire went out long ago. Still, I cannot fault you for stoking one of your own. So no, I'm not angry."

Rae exhaled in relief. "Thank you, Father."

"That doesn't mean I condone your behavior," he added sternly. "It has not been safe in Sakesh since the Unification—and it's even less so now. Trouble enough will find you without you looking for it. Find another way to cool your passions, Raetawy. I cannot lose you too. Understand?"

Rae nodded, contrite. "Yes, Father."

"Good. Now get the bread—and be quick about it."

After a hurried trip into the city, Rae headed back to the farm with two still-warm loaves in her shoulder sack. She walked along the river road, thinking of the conversation she had with Omari the day before. Her anger had burned itself out overnight, leaving worry behind in its ashes.

He had spoken passionately about this group of "like-minded men" and their collective calling to fight for Low Khetara. But he was a fool—a fool she loved dearly, but a fool nonetheless. There was nothing a few farmers and artisans could do against the immense power of the throne. He would only succeed in getting himself killed.

Rae shook her head that someone as even-keeled as Omari would be taken in by such a scheme. *Aren't I supposed to be the reckless one?* Then again, affairs in Sakesh were dire, and everyone had their own ways of dealing with the strain.

He's always been there to talk sense into me, she thought. *It's only right that I do the same for him.*

When the reaping was done, Rae decided to visit his workshop. Surely if she laid it out, calmly and logically, Omari would see she was right and give up his plans.

She was just approaching one of the neighboring farms when she heard raised voices.

"Have you no heart?"

She recognized that one as Baki, the shepherd who worked the land. Baki was a quiet man, so Rae was surprised to hear him speaking with such vehemence.

"Have you no sense of mercy? I have a wife, children who still wear the sidelock of youth. You would leave them to starve?"

Rae stopped at the path through the shepherd's field, where three dozen sheep stood, grazing. Up ahead, a group of people stood by the house. Baki gripped his long shepherd's crook in one hand, but the others' backs were toward her. Even so, she knew who had come calling. The nomarch's boat was anchored down by the riverbank, its ram-head sail billowing in the breeze. She took a few steps closer to better hear what they were saying.

"Watch your tongue, lest you wish to part ways with it," replied the nomarch. "It is very simple, so I'll say it again, more slowly so you understand. You will pay the king's tax and hand over half your flock in two days' time. The welfare of your women and children is your problem, not mine."

"The king's tax!" the shepherd exclaimed. "When is the last time King Amunmose has observed the Shemsu Hor and paid Sakesh a visit? How do we know that you aren't simply taking our livelihood for yourselves in his name? How do we know the king still lives? There are men who say he is ill, that his death comes on swift wings, that it is only a matter of time before—"

He never finished the sentence.

Quick as a flash, the nomarch pulled a leather flail from his belt and whipped Baki across the face. The shepherd cried out, and his crook clattered to the ground. Startled, some of the sheep bleated and scattered.

"On his knees," the nomarch said to his men. He sounded almost bored.

Two of the nomarch's guard stepped forward, grabbing the shepherd by the arms and forcing him to the ground.

Rae's fists clenched at her sides.

Father is waiting for you at home, she told herself.

A moment later, a naked boy, no more than four years old, came tearing out of the shepherd's house. The long braid that trailed from one side of his head bounced as he ran.

"Yati!" He ran to wrap his arms around the shepherd's neck.

"No, no!" Baki cried. "Go inside!"

The shepherd's wife appeared in the doorway, an infant in her arms and terror in her eyes. Rae watched her clutch the child to her breast, watched her realize she dared not intervene if she wanted to keep her children safe.

Rae's body trembled.

Don't you ever think about it, Rae?

Ignoring the presence of the little boy, the nomarch raised his flail again to bring it down on the man's back. His son, still clinging to him, let out a high, thin wail.

Rae's peripheral vision faded, until all she saw was the nomarch's face and the smile touching the corner of his lips. He was enjoying himself.

Don't you ever wonder why you're so angry?

"Stop!" she shouted.

Before she fully knew what she was doing, Rae had dropped her sack and run up the path toward the nomarch and his men.

The nomarch paused in mid-swing. He and his entire guard turned to her, but she closed the distance between them before they could respond. Catching the nomarch's arm under hers and pinning it to her body, she swiveled her hips until the flail fell from the man's grip. Then she stumbled back, stunned at what she'd just done.

Nobody moved. When the blow didn't come, Baki raised his head. His eyes widened at Rae standing there among them.

The nomarch stared at her, his face scarlet with rage. "By Amun, look who it is," he said through gritted teeth. "Ankhu's girl."

Rae raised her hands in the air. *Shit, shit, shit. What was I thinking? Father is going to kill me.*

She spoke quickly. "My apologies, nomarch. But I was worried for the boy. He could have gotten hurt."

Rae knew she should stop talking, but the words kept coming. "You can't blame the shepherd for his anger. He only speaks out of concern for his family."

The nomarch blinked, as if deeply considering her words. Then he nodded to the guards, who released Baki and grabbed Rae instead. She grunted as they shoved her forward, her arms pinned behind her back.

"Well, Raetawy," the nomarch said, calm and in control once more. "I knew you were stupid, but this…" He opened his hands to encompass the entire situation. "This is really something, even for you."

Rae struggled in the guards' grip, and one of them wrenched her wrist higher on her back until her shoulder nearly broke.

"Be still, woman," the guard hissed.

Her lip curled into a snarl, but she made no sound.

The nomarch bent to retrieve his flail from the ground, then walked toward her with slow, deliberate steps.

"You want to save this man and his child from his punishment, eh? That is very generous. Very generous, indeed. But *someone* must pay the price for his insolence. I suppose now that someone is you." He smiled. "I should thank you. I will enjoy beating you a great deal more."

He turned to the guards. "Strip her."

They ripped the tunic from her body and threw it to the side, leaving her in only her loincloth. She tried to fight back, but there were too many of them.

The guards shoved her face down in the dirt. Sharp pebbles scraped her breasts and belly, and she coughed as sand went down her throat. She made to get up, to run, but a foot came down on the back of her neck. Panting, she felt a shadow fall over her, as the nomarch's fine beaded sandals stepped in front of her face.

"Hmm," he growled. It was a hungry sound, full of hatred and desire.

With a whistling and a crack, the flail came whipping down on her back. The pain was sudden and searing. Before she could react, the sensation came again. And again.

Don't cry, something inside her commanded. *Don't give him the satisfaction.*

She clenched her teeth until she felt that they would shatter.

He whipped her. Again, and again, and again, until she lost count. Until time lost all form as her flesh parted from itself, first in one place, then another. A curtain of warm blood coated her, dripping down the curves of her shoulders and pooling between her breasts. She drooled, the saliva intermingling with the blood and the sweat and the silent tears streaming down her face.

But she didn't make a sound.

Dimly, she heard the nomarch panting with exertion above her. The strokes came less and less frequently, and with less force. Still, each felt worse than the last. She tried to hide inside her mind, to untether herself from the pain, but her body kept her present. She never went numb. She felt everything.

The strokes slowed until, with one final gasp from the nomarch, they stopped altogether.

It was quiet then, broken only by the occasional bleating of a lamb.

Rae's back pulsed with the beating of her heart, each time spilling a little more blood down the sides of her naked body. Fingers dug into her scalp and pulled her head up by her hair. Her eyes fluttered, and through the mist of pain, she saw the nomarch kneeling at her side.

"That's very good," he cooed, licking his thin lips. "But I would have enjoyed it more if you screamed."

Rae stared at him, a long string of spit dripping from her chin. Then, with effort, she chuckled.

The nomarch's smile dropped from his face. "Are you… laughing?"

"You've used all your strength," Rae said, pink-tinged spittle spraying from her mouth, soiling his pristine white robes. "And you still can't break me."

The nomarch recoiled in disgust, dropping her head to the ground. His foot made contact with her temple, and everything went black.

Rae had no idea how long she was out, but it couldn't have been very long.

Sound returned first, like a rush of wind in her ears. For a moment, she couldn't remember where she was or what had happened—then the blinding pain in her back and head reminded her. She opened her eyes to a blur of noise and color, and her stomach twisted with disorientation.

"You have two days to prepare your flock for transport," a voice said, distorted and strange. "Your fields are unburned, and the girl still breathes. Is that not mercy, shepherd?"

There was a pause, and then: "Yes, Nomarch."

Rae felt a cloud of dust pass over her, stinging her eyes, as the nomarch and his guard departed.

Baki's stricken face appeared before her. She watched his eyes rove over her body, his nostrils flaring, before he reached for her tunic and laid it gently over her.

"Yati?" a tiny, frightened voice said.

Baki looked up. "Go to your mother, son."

After the little footsteps receded, the shepherd looked back at her, grim. "I'm so sorry, Rae, but this is going to hurt."

Pulling her gently onto her side, he laced his hands underneath her legs and shoulders and lifted her into his arms. The movement stretched her torn skin, and the pain was white-hot.

This time, she screamed.

Then Baki was running, as fast as his legs could carry him. Rae's head lolled on his shoulder, and she saw the grazing fields turn to wheat.

"Ankhu!" the shepherd shouted. "Ankhu, you must come quickly!"

She couldn't bear to see the look on her father's face as he emerged from the fields, but thankfully, she didn't have to. Her body, knowing that the worst was finally over, released its stranglehold on her mind, and she fainted.

"Will she be all right?"

It was the first thing Rae heard when she came to again. She was lying on her sleeping mat, dressed in a fresh tunic and covered in a thin blanket. She no longer felt sticky and gritty with dirt, and she wondered who had bathed her. When she turned her head, her father was standing at the door of their house with a portly man who she recognized as the local healer.

"The blow to her head was not hard enough to cause permanent damage, so I would leave that alone," the healer replied, hiking his leather satchel up onto his shoulder. "But I've applied a linseed ointment over the injuries to her back and left you a bottle of willow, dill, and myrtle extract that she can take with her beer for the pain. A few drops will do. Still, the damage was extensive… She may always experience some discomfort due to the scarring."

Rae shifted. Her entire torso was wrapped in linen bandages.

Her father nodded, looking at the floor. "Thank you for coming. I will have the brewer deliver a week's worth of beer to your household as soon as possible."

The healer waved away her father's words. "Do not worry yourself about payment now, Ankhu. You have your hands full finishing the harvest. Rae shouldn't move from her bed for at least a couple days, until the wounds begin to heal."

There was a pause. "I do not know how I will do it without her," her father whispered.

Rae winced.

The healer put a beefy hand on Ankhu's shoulder. "The tale of what Raetawy did for Baki has already swept through the farms, my friend. I have a feeling there will be many hands to help."

Her father put his hand over his mouth and nodded.

After the healer left, Ankhu came to her side. Rae closed her eyes, feigning sleep. She felt like a coward, but she wasn't ready to face him. Wasn't ready to answer the questions he was bound to ask.

Why?

Why couldn't you let it be?

Why did you have to fight?

She listened to his short, shallow breaths. She felt his hand touch her hair, brushing it from her eyes. Then he said something that made her feel worse than any angry words or threats of punishment ever could.

"My brave girl," he whispered. "I'm so sorry."

Rae waited until her father had gone to sleep.

She rose from her sleeping mat, quietly so she wouldn't wake him. Her legs were weak at first, and every movement set fire to the wounds on her back. She was dizzy too, so she grabbed a jug of water and drank half of it, tipping it until cool rivulets spilled over the edges of her lips. It helped, a little.

She peered out the window. There was still some light left. She'd passed the remains of the day in and out of fitful sleep, dimly aware of voices speaking in hushed tones outside the house. Curious neighbors, most likely. Her father must have been so exhausted from the ordeal that he turned in early.

Perfect. Omari will still be working.

It was a short walk to the workshop, but it felt unbearably long. At one point, she lost her balance and nearly fell, but managed to catch herself against a palm tree. She felt one of her wounds reopen beneath the bandages and gasped. But she kept going.

The workshop was a long, low structure, kept in pristine condition—exactly what you'd expect from a family of carpenters. Firelight flickered from the open doorway, and the rhythmic strike of a hammer echoed from within. Taking a deep, steadying breath, she stumbled through the door.

Omari looked up, his hammer poised over a wooden peg. Tools lay all around him in neat lines—pull saws, adzes, bow drills, and small jars filled with glue and more wooden pegs. Wood in all shapes and sizes leaned against the walls, where several lit torches burned, filling the air with the smell of smoke and sawdust. Despite only wearing a small loincloth, Omari's whole body was shiny with sweat.

He dropped the hammer to his side and hurried over to her.

"Rae?" Omari asked, clearly alarmed. "What are you doing? I came to your house as soon as I heard what happened, but your father said you weren't seeing visitors. He said you weren't to move for two days! Ay—what were you thinking, coming here?"

She thought of the broken soldiers, muttering on street corners about the lives they used to have.

She thought of Tamerit, and how she'd fled with her family from a place even worse than Sakesh, seeking refuge from the despair that seemed to spread like a plague across Low Khetara.

She thought of Baki, armed to defend his family with nothing but impotent rage.

And finally, she thought of her father. His expression when the healer told him she'd be scarred for life. The sound of him crying at her side. The weeping stump of his arm, and how he strapped that sickle to it each day without complaint.

She thought of his fire, no longer burning.

And hers blazed brighter.

"Omari," she said, ignoring her friend's questions. "Those secret meetings you mentioned, with the 'like-minded men'—when is the next one?"

Omari blinked, surprised. "Why?" Then his gaze was redirected. "Rae, you're bleeding," he said, gesturing toward the side of her leg. "Let me take you home—"

"Never mind that now!" Her legs went weak again and she grabbed onto Omari's arm for balance. He dropped the hammer to the floor and steadied her. "The meeting..." she pressed.

Omari scoffed. But he'd been Rae's friend long enough to know it was easier to do what she asked. "Tomorrow. The next one is tomorrow. Why?"

Rae swallowed, forcing herself to stand up straight.

Find another way, Raetawy, her father had commanded.

"Because," she said, "I'm coming with you."

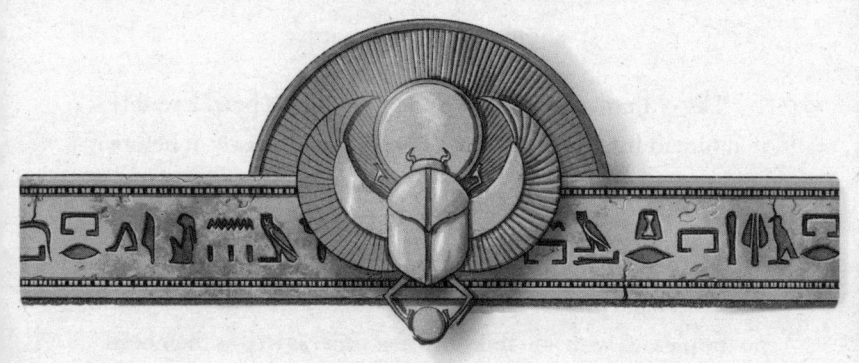

9
KARIM

Karim could have slept the whole morning—maybe even the entire day—except something was licking him.

"Ugh," he grunted, opening his eyes to see the black dog standing over him, slathering his face in slobber. Karim propped himself up on an elbow and shoved the dog's snout aside with one hand. Behkai, not to be dissuaded, started licking his hand instead. "Get away, will you?"

Karim sat up from his makeshift bed on the ground. He winced as his body not-so-subtly reminded him of the previous day's activities.

Finally taking the hint, the dog sat on his haunches and regarded Karim, head tilted, tongue lolling.

"Don't be angry with Behkai," Pa said from where he sat nearby, finishing his breakfast. "You're the one who overslept."

"Overslept? The sun has barely risen." Karim groaned. His body felt like a rug that had gotten the dust beaten out of it. With a stick. Named Babu.

The old priest plucked something from his bowl and threw it at him. It bounced off Karim's head, but he caught it before it could fall to the ground. A date. Pa tossed another date into his mouth, chewed it, and spit the seed onto the sand. "Then we are not yet too late. Break your fast and make it quick. The least you can do is make yourself useful while you're here. The gods would not be pleased with you thieving their time, as well as their dead."

Karim touched his knuckle to his nose in thanks and gobbled up a few dates and a chunk of bread, washing it down with a cup of sweet beer. Behkai stared at him the entire time with huge soulful eyes, until Karim relented and tossed him the crust. The dog caught it in his mouth and swallowed it without chewing. Or tasting, probably.

Pa tutted. "Now you've done it. He'll never give you peace again." The old priest stood, stretched his creaky legs, and turned toward the temple. "Come along now. We have much to do."

Karim stood—carefully—and followed the priest up seven stone steps, the dog padding at his heels. He passed under the archway and into the dim temple, where the air was cool and somehow heavier, smelling richly of cedarwood and flowers in late bloom. Despite his distaste for the Khetarans and their gods, Karim felt his body tense in response, as if he was in the presence of some powerful force. His life, thus far, had been practically bereft of awe, but even he recognized that if magic had a smell, a sensation—this was it.

Four square support columns stood at the center of the hall, a stone altar between them. Light streamed in from between the exterior columns, illuminating a tidy gathering of items on the altar—small stone jars of various sizes and colors, a neatly folded pile of linen, and bowls of more dates, bread, beer, and water. Pa stood at the altar, humming, gathering some of the items onto a round ceramic tray. Karim cast his eyes around the hall, amazed at the profusion of color and design painted on every surface. On one wall, a parade of boats carried standing gods across a field of blue, while on another, fantastic beasts roamed—winged snakes, a bird with a crocodile face, and a man with a donkey's body and a scorpion's tail. But although the paintings were in fairly good condition, Karim could see that the temple was old—the color faded in places where the sun shined brightest, and crumbling in dark corners where the light didn't reach. He could hardly imagine how splendid it must have been in its heyday.

"Well?" Pa asked, hefting the clattering tray into his arms. "Are you going to help me, or are you going to stand there like a goose?"

"Oh—um, yes," Karim grabbed the pile of linen and bowl of water that remained, nearly upsetting it in his haste.

"For gods' sake, be careful!" the priest barked. He examined Karim critically, taking in his stained robes, stubbled chin, and sleep-mussed hair. He frowned. "You're filthier than the dog, but I suppose it can't be helped. Better to come into the god's house with dirty feet than to never visit at all. Come on, thief. Khnum forgive me…" He then made his way toward the far side of the temple, where three more steps led to a curtained inner sanctum. Karim followed obediently, setting the items down just inside the curtain as directed by the priest.

"Only I may enter the holy of holies and approach the god. You must remain here until I'm finished," Pa commanded. He glanced meaningfully toward the palm stem broom leaning against the wall. "I encourage you to stay busy and earn your keep." With that, he vanished beyond the veil.

Sighing, Karim took up the broom and began sweeping sand into a little pile. Behkai, seemingly accustomed to this daily ritual, turned three times and curled up in a sunbeam. Soon, the sound of Pa's voice filled the air.

"Greetings to you, O Khnum!" he chanted. "Divine Potter, who shapes all men on his Wheel! Look north upon a new day!"

Curious, Karim crept back to the curtain and peeked through the edges, trying to get a glimpse of what lay within. The priest knelt on the floor, alternately kissing the ground and raising his arms into the air. Before him stood a golden statue in the shape of a crowned, ram-headed man, surrounded by cups of burning incense and the various offerings from the tray. Karim's eyes bugged at the sight of all that gold. *How has the old man kept such a treasure from being stolen all these years?* Then he remembered how comfortable Pa seemed wielding that spear and wondered how many other "thieves" like himself had perished at the end of it.

The gold wasn't the only unique feature. The ram-headed statue also had four faces, each pointing in a different direction.

Talk about an all-seeing god, Karim thought.

Pa continued, "Greetings O Khnum, Lord of the Great River! Look south upon a new day!" He rose and began wrapping the linens around the statue, as if clothing it.

Having seen enough, Karim wandered away from the door, sweeping absently and thinking about what he was going to do next. Was it worth the risk of trading some of the tomb's treasures in the nearest city? Or should he lie low and look for work in the next village? He darkened at the thought of herding sheep, after all his attempts to avoid doing just that.

Such were his thoughts when his gaze fell upon a scene on the wall. "What... ?" he breathed, moving closer to the painting.

The scene showed a man with one arm outstretched, as if summoning something. Unlike the other figures on the wall, his skin was a different shade of red ochre, his chin bearded, his robe long and dark. The man stood before a long black box marked with what Pa had called a "shenu"—an oval with a line across one end. Inside the shenu were two symbols. There might have been others, but time had worn them away. Karim recognized the symbols immediately—the folded cloth, the loaf of bread. They were the same ones engraved on the amulet he'd taken from Setnakht's tomb.

"Greetings O Khnum, God of Hidden Things, Father of Mystery," Pa's voice rang out. "Look east upon a new day!"

Karim's heart began to pound. What made him almost run from that place was not the symbols, but the man. Despite the strange Khetaran style, the simplicity of line and color, Karim recognized him.

"Greetings O Khnum, protector of the living and the dead, who sets every soul on their path! Look west upon a new day!"

The broom slipped from Karim's hand and clattered to the floor as every thought fled his mind but one.

That man is me.

Karim still hadn't moved by the time the old priest completed his rituals. He remained in front of his likeness, his mind attempting to make sense of what he was seeing.

There was a scraping sound as Pa pushed the tray of offerings out through the curtain, and then emerged from the inner sanctum backwards, bent low, sweeping away his footsteps as he went. When he straightened, he saw Karim's stare.

"I wondered when you'd find it," he said with an enigmatic smile.

Karim suddenly felt trapped and confused. He still did not trust the priest, and with the appearance of such strange magic, he trusted him even less. He considered bolting—the old man would be hard-pressed to stop him—but in the end, his curiosity won out. "That... that picture," he stammered, glancing back at the image. "It..."

Pa patted the perspiration from his forehead with a clean cloth. "It looks remarkably like you, doesn't it?"

Karim felt as if the floor had dropped out from under him. "You *knew* about this?" he exclaimed.

The priest scoffed. "Of course I did. I know every fingerbreadth of this temple like the back of my own hand. The moment I saw the engraving on that stone of yours, I knew Khnum had sent you to me. The first two symbols match the wall exactly, and the man in the painting is your perfect likeness. I wasn't prepared to tell you about it right away, though, not before I knew you wouldn't murder me in the night. Thieves like you can't be trusted. But now that you've found it, I might as well tell you everything. After all, you're part of this now."

Karim fought a wave of dizziness as the priest's words swirled around his mind. It was almost too much to take in, and so unexpected that he hardly knew how to react. "Part of what?" He gestured at the wall. "I hail from the Red Lands, hey? These are not my ways. If you could please… explain what this is?"

"It's the oracle I mentioned to you last night, given to us by Khnum himself. The Oracle of the Lamb."

"'Oracle?'" he repeated. He'd heard Pa use the word but didn't quite understand what it meant.

"It's a, hmm," the priest said, rubbing his chin thoughtfully, "a message from the divine. A foretelling of our future, yes? Like I said, it was the reason this temple was constructed more than a thousand years ago. It shows four scenes surrounding a central image, and a bit of writing along the left side of the wall." He pointed to the central image of a lamb with a bloody wound in its side. A man knelt before it, his arms raised in reverence.

"Look here," the priest went on. "Above the dying lamb is the symbol of Khnum, a ram—meaning that this creature represents the god on earth. And above the man is a mesedjer—an ear. Which tells us that the man is meant to listen to the word of Khnum and bring his message to the people."

"So, what's the message?" Karim asked, though he wasn't sure he wanted to know.

Pa cleared his throat. "That is not so easy to answer. Not that I and a hundred priests before me haven't tried. The writing here is quite vague and open to much interpretation." He began to read from the writing on the side of the images.

"'Beware,' it says, 'for soon the Great River of Khetara will turn to blood. Lies will grow fruitful as wheat in the fields, and where once there was order, chaos will reign. A secret shall rise from beneath the earth, and the Red and the White Crowns will be forever broken.'

"It goes on a bit more about general disaster, but nothing in the way of dates, names, or specific details. Other than that, all we have to go on are these four scenes that surround the central image."

Karim's stomach twisted at the ominous words, but before he could think more about it, Pa continued, pointing to the scene painted directly above the lamb. Three figures stood in profile, two men and one woman standing between them.

"I believe these are King Amunmose's three children: Meryamun, marked with a red cobra; Sitamun, marked with a black cobra; and Bakenamun, marked with the seated Anubis animal. Though I cannot tell you why Sitamun is painted larger than the other two. Perhaps she is connected to the oracle in a way her brothers are not?"

"What's that she's holding?" Karim asked, squinting at what looked like a jar with square handles on either side.

"That is an ieb—a heart. That which is weighed against the feather of Maat at the time of judgment." He sighed. "You know, I went to the king seventeen years ago, once the news of his children's miraculous birth reached me. Triplets! Clearly, it was a sign that the oracle would come to pass during their lifetime. It was my duty as a Priest of Khnum to tell the pharaoh. So I left this place under guard and traveled to Thonis to see him. But when I was finally granted an audience, he dismissed the oracle entirely!"

"'Khnum has no power in the City of Amun,' the king sneered, as if I were some common spell-scroll salesman from the market. 'It has nothing to do with me or my family.' He accused me of darkening his house with gloom and sent me away, commanding me never to return." Pa sneered with obvious disgust. "The fool! He calls himself a god-king, but he is nothing but a pretender."

His dread deepening, Karim studied the image below the lamb. It depicted a group of men, some wielding spears and knives, some on their knees with their wrists bound behind their backs, and others prostrate on the ground, felled by their enemies' arrows. All the figures wore identical white schentis except for one—a woman in a white sheath dress, who was painted larger than the men.

"What kind of weapon is that?" Karim indicated the blunted spear in the woman's hand.

"Not a weapon, exactly," Pa answered. "It's a sekhem scepter, a symbol of Sekhmet, the lion goddess. Whosoever holds it is said to wield great power and strength. Sekhmet is the warlike side of Bast, the patron goddess of Bubas. The two are like day and night—one loving, one fierce—but both great protectors, particularly of women and children." He pointed. "Bast herself appears in the third scene on the right."

In it, a cat-headed goddess placed a feather above a bald-headed child.

"The feather of Maat?" Karim guessed.

Pa nodded. "Not bad for a thief," he said approvingly. "The child appears to be a priest of some kind, though it would be rare for one so young, and a girl too."

They were both silent as they gazed once again at the painting to the left of the lamb, of the man and the black box. Karim desperately wanted to believe everything the priest had told him was superstitious Khetaran nonsense, but he couldn't deny the image right before his eyes. It was undeniably him, and it had apparently been there for more than a thousand years.

He remembered the relentless pull he'd felt toward the tomb back in the valley. Was it his gift for finding treasure that brought him to that hidden door? Or something else?

"You must tell me everything that happened down in that tomb," Pa pressed him. "You promised to give me answers—now is the time to deliver them. I cannot stress how important it is not to miss a single detail, thief. It could be important."

Karim sighed. "As you wish," and he began the story.

He told Pa about the hidden door. About the treasure room and the chariots and the wine. He told him about the statue and the little soldiers, and the black coffin where he found the amulet. But when it came time to tell the priest about the blood, and the dark presence that rose from its grave, Karim hesitated.

He glanced back at the painting, a testament to his crime. In the rendering, the man's expression was passive as he reached out to whatever was hidden inside the box. *I didn't really summon it, did I? I know nothing of Khetaran magic. How could I have done such a thing? All I did was open the box!* He rubbed his finger, still smarting from where he'd cut it on the chisel.

"Well?" Pa asked, impatient. "Is there more?"

Karim opened his mouth to continue, but found himself saying, "No, that's all. Djet went back with the other Jackals after we fought, and that was the last I saw of him."

Liar.

Pa regarded him with suspicion. "Are you sure there's nothing else?"

Karim shook his head.

Coward.

He wasn't exactly sure what kept him from telling Pa the whole story. Fear of retribution? Of judgment? Or perhaps it was simply easier to tell a version of the story where he hadn't released a terrible curse into the world. A story where Djet hadn't died alone in the dark.

He shivered, remembering the chill he'd felt down in the tomb, when he'd been certain the thing had been lurking just behind him. *Where is it now?* he wondered.

"Do you really believe all this will come to pass?" he asked Pa. "That Khetara could be destroyed?"

"The oracle only foretells the beginning of the story," Pa replied gravely. "It's up to us to decide how it ends."

Karim spent the rest of the morning helping Pa with his chores and listening to him make grand plans about his future—and Karim's too.

"I'll leave for Thonis first thing in the morning," Pa said as they pulled the day's water up from the well. "After we finish this, I'll go tell my friend in the village that I need him to watch over the temple while I'm gone."

"Wait a minute," Karim said. "I thought you were too old to travel. You said so yourself."

Pa batted the words away. "I've changed my mind. After hearing what you've had to say, I can see this is too important to ignore. Besides, until you brought me that amulet, I never had the full name of the king engraved on the temple wall. It was incomplete, you see. Now, we know the name of Setnakht. We need to visit the Great Temple of Amun for answers about him, and at least try to get another audience with the king. If he won't see me, perhaps one of his children will. Perhaps the princess herself, since she's clearly involved in the oracle somehow." He spoke quickly, more to himself than to Karim.

"Did you say 'we?'" Karim retorted. "What makes you think I'm going with you on this expedition, hey?"

Pa turned on him. "Have you not listened to a word I've said? This oracle foretells disaster on a grand scale! Perhaps you care nothing for Khetara, but how about your own people? Do you really think the coming war and bloodshed will leave your fellow tribesmen unscathed? Is that a risk you're willing to take? Spreading Khnum's word is my life's work, thief, and if you care at all about the future of this land, you'll accept that it's yours now too."

Karim rubbed his temples. He wanted an excuse to get out of this obligation but found that he had none. Although he worried for his family and would have loved to raise a small army to go back and slaughter Babu, he knew that returning home wasn't an option. Not yet, at least. So why not go north? Even if the priest's mission failed, Karim could probably make a small fortune trading the rest of his treasures at the Thonis market, which he knew was the largest in the land.

"I'll come with you to Thonis," he said, "But that's all. If you don't find the answers that you're looking for, we part ways."

Pa looked relieved. "Good." He dried his wet hands on his tunic. "Perhaps if we're lucky, Khnum will place the other two people from the oracle in our path. Each of you have a role to play, you see."

Karim shrugged. "Whatever you say, sen. How are we getting there, anyway? Isn't Thonis far north of here?"

"I have a fishing skiff moored by the river. We'll bring supplies to eat on the way, so we don't have to stop to trade. Of course, you'll have to share yours with the dog."

Karim glanced over to Behkai, who was watching him from the steps of the temple. "You put me on the same level as the dog?"

"Oh, you are below the dog, my friend," Pa replied. "The dog *begs*, but he does not steal."

They worked until the sun set. Karim was so exhausted he barely tasted his dinner. *Who knew that a priest's work was so hard?* As soon as it was finished, he lay on his mat and was asleep. The next day promised to be a long one.

The dog woke him.

Karim sat up with a gasp. It was still full dark, the desert lit only by moonlight. Behkai was barking. Karim looked around, but he couldn't see the dog or the priest anywhere. Perhaps Pa had gone to make water, as old men often have to do in the night, and Behkai had gone to guard him from predators. But as Karim turned over to go back to sleep, the barking continued, transforming from a guttural alarm to a shrill, yelping cry. Dog or not, Karim knew that sound.

Behkai was afraid.

A terrible thought struck him. *What if Babu and Hager tracked me here? Have they been lying in wait to attack?*

Scrambling to his feet, Karim ignored the aches and pains in his body and ran toward the sound, the blue amulet heavy against his leg.

"Pa!" he shouted into the murk.

The temple glowed white in the moonlight. Karim dashed along its western wall, listening for the old man's response.

Nothing.

"Pasenhor!"

Behkai's cries became more frantic.

Perhaps if he'd had time to think, or if he hadn't still been half asleep, Karim would have been more cautious. Perhaps he wouldn't have announced himself. Instead, he ran straight toward the front of the building, right out into the open path leading to the temple steps.

Behkai, blacker than the night itself, stood guard there, his back arched, tail tucked between his legs, his teeth bared as he barked at something Karim couldn't see. Beside him, lying in a pool of moonlight, was Pa.

"No…" Karim rushed to the priest's side.

The dog wheeled toward him, mistaking him for another threat, and lunged, snarling.

"Hey! Hey!" Karim exclaimed, backing away. "It's me, sen," he said softly, reaching out a hand as a peace offering. "Just me."

The dog sniffed him and began to whine, keeping his eyes trained on the two stone pillars flanking the path, their tops marked with pyramids pointing to the sky.

"It's all right. It's all right," Karim murmured, rubbing the dog behind the ears. He dropped to his knees next to the old priest, fearing what he would find, but Pa didn't seem to have a single wound on his body. Karim gently lifted his head from the ground. The priest's skin was cold and clammy, but his mouth was moving, as if in silent prayer.

He was alive.

"Pasenhor! Wake up, holy man. Wake up, your god still needs you. We have a long trip, tomorrow, remember?"

The priest's eyes fluttered before focusing on him.

"Thief."

The word was barely audible, more a memory than a whisper.

"What happened to you? Come on, get up. Let's get you back to the temple, you need water—"

The priest shook his head. He strained, his neck muscles

bulging, struggling to speak. Karim bent so his ear was close to the man's lips.

"You lied to me."

Karim's whole body tensed. "What do you mean?"

"Something happened in that... tomb," the priest gasped.

Karim shook his head, desperate to deny the truth. "No, I didn't *do* anything, I didn't—"

"'A secret shall rise from beneath the earth,'" the priest quoted. "It's in the oracle. I should have... known..."

Karim's heart began to race. Behkai hadn't moved, and was watching the shadows, a growl deep in his throat.

Someone did *follow me. But it wasn't Hager or Babu.*

"It's too late now. It's... here."

In a panic, Karim grabbed the priest under his arms, trying to drag him to his feet.

"We have to go, old man. Come on—"

Suddenly, the priest cried out in pain. "Don't move me!" he insisted, grimacing. It was only then that Karim noticed his teeth were tinged with blood. "Don't..."

"What?" Karim exclaimed, scrambling back as a gush of dark blood spilled from beneath the priest's body, as if by lifting him, Karim had unstopped a bottle of wine that was now pouring freely onto the sand. In a matter of seconds, Pa's face had gone from pale to deathly gray.

Karim went cold. He'd only glimpsed it for an instant—but that was enough. There was a small hole, deep and fatal, in the priest's back. As if someone had come up behind Pa and punched straight through his flesh to the soft viscera within.

"Nothing to be done now," the priest said, the words garbled and wet. A thin trail of blood slipped from his lips as he spoke, but somehow he still had the strength to grasp Karim by his robes and pull him close.

"Now get out of here, thief," he said with gruesome ferocity, "Quickly, while you still can. And promise me you will go to Thonis and do as I meant to do!"

"I promise! I promise!" Karim sputtered, alarmed and afraid.

"It gives me… no pleasure to leave this in your hands." The priest's voice weakened with every word. "But I have no choice. There is no one… you must… the oracle…"

The priest's body went slack, his eyes stilled on Karim's face. The blood beneath him had grown to an immense black pool.

Karim lowered the priest's head back to the ground, his heart hammering. Behkai whimpered next to him and nuzzled his master's hand.

All around them, the desert mourned in silence.

Then, one of the shadows moved.

Karim jumped to his feet, nearly stumbling over the dead man's legs in his haste. He squinted into the gloom beyond the stone column, desperate to discern the shape of his enemy. From within the darkness, two eyes flashed.

Terror seized him, like fingers around his throat.

With a strangled sound, Karim took one step back, and then another, before turning and running as fast as he could. He tore back the way he came, Behkai galloping at his side, stopping only to grab his readied pack from beside the sleeping mats.

He ran toward the river, the khamasin wind pulling at his robes as he crested the dunes, his chest burning with exhaustion, the primal terror like lightning in his veins.

He only dared to look back once, squinting into the biting wind. What he saw, bathed in moonlight, burned itself onto his memory, its afterimage appearing like a phantom every time he closed his eyes.

It pursued him, as inevitable as death itself.

The river came into view, a dark glittering serpent winding

its way to the horizon. Karim nearly tumbled down the dune toward it, the dog nimbly leaping along beside him. He spied Pa's fishing skiff pulled ashore nearby, constructed of little more than bundles of dried papyrus reeds molded into a boat shape, one end turned up like a scorpion's tail. Without hesitation, Karim tore its mooring from the ground, tossed his pack aboard, and jumped on.

Hoisting the single wooden oar into his hands, Karim was about to push away from the shore when he saw Behkai standing on the riverbank, panting, eyes brimming with fear.

"Absolutely not," Karim said with finality, "I don't have time for a pet."

The dog whined. His pointed ears flattened along the sides of his head.

A shadow rose over the nearest dune, growing closer.

Karim cursed. "I am going to regret this." He grabbed the dog by the scruff and hauled him onboard. Behkai licked his face, and cursing again, Karim pushed away the dog's snout and snatched up the oar. With one mighty shove, he pushed the skiff into the current and began feverishly rowing away from the riverbank.

The creature stood on the edge of the water, watching them drift downriver, north toward Thonis.

Karim didn't stop rowing until he could no longer see it, until it had melted back into the shadows and vanished into the night.

10
RAE

When the brightest star crossed its zenith, Rae set off. Her father didn't stir when she rose from her sleeping mat. It had been an emotional, exhausting day. He'd gotten up first thing in the morning, and prepared to work all day to harvest enough wheat to meet the nomarch's unreasonable demands. When Rae offered to assist him, they'd argued—only to be interrupted by the arrival of several neighbors and their families, including Omari and Baki. As the healer had predicted, word had spread of Rae's good deed, and many in the community had shown up to help.

Seeing them out there, working together to harvest a neighbor's grain despite their own troubles—for the king's tax spared no one—made Rae feel a fierce pride for her fellow Sakeshis. Like the wheat, her people bent in the wind, but did not break.

When he'd first arrived, the shepherd had grasped her hand. "I don't know how to repay you, Raetawy. That beating should have been mine."

Embarrassed by Baki's gesture, Rae shrugged. "Anyone would have done the same."

"No," Baki said, ardently. "They wouldn't have."

Ankhu watched the exchange with an expression Rae couldn't identify. Pride? Anger? Dread? It could have been all three.

Despite everyone talking about the incident with the nomarch, Rae and her father didn't speak of it. In fact, besides the argument, they hardly spoke at all. At sundown, they'd stopped work, settled the zebu for the night, and eaten supper in silence. And after shoving bits of bread and salted fish into his mouth, her father had finished his beer, gotten up from the table, and went to lie down on his mat. Within moments, he was asleep.

Rae had cleaned up the meal, washed her face and hands in the basin, and then lain down next to him. She watched over him for hours, just as he must have watched over her the night before.

She remembered how impossibly large he had seemed when she was growing up. To her, he was the strongest man alive. A bulwark against an increasingly wretched world. He'd kept them both clothed and fed until she was old enough to help with the farm, and sheltered her from the ugly reality of life in Sakesh to give her the gift of a happy childhood.

It had been a shock to them both when Rae grew not only as tall as her father, but surpassed him by a fingerbreadth or two.

"Don't be smug, lest you be humbled," he'd said the first time he'd realized it, wagging a finger at her. "You're still my little girl, and always will be."

Watching him sleep, she couldn't help but notice how small he looked, his thinning, work-hardened body curled under the thin blanket.

I'm sorry, Father, she thought. *But you can't protect me anymore.*

When it was time, she left her bed and padded softly to the door, stopping to don a shawl and pluck her father's knife from his belt. It was a fine bronze blade with a blackwood handle—one of the only relics left of Ankhu's life as a scribe in King Rahotep's court. The hilt was engraved with geometric designs and a large wedjat eye, its pupil inset with carnelian.

Some mornings, she'd catch him praying, knife in hand and eyes toward the dawn, the last vestige of his crumbling faith. "Hear me, Ra," he'd say. "Maker of Hours, Lord of Days—hear me and cast your light upon me. Burn away the fear in my heart, and watch over me so that I may see you again tomorrow."

Rae whispered her father's prayer as she pushed the knife into her own belt and stepped into the chill night. She rubbed her arms, her teeth chattering, and wrapped the shawl tighter around her shoulders as she walked toward Omari's house. She dared not bring a torch, so she relied on the moon to light her way. Khetarans generally avoided travel at night, as anything done after sundown was generally viewed with suspicion.

"Only jackals and criminals lurk in the dark," people said.

I wonder what that makes me? Rae thought as she approached the workshop.

Omari was waiting for her outside, also wrapped in a dark shawl. When she tried to greet him, he pressed a finger to his lips. He pointed toward a path into the mountains and motioned for her to follow. It wasn't until they'd left the workshop far behind that he finally spoke.

"Are you sure about this? There's still time for you to turn back."

Rae adjusted the hood of her shawl. The movement caused the torn flesh on her back to stretch and sting. She winced, but the pain served as a reminder of why she was there in the first place. "'My eyes have been opened to injustice I can no longer tolerate,'" she said wryly, throwing his own words back in his face. "You want me to close them again?"

Omari's jaw clenched in exasperation. "Curse you, Ay. I only told you about this because I wanted you to support my fight against the High Khetarans. I never intended for you to *join* me in it. These men... they won't look kindly on me bringing a woman into their midst. For all I know, they'll throw you out the moment you arrive."

Rae put a hand to the hilt of the knife at her side. "Let them try."

Omari sighed. He didn't call her "donkey" for nothing. Still, Rae caught him casting worried glances at her when he thought she wasn't looking.

They walked across the barren terrain, having left all vegetation behind. After a while, Rae crested a low hill and saw a large landform ahead. It looked like a ragged, oddly shaped mountain—except it seemed to have a perfectly rectangular man-size doorway cut into it. She could see moonlight shining through from the other side.

"Is that where we're headed?" Rae asked.

Omari nodded. "It is the Hesep-Mut—the Garden of the Dead. Thousands of years ago it was a vast necropolis, but now it's a ruin. No one goes there, and it provides a great deal of cover, so it's the perfect meeting place."

"A necropolis, you say," Rae said, feeling a tingle up her spine.

"Yes, so watch your step."

As if on cue, Rae's foot caught on something under the sand that almost sent her sprawling. When she looked back to see what it was, the top half of a human skull peered out at her, the holes of its eyes filled with sand.

"Come on," Omari urged. "Hurry up or we'll be late."

Rae tore her gaze from the skull and rushed to follow. He didn't have to tell her twice.

As they approached the door, Rae could see that the structure was a monument of incredible size, built with thousands of mud bricks, their edges softened by time. In its heyday, the Hesep-Mut must have been an awesome thing to behold—even now, its sheer size nearly took her breath away.

In fact, she was so distracted by the sight of it that she didn't notice the man slip out from the shadows toward them.

Rae gasped as a knife pressed against her throat. She went to reach for her own weapon, but the blade pressed harder against her flesh.

"Don't," a gruff voice said from behind her.

In the next moment, an archer appeared silhouetted in the doorway, an arrow nocked in his bow and ready to fly.

Omari ripped the hood from his head and raised his arms in surrender. "Please, we come in peace! It's me, Omari! I attended the last meeting. My friend wishes to join our number."

The archer called out to them without lowering his arrow. "The falcon sails across the sky."

Omari licked his lips, his eyes flicking to Rae. The man's arm held her firmly to him, and she stood rigid, trying not to inhale his sour breath.

What is that supposed to mean? Rae thought.

"We shall meet him on the horizon," Omari answered.

There was a pause before the man's grip loosened and the blade dropped away. Rae whirled on her assailant, a wart of a man who she could toss over her shoulder without much effort. He had scraggly whiskers and absurdly large ears, which gave him the overall impression of a donkey. She shoved him.

"Son of a dog!" she spat.

"Rae!" Omari barked. "Leave him alone. He was only doing his job."

"And what job is that?" Rae muttered, still glaring at Big Ears.

"An important one," the archer replied. "Keeping spies out of our midst." He lowered his bow and stepped out of the shadows. "Which, in turn, keeps us all alive."

Unlike his friend, the archer was a strapping man of about her father's age, his short black hair and beard shot through with silver. He wore a short schenti and a coarse, sleeveless black robe that seemed cut from the night itself. A green scarab amulet, laced on rough cord, rested on his bare chest. He moved with assurance, and Rae thought he would have looked quite at home riding a chariot. The archer seemed unbothered by the cold as he reached out to grasp Omari's hand at the wrist.

"I welcome you," he said, one eyebrow raised. "Though I'm beginning to question your judgment." He shot a glance at Rae.

"You're not alone in that…" Omari admitted.

Rae scowled, a thousand curses on the tip of her tongue.

"However," Omari went on, "I have known this girl for many years. She can be trusted. I give you my word, Asim."

Rae swallowed the curses as Asim approached her. He was a little taller than her and gave off a powerful but not unpleasant scent of burning wood.

"You may join the meeting, kitten," he murmured. "But if you breathe a word of it to anyone, I will find out, and I will not hesitate to slit your throat from ear to ear. Do you understand?"

She stared back at him, unflinching. If this was Asim's way of scaring her off, it wasn't going to work. "The name is Raetawy."

A smile quirked at the edge of his lips. "Do you understand… Raetawy?"

Instinctually, Rae's hand came up to touch the tiny wound where the other man's blade had pierced her throat. "I understand."

Asim nodded. "Very well. Then come with me—we are about to begin."

Letting out a shaky breath, Rae followed the three men through the doorway into the Hesep-Mut. Beyond it, the structure opened into a massive courtyard, surrounded by towering, uneven walls. Here and there, the broken remains of pyramid-topped pillars stood, along with wide altars nearly buried in windblown sand. A group of more than two dozen men waited by one of the altars, talking among themselves.

Rae recognized quite a few of them—fishermen, farmers, the brewer, the potter's son. Others she'd met once or twice because they were acquaintances of her father, ex-soldiers in King Rahotep's army who would sometimes offer to work in exchange for a meal. Their sinewy arms, trained to wield a khopesh in the heat of battle, were forced to make do swinging a sickle instead.

The murmurs fell silent with Asim's approach. The archer—who Rae recognized must be their leader—dropped his bow beside the altar and nimbly leaped onto it.

"My brothers," he declared, "Esteemed members of the Horizon. I have heard about the nomarch's visits to your fields and workshops, and about the pharaoh's merciless ultimatum. As if the drought was not bad enough—now Amunmose wishes to steal the very food from our children's mouths!" There were angry murmurs in reply. "Brothers—this cannot stand!"

A rallying cry went up from the men.

"A generation ago, Sematawy, the so-called Great Uniter, and the armies of High Khetara invaded our land and slaughtered our king, leaving Sakesh in ruins. Even now, there are ghosts among us! Men whose bodies still walk the earth, despite their souls having died the day the war was lost! And now Amunmose, a pretender who has never carried a khopesh in his life, he wears the White Crown of our kingdom and calls himself a god-king! But he is no god, is he, my brothers?"

"No!" the crowd replied.

"This tax increase is the act of a coward and a fool, and we must not accept it—lest we too become cowards and fools! And so, I propose we send a clear message to Pharaoh with a raid on the House of the Medjay, the very men who help him enforce his laws and keep us defenseless. We have been waiting for the right moment to act—my brothers, this is that moment! My messengers tell me that Amunmose is very ill. In his weakness, he has allowed his soldiers to become idle. Fewer guard the House of the Medjay than ever before! If we follow my plan and work together, we can cut them down like wheat in the field before they can raise an alarm." Asim paused for breath. "Now," he cried, "Who's with me?"

The question was greeted by an uncomfortable silence.

Rae stood at the back of the crowd, watching the men stare at the ground or each other, mumbling softly and shaking their heads.

Asim was looking at them too, consternation clear on his face. "I'm disappointed in you, brothers. You have been coming here for months, airing your grievances, and now that I ask for your help to allay those grievances, to fight back against this injustice—suddenly you're at a loss for words? Where is your passion? Is there nothing between your legs but the wind?"

Again, silence.

"I'm with you."

The words tumbled out of Rae's mouth before she could think better of them.

Omari elbowed her. "What are you doing?" he whispered harshly.

"What?" she whispered back. "You said you wanted to fight, why didn't you volunteer?"

"I was *about* to, but then you—"

"Who speaks?" Asim called out, scanning the crowd.

The people in front of her parted, leaving a clear path to the front. But when the men saw who she was, they erupted with exclamations of surprise and irritation.

"Is that Ankhu's girl?"

"Raetawy, this is no place for you!"

"What fool brought her here?"

"That fool brought her." Asim pointed at Omari. Omari ducked his head as the jeers were diverted in his direction. "But *this* fool let her in." Asim pointed to himself.

The crowd quieted.

"And with good reason, it seems, if it takes a farmer's daughter to shame you all into action."

"It's not that we don't agree with you, Asim," the brewer called out. He was a short man, shaped like a barrel. "But what chance do we have against the Medjay?"

The other men nodded their agreement.

"We all want change," the brewer continued, "but there must be a way to achieve it that doesn't put all our lives at risk. It's all very well for this girl to volunteer, but she can't really *fight*, so—"

"I can fight," Rae broke in.

The brewer scoffed.

Omari must have caught the set of Rae's jaw, even in the dark, and uttered a warning. "Ay…"

Rae ignored him. Her pride had run away with her, leaving caution far behind. She threw off her shawl, dropping it in a heap on the ground. Her wounds stung in protest, but she ignored them too.

Two farmers stood nearby, leaning on their walking sticks, watching the scene unfold.

"Do you think I could borrow those?" Rae asked them.

Puzzled but curious, the men agreed. With the long palm-wood sticks in hand, Rae turned to Asim.

"I *can* fight," she said. "Give me a chance to prove myself in a match of tahtib. I challenge any man here who wishes to make me a liar."

A roar of excitement greeted her offer, but Asim silenced them. "Are you sure you want to do this?"

His voice was kind, and that annoyed her. "My challenge stands," she replied.

Asim shrugged, his eyes glittering with amusement. "Very well, Raetawy. But as you can see, I am the leader here. If you're to fight anyone in this company, it will be me." He held out his hand.

Rae's breath caught in her throat. As usual, her ego had led her into deep waters. She'd occasionally participated in tahtib matches in the street fights, so she was comfortable with an asa—plus, she'd already sized up the men in the crowd and felt confident she could hold her own against them. But she'd never considered Asim. Aside from Omari, he was the largest man there, and despite his age, he looked as fierce as a lion.

No turning back now, she thought grimly, and tossed one of the improvised asa sticks to her opponent. Asim caught the asa and spun it, rolling it over his hand and catching it again with fluid dexterity. Hopping down from the altar, he approached and the crowd backed away, leaving them a wide berth. Holding the long sticks by their ends, Rae and Asim circled each other, swirling the weapons around their bodies, like a dance. The crowd began to chant and beat their hands against their thighs in a steady rhythm.

Rae and Asim met in the center of the circle and struck their asas together three times with the beat.

Clack! Clack! Clack!

"Begin," said Asim.

The amusement in Asim's eyes set Rae's fury aflame. With a guttural cry, Rae spun away, sweeping her asa into a low arc to strike at Asim's knees. But Asim was ready for her, nimbly dodging the attack and lunging forward, thrusting his weapon under her guard. It struck her full in the chest and took her breath away.

Gasping and enraged, Rae lunged wildly, slicing her asa through the air toward Asim's shoulder, but he easily parried it away and gave her a smack on the back for her trouble.

Rae sucked her teeth as her wounds sizzled with pain. The crowd of men laughed and hooted, spurring on the fight. Rae thought Asim would laugh with them, but his eyes never left hers.

"Focus, Ay!" Omari called out. "He's trying to rile you up—don't take the bait!"

Rae was about to ignore him like she usually did, when she remembered all the fights she'd lost, not because she wasn't good enough, but because she'd lost her temper. Those fights had cost her a few baubles. Losing this one would cost considerably more.

She felt the weight of her father's knife at her hip. When she turned ten he'd taught her how to use it, and pointed out the wedjat eye painted on its hilt. "You must treat your weapon with respect," he'd said. "For just as Ra's light can both create and destroy, so can the blade be used for good and for ill. It can cut you as easily as it can your enemy."

Rae felt the familiar rage burning through her veins, urging her on as she circled Asim, who hadn't even broken a sweat.

Use your rage, she told herself. *Don't let it use you.*

So instead of allowing her fury to overtake her, she closed her eyes and felt its power within her.

"What are you doing?" Omari shouted. "Are you out of your mind?!"

But Rae barely heard him. She focused on the weight of the asa in her hands, and the sensation of Asim moving near her, his shadow passing over hers as they continued to circle each other. In the darkness, she could feel the way their bodies made curving, sinuous ripples in the cool night air, which was scented with smoke, honey, and wine.

She felt a disturbance in those ripples. Asim was about to attack.

She opened her eyes and sidestepped as Asim's asa came slashing down toward her. His stick hit the ground, and Rae lunged to strike at her opponent's shoulder. The hit was clean and took Asim totally by surprise.

The crowd shouted in dismay, and Rae smiled. Asim recovered quickly and moved around her with greater caution. His casual amusement was replaced with intensity. The crowd sensed a change between them and quieted, though they kept the steady drumbeat going.

Rae matched her breath with Asim's, watching his chest rise and fall, rise and fall. And when she saw that quick intake, saw his muscles grow taut and his eyes narrow, she moved in parallel with him, curving her body away to allow his asa to pass by her. They moved that way together for several minutes, their feet throwing up clouds of sand, in a dance that was both elegant and brutal.

Rae landed several more strikes, but nothing that made Asim pause, and she was getting tired. Despite her improvement, Asim clearly had superior strength and technique, and fatigue was making her sloppy. After a frenzied exchange of blows, Asim seemed ready to thrust his weapon toward her, so Rae dodged away. But his attack was merely a feint, and as soon as she was exposed, he whirled, sweeping his asa into another blow to her back.

Her wounds reopened on impact.

A white-hot bolt of pain was followed by a gush of warmth beneath her bandages. She tried to raise her asa once more, but it was too much. Every movement caused her skin to feel like it was ripping apart. Because it was.

The world spun, and she fell to her knees.

Omari was next to her in an instant, laying her gently on her side until her dizziness passed.

Asim looked bewildered, his asa forgotten. "I don't

understand," he said, and gestured at the bloodstains spreading across the back of her tunic. "I didn't hit her that hard."

"You didn't," Omari said. "Someone else did. Yesterday morning."

Asim dropped to one knee next to them.

"May I see?" he asked Rae, his voice soft.

I've already lost, Rae thought miserably. *Why not?* She nodded.

Gingerly, Asim pulled her tunic aside and examined the bloody bandages covering her back. He grimaced and got back to his feet. "Who did this to you?"

"The nomarch," Rae replied. Her teeth chattered with sudden cold.

Asim's expression darkened. "Why?"

"She did it for me," a new voice called out. Rae lifted her head as Baki the shepherd pushed to the front of the crowd. "I'm sorry I'm late, Asim. I had a bit of trouble getting away from home—my son is ill. But it appears that I've arrived just in time."

"What do you mean, she did it for you?" Asim asked.

"The nomarch came to make his demands, and I gave him a piece of my mind. He was going to beat me and my little boy both, but Raetawy stopped him, so he beat her instead. I thought she'd be bedridden for weeks after the lashes he gave her… and yet here she is, up and fighting the very next day."

"She can't be stopped," Omari said helplessly. "Believe me, I've tried."

"Fight with me, then," Rae said. "Fight for Sakhesh." She tilted her chin toward Asim. "This man has a plan to raid the House of the Medjay, and he seems to know what he's doing."

"Quite the compliment," Asim said with a chuckle.

"Come on, now," the brewer retorted from the crowd. "This is obviously a suicide mission. Think of your family, Baki—your son!"

The shepherd shot a fierce look at his friend. "In the name of Ra, brother—I am thinking of nothing else! Do you expect the High Khetarans will stop increasing our tax? They won't stop until everything we have, everything we are, has been ripped from us."

Rae winced as Omari removed her soaked bandages and tore fresh strips from his shawl to try and stop the bleeding. Rae pushed herself upright, clutching her shawl to herself to cover her nakedness, the pain nearly forgotten with the men's exchange.

Baki gestured to Rae. "You have a girl about her age, don't you?" he asked the brewer. "What if the nomarch had beaten *your* girl? What if it had been *her* blood soaking into the sand? Would you tell me to think of my family? Or would you pick up your khopesh and seek retribution, no matter the cost?" He shook his head. "I'll do it. I'll fight for Sakesh. And for you, Raetawy."

Many of the men in the crowd nodded in agreement, and Rae could sense the energy around them shifting, gathering strength.

Asim must have noticed it too.

"What say you then?" he cried, walking in a wide circle, looking every man in the eye. "A shepherd and a farmer's daughter have made cowards of you all tonight. Will you let that stand? Or will you find your courage and join them?"

"I will," Omari declared, as if he'd been waiting for the moment to speak.

"And I," said another man.

"And I."

Dozens of men stepped forward, until nearly every single one had offered his hand in battle. Even the brewer, who watched with growing unease as the men around him volunteered, relented and said, "Gods help us, I'm with you too."

The men loosed a cheer, and then immediately broke into smaller groups to discuss inventories and strategies for the raid.

"I should get you home," Omari said to Rae, pulling the bloody tunic back down over her torso and draping her shawl over her shoulders. "We need to change your dressings properly."

Rae wanted to stay, but she knew Omari was right. She let him help her gently to her feet, but that was all. She refused to be carried.

The amusement was back in Asim's eyes. "Well," he said, his hands akimbo. "I guess it wasn't so bad after all, letting this fool bring you here."

Rae blushed and was glad it was too dark for Asim to notice. As they made their way back to the stone doorway, she took one last look at the group of "like-minded" men, talking and planning. They seemed different somehow, their faces brighter, like embers catching fire after having nearly gone cold.

"What have we done?" Rae whispered, shaking her head.

She hadn't meant for Asim to hear it, but he did.

"My dear girl," he rumbled, the words a deep rumble. "You've gone and sparked a rebellion."

11
NEFF

"Nefermaat," the priest barked. "Are you listening, girl? We've no time to waste. The barge arrived late, and it will be my hide—and yours—if these deliveries are made in error."

Neff groaned inwardly. It had already been a busy morning and she longed for the midday meal. *I thought standing all day in Yati's stall at the market was tiring—but it was nothing compared to this!* "I'm listening," she said.

"Papyrus scrolls to the scribes in the House of Life," the priest said, piling her arms high with bundles. "Incense pellets and fresh linen to the sanctuary, and this goes directly to Master Montuhotep." He handed her a long-necked wine jar, painted carnelian red. "He asked that you be the one to bring it to his chambers."

Neff nodded her understanding and went on her way. She'd made so many deliveries in the days since she'd arrived that she already knew the temple layout, and many of the priests' names, by heart. She wondered if that had been the master's intention when he'd given her the assignment. Or perhaps he was trying to test her mettle, to see if she was truly up to the task of becoming a priestess. Either way, she'd fallen into bed each night and slept like the dead, only to be woken by the Wabet at the break of dawn to bathe and scrub herself until she was raw. Her skin had already begun to take on the polished sheen of everyone else at the temple. To her dismay, she'd been so busy that she hadn't had time to serve as Prince Kenna's assistant, as promised. She'd seen him several times in passing but only long enough for a hurried greeting. She hoped that soon that might change.

She threaded her way through the crowds, taking the shortcuts she'd discovered. As she was about to round a corner, she stopped short at a familiar voice.

"The healers are hopeless," the man said. "They've tried every potion, administered every amulet. His condition only worsens. He is asking for us now, though I worry even we have little hope against such a demon. I've seen the awful brown marks on his hands and feet—he tries to hide them under sandals and makeup—and his behavior is... erratic."

Peering around the corner, she spied the Heka priest she'd crossed on her first day at the temple and his two companions as they proceeded through the corridor. Though Neff was still in awe of them, they looked far less intimidating without their animal masks.

Who are they talking about? she wondered. Interested, she remained hidden behind a statue as they walked past.

"We must be careful," one of the other two said. "He may be ill, but he could still have us beaten for failing to cure him. Or worse."

The third priest scoffed. "He doesn't have it in him."

The first priest made a harsh noise, like a curse. "Watch your words. The walls have ears." He peered into the shadows near where Neff was hiding, but moved on.

Neff waited before emerging. Was it possible they were talking about the king? She remembered gossip about his illness back in Bubas. But a demon that even the most powerful Heka priests in the land could not vanquish? Her curiosity about the situation, and about the Heka priests themselves, grew. She knew she'd been brought to the temple to learn to be an Hour priest, but she couldn't get the image of that living snake staff out of her mind. For now, though, she needed to hurry before the master noticed she was late.

She dropped off the papyrus, incense, and linen in short order, then made her way outside toward Master Montuhotep's chambers. She'd made many mistakes that first day but learned quickly from them. For all her complaints about the many long days she'd spent at the market, her father's insistence on hard work and tenacity was serving her well in her new role.

She weighed the wine jar in her hand—her last delivery. She hadn't spent much time with the master since her arrival, but Neff got the feeling that his opinion of her hadn't improved. Once she'd recovered from the trauma of that first day and gotten accustomed to her reflection in the mirror, Neff had focused on learning whatever she could at the Temple of Amun. She'd tried more than once to ask the master when her lessons would begin, but he'd simply batted her away like a gnat humming at his ear.

At the flat-roofed white building just outside the temple courtyard, she took a deep breath before knocking on the polished wooden door.

A strident voice called out from within. "Enter."

Neff licked her lips and went inside. She was greeted by an oppressive darkness. The wooden shutters on both windows were closed and covered with thick curtains, effectively transforming the chamber into a shadowy cave. Master Montuhotep sat on a reed mat in the center of the room, his face lit by a flickering oil lamp burning on a low table before him.

"I-I'm sorry to interrupt, Master," Neff stammered, suddenly feeling that she'd blundered into the middle of a ritual. "I was told to deliver this parcel to you right away." She hurriedly set the wine jar on the low table next to a small golden cup and was about to withdraw when Montuhotep spoke again.

"Shut the door, and sit down."

Neff felt uneasy, but knew she must obey. With a bow, she turned and closed the door softly, before seating herself on a mat opposite him.

The master's eyes, alive with reflected fire, regarded her briefly before taking up the lamp and holding the flame to a bowl filled with small yellow rocks—some kind of resin. Soon, the resin began to burn.

"What do you know of dreams, child?" he asked.

Neff coughed as a plume of pungent, bittersweet smoke filled her nostrils. "I don't know much," she began, recovering herself. "Only that they are messages from the gods, and that Hour priests can tell us their meaning."

"Correct," the master replied. "The gods do not speak directly, as men do. They speak in images and symbols, and so Hour priests must become fluent in the divine language. To be given this opportunity is a rare honor—not everyone is suited to hear the word of a god."

He paused, folding his hands neatly on the table between them. "The high priestess delivered you here with assurances that you were touched by Bast. Still, the journey from layman to priest is long—longer for a common girl like yourself. Do you truly wish to drink from the primeval waters, child? To fill yourself with its secrets? Or would you rather I send you back to Bubas and your mother's knee? I could bear the high priestess's wrath. You have seen for yourself the hardship of temple life. I will not make it easy for you, nor will any other priest in this place. It is understandable that you would not wish to remain here. No one would blame you for going home. Not even the goddess."

His mouth tightened, and he regarded her with glittering black eyes. "I warn you: once you drink from those waters, the act cannot be undone. For the right person, it can bring about enlightenment, but for the wrong one—it is a poison that will destroy you from within."

Neff's brow furrowed. When she'd come to the temple, she'd imagined learning to read the gods' words, poring over scrolls, unlocking the mysteries of the divine. But what Montuhotep spoke of was very different from long days spent in candlelit libraries.

It sounded dangerous.

Perhaps she should accept the master's offer and leave this place while she still had the chance. Isn't that what she'd wanted when they cut off her hair and turned her into a stranger? Wouldn't it be wonderful to be home again? Back to her own sleeping mat, to her family and friends, to days spent selling spells at the marketplace with her father?

She paused.

How would Yati react if I returned home from the temple? To know that I gave up on the priesthood before even trying? Mother would be thrilled to have her back, but would he?

No. He'd be disappointed.

The master was wrong. The goddess *would* blame her for leaving, and she wasn't the only one. So why would Master Montuhotep make her such an offer?

He doesn't want me here. He's trying to drive me away. First with the endless errands, and now with this ominous warning. Stepping outside of her emotions, it all seemed so clear. So obvious. *I might be young, but my father didn't raise a fool. The goddess brought me here for a reason, and I promised to see it through. It will take a lot more to get me to break that promise.*

Neff cleared her throat. "I want to stay."

The corner of the master's lip twitched, almost imperceptibly. "Very well. Then we will begin."

"Begin what?" Neff asked.

"You wish to drink from the waters," the master said, lifting the wine jar and pouring something dark and thick into the golden cup. "This elixir opens your mind to the divine. Visions are capricious things—they don't always come when they're called, especially to a novice. The elixir brings them to the fore. Once you drink it, I will ask you some questions about dreams I have interpreted in the past. I already know the proper meaning of these dreams, and what came to pass after the dreamers woke. If the gods wish to speak to you, the correct answers will come. If not…" He handed her the cup. "May Amun have mercy upon you."

Neff accepted the cup with trembling hands. She brought it to her mouth and hesitated, glancing over the rim at Montuhotep.

He wants you to fail.

The thought stoked a fire in her belly. All at once, she drained the wine to the dregs.

The elixir stung the back of her throat. It was cloying, the sweetness disguising a bitter, herbaceous flavor and a coppery tang that reminded her of blood. She gritted her teeth and swallowed it down, grateful she was able to do so without gagging. She placed the cup on the table and folded her hands on her lap, then returned Montuhotep's stare. His expression tightened, and that pleased her.

"Look to the lamp," the master intoned. "Soften your gaze and concentrate on the flame. Look to the darkness at the center of the light. Let it surround you; let it become your world. It is there you will be found—or lost."

Neff focused on the lamp. With the windows covered, no breeze blew through the chamber, so the flame did not flicker. It was so still, it seemed almost solid, like an object she could hold in her hand.

Time passed as she stared at the flame. Slowly, she began to feel a strange weightless sensation, which intensified with each passing second. Then a breathless wave of pleasure, the likes of which she'd never felt before, crashed over her. It sharpened her focus, making the flame brighter, richer—a sublime array of gold and violet light. She wanted to touch it, to taste it, to crawl inside and become one with it.

The room around her darkened, then fell away altogether. She could no longer see Montuhotep sitting across from her or the table between them. Even her body, the weight of her flesh and the places where it touched the floor, disappeared. There was nothing but the flame.

From across an ocean of nothingness, a voice reached her. Dimly, she recognized it as the master's.

"The dreamer is climbing up the mast of a great ship. What do you tell him?" Montuhotep asked.

The flame guttered. In her mind's eye, Neff saw shapes appear within it—a man rising up, lifted by animal-headed figures that danced in the flickering light.

"He will rise above his people, held aloft by the hands of the gods," she said. Her voice belonged to a stranger, as if something huge and foreign were speaking through her lips.

"He sees himself in a mirror."

Again, the images came, shifting within the flame.

"This man will have great sorrow—he will lose his wife."

"His face is not his own," the master said. "But the face of a leopard."

"He will become a leader among his people." The answers were coming more quickly now, flowing out of the flame and into her mind like water.

"He is in a deep well."

"He will be imprisoned for his crimes."

"He sees a shining moon."

"The man will be forgiven."

The wave of euphoria was cresting, burning through her senses, filling her mind with color and light so vivid that it was almost unbearable. She tried to look away, tried to break her connection with whatever it was that spoke through her, but another image appeared at the center of the flame.

"The lamb," she whispered.

There was silence for a moment, then Montuhotep spoke again. "The lamb from your vision? The high priestess mentioned this. Tell me what you see."

Neff wanted to stop. The longer she stared into the flame, the more it clung to her, pulling her from her world into an abyss from which she was uncertain she had the strength to return.

"No more," she begged. "I can't..."

"You can and you will," Montuhotep commanded. "Tell me what you see!"

Neff moaned, trying to focus despite the overwhelming sensations. Dozens of images passed through the flame, almost too quickly for her to register them.

"I see war," she said with difficulty. "I see a long journey. I see betrayal and death—so much death..."

"What else?" The master's voice was impatient.

Neff searched through the chaos, trying to see beyond it. Four figures emerged. One wore a crown, another carried a scepter, the third had two shadows, and the last... the last...

She was small.

"Tell me!" Montuhotep shouted.

A second later, there was a loud bang, and Neff's world exploded with light. A sudden wind blew through the chamber, and the flame went out. She blinked into the sunlight, gasping as reality came crashing back. Neff turned. A strong wind had blown the door to the chamber wide open.

The euphoria quickly soured into a bleary daze that made Neff's head hurt and her stomach churn. Across from her, Montuhotep cursed and reached across the table to grasp her wrist.

"What did you see, child? Tell me before the vision fades!"

Neff met his gaze. Then she vomited on the floor.

It took the work of several Wab priests to clean Montuhotep's room to his satisfaction. Neff would have helped, but she was too ill to move. The master continued to prod her about her vision of the lamb while she recovered, but she simply shook her head.

"I'm sorry, I can't remember," she lied.

In fact, she remembered everything. But the timing of the wind, the way the door blew open on an otherwise windless day, made her think she was meant to keep that particular vision to herself. Or at least, not to share it with Montuhotep. Until she found someone worthy of her trust at the temple, it was her secret to keep. Clearly, the goddess had called her to that place to interpret the lamb's message—and to somehow use that information to avert disaster. Her dream had been nothing but grim portents, but the vision had provided something new.

The four figures.

She hadn't been able to see their faces, or anything beyond the small details she remembered, but she knew one thing for certain: the last one was her.

But what role could a girl like her possibly play in such a grand design? She wasn't a leader or a warrior, and other than her wits, she had no particular skills.

Then she thought of the Heka priests and the snake—wood one moment, flesh the next. *Real magic.*

Hadn't Prince Kenna said he'd studied every element of the priesthood in order to choose which one he liked best? If he could learn them all… two couldn't be so hard, could it?

It was the better part of an hour before she felt well enough to return to her chambers. Before she left, Montuhotep stopped her, his large hand gripping her shoulder.

"You will go to the House of Life tomorrow, after your deliveries are done. The scribes will begin instructing you in the gods' words." He added, "It is one thing to see—but it's another to understand what you're seeing. If you are to be any use to me at all, you must have discipline and control. You must learn from the scrolls."

Neff nodded, excited by this development. "But… my interpretations of the dreams," she said. "Were they correct?"

Montuhotep was quiet, but his expression said it all. "When you are stronger," he said, irritation clear in his voice, "we will do this again."

Then he sent her away.

Neff stumbled back to her chambers, her stomach still roiling. Despite her nausea, she felt deeply satisfied. She knew her interpretations had been correct. Montuhotep had tried to frighten her, but she'd proven herself worthy of a place at the Great Temple. Finally, she arrived back at her rooms, and without answering the Wabets' prattling questions, she collapsed onto her mat and fell asleep.

Neff spent hours in the seventh sleep.

By the time she woke up, she was starving. She'd missed the midday meal, and the sun was already low in the sky. After convincing the cook to wrap up a hunk of bread, a boiled egg, and a wedge of cheese for her, she took the little parcel over to the temple gardens to eat.

Settling down under a fruit tree, she tore into the bread and egg, and took small bites of the squeaky white cheese to make it last longer. She'd almost finished when she heard people approaching on the path.

"How could you miss the Bast Festival, Kenna?" a female voice asked. "All of Thonis was there—everyone except you!"

"I'm not one for festivals, sister," Prince Kenna replied in his raspy voice. "You know this. I was there to see the goddess on her way—that is enough. Besides, I suspect my presence wasn't missed."

Sister?! Neff scooted herself behind a jasmine shrub and peeked through its leaves. Prince Kenna's hair was as wild as ever, and he was dressed in a plain black linen tunic belted with fine leather. He wore no adornment, aside from a simple Anubis collar, beaded in black, white, and blue. The girl facing him was dressed differently than when Neff had seen her at the opening ceremony of the Bast Festival, but there was no mistaking who she was. Princess Sitamun.

Unlike her brother, Sitamun looked very much like royalty. She had a prominent aquiline nose like her brother's, but where it looked beakish on Kenna's narrow face, it made the princess look regal. Her lustrous black hair fell to the middle of her back and glittered with golden beads, and she wore a blousy green linen dress with a plunging neckline that accentuated her curvaceous figure. Her jewelry, by contrast, was quite simple. Two amulets strung on black cords—one a red Isis knot, and the other a simple green scarab. It was hard to look away from the princess. She was like a chameleon—exotic, vivid, and ever-changing. Neff felt a pang of envy.

"I just think it would be good for you to visit the palace once in a while," Sitamun said, glancing toward the temple with a look of unease. "You can't hide in here forever."

"I'm not hiding," Kenna shot back. "I'm *working*. You should try it sometime."

The princess pursed her lips. "You know, brother," she said. "Maybe if you spent a little more time around the living, you'd know how to speak to them properly. You didn't used to be so cruel."

Kenna closed his eyes and sighed. "Forgive me, Sitamun," he said with deliberate patience. "I thought I'd made it very clear that I have no interest in palace life. I ask for nothing except to be left to my work. Mother may not understand the importance of what I do— hardly anyone gives the Men of Anubis the respect they deserve. But when I joined their number… it made a difference. The other priests' behavior toward them began to change." He shook his head. "The embalming chamber might be the only place in the kingdom where my presence shines a light instead of casting a shadow. So I'm sorry for disappointing you, sister, but I think I'll stay here."

Sitamun fiddled with a lock of her hair. "But Kenna… I'm worried."

"About what?"

"About Father."

Kenna's shoulders fell. "Ah." He put his hands up in a helpless gesture. "The priests are doing all they can, Sitamun. There's certainly nothing I can do that isn't already being done."

"But what if… what if they're wrong about what's afflicting him?" Sitamun asked. "What if it's not a disease demon, but something else?"

Kenna scoffed, offended. "I understand you're worried, Sitamun, but you should not question the priesthood. Where is this coming from, anyway? Have you been reading those stories again? I know you're prone to flights of fancy, but I should have thought you were old enough not to allow your imagination to run away with you."

"It's not my imagination!" Sitamun's cheeks reddened with anger.

"Then what is it?" Kenna asked. "Can you give me one reason to believe the priests are wrong about Father's illness?"

Neff leaned forward, waiting to hear what the princess would say.

A pained expression crossed Sitamun's face as she opened her mouth to speak. But in the end, she simply shook her head.

Awkwardly, Kenna placed his hand on his sister's shoulder and gave it a pat. "I realize this is hard for you. Father's health may improve, or it may not. Sometimes the gods simply wish to call their children home, and there is nothing anyone can do about it. But if he must go West, I will be there to prepare him for his journey. As it should be."

"And Mery will take the throne?"

At that, Kenna turned to the fruit tree and plucked a ruby-colored orb from its branch. "And Mery will take the throne."

The princess nodded.

"Go back to the palace, sister," Kenna told her. "And stop worrying yourself about things you cannot change."

That advice seemed to hurt the princess the most. Without another word, she walked out of the courtyard.

Kenna watched her go, his hooked nose set in profile against the setting sun. After a moment he said, "You can come out now."

Neff blanched. Then, she peeked out from her hiding place, abashed. "How did you know I was here?"

"Generally, jasmine bushes do not wear sandals," Kenna said with amusement, nodding toward her feet sticking out from behind the shrub.

Neff stood up, her cheeks hot. "I-I'm so sorry, my prince. I came to eat in the garden. I didn't intend to eavesdrop."

"No need to apologize," the prince replied to her immense

relief. "All you heard were the lamentations of a girl who has everything and wants more." He pulled a small knife from his belt and started to carve his fruit.

Neff moved to watch him, having never seen that kind before. "What is that?" she asked.

"A pomegranate."

"Mm," she murmured. "She's really pretty, your sister."

Ruby red juice slipped down the prince's blade. He licked it clean. "She is."

"It's nice that she wants to spend time with you."

Kenna pulled a slice of pomegranate from the whole, exposing a cluster of glistening seeds within. "I suppose."

Neff knew she shouldn't say more, but she couldn't help herself. "So… why don't you spend time with her at the palace? You could visit and still do your job here, couldn't you?"

The prince popped a few seeds into his mouth. "Why do you ask me these questions, Nefermaat?" he asked after chewing.

Neff thought a while before answering. "My mother wanted five children. One for each finger on her hand. But Father was only able to give her one child. Sometimes I wonder if that's why he's always been so desperate to make us rich. To make up for not giving her what she really wanted."

She'd had nothing to drink with her meal and her throat was dry. She licked her lips, then continued, her voice a bit quieter. "For as long as I can remember, I've never wanted anything more than a sister. So it's hard for me to understand why you'd turn yours away."

The prince stopped chewing. His nostrils flared.

Neff suddenly wished she could take it back. He was kind, it was true, but the prince could still have her thrown to the crocodiles. And here she was, scolding him for not being nice to his sister. What was she thinking?

"I shouldn't have said that," she blurted, taking a step back from him. "I'll go." She turned and started back toward her quarters, hoping to escape before he decided on a punishment.

"Wait."

Neff froze. She turned, and one glance at the prince's face told her he wasn't angry, just troubled.

"I'm sorry you have no siblings, Nefermaat," he responded. "But there is something to be said for being so special. So *wanted*. The waters of your parents' love all wash upon your shore, and yours alone. I am one of three, born all at once. My father spent the first year of our lives spreading the story of our births far and wide, sharing how the gods blessed him with abundance and sanctified his place on the throne. Yet I have always felt like an afterthought.

"I love Sitamun. But she lives for parties and finery and stories of passion and romance. That is not my world, and I won't have her dragging me back into it. The fact is, Father might die. It is sad, but death is a part of life, and like everyone else, Sitamun must learn to face it without behaving like a child. We all need to grow up sometime."

He glanced at Neff, and his expression softened. "Perhaps you'll never have a sister, but you can call me brother, if you wish."

Neff could hardly believe her ears. "I'm just a girl from Bubas. You're a prince. You'd call me your sister?"

Kenna shrugged. "Crown or no crown, we are all children of Khetara." He held out a seed from the red fruit.

A crown, Neff suddenly remembered. *Wasn't the first figure I saw wearing one?* Perhaps one of the three young royals had something to do with the lamb's prophecy. If so, her friendship with Kenna was meant to be.

Neff took the seed from him and inspected the tiny jewel-like fruit. "I've never tried one of these before," she said, before popping it in her mouth. It was unlike anything she'd tasted—crisp and sweet and tart, with a hint of bitterness at its center. It was wonderfully refreshing.

"I have a feeling you'll try a lot of new things in the coming days, little sister," Kenna said.

"May I have more?"

"You can have it all," Kenna replied, handing her the rest of the pomegranate.

Neff took it and sunk her teeth deep into the fruit, suckling the flesh until its juice dripped down her chin.

12
SITA

By the time she returned from her visit to the temple, Sita's hands were shaking so severely she was afraid one of the servants might notice. She'd avoided taking the Royal Road to get back, favoring one of the less-used side paths instead, so luckily she hadn't met anyone on her way home.

She needed something to calm her nerves. Her thoughts turned first to wine, and then to another one of her recently acquired diversions.

Yes, that's exactly what I need, she thought.

Late that evening, after her attendants had retired to their rooms for the night, Sita was in her chambers when Nebet came rushing in looking for a misplaced hair comb.

"I'm so sorry to intrude. I must have left it here earlier—"

Sita hurriedly sat up in bed, pulling a thin linen blanket over her bare chest. She gave Nebet a tight smile. "It's there," she said with a nod toward her ebony dressing table.

"Oh, thank you, thank you." Nebet plucked up the comb.

"Wake up to benevolence, Sitamun." She gave a quick bow and departed.

As soon as she'd left, Sita let out the breath she'd been holding.

"She's gone," she said.

One of the heavy curtains covering her window flicked aside, revealing Femi hidden behind them. He puffed out his cheeks. "Thank Amun she didn't stay to chat."

Sita bent to reclaim the cup of wine she'd hidden under the bed. "How is it that such a strapping man as you could be afraid of little old Nebet?" she asked, taking a sip. It was her second cup, and her head already felt pleasantly light.

Femi chuckled. He still wore his usual short schenti and Eye of Horus collar, though it was a little askew. "It is Nebet's mouth I'm afraid of. Despite her size, she is quite capable of seeing us together and telling someone. I risk everything every time I come to you, my princess."

"And still you come," Sita said with allure, handing him his own cup and letting the blanket slip from her chest.

Femi took the cup and drained it lustily. "And still I come."

She beckoned to him, and he obeyed, moving to stand at the foot of the bed.

"What would you have me do, Sitamun?"

Sita spared a thought for the maidservant from the garden. The girl may not have appreciated Sita monopolizing her lover—but then again, was she really going to complain? Sita was the princess.

"You'll do anything I say?" Sita asked.

"Anything."

"Remove your collar."

He did.

"Now your belt and schenti."

He licked his lips. So far, since that night at the festival, they had only touched and kissed during stolen moments in shadowy corners of the palace. What she was suggesting that night was a step into unknown territory.

After only a moment's hesitation, Femi complied, letting the schenti slip soundlessly to the floor.

Her breath caught in her throat as she beheld him, the taut angles of his body catching shadows in the candlelight. He was like the wine—thick, smooth, and intoxicating. But unlike the wine, she could drink as much of him as she liked and it would never stop feeling good.

Lying there, looking at him, all she wanted to do was drink, and drink, and drink.

"What shall I do next?" he asked, his voice a quiet rumble.

"Come here and kiss me."

In an instant, he was there on the bed, slipping on top of her.

"As you wish," he murmured.

His lips met hers, and in the sunburst of sensation that followed, she tried to forget.

Forget that night.

Forget the Bast Festival.

Forget Mery's confession.

Her brother had been drunk. There on the boat, amid the festivities and indulgences, she'd first thought his claim that he was poisoning their father was another one of his cruel jokes. But then he'd leaned forward, his lips nearly touching hers.

"Murder is quite an exciting game, dear sister," he'd whispered. "And now you're playing it with me."

He'd shared that truth with her for a reason. They'd suckled milk from the same breast, played with the same toys, grew up in the glaring light of the same expectations. And when it came to killing the king, Mery wanted to do that together too.

"How? How are you doing this?" she'd asked him once she'd recovered her voice.

Mery's eyes had twinkled with mischief. "The same way one eats a hippopotamus. A little at a time."

Sita's first instinct had been to tell someone. To go to the first palace official she saw upon disembarking and admit everything. But by the time the boat reached the shore, she knew it wasn't that simple. Mery probably wasn't working alone, which meant others in the palace were loyal to him. She thought of the oft-maligned viziers. How could she know who to trust?

Set himself gathered seventy-two conspirators when he plotted to kill Osiris, Sita had thought, remembering the legends of the gods.

Besides that, Father was so sick, he could die at any moment. If she revealed that the son in line for the throne had murdered the pharaoh, what then? Such knowledge could easily throw the entire kingdom into chaos—and war. She had studied enough Khetaran history to know that such revelations almost always ended in bloodshed. Was she prepared to have all those innocent people's deaths on her conscience? And if Mery ended up facing execution for his actions, who was to say she wouldn't meet a similar fate? Wasn't that part of the reason he'd told her in the first place?

Murder is an exciting game, dear sister. And now you're playing it with me.

One after another, her thoughts tightened around her like the coils of a snake until she could hardly breathe.

There's no way out.

Sick with horror and excessive drink, she'd stumbled back to her chambers without saying a word to anyone.

The days since had been a waking nightmare. The day following the festival, she'd walked around in a daze, feeling as if she were floating above her own body as it went from place to place, woodenly eating meals and nodding blithely as some courtier spoke about hunting expeditions and chariot racing. On the second day, she'd begun drinking wine at every meal, and found that with enough of it, her mind softened like butter, and she didn't have to think quite as much. On the third day, she'd spirited a jug of wine into her chambers for mornings and late nights. On the fourth day, she'd needed a fresh jug.

On one of those nights, she couldn't really remember which, Sita had lured Femi to her quarters to finish what they'd started at the Bast Festival. He'd been terribly nervous at first, keeping one eye on the door even as she pulled him to her, but she'd assured him that Mery no longer posed a threat.

I'm keeping his secret, she'd thought, *he'll keep mine*.

She became skilled at covering up these excesses, making sure no one knew that she was sneaking wine from the kitchens and liaisons with Femi. Forgetting, however, was proving to be extremely difficult. That morning, she'd woken in a panic, and had the idea to speak with Kenna.

She'd never been particularly close with her strange, quiet brother, but defying their parents' every expectation took courage. She may not have understood his obsession with funerary rites and the priesthood, but she still respected his ability to ignore custom and do what he wanted.

It was an ability Sita never had.

If she could hint to him that something was amiss at the palace, maybe he would come investigate. Knowing Kenna's talent for deduction, he'd probably figure out what was going on and find a way to fix the situation. Somehow.

But Sita realized her error the moment they started talking. Kenna only cared about his work, and he still saw her as a silly little girl. Her brother may be extremely intelligent when it came to scrolls and rites, but he knew nothing about navigating palace life. If she told him the truth, he'd only see it in black and white.

For all she knew, he'd make things worse.

The visit had been a mistake. Not only that, the entire time they were talking, she'd had the distinct feeling of being watched. So she'd left without telling Kenna the truth, feeling more alone than ever.

With those intrusive thoughts crowding her mind, Sita wrapped her legs around Femi and pulled him closer in an attempt to block them out. She could feel the urgency of his desire, but he gently shifted his body away, kissing her all the while.

"Don't you want me?" she asked, feeling slightly hurt.

"More than anything," Femi replied, stroking her cheek. "But you've had too much wine, Sitamun, and I don't want you to do anything you'll regret."

Sita sighed. Why did he have to be so *good*? Somehow it felt like more than she deserved.

"However," Femi said roguishly, "There are other ways for me to satisfy your appetite."

Sita stifled a laugh as he slid his head beneath the blanket.

Afterward, Sita lay on the bed, feeling sleepy and muddle-headed. She stared at the elaborately painted frieze on her wall, which featured a group of men in the marshes, capturing wild birds in a clap net.

Femi bent down to refill his cup from the jug on the floor. When he straightened again, he was holding a papyrus scroll in one hand. "What's this?"

Sita's eyes widened. "Hey! Give it here!"

"'How do I name this love that we share?'" he recited, his eyes scanning the scroll. "'A love that spills over me like water, and warms my heart like a flame? It has no shape. It is everywhere at once. I breathe it from your lips when we are together, and when you are gone, I feel it in the wind…'"

"Give me that!" Sita said, snatching the scroll, her cheeks reddening.

"A love poem from another man?" Femi teased.

"It's not from a man," Sita retorted. "*I* wrote it."

Femi's eyebrows shot up. "Princess Sitamun, you are full of surprises."

Sita stuffed the scroll back under the bed where more than a dozen others were stored in a messy pile. "I've always loved reading stories about the gods, so a few seasons ago I started writing some of my own. Poems and retellings of the great legends, things like that. I'm working on *The Death of Osiris* now. It's always been my favorite. It's so… romantic."

"Is it?" Femi echoed, sounding unconvinced. "Doesn't Osiris's brother Set murder him and cut his body into a dozen pieces?"

"Fourteen pieces," Sita corrected him, staring at the stars painted on her bedroom ceiling. "Which he scatters all across the kingdom. Instead of simply mourning her husband's death, Isis turns into a bird and takes to the skies in search of the pieces, and she finds them all except for one. So she fashions the missing part out of gold and puts Osiris back together again.

"Then, with her magic and her love, she stops time and brings him back to life. In that frozen moment, they make love and conceive Horus, the avenger. But when time restarts, Osiris dies again, and they are forced to part. Osiris enters the Duat, and from that day forward, reigns as the Lord of the Dead."

She smiled. The story and the kissing and the wine were all a comforting distraction from the world outside her bedroom. "Can you imagine loving someone enough to stop time for them?"

Femi looked at her, a bit of sadness in his eyes. "I can imagine it."

Sita wondered if she'd said something wrong.

He sat up and picked up his schenti from the floor. "I beg your pardon, Princess, but I must be going. The captain of the guard has been keeping a closer eye on the men lately, and if I'm gone much longer, I'm afraid I'll be missed. A few of the other guards have been sent away recently, for reasons unknown, and I'd rather not join them."

Sita thought of the empty wine jug and her soon-to-be empty bed. Already she could sense dark thoughts seeping back into her mind. She felt cold.

"Very well," she said dully, pulling the blanket tightly around her.

He stopped in the doorway and looked back at her. "Perhaps I could return tomorrow?"

"Tomorrow night I must attend a banquet," she replied, rubbing her temple. She felt a headache coming on. "Some ambassadors and a prince are visiting from Tash."

"Ah," Femi said, nodding.

"I will call upon you again soon," Sita said, the formality returning to her voice.

It was a dismissal, and Femi knew it. She could tell by the way he straightened his shoulders and nodded crisply, his jaw set.

"Of course, my princess." And then, "I look forward to it."

When he'd gone, Sita went to the basin and poured herself some water. She drank three cupfuls, but her mouth remained bitter and dry.

He gives himself to you, and still you treat him cruelly.

Despite his valid reasons, she hadn't liked that he'd left before she'd wanted him to, so she'd punished him with her coldness.

You're using him.

She stared at her reflection in the brass mirror, her thick hair pleasantly tousled, her copper skin tinged with the blush of pleasure and drink.

She was beautiful and perfect, and she hated herself.

But what else could she do? Carrying Mery's secret became more difficult with each passing day. It had nearly gotten to the point where no amount of wine or distraction could prevent the dread from spreading through her every waking moment. She had to do something to keep from going mad. *Besides, I'm not hurting Femi, not really*, she reasoned.

But the thought didn't ring true.

Sita blew out the lamp on the table and fell back into bed, praying for a dreamless night. But sleep stayed far from her chambers, and she turned to gaze at the frieze again, illuminated by the moonlight. In the hunting scene, the colorful, elegant birds were painted midflight, their wings spread as the net closed around them.

For the birds, time had stopped. Their eyes were forever turned toward the sky, but they'd never reach it. They were trapped.

She closed her eyes, but the crisscrossing clap net remained like an afterimage, tightening around her in the darkness of her mind.

The Tashan prince was speaking to her.

"What?" Sita had to shout to be heard over the music of flutes, harps, and drums.

"I said, 'Do you want some lentils, princess?'" the prince shouted back.

"Oh. No, thank you," she replied, and turned back to her cup. The shedeh she was drinking—a kind of fermented pomegranate juice—was a nice change from the wine. Though she'd had so much of it already that she'd ruined what was left of her appetite. Normally she loved the savory lentils they served at banquets. They were stewed with onion, garlic, and cumin—but that night, the mere sight of them turned her stomach.

She'd been seated between Harsi, the Tashan prince, and a sleepy old vizier who nodded off after the first course. She was certain her mother had put her there on purpose, in the hopes she and Harsi would strike up a rapport. After all, the prince was a striking figure in his bright green sash and emerald-encrusted circlet, and the queen was eager to find a suitable match for her only daughter. The prince was handsome, with a broad, elegant face, an easy smile, and deep brown skin. He was also courtly, and, most important of all, he was the next in line to the Tashan throne.

Unfortunately for the queen, enticing the visiting prince was the furthest thing from Sita's mind.

She'd managed to engage him in some banter when he'd first arrived, placing a garland of flowers around his neck, but now that she was five cups into her shedeh, her charm had faded. Harsi was courteous to a fault, but Sita was certain he'd noticed.

Despite her many years of diplomatic instruction at the hands of her mother, she couldn't bring herself to care. The mounting sense of unease had so completely overtaken her life that even polite conversation felt like an impossible task.

The banquet table overflowed with dishes piled with roast oxen and goose, bowls of plump figs and red grapes, bright radish and cucumber salad mixed with vinegar and parsley, and honey and tiger nut cookies baked into crescent shapes and dotted with sesame seeds. The table stretched nearly the full length of the open-air hall, with guests seated on each side, one and all bedecked in their finest robes and gowns, their necks dripping with gold. Many of the women wore head cones over their wigs, which melted with the heat of their bodies, releasing a spicy-sweet fragrance into the air. Made of a combination of myrrh, wax, and resin, the cones got smaller and smaller as the night wore on, ticking away the minutes until the party was done.

Sita adjusted the silver circlet around her head, which was inlaid with white papyrus flowers in mother-of-pearl. There was silver thread woven into the fabric of her dress as well, a long formfitting indigo kalasiris accented with ostrich feathers that her mother had procured for just such an occasion. She nibbled on a cookie, unable to tear her eyes from her father seated at the head of the table, his sunken face ghoulish in green eye paint and rouge. He wore the double crown, and his neck strained visibly beneath it. The tall White Crown of Low Khetara, crafted of electrum and diamond, sat within the curved crimson-gold basket of the Red Crown of High Khetara, the rearing cobra upon its brow staring upon the scene with sparkling garnet eyes. He'd taken to only wearing it for special occasions, favoring a simpler gold circlet the rest of the time. Sita could see why. The double crown was so heavy, her father looked as if he might collapse under its weight.

While the rest of the guests chatted and ate, the king spoke to no one. Once every few minutes, he ate a grape or a piece of one of the little cone-shaped honey cakes that he favored, but otherwise he was very still.

Sita's stomach lurched again, and she set the cookie down, unfinished.

Her mother sat nearby, doing her best to sweeten the sour-faced Tashan ambassadors with bottomless cups of shedeh. They all wore richly patterned robes in the same bright green as Harsi's sash. The queen's smile was dazzling, but Sita could see her casting anxious glances toward the king.

She's doing his job, and everyone knows it, Sita thought.

In the absence of conversation, Prince Harsi had turned his attentions to the dancing girls. There were four of them, naked except for translucent loincloths and white beaded necklaces, their braided hair swinging in time with the music. They moved with practiced ease, contorting their lithe bodies into deep backbends and high kicks while maintaining eye contact with any guest that glanced their way. Among the dancers was Tadia, one of her father's favorite concubines. She made the most of her voluptuous body, managing to catch Amunmose's eye as she rotated her hips invitingly in his direction. He gave Tadia a weak smile and raised his cup to her.

Suddenly Sita felt hands gripping her shoulders and heard her mother's voice in her ear. "What has gotten into you? The prince has been trying to engage you all evening and you've been as charming as an ox! I've got my hands full as it is without you dishonoring this house with your behavior. Are you *trying* to make me look like a fool? Stop drinking and compose yourself. *Now*."

Sita's cheeks reddened. She'd forgotten that the queen noticed everything.

"Yes, Mother," she murmured, her voice thick.

With that, the queen stood, offered Harsi another dazzling smile, and melted back into the crowd of lesser courtiers and attendants who mingled around the banquet table.

Sita didn't think Harsi had heard her mother's blistering reprimand, but he must have sensed the tension. He glanced at Sita uncertainly.

Just then, Maet bounded up to the king, having wriggled out of her mother's grasp from where she sat with the other lesser wives. Sita watched her father's eyes brighten. With great effort, he pulled the girl onto his knee and offered to share his cake with her.

Seizing the opportunity to make conversation, Harsi said, "Sweet girl. The king seems quite taken with her."

"He is," Sita replied, hoping the prince wouldn't notice the pain in her voice. She knew she shouldn't be jealous of little Maet—she loved her too. Everyone did. But Sita couldn't help it. Seeing her father lavish affection on the child, something he'd never done for Sita, tore her heart to pieces every time. Maybe the little girl represented freedom from the constraints of the throne, of which Sita was a constant reminder. Maybe he'd reached a time in his life when he could appreciate the simple pleasures of a child—something he couldn't do in the early days of his reign when Sita was young.

Or maybe the king just liked Maet better.

Sita looked away from the pair, forcing her thoughts back into the dark where she kept them. *Harden your heart*, she told herself. *Make it as a stone that grief cannot penetrate.*

"My father was surprised to receive the invitation to visit your kingdom," Harsi began again, trying a new tack. "There hasn't been much exchange between Tash and Khetara in many seasons—and suddenly we find ourselves here. I wonder why that is?"

Sita licked her lips. He was fishing. Perhaps he hoped the shedeh would have loosened her tongue and he'd get some valuable information out of her. She knew the invitation was her mother's doing, having convinced the king that it had been his idea all along. The viziers were only too happy to oblige. Normally, Sita wouldn't have paid attention to any of these political machinations, but since Mery had so effectively revealed her ignorance about matters of import when he'd confessed his plans, Sita had made it a priority to learn everything she could about the state of the kingdom.

She'd begun eavesdropping on conversations and writing what she'd learned on scrolls kept under her bed, hidden among her love poems and stories. Even if Nebet or one of the other attendants came across them, she wrote them in the gods' words instead of the common script, so none of the servants would be able to decipher them. She had even asked her tutor to give her an overview of Khetaran current affairs during their last lesson. He'd been surprised, perhaps even a little frightened, by the request—as if she'd asked for a weapon that might one day be used against him. But she *was* the princess, so in the end, he'd complied.

What he told her was shocking.

The ongoing drought leading to crop reductions and mass hunger across the Two Lands.

The weakening of trade and relations between Khetara and the surrounding kingdoms.

The unrest in Low Khetara, where the king's nomarchs had been receiving growing resistance to Amunmose's steep tax increases.

Mery was right, she'd thought. *While he sits and eats cake, outside the kingdom falls.*

By killing their father, Mery believed he would save Khetara from the poor leadership that was driving it into ruin. Sita had thought he was exaggerating, but the more she learned, the more she saw she was wrong.

The queen had likely arranged the visit from Tash in an attempt to strengthen ties with the kingdom at their southern border, so that in the event of violence in Low Khetara, they would have an ally to come to High Khetara's aid.

A marriage between me and their eldest prince would certainly do the trick. But she didn't say any of that to Harsi.

"Time rushes by so quickly, does it not?" she said instead, nimbly sidestepping the question. "Sometimes we blink and seasons have passed without our notice, and we've failed to reunite with old friends."

"Indeed," Harsi said with a small smile. Despite not getting the information he wanted, he seemed to appreciate the clever deflection.

Even after five cups of shedeh, Sita thought with satisfaction, *I can still play this game.*

"Harsi, my friend!" Mery waved from across the table as he flitted around the room like a peacock. "Are you enjoying yourself?" He was resplendent in a midnight-blue robe and a collar decorated with blue and white lotus flowers. A golden scarab made up the center of the collar, its shell a great emerald that subtly honored the visiting Tashans. Sita couldn't help but notice that he'd adopted a familiar tone with the prince, calling him "friend" despite their never having met before.

"Very much, Prince Meryamun, very much," Harsi replied, raising his cup in appreciation.

Mery then turned his attention to her. "Sitamun, it's not like you to remain hidden behind the table during such a feast. Come, allow me to introduce you to some of our other guests."

"Ah, but I'm keeping Harsi company at the moment," Sita demurred. "Perhaps I shall join you later." It was true, she and Mery were normally joined at the hip during formal occasions, but she couldn't bear the idea of prattling on about fashion and perfume with the lesser nobility that night.

Mery's eyes narrowed for only a moment before he grinned and said, "Very well—later then," and moved on. She watched him work the crowd, his slender body glowing with health and vitality, and his infectious smile spreading to each person he spoke to, disarming one scowling Tashan ambassador after another. The queen was never far from his side—clearly relieved to share the burden of diplomacy with her very capable son. With every laugh, every shared whisper, every cup poured in fellowship, Sita saw the crown shift invisibly from her enfeebled father's head to Mery's.

She couldn't help but wonder who else saw it too.

"Your brother cuts a fine figure," Harsi said after a moment. "As do you. The two of you are alike in many ways, no?"

Sita picked a fig from the bowl in front of her and inspected it carefully before taking a bite. The shedeh was making her wistful for better days.

"We are," she said finally, gazing into the fruit's soft pink flesh.

"In looks and in temperament, I've been told. Mother tells us we were most unmanageable children. Though Mery was always better at getting away with things than I was. We both love the old stories, perhaps I more than him; and we both love a hunt on the river, perhaps him more than me. I prefer watching the birds to killing them, though given the chance, I can throw a spear as well as any man."

The musicians finished their song and started a new one: the mirror dance. The four dancers faced each other, two by two, and began to move, each pair mirroring the other's movements in perfect harmony. Slow and seductive, each musical phrase was punctuated by a tinkling of the tiny silver bells each dancer wore on their fingertips. The boisterous chatter quieted somewhat as the guests turned to watch, mesmerized by the sway of the dancers' hips.

"But we're different too," Sita added.

"Oh?" Harsi said, his eyes still on the dancers.

Not everyone was watching the performance, though. Mery stood across the room, and while the other guests were drinking in the sight of those sleek, light-footed bodies, he was looking at her.

"Mery has courage," Sita said, trapped in her brother's gaze. "I do not."

"I'm certain that isn't true, Princess," Harsi replied with a good-natured chuckle. He popped a fig in his own mouth and chewed it with vigor, as if he wished it were something else. "And even if it is, you are young. Perhaps in time, you will find your courage, as your brother has done."

Mery's secret sat on the tip of her tongue, bitter and unmoved by the sweetness of the fruit. She could be free of it—all it would take was a few words to unburden herself. But it had seeded in her belly and grew there like an unwanted child. What chaos would she bring into the world if she let it be born? And what tragedies would come if she didn't?

The dancers continued to move in unison as the song went on—when one raised an arm, so did her reflection, and when she tilted her head toward the sky, her reflection did the same. And at the end of every phrase, the little bells chimed.

Sita considered Harsi's words and the elusive nature of courage.

"Perhaps I will," she said, uncertain. She could feel the force of Mery's will tugging at her, willing her to get up and take her place by his side. Instead, she took up the shedeh jug and poured herself another drink with a trembling hand.

13
NEFF

"Again."

Neff rubbed her eyes. They were painfully dry, much like her throat, but there was no water in the House of Life. No sunlight either. Nothing that might damage the thousands of delicate papyri stored there. A few other scribes worked nearby, copying words from old papyri to fresh scrolls, either to protect the wisdom from deterioration or to send to another House of Life elsewhere in Khetara. They mumbled the words to themselves as they wrote, never looking up, almost as if they were in a trance. The walls of the chamber were honeycombed with apertures for storing papyri, each one marked with a short line of sacred text to identify the scroll within. It was a strange place, like a dark beehive, humming with concentrated activity.

She'd been spending endless hours in the subterranean chamber, being instructed on the gods' words by the chief scribe. He stood beside her, his skin pale to the point of translucence, his thin body bent like a shepherd's crook. He watched her read with round protuberant eyes, reminding Neff of a fish, or some other deep-sea creature who spurned the sun.

"Again," the scribe repeated, tapping the top of her scroll with a skeletal finger. "From the beginning."

Neff sighed. She stood at a waist-high wooden table, the papyri lit by several carefully tended oil lamps placed nearby. After introducing her to each of the gods' words, their sound and meaning, and how to read them—"find a symbol with a face and read in that direction"—the chief scribe set her to reading simple passages aloud. She'd been working on the one before her, "The Forty-Two Ideals of Maat," for so long that she'd nearly memorized it.

When she'd first come across the symbol for *Maat*—an upright ostrich feather with a bent tip—she'd stopped.

"It's like my name," she'd said. "Nefermaat."

Because she was already versed in the common script, learning the formal script came to her more quickly and easily than the chief scribe had expected. After all, the common was just a simplified version of the sacred language. Learning it was like moving in reverse, from the curving line she was familiar with back to the bird or the hand symbol it had once been. The chief scribe had nodded sagely at her observation about the ostrich feather and dipped his reed pen into the inkwell on his palette.

"Nefer," he intoned, drawing a shape that reminded her of a lute, "Maat." Next to the lute, he drew the feather. "That's your name, written in the gods' words."

"Why a lute?" she'd asked.

"It is not a lute," the chief scribe corrected her. "That is the heart and the windpipe that allows us to speak. It signifies the voice of the spirit. And the feather, of course, is the symbol for Maat—goddess of truth and justice. Her husband is Thoth, god of writing and lord of all knowledge. The two are inexorably joined. There is no knowledge without truth. That's why you must learn to read, girl, if you are to correctly interpret the messages of the gods. Please continue."

She'd passed several days that way, from dawn until dusk, leaving the House of Life only to take her midday meal in the temple garden with Prince Kenna. They'd eat in the shade of the pomegranate trees, and sometimes he'd tell her about embalming—how much natron it took to mummify a body, which organs were left inside and which were removed—and sometimes about Heka, but most of the time he preferred to listen. He'd sit on a rock with his bread, his legs folded neatly under him, attentive to her stories about the market in Bubas and her father's wild schemes. So far, her company seemed to be all the prince required from his new "assistant," and that was fine with Neff.

Thinking about food made her stomach rumble. Given the lack of natural light down in the House of Life, she had no idea when she'd be released for the midday meal, but she hoped it would be soon. Blinking her dry eyes, she prepared to read the "Ideals of Maat" for the third time that morning. Each of the forty-two ideals was a statement intended to be spoken to judges, both earthly and divine, attesting that the speaker was worthy enough to enter the Duat, where all good souls went after death. They were simple enough to read, but extremely repetitive.

She stifled a yawn and read the lines, which attested to various gods that she had not been guilty of sin, told lies, done any wicked magic against the pharaoh, or eavesdropped upon others, and many other transgressions. She always choked a little on the eavesdropping line, as she had listened in on quite a few conversations since she'd arrived at the temple. She was in the middle of the twenty-fifth ideal when she was interrupted.

"Excuse me, Chief Scribe?"

Neff and her teacher turned toward the door. Master Montuhotep hovered on the threshold, as if unwilling to enter the dusty chamber for fear of soiling his garments.

The chief scribe bowed his head in obeisance. "How may I help you, Master?" he asked.

"The girl is required at the palace," Montuhotep said bluntly.

"By whom?"

Montuhotep sighed heavily, as if he was less than pleased about the answer. "The pharaoh has gotten wind of the girl's… talents, and he wishes to meet her."

The chief scribe's eyes bulged, until Neff thought they might pop right out of his skull.

"Ah!" he chirped, nodding more than necessary. "Well! Indeed!" He picked up "The Forty-Two Ideals of Maat," rolled it into a tight scroll, and slipped it back into its hole in the wall. "Return tomorrow and we will continue," he said to Neff, patting her weakly on the shoulder.

Neff gave him a stiff little bow before turning away. *Why would King Amunmose be interested in me?* Obediently, she left the dim chamber and climbed the steps, squinting into the brightness of day. Montuhotep strode ahead, and she had to rush to catch up. The head of his leopard skin bobbed side to side as he walked, its ebony eyes glaring at her with disapproval.

"M-master…" she began.

"When you approach the throne, do so with reverence," Montuhotep commanded, cutting her off. "Keep your head bowed and eyes downcast. Do not speak unless spoken to. And if you are addressed, keep your responses brief. The king is in a delicate condition, and you must not upset him in any way." He stopped abruptly, and Neff nearly ran face-first into the scornful leopard head. "I will be listening very closely, so I strongly suggest you watch your words."

Neff swallowed. They walked on, exiting the temple complex and following the wide tree-lined Royal Road to the palace. Guards patrolled the area, swatting away beggars and malcontents, each of them armed with a khopesh and wearing an Eye of Horus collar. They passed the temple bakeries and storehouses, the stables where the pharaoh's personal and military horses were kept, and another complex of government buildings in the distance. It wasn't anywhere near as crowded as the Thonis city streets she'd seen from the boat, but it was busy nonetheless. Officials clothed in white robes and fine black wigs argued vigorously under the shade of palm trees, while bare-chested young scribes dashed from place to place carrying bundles of papyri. Soon, they were welcomed through the palace gates and entered the sumptuous courtyard, then the main columned hall, before being led to the throne room. A fine-boned attendant with kind eyes and delicate hands met them at the portal.

"The king awaits you," he said, waving her inside with practiced elegance. Montuhotep moved to follow, but the attendant put up a hand. "Pharaoh appreciates you accompanying the girl here, Master Montuhotep, but he prefers to speak to her alone. You may return to your duties. I will ensure she is conveyed back to your care the moment her audience with the king is concluded."

A red flush appeared on Montuhotep's cheeks. "Of course," he said with a curt bow. "I serve at the pleasure of the king." With one last warning look at Neff, he turned on his heel and was gone.

"Don't worry," the attendant said softly, guiding her lightly with a hand on her back. "The king has a soft spot for young girls. You have nothing to fear."

Neff nodded, though his reassurance made her considerably more anxious, not less.

Compared to the vast colonnade hall, the throne room felt

intimate, with only six columns lining the central aisle. The columns were painted in vivid shades of red, sky blue, and gold, their capitals carved into blooming lotus. Sunlight filtered in through high diamond-patterned windows, illuminating paintings that covered every wall from floor to ceiling. She saw armies of painted men, their faces pointed toward the throne, and above them, a parade of animal-headed gods all seated on thrones of their own. At the end of the aisle, a ramp led up to a platform inlaid with rich blue tile, flanked by two tall flaming braziers. There, under an ornate canopy, the king slouched in a low-backed golden chair, staring into a bowl of soup while being fanned by a two lanky male servants in loincloths.

"Pardon me, my king," the attendant said.

The king looked up and straightened when he saw who it was.

"As requested, may I present Nefermaat of Bubas," the attendant announced, dipping nimbly into a low bow.

Neff bowed too, trying to match the man's elegance.

"Yes, yes, thank you, Ineni—you may go," he said, and turned to the servants. "You too. Go on. Out!"

The three men left soundlessly. Neff and the king were alone.

"Come closer, young lady," he said. "Come, come." He spoke in an odd, uneven manner, repeating himself and gesticulating jerkily with his hands.

What's wrong with him? she wondered, and then remembered the conversation between the Heka priests. Whatever had infected the king's body must be affecting his mind too.

Squeezing her trembling hands into fists, Neff approached the throne, keeping her eyes on the floor as her master had instructed.

"Am I really so terrible that you won't even look upon me?"

Neff was suddenly seized with panic. *I've only been here a moment, and already I've bungled it!* "N-no, my king, not at all," she stammered, unsure what to do. She glanced up at him without lifting her head, and saw he was smiling. Instinctively, she smiled back, though she worried it was more like a grimace.

She had always wondered what a pharaoh might look like. He was, after all, a god on earth. Would he shine with an inner light? Would he be as regal as the statues made in his likeness?

The reality was nothing like that.

Looking at King Amunmose, she was reminded of the small beeswax figurines her father sometimes made for his customers. He'd carve them in the shape of an enemy of their choosing, then instruct them to take the figurine in hand, abuse it to their liking, and toss it into a fire. By doing so, the idea was that their enemy would suffer terribly, just like the figurine. Neff had watched him demonstrate the ritual a few times, watched the little wax faces grow soft in the flames, slowly melting away to nothing.

The king's face looked just like that. As if it had been molded to resemble life, but was all too rapidly falling apart. He seemed to be disappearing into his rich robes, his jewel-encrusted gold cuffs hanging loosely from his bony wrists.

"Come, come," the king repeated impatiently, coaxing her closer. "Don't be shy."

Working to maintain her smile, Neff took a few obedient steps up the ramp onto the low platform, until she was close enough to catch a whiff of the king's heavy perfume. It was sweet, but did not cloak the sick, sour smell wafting from his body. Her stomach twisted in disgust, and she stopped.

"That's better," the king said, settling back into his seat. "Your reputation precedes you, my girl—despite Montuhotep's attempt to keep you his little secret." He wagged a finger. "That was very naughty of him! But… it's very hard to keep a secret from me for long. Very hard!"

He coughed, a wet, bone-shaking sound. "I heard you were a gift from the high priestess of Bubas, and that you have the makings of a very talented seer." He paused, his yellow-tinged eyes studying her closely.

"I hope so, my king," Neff replied.

The king nodded and fussed with the bowl of green soup on a small table by his side. "Do you see this, Nefermaat? Here I am, the pharaoh, and what do they feed me? This… *sludge*. Boiled mallow leaves. They say it settles the stomach, but I feel queasy just looking at it."

The savory soup was likely the only pleasant smelling thing in the room.

"I'm sure it's quite delicious, my king."

Amunmose chuckled. "Yes, perhaps you're right. Perhaps I should take my medicine like a good boy. But first—" He broke off a piece of a mound-shaped honey cake from a little plate on the side table and popped it into his mouth. He chewed it and winked at her wickedly.

"You're probably wondering why I've called you here. Well. You see, Nefermaat… It's a lovely name, did I mention that? A lovely name for a lovely girl. What was I saying? Oh, yes." He leaned forward, his eyes darkening. "I've been having the strangest dream. Every night. I was hoping you could tell me what it means. Montuhotep has ideas, of course, but sometimes he can be an absolute brick. No fun at all. So I'd like to hear what *you* think."

Neff felt her palms grow slick with sweat. She wanted to tell him she wasn't ready. That despite her work with Master Montuhotep and her studies with the chief scribe, she still had so much to learn. But she knew none of that really mattered. Disobedience wasn't an option.

"I'll do my best, my king," she said.

King Amunmose gazed up at the painted ceiling and chewed a second piece of cake. "The dream starts right here, in this room. I'm on the throne, and outside, the sun is setting. I'm wearing the double crown, but there's something strange about it. Instead of the serpent and the vulture, my uraeus has two serpents—one red and one black. After a moment, the red serpent slithers down from its place on my brow and bites me on the neck. But the black serpent doesn't move. It just sits there, watching."

The king suddenly frowned and clutched his stomach until whatever pain he was feeling seemed to pass. "What does it mean, child?" he asked, a little breathless. "What are the gods trying to tell me?"

"Two snakes," Neff murmured. She closed her eyes and steadied her breathing, as the master had taught her. "One red, and one black." She cast her mind into that in-between place she'd first encountered in Montuhotep's chambers, the place inside the flame where she could hear the whispers of the gods. It didn't happen right away, and she began to worry that the vision wouldn't come. But finally, in the shadows behind her eyes, she envisioned the two serpents on the king's crown, and saw the whole scene play out before her. The red serpent's fangs. The bite. The king's open-mouthed silent scream. The black serpent, still and watchful from its seat on the crown. Then, the words came.

He is betrayed by those closest to him.

The message hit her like a gale in a storm, nearly making her stumble.

He will die at the hand of one, while the other bears silent witness.

The vision vanished. Neff gasped and opened her eyes.

"What is it?" the king exclaimed, leaning toward her.

Neff felt sick with horror. She couldn't possibly deliver such a prophecy to the king. Montuhotep told her not to upset him in his fragile state, and she couldn't think of anything more upsetting than the prediction she'd received.

Such a message would cast suspicion upon his family and his closest advisers here in the palace, she thought. *What if I'm wrong? It could cause all kinds of trouble, terrible trouble.*

She had no idea what to do.

So she lied.

"The gods are telling you to trust the priests," Neff blurted out. "The red serpent is your doubt and will harm you if you choose not to heed their advice. The black serpent is patience. The black serpent waits for happiness to return, and it will be rewarded."

The king regarded her with an odd expression. "Incredible. That's exactly what Montuhotep said."

Neff's shoulders sagged with relief. "The master is very wise."

In her peripheral vision, a shadow moved. Her gaze flicked to the portal to the left of the throne, where the two attendants had exited. *Had someone been lingering in the doorway?*

"Very wise, very wise," the king murmured. For a moment he looked confused, as if he'd forgotten where he was, before he looked at her and seemed to remember. "Do you know, Nefermaat? There is something else in the dream—a sound. The bleating of a lamb. What do you think of that?"

Neff felt her knees buckle.

He continued, muttering to himself. "That rough-looking priest that came to the palace, all those years ago, he'd been ranting about a lamb, hadn't he? What a fool." He turned his gaze back to Neff. "Funny, though, that I would hear a lamb in my dream, isn't it, child?"

He frowned again, as if his pain were returning. Even with the thick makeup that covered his face, it still looked a little green. "I must..." he gasped, struggling to speak, "return to my chambers... now. Ineni!"

The elegant attendant appeared, along with four litter bearers carrying the king's palanquin. Neff was quickly forgotten among the activity, so she took it upon herself to back out of the room.

In the main hall, she leaned against one of the columns and

tried to catch her breath. Small groups of courtiers and palace officials spoke in the corners, but they seemed oblivious to her presence. She closed her eyes.

A dozen questions whirled through Neff's mind. If her explanation of the king's dream had been a lie, did that mean that Montuhotep had been lying to him too? She worried about her vision being wrong, but what if it was right? What if it wasn't a disease demon making the king sick, but someone in his inner circle? What if Montuhotep himself was involved somehow, and that's why he lied about the dream?

Neff's heart began to race at the thought.

But even that wasn't the most terrifying part of the king's dream. What frightened her most was the fact that the king was dreaming of the lamb.

Take heed, Thonis, Great House of Amun!

The lamb's words came back to her like the sting of a snakebite, the words and the blood and the terror.

Sorrow and ruin to the Children of the Two Lands!

"Are you all right, little priestess?"

The voice was so close that it made her jump.

Neff opened her eyes to see Prince Meryamun standing before her. She recognized him from the Bast Festival, when he and the princess had come to the temple to pay their respects. He was dressed in a beautifully pleated green schenti and a gauzy shirt that was open at the chest, revealing an intricately beaded carnelian collar around his neck. His eyebrows were thick and dark over his hooded eyes, which studied her with amusement.

"Oh! Greetings to you, my prince," Neff said, dropping her head.

"You were just in the throne room, interpreting your first royal dream, were you not? It seems it took a lot out of you."

"I was," Neff replied, steadying her voice. "I am honored by the king's faith in me. I… I was a little nervous, that's all."

"That's not what I meant," the prince whispered, leaning close. "I meant it must have taken a lot out of you to lie to the king's face. That's not an easy task—nor a safe one."

She froze. The shadow in the doorway—had the prince been watching them? Even so, how could he know that she'd been lying?

As if reading her mind, the prince grinned. "You see, words may lie—but the body speaks the truth. When you've been lied to all your life, you learn what deception looks like."

Neff's entire body began to quake. She thought she'd done the right thing to protect the king's health, to protect herself, but now—

"Do you know the penalty for such a crime? It's *quite* severe. Perhaps you believe he'd be merciful to one so young, but—" He crinkled his nose. "I wouldn't count on it."

Tears welled in Neff's eyes.

"You must have had an *awful* vision to take such a risk," the prince mused. "What was it?"

She felt like a bird in a net that was slowly tightening all around her. But the prince left her with no choice but to tell him the truth. Perhaps if she did, he'd show her mercy. And perhaps if her vision was correct, the prince might be able to use the information to help save the king.

"The gods told me that the pharaoh will be betrayed by those closest to him," she finally said. "He will die at the hand of one, while the other bears silent witness."

Neff saw the prince's pupils constrict.

"Fascinating." He licked his lips.

"You'll help him, won't you?" Neff said quietly. She knew she should keep quiet, but she couldn't stop herself from asking.

"I'll make sure that the king is taken care of, don't you worry," the prince replied soothingly. "Now, what if I ask you to decipher one of *my* dreams, young Priestess of Bubas? Are you going to lie to me too?"

"No, my prince," she said.

"Good," Prince Meryamun said, and leaned against the column next to her. "Then hear this: for the past two nights, I've dreamed of Sobek. I cannot tell you more than that—only that I know it is him." He stared at her, expectant.

"Sobek," Neff repeated. She knew the name from her father's spells, some of whom he'd directed to the fierce crocodile-headed god. Most of the time, he'd sell those spells to traders and fishermen who wanted protection from the various dangers of the Iteru River.

Once more, she closed her eyes and cast her mind to the in-between place. She imagined the reptilian face of the god crowned with feathered plumes, ram's horns, and the shining disc of the sun—

"When you are confronted with the power of Sobek," Neff found herself saying, "kneel."

The prince blinked. "That's it?"

Neff sagged against the column, feeling weak in the knees. The message had come more quickly this time, but the experience was no less exhausting. She nodded.

Prince Meryamun scoffed. "Not terribly illuminating, is it?"

"That is the message, my prince," Neff murmured. Her stomach growled. She'd long since missed her midday meal.

Noticing her distress, the prince seemed to relent. "I suppose they'll be expecting you back at the temple. Go, then. But now that you've told me this prophecy about my father, it is imperative that you keep it to yourself. One never knows who to trust, so you must guard your secrets with care. You were right to keep it from him—which is why I'm not having you whipped for lying to the pharaoh. I will handle it from here. Do you understand?"

"Yes, my prince."

The prince grinned, his face lighting up with pleasure. It was terrifying how handsome he was when he smiled.

"Good girl," he cooed, and lifted a ringed finger to his lips as a reminder.

Neff bowed and turned, walking slowly out of the hall, through the courtyard, and past the palace gates. When she was out of the complex, she began to run, her sandaled feet slapping the ground until she reached the temple gardens. She was going so fast that she nearly crashed directly into Prince Kenna.

"Hey, hey, hey!" he exclaimed, grabbing her by the shoulders. A basket hung off one arm, with what looked like the remains of a simple meal inside. "Where have you been? I waited, but you never showed."

"I was… at the… palace," Neff said between panting breaths.

Kenna's face drained of color. "Why?"

Neff opened and closed her mouth, unsure of how much to say.

"The king," she began. "He wanted me… he wanted—" She looked at the prince's sharp, angular face, and his wild nest of black hair. He wasn't handsome like his brother. But he was a most beautiful and welcome sight.

She couldn't help herself. She fell into Kenna's arms and sobbed like a lost, terrified child.

The prince's body went rigid at her embrace, but slowly Neff felt him relax. Then, she felt his arm wrap around her shoulders. He patted her gently. For what seemed like a long time, he just let her cry. Neff finally understood why he'd cloistered himself at the temple, far from the machinations of the palace.

They were both part of something so big and so terrible that she could only see it in pieces, like watching a sandstorm approach through a keyhole. Whatever was coming was just as unstoppable. Just as catastrophic. She wanted to tell Kenna everything that had happened, but she'd promised Prince Meryamun that she wouldn't speak of it. She had to obey. Didn't she? If she told Kenna and his brother found out, surely she'd be severely punished, and it might even put Kenna himself in danger.

No. She had to stay silent.

When her sobs finally faded to sniffles, Kenna spoke.

"It's all right," he said softly. "You're safe now."

Neff held on to him tighter, as if doing so might keep them both from blowing away in the coming storm.

"No," she whispered into his chest. "I'm not."

14
SITA

The dead geese lay in a pile on the prow of the hunting ship, their pink legs curled under them, golden eyes staring. Sita lounged under a canopy nearby, nursing a cup of wine. She gazed at the birds, their downy feathers blowing in the breeze coming off the river, amazed that moments ago they'd been soaring through the air, blood churning through their veins.

Alive and free, she thought, *until—*

"Got you!"

Mery stood on a papyrus skiff next to the larger boat, a polished wooden stick gripped in one hand. He was naked aside from a short pleated schenti. Bending down, he pulled a dead goose from the marshy waters and held it up, raising a cheer from the revelers on the ship.

Fowling with sticks was one of Mery's favorite pastimes, and Sita wasn't sure what he loved more—the art of the hunt or the glory of the kill. Sita enjoyed sailing, and the heft of a spear in her hand, but never really developed a taste for the hunt itself. Still, she almost always accompanied her brother on his expeditions. After all, it was a rare chance for her to get away from the palace for a long afternoon.

Mery locked eyes with her, his grin dimming when he saw she wasn't cheering like the others. Dropping his weapon onto the skiff, he took up the long oar and poled himself alongside the prow of the ship. From there, he nimbly hopped onboard and crouched next to her, his chest heaving with exertion. His body glistened under the bright sun, as lean and sleek as a panther.

"A gift," he said, dropping the sodden corpse onto Sita's lap.

Sita jerked upright, spilling her cup of wine. Her thin dress was soaked through. "Mery!" Repulsed, she picked up the dead goose and laid it on top of the pile with the other birds.

Her brother laughed, and some of the other revelers joined him, because the prince should never laugh alone.

"You see the thanks I get for all my hard work?" Mery called out to the group. "How very *rude*." He gave her a playful nudge before turning to the others to accept congratulatory pats on the back.

Sita's head swam. She'd gotten used to being intoxicated, so much so that being sober had become too awful to bear, but there was something about the goose's soft, heavy corpse and the constant sway of the anchored ship that made her queasy.

I won't have any more to drink, she thought, knowing it was a lie.

"I don't like it either, See-see," said a small voice. Sita turned to find Maet clambering up to the prow, her black braid swaying with the movement. She clung to Sita's side, scowling at the dead birds. "I liked them better when they were up in the sky," she said, pouting. "Now they're all broken. Mamet says if I break my toys, I won't get to play with them anymore."

"That's true," Sita agreed. "If we love our toys, we should take good care of them."

At this, Mery returned to them, tickling the little girl under the chin. "Ah, but you'll like these geese very much when Cook roasts them up for your supper tonight, won't you, little kitten?"

Maet giggled, then gave a weak smile.

Sita studied her. "Are you feeling all right, Maet? You look a little pale."

Maet shrugged. "My belly hurts. It's been hurting all the time. Mamet said to come breathe the air from the river. She said that might make me feel better." She leaned her head on Sita's shoulder. Then something caught her interest.

"Are you playing Mehen?" she called out to one of the young men on the lower deck. "I want to play! I want to play!"

She dashed over to the table where the boys were setting up the game, and Sita watched her with longing. Sita had always been in such a hurry to leave childhood, to dive into the adult world headfirst. But ever since she'd done it, since she'd reached the deepest waters and saw what lived at the bottom—she'd felt like she was drowning. She'd give anything to go back in time to those blissful, innocent days. She'd give anything not to carry the burden of knowledge on her shoulders...

Sita reached down to retrieve her cup and hefted the wine jug in her hand. Empty.

How many days until Father dies?

The thought came unbidden.

Four? Five?

Spilled wine had dried on her fingers. The stains looked like blood.

One?

She stood abruptly and went to the little table that held a plate of food and a jug of fresh water, and poured the water over her trembling hands until they were clean. That done, she turned to watch Mery. He'd poled his skiff back to the edge of the reeds and was waiting for the men trudging through the marsh to drive more birds in his direction.

Things will be better when Mery is on the throne, she told herself. This was her conclusion after days and days of internal struggle—and she felt comforted by it. Mery was always right and she trusted him. Why should that change now?

She watched him hold his hunting stick aloft with perfect stillness. He was the image of a king in his prime, a man who could command a kingdom, lead an army, bring an enemy to his knees. Their father couldn't do any of those things.

What Mery was doing was distasteful, yes, but wasn't it also necessary? In essence, he was putting the welfare of the Khetaran people above the life of one man, even though that man was his own father—and the king. Such an act took courage, and wasn't that the sign of a mighty leader? Looking at him, it was easy to believe that Mery *would* lead Khetara back to greatness. She must not do anything to threaten that future. She, too, must have courage.

Sita told herself these things, and she almost believed them.

Taking up a plate of food, she walked to the edge of the boat and sat down, trailing her toes in the water. She bit into a fresh fig and gazed down into the river, where white and orange fish swam just under the surface. Sita was relaxing there, eating and listening to the gameplay behind her, when suddenly all the fish scattered.

A dark shadow filled the water beneath her feet.

She stopped chewing.

"Mery."

Her brother didn't hear her. One of the men who'd been wading through the reeds had gone out to speak to him.

"Perhaps we should move on, my prince," the man said, standing waist-deep in the water. "I'm afraid there are no birds left in this area."

"All right," Mery replied. "We'll make one more stop before heading home."

Sita scooted back and set her plate on the deck. "Mery..." she said again, louder this time. The shadow was moving toward her brother's skiff, growing larger as it rose to the surface.

"What?" Mery snapped irritably, turning toward her.

There's something in the water, she wanted to say, but the words didn't get out in time.

In the next instant, a dark creature of impossible size erupted from the river. Its scaled armor glistened in the sunlight, and its enormous maw was open wide, revealing long rows of dagger-like teeth.

"*Crocodile!*" someone screamed, and then—chaos.

Time slowed to a crawl as Sita watched, paralyzed. The crocodile lunged at the man in the water, clamping onto his torso and tearing into his flesh. The man shrieked as he was pulled, thrashing, under the water. Half a dozen other men burst from the reeds, pointing and shouting and raising their spears and bows. Mery stood unsteadily on the skiff, trying to keep it from overturning in the churning water. On the ship, the revelers dropped what they were doing and ran to peer over the side, horrified as the horny ridges of the beast's back resurfaced, heading straight for Mery.

"Kill it!" a man shouted. "It's going for the prince!"

Sita watched one of the young archers point his bow as the great crocodile sprang from the river with incredible force. Mery gazed up at it, mouth open, eyes wide.

If that archer shoots his arrow, it won't hit the crocodile, Sita thought. *It'll hit Mery!*

"Wait!" Sita screamed, but too late.

The archer loosed the arrow.

Then, inexplicably, Mery closed his eyes and dropped to one

knee. The arrow sailed over his head and into the crocodile's mouth.

The beast twisted with the impact of the blow and fell back into the water. The resulting wave pushed Mery's skiff back to where the armed men were standing, and they caught and steadied it. Everyone stared as the injured crocodile's horny ridges cut through the water past the ship and disappeared downriver.

It was over.

Sita nearly collapsed with relief.

"My prince, are you all right?" one of the attendants asked Mery.

"Yes," Mery replied. He sounded strangely distracted. "Yes, I'm fine."

"Thanks be to Amun," the attendant continued. "Truly, he has protected you this day." He shot a nasty glare at the archer, who'd gone pale with fear. He, like Sita, must have realized that he'd almost killed the prince. If Mery hadn't dropped to his knee at exactly that moment, the arrow would have struck him square in the back.

Her brother must have realized it too, and Sita wondered if Mery would execute the incompetent archer right then and there. But the prince seemed completely uninterested in killing anyone or excoriating his men for their negligence. To everyone's surprise, he simply poled his skiff back to the boat, climbed aboard, and walked to the prow to sit in Sita's chair under the canopy. He glanced into the empty wine jar and snapped his fingers at one of the concubines sitting nearby.

"Wine," he said simply, and she rushed to retrieve some. Everyone else on the ship took that as a sign to return to their activities, and a warm chatter rose once again from the group.

Sita approached her brother with caution. Perhaps he was in shock? Once the concubine brought wine and poured some into a cup for him, Mery took a long drink and leaned back, staring at the river where the crocodile had emerged. A dismembered arm had risen to the surface and floated there. A white fish came to nibble at it. Sita grimaced and turned back to Mery.

"Are you sure you're all right?" she asked.

Her brother didn't meet her eyes, didn't react. He simply stared at the river, chewing his lip.

"Kneel," he muttered.

"What?"

"When confronted with the power of Sobek, kneel," Mery replied. "That's what she said."

"That's what *who* said?"

He looked at her, his eyes bright with wonder. "That girl. The little seer from the temple," he said. "She interpreted my dream, and she was right. When I saw the crocodile, her message was the first thing that came to mind."

Sita remembered the strange girl she'd seen at the Bast Festival and wondered if he was talking about the same person. "*That's* why you dropped to your knee when you did?"

"Yes," Mery replied. "That little priestess saved my life." He scoffed, then smiled. "Oh, this is very good."

Sita was about to ask what he meant, when someone cried out in alarm.

What now?

A few of the revelers crowded around a small figure lying on the deck.

"Someone come quickly!" one of the women shouted. "She needs help!"

Sita gasped.

Maet had collapsed.

15
RAE

The nomarch's ship sat low in the water, heavy with the remaining seventy hekats of grain promised for the king's tax. The nomarch himself sat on the deck in a fine acacia-wood chair, chewing his mastic gum while his men loaded the last of the bundled wheat. Even from where she stood on the riverbank, Rae could see that the hold was bursting with wooden chests and barrels of all shapes and sizes. The collective bounty of Sakesh, bound for Thonis.

The nomarch raised his cup of beer to her. "The king sends his thanks!"

Anger flamed in Rae's breast, but this time, she held her tongue. Ankhu stood beside her, and despite being exhausted from days of harvesting, Rae saw her father's self-control crumbling as he glared at the sneering face of the nomarch. This was the man who'd stolen his livelihood, the man who'd stripped his daughter naked in front of half a dozen men and whipped her into a bloody pulp. She could see the unreleased fury burning him up inside.

"Why don't you go inside and rest, Yati," Rae said soothingly, putting an arm around her father's shoulders and steering him away from the riverbank. "Nothing more needs to be done today. I'll take care of the zebu. Everything else can wait until tomorrow."

Ankhu raised an eyebrow at her. "'Yati,' eh? I know sweet talk when I hear it. Aren't I usually the one talking you down from a murderous rage? And yet when the accursed dog who beat you comes to collect what is rightfully ours, you just send me to bed and go tend to the zebu?" He glanced back as the nomarch's boat raised anchor and set off down the river. Then, he leaned in close to Rae, his gaze searching. "You're up to something."

Rae started to argue, but her father waved it away. "Don't bother denying it. You still think you can hide things from me? I know you've been sneaking out at all hours. It's something to do with Omari, isn't it? And here I thought that boy had a good head on his shoulders—"

"He does!" Rae covered her mouth with one hand. It was as good as an admission.

"So…" Ankhu said, stepping out from under Rae's arm. "What kind of trouble has Omari gotten you into?"

Rae felt her eyes drawn to the city on the horizon. "The less you know, the better."

Ankhu frowned. "Raetawy…" he said, his voice a warning.

"It's not something stupid like street fighting, all right?" Rae said. "It's *important*. Something has to be done."

"Oh, and *you're* the one to do it?"

"Not only me."

She'd already said too much. Her father was no fool, and he knew about Sakesh's rebellious elements as well as anyone.

Ankhu sighed and rubbed his eyes. "Haven't I ever told you about what happened during the war?"

"Only a thousand times."

"Well then, perhaps I need to refresh your memory, because you don't seem to understand the power you're dealing with."

"I do understand. You don't need to—"

"Yes. Clearly, I do."

Rae crossed her arms over her chest and looked at the ground.

"You remember how Sematawy's attack on the palace took everyone by surprise?" Ankhu began. "He distracted King Rahotep's army with a battle on Sakesh's northern border, while at the same time, he and an elite force of his best men infiltrated the palace. Rahotep hid his family away and faced them with the remainder of his guard, but they were unprepared for the brutality of the northern scourge. They slaughtered the king's guard and whoever else got in their way—attendants, servant girls, palace officials. And when they captured Rahotep, Sematawy had his men hold the king while he ran him through the belly with his blade. A fatal blow, but one that takes a long, long time to kill you."

"Father—" Rae knew the history well, but apparently her father had always spared her the gory details. She wanted him to stop.

But Ankhu held up a shaking hand. "No, you'll listen, Raetawy. While our king slowly bled to death on the throne room floor, Sematawy sent his men to root out Rahotep's wives and children from where they were hiding. The women screamed. Begged. The babies cried. They were all so afraid. And Sematawy killed them, one by one. He killed them right before Rahotep's eyes as he died on his throne, piling their bodies before him."

He paused. "Now I know Rahotep was no innocent. He'd committed atrocities against his enemies during his own wars. Perhaps, at the time, I accepted them too readily, both because he was my king and because I believed he had the blood of the gods in his veins. But hear me, Raetawy: *no one* deserves what Sematawy did in the palace that day. Least of all the children."

Rae shut her eyes. She felt sick. "Why are you telling me this?"

"Because I know you and Omari and whoever else you're scheming with think Amunmose is nothing like his predecessor. And you're right. Sematawy was a tyrant. He joined High and Low Khetara through blood and terror and lies, and it was fortunate that fate took his life in that skirmish after Unification. But just because this king seems weak and indulgent, just because he hasn't marched his armies down here to slaughter us where we stand—doesn't mean that he *won't*. A snake is a snake, Raetawy. You step on his tail? You get bitten."

Rae scoffed. "So, that's your advice? Accept the way things are? I tried that. I tried to turn a blind eye, but when I saw the terror on Baki's son's face that day…" She shook her head. "I know that I haven't always made the best choices, Father, and I know you worry about me. But I can't stay home and do nothing. I can't. Not anymore."

Ankhu sighed and stared downriver to where the nomarch's ship was vanishing into the horizon. In the matter of a moment, his anger drained away. "I know you can't. You're as stubborn as I am. But please, please for the love of Ra, be careful. You're all I've got left."

"I won't let anything happen to you," Rae said. "And I'll be fine. I promise."

Ankhu glanced back at her with tired, weary eyes. "Don't make promises you can't keep."

It took a lot of convincing, but Rae finally got her father to go into the house and rest. He slept through the midday meal and was still sleeping when she went out to tend to the zebu.

She was filling water buckets on the riverbank when she saw him.

A man on a fishing skiff, accompanied by a large black dog.

Normally, Rae wouldn't have stopped to watch a common fisherman, but there was something about the man and his dog that made her pause. She couldn't pinpoint exactly why he captured her attention—his dark robes were filthy but not uncommon, and he was sailing on a plain old reed fishing skiff. The shadow of dark stubble along his jaw was a bit unusual—most Khetaran men kept themselves clean-shaven—but that didn't mean much. Perhaps he simply hadn't had time to perform his ablutions during his journey. He wasn't particularly good-looking either, not that it would have captivated her if he was. So why couldn't she look away? What was it about him that didn't make sense?

Lean and lanky, much like his dog, the man moved about the skiff with a hint of stiffness that Rae recognized as evidence of a nagging injury of some kind. She knew the feeling well! However, whatever pain he was experiencing seemed to be forgotten when he caught sight of her studying him from the riverbank.

"Greetings to you!" he called out. As soon as he smiled, his nondescript, rugged face instantly turned boyish and charming. "You... ah... you don't happen to know anything about dogs, do you, sena?"

The man's voice affirmed Rae's suspicions. He spoke with an accent and colloquialisms she'd only heard on occasion at the Sakesh market. A tribesman, she guessed, from the Red Lands. Though from which tribe she had no idea. There were so many that most Khetarans didn't bother trying to discern one from another. She should have ignored him, but curiosity got the best of her.

"What seems to be the problem?" she asked.

Encouraged, the man paddled his skiff over to the riverbank

and pulled it ashore. The black dog leaped off the boat and came over to sniff between Rae's legs.

"Behkai, no!" the man scolded, darting over to pull the dog back by his haunches. "So sorry. He's been a terrible pest for the past couple days. He won't leave me alone, not even to sleep."

"What have you been feeding him?"

The man blinked at her. "You know, bread, bit of onion... A long journey it has been, and we haven't got—"

"Wait a minute," Rae broke in. "Isn't he your dog? How do you not know what to feed him?"

"He isn't *my* dog. He is *a* dog who is very pushy and whose company I am temporarily tolerating."

Rae blinked. "Right. Well, aren't you a fisherman?" she asked, indicating the skiff. "Dogs like fish."

Again, the man gave her a long blank look. "A fisherman, yes..." he said uncertainly.

Rae rolled her eyes. "You're not from around here, are you?"

"It is obvious, hey?"

"Painfully so."

"Ah."

"Where *are* you from?"

The man drew himself up. "From the Red Lands, sena. The tribe of the Anen," he said, with fierce pride.

Rae considered him carefully. *He's expecting disrespect. Bracing for it.* She felt that way often enough herself to recognize it on this man's face, just like she recognized hidden pain in his body language. She decided to surprise him.

"Well," she said, arms akimbo, "your dog is upset because he's hungry, which means you probably are too. Come on." She started walking back to the house.

After a moment's silence, Rae heard his footsteps, hurrying to follow.

"You're very kind, sena," he said. "Which is more than I can say for others I've met along the river. I can't tell you how many times I've been turned away."

Hearing the bitterness in his voice, Rae shot him a look. "People have every right to be suspicious. You're a strange man on a fishing boat with no fishing equipment. Or fish."

The man glanced back at the skiff. "You noticed that, hey?"

"It took me a minute, but I figured it out eventually."

"Why help me then? If I'm so *suspicious*?"

Rae thought for a moment and shrugged. "I honestly don't know. I had a feeling about you, I guess."

The man was quiet while he considered this. "I'm not sure I agree that I'm a 'strange' man, sena. Handsome, certainly... but 'strange'?"

Rae snorted. She opened a few storage barrels, pulling several dried fish from one, a handful of dried dates from another, and a round loaf of bread from a third. She wrapped the whole package in some rough papyrus paper, along with a bunch of fresh green onions. "This should hold you for a day or two," she said, handing it to the man. She tossed one last fish to the dog, who caught it in his mouth. In an eyeblink, it was gone. The dog licked his lips in satisfaction.

"Good boy," Rae said, giving him a rub behind the ears.

The man stared at the package of food, then back at her. "You wish to trade for this?"

Rae shrugged. "Just take it. We've already lost more than half of our wealth to Thonis. What's a bit more? At least this food is going to someone who needs it."

"Thonis, hey?" The man's eyes brightened with interest. "That's where I'm headed. Is it far?"

"About a day's travel—longer coming back upriver, since the winds are less reliable than the current." She cocked her head.

"What business do you have in Thonis, if you don't mind me asking?"

The man cleared his throat. "Information gathering," he said vaguely.

Rae raised an eyebrow. "Well, I'd be careful if I were you. That's the king's city. You think people here in the south are wary of strangers? It's much worse there, with the king's guard crawling all over the place."

"Don't worry," the man said. "I know better than to trust a Khetaran—present company excluded, of course."

Rae crossed her arms in annoyance. "The High Khetarans aren't like those of us here in Sakesh," she said. "We're not all the same, you know."

The man offered her a small smile, full of irony. "Oh, yes? Well, neither are we."

Rae squirmed, remembering how she'd lumped all the tribes of the Red Lands together as one, assuming they were all pretty much alike. Somewhat abashed, she turned back to the storage area and pulled one of her father's old white tunics from a hook. It was a bit worn in places, but otherwise serviceable. "Here, why don't you take this too? Those old robes of yours look like they'd be better off in a fire than on your back. Wear this into Thonis instead—it will help you blend in."

His eyebrows raised, the man took the tunic and nodded. "You've been very generous…" He looked at her, expectant.

"Raetawy."

"Yes, very generous, Raetawy. I appreciate your charity, but you must allow me to offer something in return." He pulled the bulging pack from his shoulder and knelt on the ground to rummage through it.

Rae leaned over to peer inside, and couldn't believe what she saw.

He's got to be a criminal. How else would a man like him get his hands on treasures like those?

Still, who was she to judge? She was about to become a criminal herself.

"That's quite a collection," she said. "Where did you get it?"

The man pulled a few small items from the pack and immediately tied it shut again. He stood and faced her with an enigmatic expression. "Perhaps you'll leave the information gathering to me, sena?" he said quietly. "We all have our secrets to keep."

Secrets.

Rae was reminded of the last time she saw Asim, when he taught her the code phrases used to identify other members of the rebellion.

The falcon sails across the sky.

We shall meet him on the horizon.

"Speak of this to no one outside the circle," Asim had told her. "Not your father, not your friends—*no one.*"

Rae blinked, bringing her focus back to the present.

"Yes," she said to the Red Land tribesman. "We all have our secrets."

"I'm glad we understand each other," he said, and held out his open palms to her. They held at least a dozen pieces of fine jewelry: beaded necklaces, a golden ring, a bracelet inlaid with lapis and decorated with lotus flowers. "Choose. Any one you like. They would all fetch a tidy sum at market, if you decide to trade."

Rae ran her fingers along each of the items, picking up one, then another. She'd never touched anything so beautiful in her life. It was nearly impossible to choose. In the end, though, she went with her gut.

"I'll take this one," she said, picking up a red jasper amulet on a simple black cord.

"That?" the man said, confused. "But that's nothing. A little carved lion. Can't be worth more than a couple loaves of bread."

"Then it's an even trade," Rae said, looping the amulet over her head. "Trying to trade one of those other items might raise suspicions at the market here, and I don't need more trouble than I've already got. Besides, I don't want to sell it, I want to wear it. It's a Sekhmet amulet—it provides protection from the goddess. And I could use some."

"Sekhmet," the man repeated. "Where have I heard that name before?" After a moment of consideration, he shrugged. "You may take the amulet, Raetawy-sena, but please let me offer you something of real value, for your kindness. Keep it for yourself, if you like, or give it to someone you love."

When Rae nodded in assent, the man studied the remaining objects in his hand for a long moment before selecting the gold ring. Slipping it on her finger, Rae was surprised to find that it actually fit. It was a simple, unique piece featuring a swiveling gold cube with an engraved symbol on each of its four faces. A cobra, a feather of Maat, an Eye of Ra, and a scarab beetle. She'd have to hide it at home, of course—its obvious value would attract too much unwanted attention on the streets of Sakesh. That was too bad, because it felt good on her finger. She spun the cube playfully, pausing on the face with the Eye of Ra. "It's like my father's dagger," she said.

"Is it?" the man said with interest. "Then I think it was indeed meant for you."

Deep in thought, the man walked back to the riverbank, the dog prancing at his heels. Rae followed. They stood together in companionable silence, watching the trading ships pass by on the Iteru. The man reached out to grab the prow of the little skiff, steadying it so the dog could leap aboard.

"I expect you've traveled by boat before, hey?"

"Only on short trips," Rae admitted. "Never as far as Thonis."

The man nodded. "This is my first time," he said. "It's so strange, because the river, it just takes you. The current pulls you along as it wishes, like it has a mind of its own. I can use my oars, of course—I can direct the boat this way or that way. I can pause on my journey, as I have done to see you, sena. But when I am back on this boat, as soon as I release my hold on land, the river resumes carrying me along its path. I can stall, I can stop... but I think the river will get its way, in the end." He shook his head and chuckled. "Do you get my meaning, Raetawy? Or do I sound like a fool?"

It was odd. Rae felt comfortable with the man, as if she were talking to an old friend, rather than a stranger she'd only just met. His question made her think of the night in the Garden of the Dead.

"You don't sound like a fool," she answered. "I got in this fight a few days ago—a fight I knew I couldn't win—and I felt like that. Like there was this current pulling me to do something I knew I probably shouldn't."

"So did you?" he asked. "Let the current take you, I mean."

Rae nodded. "I did. Maybe I was wrong and we're both fools, probably being carried off to be eaten by crocodiles."

The man laughed, his seriousness melting away. "I like you, sena. You are truly the greatest Khetaran I've ever met."

Rae snorted. "Given your opinion of us, that isn't saying much."

"Well, I wish you much good fortune," the man said. He leaped nimbly onto the skiff, and dropped his heavy pack onto the deck. "Maybe the river will bring us together again someday."

"Maybe so," Rae said, grasping the lion amulet in her hand.

The man shoved off to join the other boats floating downriver, and Rae raised a hand in farewell.

"Thank you again!" he shouted, touching a knuckle to his nose. The dog barked. "What, you'd rather stay with her, Behkai? Because that's good for me, you know. One less mouth to feed!"

Behkai sat on his haunches and whined.

"Ugh, fine, stay. Raetawy-sena probably doesn't want you, anyway!"

"Hey! Wait!" Rae shouted. "You never told me your name!"

The man considered this before answering. "Call me the Jackal!"

Rae watched him go, the not-fisherman with the bundle of definitely stolen treasure and a dog that wasn't his either.

She hoped he was right. She hoped she would see him again.

It was sunset by the time Rae left the blacksmith's shop. At the last Horizon meeting, he'd mentioned that he could rework farming tools into simple weapons that could be used for the attack on the Medjay, so she'd gone to his workshop in the city to drop off what she could spare. It felt strange saying the secret words to the blacksmith when she'd arrived—but exciting too. Walking down the busy street toward home, she felt as if every eye was upon her, whispers wafting like smoke in her wake. It was probably all in her imagination. Still, she couldn't help glancing over her shoulder to ensure she wasn't being followed.

"Oh!"

Rae collided with someone walking in the opposite direction and stumbled back.

"I'm sorry. I wasn't looking—" She stopped short when she saw who it was. "Tam," she murmured.

The young weaver wasn't wearing anything spectacular—a simple, finely woven kalasiris dress—but the way it hugged the ripe curves of Tamerit's body made Rae's head feel light.

"Rae!" Tam exclaimed, adjusting the basket of undyed flax fibers balanced on her hip. "I didn't think I'd see you for a while. I heard what happened." A look of tender concern creased her face. "Are you all right? I was so worried about you."

Rae's cheeks reddened with embarrassment and pleasure both. "I'm fine. I've been meaning to come see you. I've just been… busy."

Tam brushed a lock of tightly curled black hair from her face, a gesture that made Rae's chest ache with desire.

"Busy, eh?" Tam said. "On the farm, I'm sure, but what are you doing in the city at this hour?"

Between the question and the sight of Tam's dark teasing eyes, Rae's thoughts got tangled up in knots. "I, ah, I was dropping off some things for the blacksmith," she stammered, finally deciding that the truth—or at least part of it—was probably the safest route.

"The blacksmith," Tam said, as if the words were a curious food she was tasting. "How interesting."

"Is it?"

"Yes. I was wondering how long it would be before you fell in with the Horizon."

Rae snapped out of her reverie with a violent lurch. "W-what? No. I mean, how—?"

Tam leaned in close, enough that Rae could smell the jasmine oil in her hair. "All the weavers know about the blacksmith and what he does in his free time," she whispered. "Besides, you and Omari are close. If he's involved with the rebels, it's not a leap to assume you might try to join them too. After the beating you received, I'd have been surprised if you hadn't."

Rae glanced around furtively, terrified someone would overhear their conversation. "We can't talk about this here. It's not safe."

Tam nodded. "Come with me." She took Rae's hand and

pulled her toward an abandoned house nearby. Other than a ragged old soldier hunched on the street corner, there was no one around.

Rae was so distracted by the sensation of Tamerit's small strong hand in hers that she didn't question where they were going. They slipped in through the front entrance, its door battered down long ago, and into the shadowy interior. It was terribly dusty inside, littered with broken furniture and shards of pottery that crunched underfoot.

Rae recoiled as half a dozen mice scattered upon their arrival. "Are you sure there's no one here?"

"No one comes here," Tam said.

Rae squinted into the gloom. The house must have been beautiful once, with its high ceilings and colorful tile floors. The sight of it made her sad. *Once great, now ruined, just like everything else in Sakesh.*

"What is this place?" she asked.

"One of King Rahotep's viziers lived here," Tam replied. "His closest adviser, apparently. He was executed by the High Khetarans, his body left to rot in the fields without proper burial. People say that his mutu still haunts this place, so..." She shrugged. "They tend to stay away."

Rae shivered, though she'd rather a restless spirit listen in on their conversation than a member of the nomarch's guard. They moved to stand under a crumbling archway, away from any windows where they might be seen. Rae picked up where she'd left off. "First of all, Omari and I are close, but we're not *that* close. You know that, right?"

"I know." Tam chuckled. "Mamet Mut may not see what is plain as day, but I do."

"Good," Rae said, relieved. "And secondly: How do you know about the Horizon?"

"All the weavers know about them. But they don't allow women to get actively involved with the rebellion, except to pass along messages. Though it seems as though they've allowed *you* in."

"I can be quite convincing," Rae said wryly.

"Everyone's talking about how you stood up to the nomarch at the shepherd's farm. I'm guessing that had something to do with it?" Tam said.

Rae shrugged. "Maybe. I also may have picked a fight with Asim."

Tam laughed, a lovely, tinkling sound. "Did you win?"

"No. But I don't think that was the point."

"Two beatings in two days. You really are a glutton for punishment, Rae."

Rae grinned and looked at the ground. What was it about this woman that made her so shy?

Tam glanced down into her basket of wool and sighed. "I wish they would let me fight too."

"Really?" Rae asked, surprised. "But you seem so… soft."

"I can be," Tam replied sharply.

"Oh, no, I didn't mean to suggest that you're weak," Rae quickly added, the words clumsily tumbling out of her mouth. "You're just so, you know, elegant. Not a ruffian like me."

A small smile quirked the corner of Tam's mouth, and she moved closer. The dusky shadows on her face made her look otherworldly, like something out of a dream. "Is that how you see yourself? As a ruffian?"

Rae shrugged. "Why not? Beauty isn't a tool available to me, so I have to use what I've got."

Tam regarded her with a look that made Rae's chest tighten. "Has anyone actually told you that? That you're not beautiful? Or is that something you tell yourself?"

Rae didn't trust herself to speak.

"People can be more than one thing, you know," she said, reaching to touch Rae's lion amulet. "Like Sekhmet. She can be the killer of men, the bloodthirsty, the mistress of slaughter. But she can also be Bast. The protector. The mother. Goddess of joy and pleasure. She's both, all at once."

"And you?" Rae murmured, Tam's hand still on her chest. "What's on the other side of your softness?"

"A fierce heart," Tam replied. She was so close that Rae could taste her breath, which had turned cloudy as the chill of night approached. "A heart that burns."

Rae covered Tam's hand with her own and gripped it tightly. She wondered if the weaver could feel how fast her heart was beating, or the heat pouring off her body. She was acutely aware of how alone they were. The privacy felt both tantalizing and disorienting.

She'd never had those feelings for Omari, or any other man, for that matter. She'd nearly resigned herself to the thought that she wasn't meant for love—until the day she met Tam, and her world turned upside down. Still, it was one thing to long for the beautiful weaver, and entirely another to be alone with her in that forgotten place, with no curious eyes upon them. It was all she could do not to throw open the doors of her heart and let fly everything hidden inside. But still something within her resisted and was afraid.

"I have no doubt that you are all of those things and more," Rae said. "But that's exactly why you must not get wrapped up in the rebellion. It's too dangerous, Tam."

Tam's eyes narrowed. "Dangerous? They're planning something, aren't they?"

Instead of answering the question, Rae said, "Tam, please. You came to Sakesh to be safe—I want you to stay that way."

"Oh, so it's all right for you, but not for me?" Tam argued. "You sound exactly like the men!"

Rae blinked. "I'm sorry, you're right. If things go well and I prove myself to Asim, I'll mention your request to him. I make no promises, but—"

"You don't need to promise," Tam said, her voice warm with gratitude. "I can wait for the Horizon to come to their senses. But in the meantime, you have to give me something else."

Rae swallowed, her pulse picking up speed. "What do you want?"

"The gift you've been keeping for me all this time," Tam said, weaving her fingers through Rae's hair.

Rae let out a shuddering breath. She'd been holding back for so long that when she finally let go, the force that drove her into Tamerit's arms was as strong as the khamasin wind.

When their lips met, it was tentative, barely a touch. But once Rae felt Tam's body pressed against hers, felt it fill all her empty spaces, she kissed her with a hunger that couldn't be sated. Everything beyond sensation fell away—the pain of her wounds, the dark room, the city that balanced on the edge of violence—it was all gone. There was nothing but breath and heat and softness and desire.

The doors of her heart were hopelessly, blissfully open. *Come inside*—her body spoke the words even if her voice did not. *Come inside and see everything that I am, take everything that I am. It is yours, it is yours, it is yours.*

They held each other until the sun went down, and all the light went out of the world.

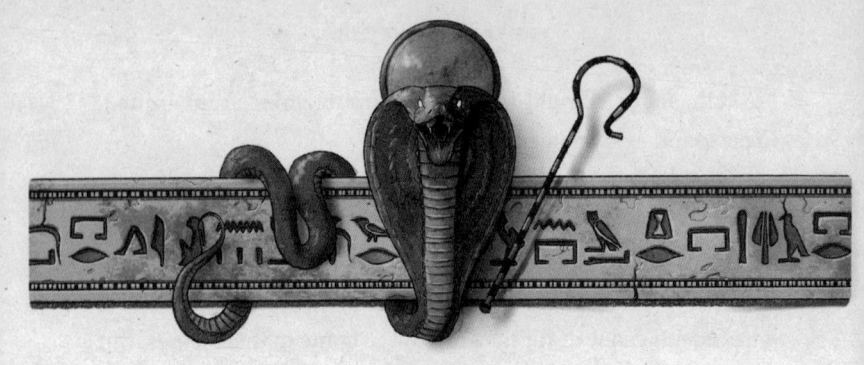

16
SITA

The sight of Maet's still form lying on the ship's deck sobered Sita in an instant. Without hesitation, she leaped into action.

"Oarsmen," she shouted, "Take us back to the palace at once!" She turned to one of the servants. "You—take a skiff to the temple and summon the physician-priests. Tell them to meet us in Maet's bedchambers. And someone bring some water! We must try to rouse her."

The servants, unaccustomed to taking orders from Sita, all hesitated.

"What are you waiting for?" Sita exclaimed. "Go!"

With the application of a cool compress to her forehead, the little girl's eyes fluttered open. "My belly hurts so much, See-See."

Sita pulled the girl's head into her lap and rubbed her arm. "I know. We'll be home soon, and the priests will take good care of you."

Maet groaned and closed her eyes again, falling quickly into a restless sleep.

The ship was moving swiftly now, the oarsmen keeping a brisk stroke as they cut through the water.

Mery appeared at Sita's side, looking no worse for the crocodile encounter that had nearly killed him a few minutes earlier.

"For a moment," he said, "I thought it was Mother here on the ship, ordering people about! I didn't know you had it in you, Sitamun."

Sita blushed. "What was I supposed to do? Maet needs help." In fact, she'd surprised herself. Normally, she wouldn't think about taking command of a critical situation like that. There was always someone else to do so instead.

Mery's eyebrow quirked. "Your concern for the girl is… admirable."

It sounded like a compliment, but Sita knew better than to accept her brother's words as they appeared. He often used language like pawns in a game, to feel out his opponent's weaknesses. And he'd played with Sita enough times to know hers by heart. Mery knew her true feelings, sometimes before she even knew them herself.

Was she really acting out of love for Maet?

You feel guilty, don't you?

The truth stung.

She'd been bitterly jealous of the little girl and the way her father favored her. Loved her. She was only six years old, and yet Sita remembered wishing the little girl would disappear, so she wouldn't have a constant reminder of the relationship she didn't have. And now, it felt as if her jealousy had taken physical form and inflicted pain upon an innocent child. Sita knew it wasn't true, but it *felt* true.

You're just helping her to make yourself feel better. You're not doing it for Maet.

She looked down at the girl's pale little face, her eyes moving rapidly beneath the eyelids as if caught in a nightmare.

Perhaps Father was right not to love me, after all.

"Away, disease demon!" the old priest commanded. "Be gone from this place, and injure this child no longer. She is a child of Amun and is protected by his unseen hand. Away!"

Sita watched as the man used a polished stick to draw a circle of protection on the ground around Maet's bed as he repeated the spell over and over again. The girl looked very small, wrapped in fresh bed linens. The old ones had been taken outside and burned. Sita had remained with her since they'd arrived back at her bedchamber. Several bald-headed priests had arrived shortly after, filling the room with frenzied activity. Sita backed out, feeling like she was in the way. They closed the curtains, and Sita watched through the gauzy fabric as they bade Maet drink a cup of water poured from a jug painted with images of Isis. She reluctantly obeyed, rivulets spilling over both sides of her tiny lips before collapsing, exhausted, back onto the pillow.

"What happened?"

Sita jumped—she hadn't even heard her mother approach. Then again, the queen had a reputation for being the first to know everything, so Sita wasn't that surprised to see her. Once, she'd overheard an official at a banquet say that Queen Bintanath painted little ears on the walls of every room, so she could listen in to any conversation she liked. Obviously, the queen's ears had picked up the news about Maet.

"We were fowling on the river, and she fainted," Sita explained. "She told me she'd been having some stomach pain, but other than that she seemed all right. Her mother was at the market on the other side of the city—I've sent a messenger to retrieve her."

Now was not the time to mention the incident with the crocodile, Sita decided. Her mother would have a hundred questions if she brought *that* up, and Sita was too tired to answer them. She'd sobered since Maet collapsed, but now that all the excitement of the voyage home had passed, she was left with a headache.

The queen sucked her teeth. "The king will be terribly upset when he finds out she's ill," she said, more to herself than to Sita. "Better not to tell him until we know more. I'll see that his attendants don't speak of it." She made to leave but then saw something that made her stop abruptly. She sighed. "Ah, well. Too late."

Sita turned to find the king lurching toward them, wraithlike without his thick makeup, trailing two desperate-looking attendants in his wake.

"A lion fetch that man," the queen mumbled. "What does he think he's doing? He should be in bed…"

"Where is she?" the king demanded, his eyes wild. "Where is my girl?" His gaze passed over Sita like she was a painting on the wall and alighted on the priests inside Maet's bedchamber. The king blundered inside, unsteady on his feet.

Ineni, one of his attendants, hurried forward with an apologetic look. "I tried to stop him," he said to the queen, "but Pharaoh wouldn't hear of it."

The physician-priests looked up from their work. "My king," they chorused, bowing their heads.

Amunmose ignored them. He sat on the bed next to Maet, placing one skeletal hand on her arm. "Hello kitten," he said, wheezing with exertion. "How are you feeling?"

"It hurts," Maet whined. "I'm scared."

The king patted her arm. "Well, I'm going to tell my friends here to make sure you get better right away, all right?" There was comfort in his voice, but an edge too.

The priest standing behind him flinched.

"What if, later on, after you've gotten some rest and seen your mother, I bring you a brand-new doll? I can send one of my fastest messengers to fetch one from the market, just for you. Would you like that?"

Maet nodded.

"And maybe a honey cake too?"

"I'm not hungry," the girl said sadly.

"Oh, but you've always got room for a honey cake," The king tickled the girl under her chin. "They're our favorite. They make them special, just for us! I can share it with you, like always. And maybe your new dolly can have some honey cake too."

Maet managed a weak smile.

Something clicked inside Sita's mind.

But before she could think further on the conversation she'd overheard, her father struggled back to his feet and exited the room. Ineni rushed to assist, but the king waved him off, gesturing for the chief priest-physician to follow him into the corridor, leaving the other priests to finish attending to their patient. Sita moved aside, still listening.

The king demanded, "What is it? What ails her? And where is Montuhotep? He should be here."

The priest wiped his brow with one hand. "Ah, I'm afraid Montuhotep was in council with the prince when we received news of Maet's condition, so he tasked me to attend to her in his stead. Meryamun called on him with an urgent matter."

Sita was surprised. She'd left Mery at the riverbank when they'd returned from the hunt, and he hadn't said anything about a meeting. Although his behavior *had* been strange... She'd expected him to have been shaken after the crocodile attack, or at the very least, furious. But instead, he'd seemed almost elated. Calling for a private meeting with the king's most trusted adviser, without consulting the king, was a brazen act. What could have driven him to do such a thing?

Her father appeared equally confused by this development but didn't seem to have the energy to pursue it.

"What ails her?" he repeated.

The priest cleared his throat. "We... don't know yet. Maet is extremely weak and experiencing pain in her stomach and chest. She vomited shortly after waking and has refused to take food or any drink other than water."

"Has the food on the ship been checked?"

"No one else has taken ill, my king, and everyone on the fowling expedition ate of the same provisions. In fact, it very much reminded me of... of..." He sounded as if there was something he was reluctant to say.

"Spit it out, man!" the king said, impatient.

Sita saw beads of sweat beginning to form on the priest's forehead.

"It reminded me of when you first fell ill, King Amunmose. We also had all the food and drink checked, but no corruption was found, and no others fell sick. And the symptoms are the same. Of course, stomach pain and weakness are common, but"—he paused to lick his lips—"we found light brown spots on the palms of her hands and feet. They are remarkably similar to yours, my king. And those... those are not common."

Sita felt the words like a blow.

What's killing Father is killing Maet too.

Mery had told her about the poison, but he hadn't divulged how he was administering it.

Now I know.

The king's already pale face went gray at this news. He gripped the priest's shoulder, steadying himself.

"Is it possible... she could have gotten this from me?" he

asked, his voice full of dread. "That I passed this curse onto her somehow?"

The priest looked horrified, unable to tear his gaze from the king's ghoulish visage. "It's, ah, possible a demon or curse is to blame, but I assure you, we are doing everything we can for her, and for you, my king. The most powerful healing spells, spells of protection, sacred water poured over the image of Isis... We are working day and night, scouring every scroll in the House of Life to find a cure—"

"Did she get this from me?"

Everyone in the corridor started at the king's angry shout, which echoed down the hall. Inside the bedroom, the other priests' prayers fell silent.

The head priest opened and closed his mouth several times. Finally, he said, "I'm afraid only Amun knows that answer, my king. I'm so sorry."

Sita watched as her father's hand dropped from the man's shoulder, his eyes darkening.

"You've overexerted yourself, imi-ib," Queen Bintanath said, sweeping forward with exaggerated affection. "You need rest."

The king nodded, but otherwise didn't acknowledge her presence. "Take me back to my chamber, Ineni."

Ineni rushed in, dropping into a respectful bow as he passed the queen, and gently guided King Amunmose down the corridor.

A moment later, Maet's mother appeared, followed by a servant carrying a basket of fresh flowers from the market. The yellow blossoms felt like an omen, and not a good one.

Yellow is for mourning, Sita thought.

Maet's mother stopped to greet the king before making her way toward them with fear in her eyes.

"She's awake," the Queen Bintanath told her, and gently led the woman inside the bedchamber.

Sita stood in the doorway, cold despite the late afternoon heat. She could think of nothing but her father's words about the honey cakes.

They're our favorite.

They make them special, just for us.

She ran to find Mery.

She met him passing through the main hall, so distracted by his own thoughts that he didn't notice her until Sita was right in front of him.

"It's the cakes, isn't it?" she blurted. "You're putting it in the honey cakes."

Mery's eyes flashed from distant to focused. "Quiet!" he growled. Glancing around to see if anyone was watching, he seized her by the arm and dragged her across the hall into the pleasure garden. "Your mind is like an empty room, Sitamun…" he muttered once they were outside.

"Don't you speak to me that way!" Sita retorted—though she did lower her voice. "Tell me the truth, Mery: Have you been poisoning Father's honey cakes?"

Mery crossed his arms, looking bored. "*I* certainly haven't."

"But someone else did," Sita pressed. "By your command."

Mery shrugged.

Sita covered her mouth with her hand. She was so stupid. *Of course* that's how he did it. The cooks made the king's honey cakes especially for him because he adored them so much—and they were so sweet that they could easily disguise the bitterness of poison. It was such an obvious choice that it irritated her to not have thought of it sooner.

Still, knowing the cakes were poisoned didn't explain everything.

"I still don't understand how the poison could go unnoticed," she said. "The priest said they tasted all the food when Father first got sick, and no one else was affected. They must have tasted the honey cakes too—Father's the only one who eats them."

Mery smiled. "It's a *delicious* puzzle, isn't it?" He bent to pluck a red poppy from a flower bed, twirling it in his fingers. "Some might say that poison is a coward's weapon. That the only honorable way to kill a man is face-to-face, with a blade. But I would argue that if done well, poisoning is an art unto itself."

He lifted the flower to his nose and smelled it with his eyes closed. "First, you must consider which poison to use. There are dozens, you know—plants, minerals, venom—each with their own gruesome effects. Only by making yourself a regular at the House of Life can one study all of them in detail, and only after many hours of research might you find the perfect poison for the job. A common additive, for instance, used to make yellow paint, and often mixed with copper to make tools more durable. Few even know it's poisonous at all. Its harmful effects are only mentioned in a single obscure papyrus.

"Next, the dosage. It's easy to kill someone by pouring poison into his wine cup and watching him die on the spot. You've done the job—but at what cost? Everyone will know it was murder, and unless you're very, very lucky, or everyone around you is very, very stupid, they'll eventually figure out it was you who did it."

Sita sat heavily on a stone by the fishpond, feeling like she often did after losing a game of Hounds and Jackals, and being forced to listen to Mery explain exactly how he beat her.

"No," Mery went on, "if you want the job done right, you can't be so artless. You have to choose a poison that's not only obscure, but also harmless in small doses. So harmless that if someone ate, for instance, a single poisoned honey cake—or even *two* poisoned honey cakes—they'd feel just fine. But if you ate them every day, one little sweet at a time, well…" Mery opened his hands, as if to reveal a wonder inside. "At first you'd simply have a little stomachache. But then it would get worse, and worse, and *worse*."

He took one last look at the poppy and cast it to the ground. "Until one day you'd just die. And everyone would be awfully sad and blame it on a demon or a curse or the annual pest, and the priests, having given their very best effort, would shrug their shoulders and say that the gods work in mysterious ways." He chuckled. "That's all conjecture, of course. But if someone I knew came up with a plan like that, I'd applaud their ingenuity. Wouldn't you?"

Sita closed her eyes, her mind reeling with the implications of her brother's words. "Mery," she whispered, trying hard to control the growing hysteria in her voice. "Father isn't the only one eating those cakes."

Mery's eyebrows rose, and for once, he looked surprised. She took a grim satisfaction in that.

I guess you didn't plan for everything, did you? she thought.

"Maet," he said, realization dawning.

"Yes, Maet! She could die because of you! Father has been sharing those cakes with her. He's still doing it, even now! We have to stop this! Maybe if she doesn't eat any more, she could survive, and then—"

"No."

The word was solid. Final. Like a stone being laid over a grave.

"No one can know." Mery took her face in one hand and pulled her toward him, as if for a kiss. His hand still held the scent of the poppy, earthy and sweet, with a hint of smoke. "And we don't stop until it's done. If we tell them the cakes are poison—if anyone finds out—they'll kill us, Sitamun. Not just me. They'll kill you too. Do you understand? Or do you think your throat is too pretty to cut? You may have the purest blood, sister, but there are a dozen other girls waiting to take your place."

Sita let out a choked sob. "I can't keep doing this," she said, gripping the scarab amulet in her hand. "I *can't*—"

Mery's expression softened. "Oh yes, you can." Mery whispered, his lips lovingly shaping each word, "Not for me, but for the kingdom. For our people. This is the hard part. But soon, this will all be in the past. Remember all the fun we used to have? We'll have it again, you and me, I promise. And we'll bring all Khetara along with us. All right?"

Sita sniffed, tears rolling down her cheeks. There was something unsettling, a hidden message that she couldn't decipher in what he said. But she was too sad, too tired, and too confused to fight him. He was Mery the beautiful, the brilliant, the future king. Who was she to question his decisions, no matter how monstrous they might seem?

She thought of the pile of dead birds on the ship, and how much she abhorred fowling.

Ah, but you'll like them very much when Cook roasts them for your supper tonight, won't you, little kitten?

Mery had done the vile deed, but she and the rest of the kingdom would benefit from it. Perhaps it was cowardly to enjoy the meat her brother provided for the table, while complaining about what he had to do to get it there.

Have courage, she told herself, wiping the tears from her face.

"All right," she replied.

Her brother replied with a heart-melting smile. "Now, forget about this ugliness and get yourself ready for the evening meal. Tonight, we feast on the spoils of the hunt!"

After he left, Sita stayed by the fishpond for a long while, staring down into the water. Finally, she stood, and there was a sudden flutter of wings. A falcon rose from a rosebush, launching into the air. There was something small and wet lying on the ground nearby. Sita stepped toward it and saw the half-eaten remains of one of the long-tailed monkeys, its little mouth open, its glossy innards spilling out onto the stone tiles. Feeling sick, Sita glanced over to the sycamore tree, where she could see the other monkey watching from the branches, silent and alone.

Above, the falcon wheeled through the sky, waiting, crying out for more blood.

17
KARIM

Karim sat on the riverbank, eating bits of bread and fish and holding a speared onion over the fire he'd built for the night. He chewed each piece slowly, trying to make them last as long as he could. Behkai watched him, rigid with concentration, a long, pendulous string of drool suspended from his mouth.

Karim tried to ignore the dog, focusing instead on the flames blackening the onion skin, releasing a savory smell into the air.

Behkai let out a high, piteous whine.

"Fine! Fine!" Karim tossed him a piece of bread and a hefty chunk of fish. Behkai swallowed them without chewing, then looked back at him, hopeful for more.

"That's all you're getting. This food has to last us until we get to the city, and we've already gone through more than half of it. If you're still hungry, go catch a rat."

Behkai cocked his head, like he was offended by the suggestion. Snuffling, he turned around three times and curled into a tight black circle of fur by the fireside.

Karim sighed, then noticed his onion was on fire. Cursing, he quickly pulled it from the flames and blew it out. Luckily, it still looked edible, so he waited until it stopped smoldering and took a bite. The burnt skin was crispy, and the hot, savory juices inside burst in his mouth. *Not bad at all.* As he ate, he thought about the farm girl who had given him the food. There was something about her that stayed with him, something more than her act of kindness and the boldness of her manner. He felt as if he was always supposed to meet her on that riverbank, that it was a passage in a story already written long ago.

Karim swallowed the last bit of onion and threw the skewer into the fire. He was still having trouble reconciling his involvement in the ancient Khetaran oracle with his own spiritual beliefs. The Anen, like most of the other tribes of the Red Lands, had neither the time nor the patience for a host of fickle gods and their ill portents.

They had one god. A creator and a destroyer, both—a god of all. Any more seemed unnecessary.

The same god who protected his flock one day might slaughter it the next, just as the shepherds in his tribe might do. And as the sheep couldn't possibly understand the reason for their fate, man couldn't hope to understand his either. In this way, the tribes accepted the harshness of life, while celebrating blessings when they came. They knew that in the end, fate rendered its will upon you, regardless of whether you deserved it or not.

In comparison, the Khetarans' faith seemed complicated to the point of absurdity. But if their gods were false, then how had the Oracle of the Lamb come to be? The whole situation had thrown his thoughts into disarray. How was he to know what to believe? The image of the creature standing on the riverbank was never far from his mind, though the farther they drifted from that temple in the desert, the harder it was for Karim to believe that it all had really happened.

He'd initially embarked on the voyage to Thonis because of his promise to Pa. But the closer he got to the city, the more he wanted answers for himself too.

Having finished his meal, Karim sat back and brushed the crumbs from his hands. He'd been doing a lot of thinking during those days floating down the river. Traveling on the skiff made him realize that in all his life, he'd never really been alone before. Back with the Anen, he'd always been around other men or his family—and later, with the Jackals. Other than the occasional solitary hunting expedition, there'd always been another voice in his ear. But on the river, there was nothing. Nothing but the sound of water rolling over rocks, and the urgent cries of ibis flying overhead. Other boats would often pass them by, but aside from a few polite greetings, no one stopped to talk.

When the solitude got to be too much, or when he couldn't sleep for fear of what waited in dreams, Karim had gotten in the habit of talking to the dog. He'd talk about the weather, tell stories about his time with the Jackals, and point out interesting landmarks he saw on the way.

Behkai turned out to be quite a pleasant traveling companion. When Karim wanted quiet, Behkai either slept, cleaned himself, or stared down at the water, transfixed by the creatures he saw below. When Karim wanted to talk, Behkai sat very still and listened, his big black head cocked in a show of intense interest.

They saw many wonders along the river. White pyramids topped with gold, vast columned temples bright with color, and enormous stone kings, carved straight from the mountains, as if a thousand artists had chipped away the rock until the man inside was freed. Karim had little love for the Khetarans, but he was awestruck by the sight of their handiwork.

It was mostly at night, when darkness threw a shroud over those wonders, that bitterness set in. What had the Khetarans done to deserve a river that offered unending bounty and asked nothing in return? What earned them the gift of greatness?

Is this what it looked like—the other side of destiny? Would the Khetarans' good fortune really last forever? His cynical side—the side that was always waiting for the next raid, the next pestilence, the next unexpected catastrophe—told him no. Nothing lasts forever. No matter how tall their monuments or how beautiful their tombs, fate, Karim knew, would come for them all.

Behkai was growling.

Karim's eyes fluttered open, having nearly slipped into a doze. The fire had burned down to embers, and only glowed enough to light a small circle around them. He glanced over at the dog, who'd gotten up and was standing at attention, growling deep in his throat at something in the darkness. Karim sat up at once, scooping some of the embers into his torch until a steady flame rose from it. Then Karim was at Behkai's side, squinting in the direction of the dog's gaze.

Probably a snake—or a jackal, he thought mildly, but the wild beating of his heart betrayed him. He swung the torch slowly from left to right, illuminating a boulder, a cluster of thorny shrubs, the jagged remains of a tamarisk tree sticking out from the ground like a broken tooth, and—

Something moved.

He scrabbled at his waist, feeling for the knife in his belt. He found it and pulled it free, holding the blade out in front of him. It trembled.

No, it's not possible. He'd traveled so far... farther than any man from his tribe had ever gone, and the river was swift.

A hint of sweat appeared on his brow. He squeezed his eyes

shut, forcing himself not to imagine the creature whose image had been burned into his mind that night at Pa's temple, the creature he seemed to see in every shadow.

Karim cursed himself for allowing his fear to take control.

Stop it, he commanded, swinging the torch back around and finding only sand and emptiness. *Nothing could have followed you here on foot at that speed. Nothing. Not even—*

He froze.

A figure stood in front of the thorny shrubs. It hadn't been there a moment before.

A man.

The figure was cloaked in rough robes of indeterminate color, his face shrouded under a ragged hood. For a moment, Karim felt relief. This couldn't be the creature he'd seen in the desert that had killed Djet in the depths of the earth.

But then, then…

The firelight reached the man's hands. The skin was dark with decay, his curling, skeletal fingers capped with golden tips. His feet were clad in fine leather sandals inlaid with gold, sandals far too fine for a man such as this. Strips of fine linen wrappings, soiled with time, their ends shredded, dragged serpentine along the ground behind him, trailing from the body beneath the robe—

The wind blew off the river, filling the man's hood like a sail and allowing the firelight to reach his face.

Suddenly, despite being outside, surrounded by endless space, Karim felt as if he were back in the press of that suffocating tomb, with its walls closing in around him. He couldn't breathe, couldn't move, couldn't scream.

As a child in the Red Lands, Karim often imagined the face of fate, the grim visage that followed in your footsteps all your life, waiting for the moment you finally belonged to him.

That was the face that peered out from behind the shroud.

A gaunt, hairless, desiccated face, its skin stretched taut over a skull exposed in places to reveal sinew stretching between cheeks and mouth. No visible eyes looked back at him from the two black gaping holes, but only twin glints of reflected firelight, glittering with malice.

Somewhere in the distance, a jackal howled.

Then, as if the sound had broken a spell, the creature took a step forward.

Behkai shot past Karim, tearing toward the creature with a ferocious snarl.

"Behkai, no!" Karim shouted, finally finding his voice.

He imagined the dog crashing through the specter, revealing it to be nothing but a loose cloth held up by a bundle of dry sticks, a false man constructed to scare away predators. But instead, the thing reached out, grabbed a fistful of scruff behind the dog's neck, and hurled Behkai away as if he weighed nothing at all. The dog slammed into a boulder, yelping in pain before sliding to the ground and lying still.

Karim stared at Behkai's body in shock.

The creature took another step forward. And another.

Karim should have run. Should have bolted back to the skiff and left everything behind. He might have made it too. But something had overtaken him, something stronger than terror.

Rage.

In one fluid motion, he lobbed the flaming embers inside his torch at the creature. The rough fibers of its robe caught instantly and began to burn. The thing hissed, throwing off its smoking robes, revealing the horror of a half-wrapped mummified body beneath. Where the skin of its chest had worn away, a network of gray tendon and muscle crisscrossed, and beneath that, a hollow cage of bone. An intricate scarab collar hung around its neck, and an ornamental pendant depicting the same doglike creature he'd seen in the tomb—with a downturned snout and tall, blunted ears—hung from a gold belt looped loosely around its waist.

The creature turned its head toward Karim, light still burning in the hollows of its eyes. With a chilling, unearthly roar, it lunged for him.

But Karim was ready. Sidestepping the creature's reach, Karim used its forward momentum to thrust his dagger deep into its abdomen, and then upward into its chest cavity. But the dagger found little purchase with no flesh to pierce or tear. Karim stabbed again and again, but the creature took no notice. It reached up, its bony, gold-tipped fingers closing around Karim's throat.

The creature's grip was so strong, so abruptly suffocating, that the dagger slipped from Karim's fingers. He raked at its hands, using every bit of his own strength to try and pry them off his neck.

Already his head felt light and swollen with blood, each pump of his heart pulsing through his eyes as he stared into the gruesome face of the creature.

It has a name, he thought as he felt his body grow limp, his defensive blows growing weaker and weaker with every passing moment. A name he'd whispered into the night. A name like a curse.

Setnakht.

The monster held on to him as he collapsed to the ground, his vision blurring at the edges, the roar of wind in his ears. Dimly, he felt one of its hands release his throat and move to his torso, ripping his robes aside and exposing his bare chest.

What is it doing?

But before he could wonder further, there was a blur in his fading vision. Something lay in the shadows just behind where the creature knelt over him, like a wild dog hunched over its kill. It was small and white and darkly wet, and it regarded him with huge black eyes.

A bloody lamb.

"Not yet," the lamb whispered in his mind. *"Not yet."*

Karim's eyes fluttered, and the vision vanished.

The creature's hand was on Karim's chest, its fingers digging into his flesh. But with its concentration no longer on strangling him, the grip on his throat loosened enough for Karim to get a little air, a little strength. Where the lamb had been, he spotted a single smoldering ember, just within reach. He grabbed it, ignoring the searing pain in his hand, and pushed it straight into the creature's face.

The mummified skin around the ember hissed as it burned away, and the creature let out an earsplitting howl. Releasing its hold on Karim's throat, it rose up, scrabbling at the smoking hole in its face.

Wasting no time, Karim got to his feet and, with a guttural cry, charged at the creature. He struck it with his shoulder and wrapped his arms about its waist as he drove it back, back, until they both fell.

They never hit the ground.

There was a dry, splintering sound, and Karim felt something sharp nearly drive up into his belly. Nimbly, he twisted his body, rolling off the creature and onto the sand below. The impact drove the little breath he had left straight from his lungs, but he didn't stay down. Jumping back up, he squared his shoulders, anticipating another attack. But none came.

He'd impaled the creature on the broken stump of the tamarisk tree. The thick, jagged blade of wood cut a gaping hole through its body and reached, bloodless, to the night sky. The ember had burned away half of the remaining skin on the monster's face, exposing naked bone and charred sinew beneath. Karim stared, agog and gasping, into the deafening silence of the desert. He kept his distance, waiting for the figure to rise up and come for him again.

Minutes passed, and still Karim waited. He coughed, spitting bile, which lit his bruised throat on fire. But still the creature didn't move. Shuffling a little closer, Karim kicked once, twice, driving it farther onto the spike of wood.

Nothing.

Karim allowed himself a whimper of relief. He stumbled over to Behkai, who lay in a pool of starlight. The dog hadn't moved since the monster had kicked him.

Karim looked down at the animal's body and sniffed, wiping at his eyes.

"Curse you," he said, his voice thick. "Why did you have to attack it? Stupid, fool dog."

Without Behkai there to help lift it, the silence was too heavy.

Karim dropped to his knees and laid a hand on Behkai's chest.

It rose and fell.

Karim's heart soared. "Hey! Hey! Are you alive?" He bent low, pulling the dog's face toward him and rubbing it vigorously. "Come on, sen, stay with me. Stay with me, you fool dog!"

A long, long moment passed.

Then Behkai's eyes dragged open. He blinked, and licked Karim on the mouth.

"Ugh," Karim sputtered, "Disgusting." Behkai's tail wagged weakly, and Karim rubbed him behind the ears. "Good boy," he whispered.

Behkai attempted to rise to his feet but whined with the movement and lay back down.

"Stay," Karim told him, holding up a hand.

With effort, he gathered the big dog into his arms. He carried him back to the skiff, Behkai's long legs sticking comically into the air. After getting the dog settled on a blanket, he ran back to gather the rest of the supplies, and then pulled anchor, pushing back onto the gentle current of the river.

It was only then, once they'd left that cursed bit of desert behind them, that Karim allowed himself to feel the pain and exhaustion that had been waiting on the other side of terror. His body felt numb and heavy. He slid down to the floor of the skiff alongside the dog. Behkai was already asleep, his warm, silken body a comfort against the brisk night air.

Karim closed his eyes, subconsciously pressing his cheek against the back of Behkai's great black head, grateful both to be alive and not alone.

A sound woke him, or rather, a thousand sounds.

The sun had been up for hours by the time Karim opened his eyes. Blinking into the glare of day, he rose to find an astonishing sight. Instead of the emptiness of the Red Lands, the rolling fields of farmland, or the vast Khetaran temple complexes he'd been accustomed to seeing from the river, the skiff was approaching a city on the east bank. A city so huge, so spectacular, and so *white*, that he thought that he was still dreaming. He'd floated past other towns and villages on his journey, but none that rivaled this one.

Among the thousands of flat-topped white structures stretching as far as the eye could see, bursts of color splashed across walls and temples and towers pointed with electrum. There was more color too, from flowering trees and bushes to crowds of people in vivid robes of red, blue, and green. The whole of it was like a tremendous canvas painted joyously with moving, breathing life.

This was Thonis. Capital city of Khetara.

"Wake up, Behkai," he breathed. "We've arrived."

Drinking in the miraculous scene, Karim wondered if he could finally stop running, or if he'd merely traded one kind of danger for another.

18
RAE

Rae crouched in the dark, waiting for the signal. For probably the twentieth time, she felt for her father's dagger, making sure that it was solidly wedged into her belt. The black cloth mask—hardly more than a sack with holes for her eyes and mouth—was hot and itchy, but it did its job well. Between that and her dark tunic, she was practically invisible. A ghost in the night.

The House of the Medjay stood before her. She and ten other Horizon rebels, including Omari and Asim, were hidden in the shadows around its perimeter, where they all had a clear view of the low U-shaped building.

After the Great War, the new nomarch had built the solid, unbeautiful symbol of their control over the city on Sakesh's northern border. On the insides of the building's two prongs were a dozen arched portals, each hung with heavy curtains to block out the wind and blowing sand. Inside these small barracks, approximately forty soldiers slept.

Rae knew all this because the baker often delivered bread to the Medjay, and he'd made a special effort to count the men the last time he'd been there, then communicate that information to the rebels. And after several nights of surveillance, they'd also learned that only three men stood guard at the front of the building after midnight. She watched them from her hiding place, one man patrolling in front of the right prong and two others on the left. A large brazier burned next to them on each side, keeping the darkness at bay.

Most important, though, was what lay at the end of the U-shaped building, which could only be accessed through the open courtyard, past the armed soldiers packed tightly within the barracks on each side. A large windowless chamber, containing items that were nearly impossible to come by in Sakesh.

The armory.

Asim's plan was simple. Incapacitate the guards without waking the soldiers, infiltrate the armory, and steal as many weapons as they could carry.

"We are sending a message to the Medjay—to the nomarch—to the pharaoh himself," Asim told them at their last meeting. "For too long we have foundered in the ruins of our once great city. For too long we have allowed ourselves to remain powerless, toothless, offering up our flesh to feed the king's insatiable hunger. No more. We will take up arms. We will defend what is ours. Out of the darkness, the City of Ra will shine again on the horizon!"

The rebels had cheered, fists in the air, and Rae had joined them. She'd nodded at the men as they dispersed into the night, and a few of them even nodded back.

Rae's heart had swelled with pride.

I was fighting in alleys, thinking I was going to earn respect. But Buto and his stupid friends have none to give. The rebels, on the other hand, were reputable men—artisans, tradesmen, some of them ex-military. Earning their respect might actually have meaning.

If any of them were nervous about the raid, they hadn't shown it. Once the decision had been made, there was no looking back, and no one—not even the reluctant brewer—spoke a word against it. Rae had a few reservations about the plan at first, having thought about it every day while she worked in the fields. It was a simple plan—but was it *too* simple? What if something went wrong? At the end of that last meeting, she'd finally gotten up the courage to speak to Asim.

"Don't worry, I've got a secret weapon," the rebel leader had told her. He'd brought a large sack and shown her what was inside. "Might get messy if we have to use it," he'd added with a grim smile, "but it'll be a night the Medjay won't soon forget."

Rae's focus jerked back to the present as she heard a distinctive *kroo, kroo*, much like the call of a nightjar. But it was no bird—it was Asim's signal.

Time to go.

On bare, silent feet, she and Omari sprinted out into the open, keeping low and to the shadows, as Asim and another rebel emerged on the other side. The two pairs flanked the building, Rae and Omari on the left, Asim and his partner on the right. When she reached the outer wall, Rae pressed her back against it, listening to hear if either of the guards standing on the other side had heard their approach.

"So, what do you think of the job?" a young voice asked.

"Eh," a second, older voice grunted. "Sakesh is a dung heap. I'd rather work with dogs."

Rae's cheeks flushed with anger, but she was relieved. Clearly, they hadn't heard a thing. "You should have stayed in Thonis," the older man continued.

The younger one chuckled nervously. "I didn't have a choice. Our superiors made it clear that the others and I were needed here."

The second man snorted. "Sent the best of the best, did they?"

There was an awkward silence. Then: "There've been shifts in the assignments at the palace lately. We were the only ones left."

"Lucky me."

An embittered old guard and a brand-new one, Rae thought. *We can work with that*.

From the other side of the building, a deep voice called out. "I think I heard something over here. Sounded like an animal rooting around, but I'm going to have a look."

"Fine," the older man said, uninterested.

Rae glanced over at Omari and smiled.

They waited, counting silently to ten. Other than the sound of the young man humming tunelessly, there was only silence.

But the third guard did not return.

"Eh, Hasire, get back here, will you?" the older man said after a minute or so had passed. "It's your turn to mind this whelp. He irritates me."

The humming stopped.

"Hasire?"

Rae clenched her hands into fists, her body tensing with anticipation.

The older man cursed under his breath, sighing. "I'm going to find out where that fool has got to. If I don't come back in two minutes, wake the men."

"Y-yes, sir," the young man replied.

Rae listened to the faint sound of receding movement, and took a quiet step toward the corner of the building and the circle of flickering firelight.

"Hasire?" the older man said again, his voice distant. Then came a muted grunt of pain.

Rae's pulse began to race as the young guard gasped. He'd heard it too. Any moment now, he would sound the alarm, dragging every soldier in the barracks out of their slumber and down onto the rebels' heads.

Go! Now!

Rae darted around the corner. The young guard had his back to her, khopesh in hand, and was craning his neck to catch a glimpse of his companions on the other side of the building. In one fluid movement, she clamped a hand over the guard's mouth and snaked her other arm around his neck until it was tucked into the crook of her elbow. She squeezed, pulling her elbow back to create pressure on his throat. It took a moment for the guard's shock to register. Then he started kicking and stabbing the blade over his shoulder to try and get her off his back. In an instant, Omari was there. He disarmed the young guard and caught the khopesh before it could clatter to the ground. The guard's blows weakened. A few seconds later, he went limp.

Rae and Omari remained perfectly still, listening for any movement from the barracks. Their struggle had made more noise than anticipated.

The barracks remained silent.

Sighing with relief, Omari stuffed the khopesh into his belt and helped Rae drag the unconscious guard to the side of the building, where they set to binding his wrists and ankles. "Curse you, Ay," Omari whispered while they worked, "You were supposed to wait for me! *I* was going to give the signal!"

"He was about to squeal," Rae retorted, tying a rough gag around the guard's mouth. "We didn't have time for a signal." She glanced up. He was glaring at her. "What? Everything's good. Flawless execution."

Omari shook his head. "You're impossible. Come on, let's go."

"I don't know what you're complaining about," Rae whispered as they ran to the front of the building. "All you do is complain…"

Asim and his partner were waiting for them.

"Done?" Asim tipped his chin toward where the young guard had been standing.

Omari nodded.

"Good." Asim turned away from the House of the Medjay and cupped one hand to his mouth.

Kroo! Kroo!

Within seconds, six more men emerged from hiding, four carrying large stoppered jars, the other two holding rolls of rough cloth. For the next step of the plan, Asim and his partner were to keep watch at the entrance while Rae, Omari, and the six additional men made their way into the courtyard.

Easy, Rae thought to herself, focusing on the armory doors. It was only about fifty cubits away, give or take, but suddenly it felt a lot farther. She imagined all those men slumbering behind the heavy curtains, daggers cradled in their arms. One wrong move, and—

She took a step forward, her toes curling into the cool, hard ground, and remembered what Asim had told her. *Don't hold your breath, and don't stop. Move faster than your fear, and it will never catch you.*

Rae started walking, slow but steady, keeping her eyes forward. In her peripheral vision, the curtains covering the barracks fluttered in the breeze, but she didn't look, and she didn't stop.

Before she knew it, she'd reached the armory doors.

Omari made it too. The two cloth-bearing men were behind him, each now carrying a lit rushlight. They must have stopped to light them on the burning braziers when they arrived. Meanwhile, the other four men proceeded slowly around the inside perimeter, pouring the contents of their jars along the walls, saturating the bottom edges of the barracks' heavy curtains with a black viscous liquid. They were the same jars that Asim had shown her back at the meeting place, hidden in his heavy sack.

"What is it?" she'd asked him.

"Naft," Asim had replied. "It comes from under the water. Not easy to find."

Rae had never heard of it. "What does it do?"

Asim told her. She'd been fascinated, and wished she could see it work with her own eyes. But as she watched the men pour the evil-looking stuff onto the ground, she changed her mind. If things went as planned, they wouldn't need to use it. *Let us pass a quiet night*, she prayed, *and calamity never find us*.

Tearing her gaze away, Rae refocused on the armory, which was bolted shut. "Help me with this," she murmured to Omari.

He stepped up next to her, and together they quietly slid the wooden bolt free and pulled open the double doors. It was utterly dark inside the windowless chamber, so Rae turned to one of the cloth-bearers, holding her hand out for his rushlight. It was a simple thing, just a section of reed dipped in animal fat, but it cast enough light around the room for Rae to see what was inside. Her eyes widened.

Asim had guessed at what might be inside the armory, given what he'd seen the Medjay carrying on their patrols around the city. But it was better than that. Much better.

There were spears and javelins lined up against the wall, as well as a dozen khopesh much like the one the young guard had been carrying. Daggers and short swords lay on tables in neat, gleaming piles. They were all expertly crafted, fitted with bronze blades and fine wooden handles. Nothing like the improvised weapons the rebels had made from smelted farm tools and spare lumber. Rae was delighted to see several slingshots and two composite bows among the stash as well. But those weapons, though impressive, weren't what caught Rae's eye.

She spied a strange object tucked into a corner that glittered when the firelight passed over its surface. It looked like a pair of golden wings folded over each other, each feather an intricately formed scale of overlapping metal.

While Omari and the other men began rolling armfuls of weapons tightly into the heavy cloth they'd brought, Rae walked over to the object, transfixed. Upon closer inspection, she discovered it was scale armor. The wings were meant to wrap around the warrior's chest, secured by two crisscrossing straps of leather around the back. It looked old and impossibly beautiful. She wondered where it came from.

"Rae, come on!" Omari whispered harshly. One man had already finished bundling up the compound bows and most of the blades, effectively silencing any noise the weapons might make as they were carried. Omari and the other man hurriedly rolled up the spears and javelins.

Nodding, Rae picked up the armor and was surprised when another object slipped out from inside it. A handle with a heavy head—a mace, perhaps? Her hand shot out to prevent the thing from falling, and as soon as her fingers wrapped around its hilt, a crackle of energy passed through her body, so strong she almost dropped it.

What was that? she wondered, but the shock was gone as quickly as it came. She brought the weapon closer to the light. *It's not really a mace, is it?* she thought. It had a long head like a paddle, made of some kind of gray mottled stone and engraved with two eyes and sacred words. The handle was made of highly polished cedar, its grip wrapped in soft leather. Like the armor, it looked old and very, very valuable. She wondered if both items had been plundered from Rahotep's palace long ago, and had been sitting here collecting dust ever since.

Wait a minute, she thought. *I know what this is.* She'd seen one painted on the outer wall of the king's abandoned palace, back when she and her friends used to play there. *It's a sekhem scepter.* More a ritualistic object than a weapon, sekhem scepters were a symbol of authority and associated with the lion-headed goddess Sekhmet.

Her fingers drifted to the little Sekhmet amulet hanging around her neck, and her thoughts to the man who'd given it to her. *Strange...*

"Rae!" Omari interrupted, his tone frantic. "We have to go! We've already lingered too long!"

"I'm coming." Rae quickly threw off her robes and slipped her head through the winged armor. The metal feathers jingled softly as they settled onto her shoulders, cascading over her chest like liquid gold. Then she stuck the scepter and a few slingshots into her belt and pulled her robes back on. One of the jar men had come inside the room and was pouring the black naft over the remaining weapons that wouldn't fit inside their cloth bundles.

"Go, go, go!" Omari muttered to the man with the last cloth bundle, sending him back out into the open. He was waving Rae and the jar man out of the door when what they'd all dreaded came to pass.

"To arms!" a ragged voice shouted into the night. *"To arms! We're under attack!"*

The young guard had wakened.

Rae's heart leaped into her throat as fear and regret overwhelmed her.

I should have knocked him out cold instead of choking him unconscious.

I should have tied the gag tighter.

I should have—

Omari froze, and turned to her with wide eyes.

Calamity, it seemed, had come knocking.

"Run," she said, and tore through the armory doors, pulling Omari along behind her.

Already a few men were stumbling out of the barracks,

daggers in hand, blinking into the dark as the young soldier continued to sound the alarm. Somewhere in the din, Rae heard the urgent call of the nightjar.

Kroo! Kroo! Kroo!

The two burning braziers at the front of the building toppled with a metallic clatter, spilling their red-hot embers onto the pools of naft that had been poured at their bases. There was a *whoosh*ing sound as the pools burst into flame. In the next instant, twin fires began traveling along the trails of naft the men had poured on each side, alighting the heavy curtains as they went. There were shrieks of surprise and pain as men who'd been coming out of their barracks were torched, their clothes and hair catching fire as they tried to push through the flaming curtains. Rae had never seen anything burn so hot, so fast.

The House of the Medjay was all smoke and screaming and chaos. A second later, Rae and Omari were buffeted by a burst of force as the naft-soaked armory behind them exploded. Rae stumbled and nearly fell, but Omari yanked her to her feet and kept running. Their only chance at survival was to get away in the confusion, to vanish into the night before the Medjay got their bearings—

Someone ahead was blocking her way. The hem of his robes was aflame.

It was Big Ears, the man who'd menaced her with a knife when she'd arrived at the first Horizon meeting. He'd lost his mask in the fray, and she could see the panic on his face as he tried desperately to extinguish his robes. Then, one of the Medjay soldiers spotted him.

Rae moved to intervene, but she couldn't get there in time. The young soldier closed the distance first, spun the rebel around, and delivered a savage blow to his jaw. Big Ears reeled and would have gone down, but the soldier caught him and, in one fluid movement, thrust his dagger into the rebel's gut.

No!

Before Rae could react, Omari pushed her aside and hurtled toward the two combatants. He wrested the dagger from the soldier's grip, grabbed him by the back of the head with one massive hand, and bashed his skull against the mud-brick wall. The soldier's head bounced back, and he collapsed, leaving a circle of blood on the wall.

Panting, Omari hoisted Big Ears's arm around his shoulders and started to drag him away. "Let's go!" he shouted to Rae.

She moved to follow when another soldier ran toward her from the left, attempting to cut off her escape.

"Hey! Stop!" The soldier's face was monstrous in the firelight, ash-black and bubbling with burns. Rae reached for her dagger, but her fingers closed around the handle of the sekhem scepter instead. With a primal cry, she struck out at the soldier with a savage swing, the heavy stone paddle connecting with his shoulder and dropping him to the ground. He lay writhing and clutching his shattered arm, adding his screams to the clamor.

Rae felt fingers close around her ankle. She gasped and tried to wrest her foot free, but the grip was too strong. Then a body slammed into her hips, sweeping her legs out from under her. Rae lost her grip on the scepter as she fell and landed heavily on her back.

The impact left her breathless—but only for a moment. Her attacker still had her legs pinned, but the scepter was only an arm's length away. *If I could just reach it...*

She twisted, groping for the weapon. Her fingertips brushed its handle when suddenly the man mounted her. It was the soldier who'd had stabbed Big Ears—apparently Omari hadn't finished him off, after all.

The soldier panted, his eyes wild, and his head was a bloody mess from where he'd hit the wall. He struck her once, the blow like a thunderclap. Rae brought her arms in to protect her face. He kept hitting her, again and again, his face contorted with rage. Rae tried to block the blows, but her head was swimming, her vision darkening at the edges.

"I want to see your face before I kill you," the soldier snarled, grabbing Rae's black hood and pulling it free, "you stinking—"

The insult died on his lips as his rage transformed to confusion at her young battered face.

"A woman?"

It was only a moment's hesitation, a slight shifting of his weight on top of her, but it was enough time for Rae to reach out and grasp the sekhem scepter. Her fingers closed around its handle, and with every ounce of strength she had left, she struck the soldier's temple with a sickening, wet crack. A profusion of blood sprayed across his startled face, and his eyes, still fixed on hers, went still. Then he slumped on top of her, dead.

Rae's breath came in short bursts as her body flooded with panic. The soldier's head lay on her chest, his blood soaking her clothes, the smell of it nearly as suffocating as the crushing weight of his body.

Horrified, she pushed his corpse off her and scrambled to her feet, the scepter still gripped in her hand. She stared back at the soldier, lying on his stomach on the ground, his head a bloody ruin. The world spun.

Rae shook her head to clear her vision. There was no time to waste. She only had seconds before someone would notice her and attack. The edge of the building was just ahead. If she could just make it back into the city, she'd be safe. Many of the other soldiers were still emerging from their barracks and fighting the fire, still trying to comprehend what was happening.

She ran, feeling the weight of the scale armor under her robes.
Don't hold your breath.

There was a cry behind her. More shouting.

Don't stop.

Her robes stuck to her skin, saturated and stinking of death.

Run faster than your fear.

She ran beyond the reach of the firelight. The shadows embraced her, but even then, she didn't stop. When the job was done, the rebels were to scatter to the four winds, so that it would be impossible for the Medjay to track them to any one place. So Rae ran through the darkened streets until they fell away to farmland, until she'd made it all the way up the path to Omari's workshop. Only then, once she'd pushed through the doorway, did she stop running.

Omari was inside kneeling on the floor, Big Ears laid out before him. The rebel grimaced with pain as Omari applied pressure to the wound in his stomach. Rae dashed over to them, tearing off her bloody robes.

"Will he live?" she asked, dropping to her knees beside them.

"I can't say." Omari's voice was laced with anger and anxiety. "But I dare not call on the healer. Even if he is a good man, he's sure to ask questions, and I don't know if he can be trusted with a secret such as this."

"How about your parents? Can they help?"

"The less they know, the better," Omari replied, echoing what she'd said to her own father. "I don't want them involved."

Big Ears waved away their concerns.

"You'll call no one," he barked, his voice full of gravel. He glanced over at Rae, his eyes twinkling with mirth despite what must have been excruciating pain. "Figured you'd be pleased to see me cut, girl, after the one I gave you."

"All is forgiven." Rae put her hand over his. "Just don't die. Who will menace the new rebels if you do?"

Big Ears laughed, and a fresh spout of blood poured from the wound. He moaned.

"Be still!" Omari commanded. "If we can stanch the bleeding, you may survive. Good for you and good for us too! It would give us a lot less explaining to do come tomorrow."

The man nodded and closed his eyes. Soon, he was either unconscious or asleep, and didn't stir again while Rae helped Omari pack and wrap the wound with fresh cloth. But still, he breathed.

When they finished, they both went to the basin to wash the blood from their hands. In the quiet, the frenzy of battle began to drain from Rae's veins, and the reality of what had happened fell upon her. She felt overwhelmed. Exhausted. Numb. Her hands shook uncontrollably.

Omari, on the other hand, was luminous with triumph.

"We did it, Rae," he said, leaning against his worktable. "We took their power, and we burned their house."

"We did." Rae knew she should feel the same—after all, the mission had been a great success. In fact, using the naft probably sent as strong a message to the High Khetarans as the stolen weapons. It was what needed to be done; what no one else had the courage to do.

It was your fault the guard woke up.

Clearly unsatisfied with Rae's response, Omari went on. "Don't you see? Tonight, Sakesh burns bright with the fires of vengeance!"

"It does," Rae said, glancing back over to the sleeping rebel.

It's your fault that he might die tonight.

Omari's eyes were alight. "It was exhilarating, wasn't it? Finally getting the chance to give those cursed High Khetarans what they deserved?"

Rae nodded.

You killed that soldier.

You crushed his skull.

Your robe is soaked in his blood.

Rae was no stranger to violence. She knew what she was getting into when she'd joined the Horizon. And she'd been the one to encourage the rebels to mount this attack. It was the right thing—the only thing—they could do to fight back.

But she'd never taken a life. She'd never imagined how that might feel. She'd had no choice, of course—it had been the soldier's life or hers. But still… she couldn't stop thinking about the shock and blood splatter on his face when he died, and the weight of his lifeless body.

Stop it, she told herself. *You're supposed to be stronger than this. This is war. How do you expect the men to respect you if you fall apart after the first battle? A battle we actually won?*

Omari didn't seem to notice the internal struggle going on in Rae's mind.

"This is the beginning of our journey back to greatness, Rae," he said, glancing out the window to the starry night beyond. "Isn't it wonderful?"

Have courage, damn you, she thought, and stood a little straighter.

"Wonderful," she said.

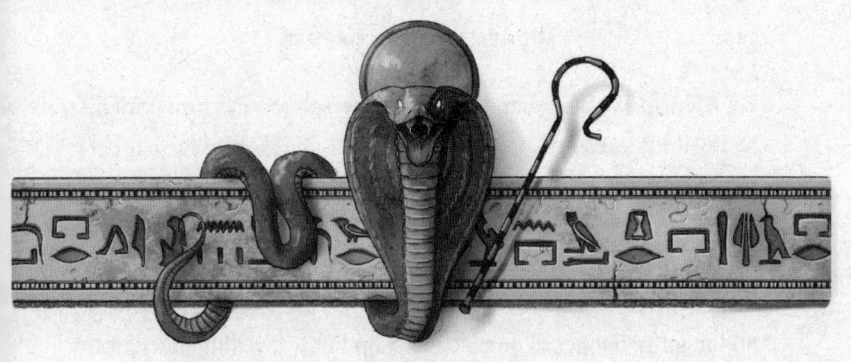

19
SITA

"Tell me what you want."

Femi's voice curled like smoke into her ear, the words winding their way into the fruitful garden of her fantasies. Sita had tended it in secret for years, but she'd only begun to taste what grew there.

She lay on the soft woolen rug in her bedchamber, and he knelt before her like a supplicant. They'd just started and already he'd begun to sweat—his moist skin glistening in the moonlight streaming in from the window. She watched a single bead of perspiration roll from the hollow of his throat, down his bare chest and stomach, and along the deep trench of his pelvis. Sita couldn't resist darting forward to lick it away.

Femi inhaled sharply at the touch of her tongue to his skin.

That sound, that gasp—it was teeth biting into ripe fruit, it was honey-sweetness dribbling down lips. It threw open the gates to her secret place and invited everything inside.

Sita reached out and pulled him to her, cupping the back of

Femi's neck with her hand, wrapping herself around him until his heavy body pressed her into the floor.

"This," she murmured as he kissed her neck, her collarbone, her shoulders. "This is what I want. What I need." There was something about the weight of him, the way his bulk held her fast to the earth, that made her feel safe. Like she was grounded, no longer in danger of being caught up in the swirling maelstrom of her life.

She felt his heart quicken at the sound of her words. He looked up and met her eyes, his pupils dark and full of adoration.

She wondered if he loved her.

She worried that he did.

Femi was no fool. Certainly, he must know the folly of a palace guard imagining a future with a princess—but that might not stop his heart from dreaming. From breaking.

Perhaps his resistance to lovemaking wasn't only for her sake, but for his own. Perhaps he was doing everything he could to keep her from imprinting on his soul.

Still, she wondered how much longer either of them could resist the temptation.

She wanted to stop.

She couldn't stop.

How many lives will I destroy along this cursed path? she wondered.

Instead, she held him tighter. Dragged her nails across his broad, sweat-slick back, and spilled herself into him until they were both drowning, gasping for breath—

A ragged wail split the night.

Sita pulled away, mid-kiss. She waited, dread dropping like a stone in her belly. Her fingers still dug into Femi's back, but now it was for a different reason.

"What was that?" Femi whispered.

Then they heard it again. A woman's voice. A cry of such total despair that it sent a bolt of terror down Sita's spine.

She was on her feet in an instant, pulling a robe around her body and running out the door with Femi at her heels.

"Sitamun, wait!" he said quietly, grabbing her wrist. "Someone might see!"

"I don't care if they see," Sita said, and jerked her hand free. "We're going."

Femi's expression changed when he heard the commanding tone in her voice. "Allow me to go first then, Princess," he asked. "In case there is danger ahead."

"All right. But we must hurry."

The intimacy between them was gone. It existed only within the confines of her bedchamber—it couldn't survive anywhere else.

They started down the hall, which had broad windows on one side and flickering torches lining the other. One of the palace cats sat on a ledge, its golden eyes curious as they followed Sita and Femi's passage.

The wailing continued, a chilling, tortured keening.

Like someone's heart is being ripped out, Sita thought with a shiver.

She rushed toward it, pushing Femi to go faster. They passed sleepy courtiers and their wives emerging from their rooms, blinking and bewildered. Finally, Sita pushed past Femi and ran.

The closer they got to the sound, the more certain Sita became about who was making it. And why.

Her dread intensified.

Please, she prayed, *not that*.

Bile rose into Sita's throat as she slowed and then stopped at the door to Maet's room.

Oil lamps and incense burned inside, but it did nothing to

mask the sour smell that permeated the room and flowed out of it like a curse. In the dim light, Sita saw Maet's mother on her knees at her daughter's bedside. She was rocking back and forth, wailing, crying, tearing the hair from her head. The sight of her was like a physical blow. There was no air to breathe. The world had suddenly become a void filled with nothing but suffering.

Sita turned away.

She didn't want to look.

If she didn't see, maybe it wouldn't be real.

You don't deserve to be spared this pain. The voice in her mind was harsh, but it spoke the truth. *This is on your hands.*

Look.

Look at what you've wrought.

With effort, she dragged her gaze to the small, still form lying in the bed.

"No," she murmured. "Maet…"

The blanket had been pulled up to the girl's chest, clearly smoothed by a mother's desperate hands, helpless to do anything else. Maet lay with her head turned toward the door, her eyes open and staring. Her lips were slightly open too, as if she were about to call out.

See-see…

I'm scared, See-see…

Why didn't you help me, See-see?

Sita's legs gave way beneath her.

Femi caught her before she could fall. "Sitamun, are you all right?"

He sounded far away, and it was several minutes before Sita regained her bearings and was able to stand again on her own, swaying unsteadily on her feet. She touched her face and found tears there.

Others arrived. Priests, courtiers, guards—and soon, the

wailing was overpowered by the hum of prayers and hushed conversations, of arrangements being made.

Montuhotep appeared, assessing the situation. He looked unusually disheveled, and there were dark circles under his eyes. Frustration coloring his face, he pushed his way past the crowd into the bedchamber.

"Out of my way," he said. "I should have been the first to know about this—the first!" Without addressing Maet's mother, he stood over the bed and began to speak. "Praise to you, O Amun, Lord of All, mysterious of form," he recited, "Take this child into thine arms, for she is ready to go West; make her heart as light as air, so that she may be judged and found worthy to enter the Field of Reeds—"

Suddenly the queen appeared in the corridor, her eyes filled with panic. Sita was surprised at the strength of her emotion—Maet wasn't her blood, after all—until she spoke, and everything changed.

"The king!" Queen Bintanath exclaimed. "No one can find him! He's vanished from his chambers. He was there moments ago…"

Father is missing? Sita could hardly wrap her mind around this new information.

At the queen's pronouncement, the crowded hallway became even more chaotic, and Femi was pulled away by other guards to launch a search for the pharaoh.

"I'm sorry," he said to Sita before disappearing down the hallway.

"She has told no lies, O Amun," Montuhotep droned on, "nor has she closed her heart to the suffering of the innocent—"

Maet's mother seemed oblivious to both the high priest and the news about the king. She continued her mournful cries, the strands of her black hair falling to the stone floor as she ripped them free. They collected around her in a soft nest of pain, one

Sita imagined she would sit in for the rest of her life. She might fly from it from time to time, but she would always return to brood there, in her profound, unspeakable loss.

Sita felt cold. She knew she'd allowed the girl to die. Keeping Mery's secret had been no different than feeding Maet the poison herself. Somehow she'd imagined that the girl might still pull through, that she'd refuse to eat any more of the cakes, that her youth would save her.

She'd been wrong, of course. And Maet had died, a lamb sacrificed on the altar of Mery's grand plans for the kingdom.

Sita watched Maet's mother, alone inside her grief.

Was it worth it? she wondered.

Her eyes suffused with tears, she tore away her gaze, taken by a sudden desire to make herself useful. *I should help them search for Father.*

She walked briskly back down the hallway, past her own chambers, until she reached the palace's main hall. Several guards were already there—one interrogating poor Ineni about how the king could possibly have slipped away—but they took no notice of her.

Something soft brushed past her legs, and she looked down to see the striped cat. She snaked around Sita's ankles, her tail erect, but when it was clear Sita had no treats nor affection to offer, she moved on, making her way on silent paws toward the pleasure garden.

Sita found herself following.

Outside, the lotus was in full bloom. The fishpond was black and still, the white flowers dotting its surface like stars on a night sky. All around, the trees huddled in shadow, and from within their boughs the nightjars sang. *Kroo, kroo! Kroo, kroo!* The green herbaceous smell and the quiet beauty of the garden seemed incongruous with everything happening inside the palace walls.

Then she saw someone sitting on a bench across the way, under the sycamore tree. A thin, huddled apparition.

"Father?"

The figure didn't move. Sita hurried under the tree's canopy, blinking until her eyes adjusted to the darkness.

King Amunmose sat on a stone bench flanked by jasmine bushes, staring past her to the garden beyond. He wore a fine white tunic, edged in crimson thread, which draped loosely over his body. He wore neither a crown nor a headdress, and his wispy, elderberry-dyed hair, the color of an old bruise, shivered in the breeze. Shadows clung to his jutting cheekbones and the hollows of his eyes. He didn't react to her arrival.

"Father?" she repeated.

He turned to her then, his eyes luminous and somehow too large. For a moment, he didn't speak. Then: "I had the dream again."

His voice was dry and so soft that Sita thought she might have imagined hearing it.

"What dream?" she asked.

He raised an unsteady hand to his forehead. "The snakes. The red and the black. The one that bites, and the one that…" He looked at Sita, actually focused on her, as if he were seeing her for the first time. "I trusted the priests. I followed their instructions. I did… *everything*." The last word came out choked with impotent rage.

Sita grimaced. Ever since the Bast Festival, she'd avoided being in her father's presence. She knew if she spent too much time with him, if she allowed herself to stop thinking about Mery's reasons for doing what he was doing, if she for one moment forgot about the future and remained in the present, if she allowed herself to *feel*—her weak heart could destroy everything.

You've come this far. You can't turn back now.

"Please, Father," Sita said, moving closer to him. "Let me take you back to your chambers. Everyone is looking for you, and—"

"She's gone, isn't she?"

Sita paused, breathing into the silence.

"I'm sorry, Father."

The king's head dropped.

After a long while, he spoke. "I know I have done wrong," he said, staring once again into the middle distance, speaking to everyone and no one, and Sita least of all. "I know I have fallen short of greatness and that a host of malevolent spirits may have brought this condemnation upon me, for both what I've done and what I've failed to do. But why…?" His voice broke, and his shoulders crumpled. "Why did they have to take *her*?"

Sita thought of Maet's little body cooling in her bed. She didn't deserve any of this.

Still, she couldn't stop the horrible, selfish thoughts from spilling out of her. All the things she wished to say, but never did.

Would you cry this way for me, Father? she wondered as he gasped and shook with despair. *I'm not innocent and pure—not anymore, but I am yours! Your flesh! Your blood! Maybe I wouldn't be so broken, if only you'd loved me!*

With a shudder, the king collapsed, tumbling forward off the bench and onto the soft, loamy ground below.

Sita stared at him, feeling once more that her anger had materialized into a weapon and struck down its target. She took a step back.

"Father?" she whispered.

Only the nightjars replied. *Kroo, kroo!*

Sita turned on her heel and ran into the palace, screaming for help.

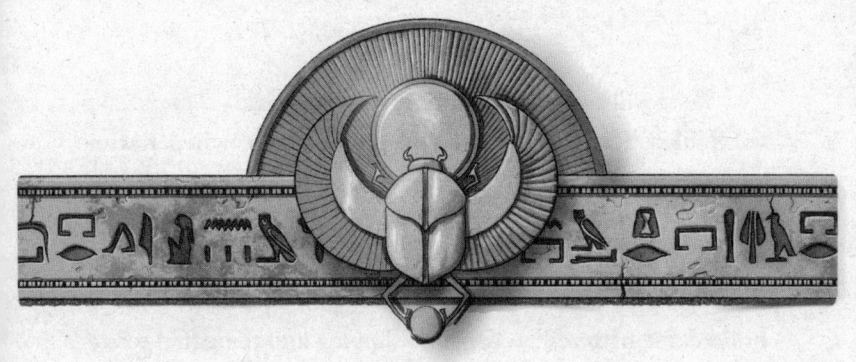

20
KARIM

"Stay."

The dog cocked his head and studied Karim's outstretched hand.

"I have to go away for a while," Karim said slowly, as if enunciating each word might help Behkai understand their meaning. "And I can't bring you with me, so I want you to *stay* with the *boat*." He pointed to the skiff anchored to the riverbank behind them.

Behkai blinked. Having enjoyed a nice long rest, the black dog seemed to have recovered from his encounter with the creature the night before. Karim hated leaving him alone while he went to the temple, but he had no other choice.

"You know how to handle yourself, hey?" Karim went on. "Don't let anyone steal the skiff, and I'll be back as soon as I can."

Behkai whined. The dog stared at him, his expression sending a message so clear that even Karim, who was still new to canine companionship, could understand.

"Yes, I will bring food," Karim said with a sigh.

Behkai licked his chops and didn't budge when Karim adjusted the white tunic Raetawy had given him and made his way toward the temple gates. After dragging the skiff onto the riverbank earlier that day, he'd stripped down to his loincloth and dipped his hands into the river, splashing the cool water over his bruised and battered body before slipping into the gifted white tunic. Thinking he might need them later, he'd scrubbed the blood and grime from his dark robes too, and hung them on the crook of the skiff to dry in the sun.

"Well," he muttered nervously as he looked up at the towering structure before him, "if not now, then when?"

Of all the wonders Karim had seen on his journey downriver, the Temple of Amun was the most alluring. A line of ram-headed lion statues led up to two massive pylons, each flanked by flagpoles sporting long flapping banners in red and green. Every fingerbreadth of the temple's high walls was carved and painted with symbols, colorful geometric patterns, and larger-than-life figures of men and gods. Crowds of people swarmed around its entrance—soldiers, peasants, vendors leading donkeys laden with merchandise, and serious bald-headed men dressed in white. Karim noticed some larger boats anchored nearby where groups of workers in loincloths labored, lifting boxes of goods from their holds and carrying them toward the temple gates.

It must be a supply delivery day, Karim deduced. It wasn't going to be easy to gain access to the temple records, but it would be a lot easier on a day when strangers were streaming in and out of the temple on a regular basis. If he could slip inside unnoticed, he'd only need to figure out where they kept the records. Bribe someone to help him, perhaps. One of the priceless objects from his pack might loosen some lips.

Unless of course, I offer it to the wrong person and get caught.

Karim gulped, the thought of losing a hand—or his head—stopping him in his tracks.

What am I doing?

Sure, he'd started this journey because he'd promised the old priest to find answers about Setnakht and his relationship to the Oracle of the Lamb, but things had changed. The monster was dead. He'd left it impaled on that tree. It wouldn't be following him any longer, nor hurting anyone else. Didn't that make an end of it? Whatever else the oracle predicted, it had nothing to do with him. Why dig into this nightmare any further? What good would it do?

I could take my treasures to the Thonis market, as I'd planned, trade them for the best weapons in the land, and sail back to the Anen, he thought. *Hager and Babu wouldn't stand a chance against a Khetaran bow and khopesh. They wouldn't see it coming. I'd cut them down, take back my family—*

Karim shook his head. No. Just because he'd killed Setnakht, didn't mean the events of the oracle would never come to pass. The old priest had warned him that the impending disaster wouldn't only affect the Khetarans. If Pasenhor was right, then Karim's family still wasn't safe from it. A few Khetaran weapons wouldn't be enough to protect them.

Despite his best efforts, his mind was inexorably drawn back to that distant valley. To a tomb that was now the final resting place of a boy who'd deserved better. *He'd* opened that door. *He* was the one who set all this in motion—or so it seemed. It was his responsibility to make sure no one else was hurt by his actions. Whether he liked it or not, he needed to honor his vow and try to find an answer.

Djet's voice came once more into his ear.

If anyone can find it, you can.

Karim sighed. Why did that boy have to go and believe in him?

"Curse you, Djet," he whispered, resuming his trek toward the temple. "If I die today, it'll be all your fault."

As big as the temple looked from the riverbank, it was nothing compared to the sensation of standing before its impossibly high walls. For a moment, he forgot himself and just stared, awestruck, at the majesty before him.

"Eh! Move it, will you?" a grating voice burst out. "Can't you see you're in the way?"

Startled, Karim turned to see a long-faced man leading an equally long-faced donkey with heavy cloth sacks slung across its back.

"Sorry," he said, sidestepping to let the man pass.

The long-faced man pulled the donkey along, muttering irritably. Karim followed them up to the temple gates, where twin statues sat on enormous thrones on either side. The statues were of a strange man with a long beard and blue skin, wearing a tall golden crown that resembled two feathers side by side.

Amun, I presume. Karim remembered what Pasenhor had told him about Thonis's patron—that he was the god of mystery, of all that was hidden and unseen.

Taking care to walk casually behind the long-faced man and his donkey, Karim advanced toward the open gates, where several shiny, hairless officials in white tunics stood inspecting all the goods coming into the temple.

"What's this?" one of them asked the long-faced man.

"Natron for the embalmers," he grunted.

The official waved him inside, and Karim quietly moved close to the donkey, laying one hand lightly on a bulging sack, as if to imply ownership. The official, assuming that Karim and the man were together, barely gave him a second glance as he passed through the gates. As soon as he was clear, Karim slipped away, leaving the unwitting natron vendor and his donkey to complete their delivery alone.

Finding himself in a large courtyard, Karim hid in the shadow of one of the painted columns to take stock of his surroundings. Directly ahead, there was an entrance to a grand roofed hall, but on both sides of the courtyard were passageways that led deeper into the temple proper.

I definitely need a guide, he thought. *There's no way I'll be able to navigate this place unnoticed.* He scanned the crowd, looking for a likely candidate. *Someone dressed like a priest, who knows their way around. Someone young and ambitious enough to take a bribe...*

His eyes passed over a girl of maybe thirteen years, bald and dressed in a simple white dress. She looked at him curiously.

Too young, Karim decided. He kept searching.

Finally, his gaze landed upon a moon-faced man leaning against a column, paring his nails and looking bored. Despite his youth, he had rough hands, the skin worn and thickened with use.

Probably a laborer of some kind. A low-ranking priest. Perfect.

Karim sidled up to him. "Excuse me," he said in a low voice. "You couldn't tell me where I could find the House of Life, could you?"

The young man glanced up at him, eyes narrowed in suspicion. "Who wants to know?"

"Just someone who's come a very long way," Karim answered, shrugging off his pack. He picked out a shiny gold buckle, studded with obsidian, and flashed it at the priest. "And one who will be happy to make it worth your time," Karim added. "Trade this, and you'll never have to do a hard day's work again."

Karim placed the buckle in the young man's palm, who studied it with interest.

"So you'll tell me where I can find the temple records?" Karim asked hurriedly. He was relieved that the priest seemed amenable, but he needed to move quickly. The long-faced man and his donkey were leaving, and any moment now, the gate official might notice his business partner was missing.

The young man looked up at him and grinned, a twinkle of mischief in his eye.

"No," he said. "But I *will* alert the gatemen of a trespasser and likely criminal. I'm sure I'll be commended for my bravery." He chuckled. "But thanks for the buckle."

Karim felt the blood drain from his face.

Shit.

The priest turned toward the gate, ready to call out and ruin everything, and there was nothing Karim could do about it.

Go looking for trouble, and you'll always find it…

He was about to make a run for the gates, when—

"Nehshi, you found him!" a childlike voice rang out.

Karim turned to see the bald-headed girl he'd seen earlier beaming at the befuddled priest.

"You know this man, Nefermaat?" Nehshi asked.

"I have been waiting for him," the girl replied. "He's come from a faraway kingdom to peruse our collection of papyri. Isn't that right?" She turned to Karim, eyebrows raised meaningfully.

Karim had no idea why the girl had stepped up to claim him, but he decided it was best to play along.

"Yes, of course," he answered, adopting a formal tone. "My apologies, sena. I did not see you when I arrived, so I offered this young man a gift in exchange for his assistance."

The young priest blinked, clearly bewildered by Karim's abrupt change in manner.

"But, you… you said—" Nehshi stammered, still uncertain.

"You may keep it, of course," Karim added, closing the priest's hand over the golden buckle and patting it.

"Master Montuhotep is aware of his visit," the girl said. "I'm sure he'd want his guest treated well, don't you think?"

"But the purification ritual—"

"His kingdom does not observe our practices," Neff broke in. "So the master has allowed him to bypass the cleansing."

Nehshi glanced back and forth between Karim and the girl before relaxing his shoulders and slipping the bauble into the pocket of his tunic.

"Apologies for my ignorance," he said, dipping his head in a stiff bow. "I hope you enjoy your visit to the House of Amun."

Karim touched a knuckle to his nose. "I'm sure I will."

Once the young priest had hurried away, the girl tilted her bald head at Karim and said, "Come with me."

Karim followed her down the left-hand passage, feeling as bewildered as Nehshi had looked. Had this enterprising girl gotten a glimpse of the contents of his pack and seen it as an opportunity to get her hands on some valuables? He acknowledged a group of scribes as they passed, chattering among themselves, then tried to address the girl once they were out of earshot.

"Hey, kid. What's the deal, hey? If it's jewelry you want, I've got rings, bracelets—"

"Why do you want to see the temple records?" she broke in, her voice low. She kept walking, her gaze forward.

Karim hesitated.

"Tell me the truth or I'll scream," the girl added. "They'll find out you're not supposed to be here, and you'll get thrown out."

I'd be lucky to be thrown out and not killed, Karim thought, but decided not to say so. Still, he was impressed—the girl only looked slightly older than his little sisters, but she was clearly quite the shrewd customer.

"I need to find out about someone. An ancient Khetaran king named Setnakht. His name is on an ancient artifact I found in the

Red Lands, but a priest I met told me there was no record of a pharaoh by that name. He said that my only chance of learning anything about him was in the papyri stored at this temple, in the House of Life. So I came to see what I could find. That's it, all right? I don't mean anyone any harm. And I'm happy to offer you a gift in exchange for your assistance."

"I don't want any gifts."

Karim was at a loss. He stopped walking. "If you didn't want jewelry, then why did you help me? What do you want?"

The girl stopped and quickly scanned the corridor to ensure they were alone. Then she turned and faced him. Her expression was defiant, but he could see the fear in it too.

"The first day I got here, someone helped me too," she said. "Besides, I know who you are. And I want your help."

"What?" He studied her face, but he was certain he'd never seen her before. The girl's eyes were strange, too old for her young face. *How could she know who I am?*

He found himself unable to tear his gaze from her stare. Her eyes were deep dark wells that had no bottom, and they pulled at him like the invisible force that led him to secret places. He felt dizzy and strange.

Who is this Nefermaat?

An image flashed in his mind. A painting in a forgotten temple of a child being crowned with a feather by a cat-headed god.

"The oracle…" Karim murmured.

Nefermaat blinked, and the spell broke.

Karim stumbled back from her and shook the strange feeling away.

The girl tilted her head, looking quite catlike herself. "What oracle?"

It took Karim a few seconds to recover from his reverie. Was it possible that fate had brought them together, as Pasenhor had hoped it would? For what purpose? If he was going to find out, he had to tell her the truth—both to convince her to help him and because he had the feeling he was supposed to.

I can't believe I have to put my trust in yet another Khetaran, he thought miserably.

"The Oracle of the Lamb," Karim finally replied.

The girl paled. "The lamb?"

Karim nodded. "Painted in a Temple of Khnum, south of here. That same priest I mentioned earlier was its caretaker. He told me a little about it, something about water turning to blood and broken crowns…" He left out the part about the secret rising from beneath the earth. "The thing is, the painting showed a man who looked a lot like me, and a girl exactly like you. But I don't know how that's possible. The priest said it's more than a thousand years old."

With every word he said, the girl's fear sharpened. "This priest, did he happen to come to the palace many years ago, to tell the king of this oracle?"

Karim blinked. "Yes, he did, actually. But your king threw him out and told him not to return. And now… the priest is gone." He didn't elaborate on the manner of Pasenhor's death.

Nefermaat shook her head. "I don't understand," she murmured, mostly to herself. "Why me?"

A priest carrying a tray full of jars and linen passed by and glanced at them curiously. The two of them quieted, not wanting to be overheard.

When the priest had passed, Karim leaned forward. "I recognized you from the painting, but you've never seen it. Yet clearly you know something about all this. You said you know who I am. How?"

The girl fidgeted uncomfortably. "That wasn't exactly true," she admitted. "I don't know your name, or where you come from, or anything about you, really. I saw you in a vision."

"A *vision?*"

The girl quickly told him about her recurring dream. The similarity to the Oracle of the Lamb was too great for Karim to dismiss. Then she told him how she'd been brought to the temple to train to be a priestess.

"The vision I experienced here at the temple showed me four people, each of them somehow connected to the lamb. I was one of them, and you were too, just like you saw in the painting. The others and me were alone, but for some reason, you—" Here her brow furrowed in confusion. "You had two shadows."

Now it was Karim's turn to be afraid.

"Do you have any idea what that might mean?" Nefermaat asked.

Karim looked away. "No idea," he lied.

The little priestess seemed trustworthy, but he wasn't ready to tell her about the monster. If he did that, he'd have to tell her about the Jackals, the tomb robbing, maybe even Djet and Pasenhor's deaths. Would she still be willing to help him, knowing so much of what was happening was his fault?

Better to keep that to myself for now.

"Out of curiosity," Karim said, "The other two people from your vision—was one of them the princess?"

Neff looked even more amazed. "One wore a crown. I assumed that meant it was one of the royal triplets. I didn't know it was Sitamun." She paused. "The last one carried a scepter."

"What kind of scepter?" Karim asked. He racked his mind to remember what Pasenhor had called the weapon he'd seen in the painting. "Was it a… sack-ham scepter? Or something like that?"

Neff nodded vigorously. "Yes! A sekhem scepter! Exactly!"

Karim thought of the girl Raetawy and scoffed. "I think… I think I may have met her. Though the odds of such a meeting are too incredible to imagine."

"Where?"

"South of here in Sakesh, on a farm by the side of the river," Karim replied.

"'Take heed, Sakesh, Great House of Ra...'" the girl murmured to herself. "What did she look like?"

"A tall, strapping young woman. She offered me fish and some other supplies, and in exchange I gave her two pieces from my collection. A gold ring, and a small lion amulet."

"A lion... like Sekhmet," Neff mused.

"Exactly so."

"Maybe the meeting wasn't a coincidence at all."

Once again, Karim was reminded of the river's current, inexorably pulling him to some unknown destination.

"Well, sena," he said, "I've answered your questions. It's time for you to hold up your end of the bargain. I need to find out whatever I can about Setnakht. The old priest seemed to think he was the key to everything."

The girl nodded. "Fine. But we'll have to hurry. Most of the priests are taking their midday meal, so they'll only be out of the way for the next hour or so." She started to walk, then stopped again. "The only problem is, I'm not good enough at reading the sacred word to find what you're looking for so quickly. It would take me all day."

Karim ran a hand over his black stubble. Time was slipping away. "Isn't there anyone who can help us? Someone who'd be willing to bend the rules a little?"

For the first time, the girl smiled. "There is one person we could try."

Nefermaat led Karim to a large airy chamber, lit by sunlight that poured in through broad windows on the far wall. As they approached the room, Karim's senses were assaulted by the smell of fragrant spices and salt, so powerful that it made his eyes water. A table ran along one wall, covered with tools arrayed in orderly lines—jars of various sizes, grass brushes fastened with palm leaf, sharp flakes of obsidian, and two thin metal shafts—one with a sharp end, and one that looked like a very long spoon. In the corner of the room, Karim was surprised to see the same sacks that the long-faced vendor and his donkey had just delivered.

Natron for the embalmers.

He shivered, understanding that grim collection must be for acting out the Khetaran embalming ritual. It was exceptionally strange, particularly in contrast to his people's custom of burying their dead within the day and marking the grave with a bed of stones. But strange though it was, the practice was also familiar. He'd seen its results dozens of times inside the tombs he'd robbed. Still, coming upon the thousand-year-old mummies out in dark desert caves was one thing. Seeing an embalming performed in person was quite another.

A small, slight young man stood with his back to them in the middle of the chamber. He wore a long schenti belted at the waist and nothing more, and Karim could clearly see the bones of his spine as he bent over the stiff, desiccated corpse in front of him. It was the body of an elderly woman, held aloft by two pedestals. Her arms were crossed demurely over her chest, and her long, neatly braided gray hair curled over one shoulder like a cat's tail. Her skin had turned the color of earth and shone with a coating of fragrant resin. The man was carefully wrapping the woman with inscribed bandages, the roll unwinding as he passed it over and under her body with practiced precision. He was so focused on his task that he didn't notice their arrival.

"Kenna?" Nefermaat said softly.

The young man stopped and turned to look at them. He had

a severe, ill-proportioned face—the nose too big, the chin too sharp, the neck too long. He reminded Karim of a vulture hunching over carrion in the desert.

"Neff," Kenna said, the skin around his eyes crinkling with pleasure. Then, his gaze flicked to Karim and turned curious. "Who's this?"

"I'm sorry to disturb you," the girl replied. "But I was hoping you'd be able to help my friend. He needs to find information about an old king who seems to have been erased from the public records. A pharaoh named Setnakht. He thinks there might be mention of him in our House of Life."

Kenna gently set down his roll of wrappings on the dead woman's abdomen. "Your *friend*…" he said with obvious suspicion.

"Greetings to you," Karim said with a nod. "I've come a very long way to be here, and I'd deeply appreciate your assistance."

"A long way, yes," Kenna replied, studying him. "You've just come off the river. I'm sure your dog was pleased to be ashore after such a lengthy journey."

Karim was thunderstruck. Did everyone in this temple know who he was? But even Nefermaat seemed surprised.

"You must be quite keen to find answers here," Kenna went on, "Men of the Red Lands aren't usually fond of traveling by boat."

"How… how do you know all this?" Karim asked when he found his voice. "You are a priest—is this magic?"

Kenna's smile was a crooked thing that hung a little uncomfortably on his face. "Ah, no. There's no need for Heka when simple observation will suffice. Despite your Khetaran garb, everything about you indicates you're from the Red Lands. Your accent, your manner—even your facial hair. And your tunic tells me all the rest. Not only is it suffused with the scent of the river, it's also covered with quite a few of these." He walked up to Karim, plucked something from his tunic, and held it up to show him. A black dog hair. "The animal must be quite devoted to you, to leave so much of himself behind."

In that moment, Karim realized lying to this man would be a mistake. Clearly, Kenna would see right through it.

"Everything you say is true, sen. I know how your people view mine, so I suppose it would be natural for you to refuse to help. But I, too, have eyes to see, and I believe you have a fondness for this girl, this Nefermaat." He'd noticed the way the embalmer had brightened when she'd walked into the chamber. "She and I have only just met, but she's chosen to trust me. To help me. Perhaps, for her sake, you could do the same?"

Kenna didn't look convinced. "What is this all about, Neff?" he asked the girl.

"I don't know yet," the girl replied. "Not exactly. But I know it's important. And I promise, when I figure it out, I'll tell you everything."

"The origin of this king is an ancient mystery, sen," Karim added. "You may be the only one who can help me solve it."

To Karim's delight, the bait had the desired effect on the curious embalmer. Kenna cast a glance back at the nearly completed mummy behind him. "I suppose she'll keep until I return," he said to himself. Then he turned back to Karim.

"Fine, I'll help you. But I will be watching you very closely, my friend. Do not make me regret this kindness." Then to Neff he said, "I hope you know what you're doing."

Neff nodded and tipped her head toward the door. "We must hurry."

Kenna suppressed a grin. "All right." Despite himself, Karim could see the embalmer was excited about this little adventure. "Let's go find your missing pharaoh."

The House of Life was as murky as the embalming chamber was bright. Once he'd reached the bottom of the stairs leading down to it, Karim had to stand still for several seconds to allow his eyes to adjust. Windowless and lit only by oil lamps, the vast room contained one long reading table, and walls marked by hundreds of round holes with rolled papyri nested inside. Karim felt an immediate sense of familiarity in the room, but it took a moment for him to understand why.

It feels like a tomb, he thought. Not a tomb for bodies, of course. But for memories. Words. A place to preserve the wisdom and stories of days past, and to honor them with eternal life.

Neff quickly made her way across the chamber to a far wall. "All our King Lists are here," she said, "But without knowing the date of Setnakht's reign, it would take too long to read through them all. These cover thousands of years of Khetaran history."

Kenna folded his arms, his expression pensive. "It's a pointless exercise, anyway. If this king were on the main list, we'd already know about him. No, I think I know where to look."

He moved to the far end of the room, bringing an oil lamp along to light the way. They came to a wall that, unlike the others, had no openings in it whatsoever. Instead, it was painted with scenes of gods and battles and rituals, not unlike the ones Karim had seen on the outside of the temple itself.

Kenna began to explain. "My father once told me that scribes, when ordered to remove certain undesirable documents from the official record, would often stow them away in secret places, rather than burn them." He moved the oil lamp very close and swept his palm slowly across the painted wall.

"That's the thing about scribes," he continued, "They have a natural aversion to the destruction of scrolls—no matter what those scrolls might say."

Karim blinked. "I'm not following. This is… a wall."

"It *looks* like a wall," Kenna went on, his hands still searching. "When I first entered the priesthood and spent a lot of time here, this wall always intrigued me. Why create an intricate painting here? It's so dark that no one can see it.

"One day, when no one was watching, I spent some time investigating and found a little hidey-hole behind a detail in the painting. There was a papyrus inside, evidence of an illicit relationship between two palace officials, I believe. So, if there's one papyrus to be found..." His hand stopped on a cluster of lotus flowers. Then, painstakingly, he pulled a piece of the wall away, revealing a deep depression underneath. Kenna stared into it and chuckled. "Then there might be more."

Not a wall, but a door, Karim thought, with a peculiar sense that the patterns of the world were revealing themselves to him.

Carefully, the embalmer stuck his fingers inside the hole and removed a papyrus, brittle with age.

Neff hurried to join Kenna at the reading table. "You see?" she told Karim. "I told you he could help!"

Although the contents of the papyrus—which, according to Kenna, detailed forbidden curses and other such evil magic—were interesting, they had nothing to do with Setnakht.

"Let's keep looking," Kenna said. "If such information exists, this would be the most likely place to find it." Replacing the papyrus in the hole, the three of them set to searching for more hidden apertures.

Over the course of half an hour, they located three more hidden documents, but none of them held any of value to their search.

Karim stepped back from the wall and sighed. "There's nothing here, is there?"

Kenna sucked his teeth. "Perhaps not. Whomever erased this king from the records must have done a very good job. I'm sorry, but unless we find what you're looking for very soon, we'll have to abandon the search. The scribes will be returning to their posts before long."

Karim rubbed his face with his hands, frustration boiling inside him as he stared at the wall. *All this way for nothing!* What was he supposed to do now? Go to the pharaoh with his doomsaying? It didn't work for Pasenhor, and it certainly wouldn't work for a thief from the Red Lands, so—

He never finished the thought.

There, on the left side of the wall, he noticed a detail he hadn't seen before. Grabbing the oil lamp from the young embalmer, he shone its light on the strange figure painted in black and blue and gold: a god with the head of a strange doglike animal with tall ears and a downturned snout.

He felt a familiar tug in his chest, pulling him toward the image.

This is it, he thought. *I know it.*

He glanced at the others out of the corner of his eye. They were both on the other side of the room, checking the wall for more hidden compartments. He turned his back to them, so they wouldn't see what he was doing.

Leaning in close, he traced the line of the god's head with his fingertips and found a barely discernable edge. Working quickly, he dug at the crevice, chipping away a little of the stone so he could wedge his fingernail inside.

Finally, he was able to pry the panel out of the wall, revealing a small aperture beneath. With trembling fingers, he reached inside the hole and rummaged around until he found two ancient papyrus scrolls inside—as delicate as onion skin.

He opened the first scroll and saw that it was covered in Khetaran writing. However, instead of being written in the picture language that Karim had become familiar with from tombs and temple walls, the document was written in a flowing script, whose symbols looked like abstract versions of the birds, hands, and cups that he was used to. It was all nonsense to him, of course, except for a series of symbols he saw repeated more than once that seemed familiar: a folded cloth, a loaf of bread, a jagged line, a vulture.

The back of Karim's neck tingled.

The symbols for Setnakht.

His instincts, as usual, had been correct. Still, the document was useless unless Kenna or Nefermaat translated it for him. But the other scroll… as soon as he laid eyes on it, his Jackal instincts took over. He knew they'd never let him take the document, even if he'd found it hidden away inside a wall. But oh, he *wanted* it.

"Did you find something?"

Neff's voice interrupted his thoughts, and he startled.

"I did, sena," Karim replied, stealthily slipping the second scroll inside his tunic. Then he turned and presented the girl with the first papyrus. "It looks like a letter of some kind. I have a good feeling about this one. Can you read it?"

The priestess brought it to Kenna at the reading table and unrolled it, weighing down each corner with small smooth stones.

"What does it say?" Karim asked anxiously.

"It's written in the common script," Nefermaat said with excitement. "Even I can read this!"

"It *is* a letter," Kenna said, his voice hushed with fascination. "From one embalmer to another, oddly enough. Dated more than a thousand years ago." He scanned the words quickly. "You were right, my friend… It concerns your missing king!"

A thrill coursed through Karim's body as his suspicions were confirmed. "That is excellent news, sen—please tell me more."

"It names Setnakht as the third king in the sixth Khetaran dynasty," Kenna explained. "This was back when the pharaoh's capital city was in Low Khetara, not here in the north. I understand now why his reign was struck from the public record. Listen to this."

He cleared his throat and began to read.

"'To Onuriseref, Man of Anubis, my brother.

"'Today we have buried the heretic king, Setnakht, and put the scourge of his reign behind us forever. How we have all endured these past seventeen years is beyond consideration. I do not think even the greatest seers of Khetara could have predicted the breadth of his heresy—that he would reject our gods, our traditions, our art, and even abandon our great capital city in favor of building his own—all in service to the master of storms, his one true god. And though I have done Setnakht's bidding here in the temple, like you, I never accepted his teachings.

"'I have spoken prayers that burned my tongue, brother. But in my soul, I knew the king would die one day, and the nightmare would end. Thanks be to Ra, that day has come. How exactly he came to his fate, I do not know, nor do I wish to. The new king has not offered details, though some suspect Setnakht did not depart from this world willingly. All that matters to me is that he is dead. And I, myself, performed the funerary rites, with the help of my assistant, Wesir.

"'Between us, I always suspected Wesir of being an adherent to Setnakht's madness, but without evidence I had no choice but to continue to share my chambers with him. We performed the embalming together with all the proper rituals befitting a king—with one exception. It was a command from the new pharaoh himself. I removed all Setnakht's viscera and put them in the four jars, but I removed his heart too.

"'Are you amazed, brother? Perhaps it seems wrong to us, as Men of Anubis, but I was happy to do it. Happy to throw that black heart into the fire and curse his name. I asked myself: *Isn't it just what he deserves?* To travel all the way West, only to be turned away at judgment? To have his miserable ka wander the earth for eternity?

"'Heartless in life, heartless in death. It is right, brother. It is good. Rejoice now, for our long suffering is over.'"

There was a moment of silence among them after Kenna finished reading.

Karim had gone cold. He thought back to that evening by the fireside with Pasenhor, to the priest reading the engraving on the back of the lapis amulet he'd pried from Setnakht's coffin.

This is the heart of a king.

Could it be that the embalmer's assistant, who the writer of the letter suspected was one of Setnakht's disciples, had written that message in hopes it would give his king the one thing he lacked for his journey to the afterlife?

It sounded like superstitious Khetaran nonsense. Then again, Karim had seen impossible things since barging into that tomb, and the theory made a strange sort of sense. It explained why the creature had followed him halfway across the kingdom. Perhaps Setnakht wakened when Karim removed the amulet from his grave, and he'd been chasing him all this time… to get his heart back.

Not that it matters now, Karim thought. *The monster is dead.*

But just in case he wasn't… Karim knew what he had to do.

"He said that Setnakht was an adherent to the master of storms," he said to the young embalmer. "Is that—" Karim tipped his head toward the dog-headed god.

"Yes, that's Set—lord of the desert, god of chaos and war. Osiris's brother and murderer. Osiris is the divine king of Khetara and god of the underworld," Kenna replied. "I have read of a small cult who once worshipped Set, but nothing like this."

Kenna crossed his arms. "The letter seems to suggest that

the entire kingdom was temporarily converted to Set's worship. I'm amazed that such a significant event in history could be so effectively erased, but then..." A look of sadness passed over his face. "Khetara remains great in part by keeping its demons and its failures hidden in shadow."

Karim regarded the man with curiosity. There was something noble and elegant about the little embalmer, despite his strange appearance.

"We must go," Neff urged them. "The scribes will return at any moment."

Karim nodded. "Of course. I don't want either of you to get into trouble on my account. I owe you both a great debt."

"Perhaps you can repay it by telling me what this is all about?" Kenna said. "The fear in your eyes betrays you. What does a desert tribesman have to do with a thousand-year-old Khetaran king?"

Just as Karim thought he must come up with an answer, a pale crooked man lurched down the stairs and spotted them.

"My prince!" the man exclaimed. "I... was not aware you were visiting this afternoon. To what do I owe this honor?" His protuberant eyes flicked from Kenna, to the girl, to Karim.

Karim was sure he hadn't heard correctly. Had he mistaken the embalmer for someone else?

Kenna cleared his throat. "I apologize for not informing you, Chief Scribe," he said. "But I needed to access a specific embalming text, and Nefermaat was kind enough to help me find it. She's grown quite conversant under your wise tutelage."

"Oh!" the chief scribe said, preening. "Yes, the girl has potential—but, erm, who is this, if I may ask?" He tilted his chin at Karim.

Kenna walked to the elderly man and placed a slender hand on his shoulder. "He is my guest," he said, in a tone that bore no argument. "And now he must be on his way. Young Neff, will you walk him out? I wouldn't want him to get lost and end up somewhere he's not meant to be." Kenna raised an eyebrow at Karim.

Karim put on a face of pure innocence.

"Of course, Prince Bakenamun," Neff said, bowing her head. She turned to Karim. "Come along."

Speechless, Karim followed her to the door, passing the perplexed chief scribe and Kenna on the way. He touched a knuckle to his nose. Kenna pursed his lips and nodded, once.

When they emerged from the House of Life into the blazing afternoon light, Karim stopped and glanced over at the young priestess. "*Prince* Bakenamun?"

"The very one," Neff replied with a smile. "We were very lucky he was with us. The chief scribe wouldn't have let you and I go so easily."

Karim scoffed as they made their way toward the temple gate. The embalmer's eloquence and noble manner made a lot more sense now that he knew he was of royal birth. "You could have told me."

"Why should I?" Neff retorted. "You would have treated him differently if you knew, and that's why he's here and not at the palace. I thought you of all people would understand. You assumed Kenna wouldn't trust you once he figured out you were from the Red Lands, but he did. What assumptions would you have made about him, if you'd known he was a prince, and not some common priest?"

Karim chuckled. "You know, I have two sisters your age, and neither of them are as irritating as you."

"Only because I'm right," she retorted. "Besides, why should I be honest with you, when you're obviously still hiding something from me? You haven't even told me your name."

Curse this child, Karim thought. *She and her prince are mind readers.*

"You may call me the Jackal."

The girl rolled her eyes. "Really? I understand wanting to guard your name, but haven't I earned your trust?"

Karim sighed. "Very well, sena. You drive a hard bargain." He paused. "My name is Karim."

"Well, where are you going next, Karim? I heard the contents of that letter, as you did. It's interesting, but how does it help us understand anything about the Oracle of the Lamb?"

"The letter mentioned that Setnakht built his own capital city, apart from the Khetaran capitals," Karim replied. "I'm going to try and find it. There's got to be more answers to be found there, even if it's in ruins."

"But how?"

Karim thought about the item hidden inside his tunic. "I have my ways," he said cryptically.

"And what about me?"

Karim remembered the way he'd felt when he looked into the girl's eyes. The depth and the darkness contained there. "I think fate has placed you exactly where you need to be. Perhaps, if you wait long enough, your path will become clear."

He glanced up at the position of the sun. "I really must go. There is a dog by the river who probably thinks I'm dead by now."

"So you *do* have a dog!"

"He's not *my dog*. He's *a* dog."

Neff snorted. "Sure he is." She walked him to the gate, ensuring he wasn't hassled by any of the officials there.

"Goodbye," she said. "I have a feeling we'll meet again, Karim of the Red Lands."

Karim hitched his pack up onto his shoulder as they reached the open gate. Most of the vendors had gone, and the temple had resumed its normal business of tending to the gods.

"Maybe we will," he said to the young priestess, and went on his way.

21
RAE

The sun rose on a new day.

Rae woke at home in the late morning, bleary-eyed and sore. At first, her thoughts drifted to the normal rituals of bread and beer and cattle tending. But then she felt the heaviness of the winged armor she still wore and saw the sekhem scepter lying next to her, and it all came rushing back. She sat up abruptly.

We really did it.

Rae remembered cleaning the scepter at Omari's workshop, washing the blood from its paddle-shaped head, and from her hands and forearms too. She had a vague memory of walking home after that and collapsing onto her sleeping mat without even changing her clothes.

She scanned the house for her father, but he was already gone—out to care for the zebu, probably. She rubbed her eyes. Her body ached from the blows she'd received, and the wounds on her back throbbed. But the pain drove the cobwebs from her mind. The shock and guilt she'd felt the night before had dissipated with the sunrise, leaving a fresh emotion in their wake.

Triumph.

Maybe the tide is turning for Sakesh, she thought, staring out onto the bright, cloudless day. What she'd done had been extremely risky, but she'd made it back home, unscathed.

This is what Omari felt last night.

They'd grown up believing their world was solid and unchangeable, composed of varying degrees of injustice, whose inviolate rules had been decided by people older and wiser than they.

Last night they struck that world a heavy blow. And sure, the damage was only a crack. But that crack proved one very important thing.

A crack meant the world could be broken.

And what could be broken could be rebuilt. Remade.

Rae changed into fresh clothing and wrapped the armor and scepter inside her dark robes before stowing the whole bundle in the woven chest where she kept all her things, including the gold ring the Jackal had given her. Then she washed her face and was out the door, waving at her father before making her way to the city for her morning chores. She was eager to avoid any deviation from the norm.

Strange that Father didn't try to interrogate me before I left, she thought as she walked the river road. Maybe he'd been so tired from the farmwork that he hadn't noticed she was out late last night.

Or maybe, he simply didn't want to know.

There was something different about the city's energy that morning. Rae noticed it right away—there was a charge in the air, like during one of Khetara's rare lightning storms. She saw groups of women whispering to each other on the street, huddled so close together that the baskets of goods balanced on their heads bounced gently against one another, as if they were sharing secrets too. She saw bright-eyed vendors handing out fresh loaves of bread to the old soldiers who usually had to beg for their breakfasts. Was it possible that everyone already knew about the raid? News did travel fast in Sakesh... If so, it was clearly having quite an effect.

Maybe we accomplished more than just a blow to the High Khetarans, Rae thought. *Maybe we've given people hope.*

Rae picked up her daily beer and bread and was passing by the nomarch's estate on her way to the weavers' workshop when she saw the brewer coming out of the nomarch's main gate.

What is he doing there? she wondered, slightly alarmed. She hurried to catch up to him as he began walking back toward the brewery.

"The falcon sails across the sky," Rae said as she sidled up next to him.

The brewer cast a glance her way, his eyes narrowing when he saw who it was. "We shall meet him on the horizon," he replied in a low voice. "What do you want, Raetawy? We shouldn't talk out in the open like this."

"What did the nomarch want with you?" Rae asked. "I saw you coming out of his house."

The brewer blinked. "Oh, that was nothing. A delivery. Have to keep up appearances, you know."

Rae sighed with relief. "Thanks be to Ra. I was worried you'd been brought in for questioning. Did you hear anything important while you were inside?"

The brewer hesitated, then motioned for her to continue walking with him. "The nomarch was in a rage. I heard him say last night was a disaster and that he couldn't believe his men allowed it to happen on their watch. Every weapon except the ones his soldiers kept in their beds was either stolen or destroyed in the fire, and they have no clues to the identities of the attackers.

"In response, he's sending a troop of men downriver to Thonis to refit with fresh arms. They won't return for several days. Meanwhile, most of the other soldiers are either being treated for burn wounds or are repairing the damage to the building. It's a mess. A total mess."

"Just as Asim had hoped," Rae said, her mind buzzing.

The brewer nodded. "The old soldier had fortune on his side this time. I still think it was a foolish plan."

"Think what you like, it doesn't matter now," Rae remarked, stopping at the corner where they would part ways. "Don't you see? This new information—we have to tell the others about it. The Horizon should strike again while the Medjay are weakened and few in number. We must make another plan right away, before reinforcements return from Thonis. Maybe the weavers could pass along a message to Asim to arrange a meeting?"

The brewer scoffed. "You're lucky to be alive after what happened last night. Running another scheme so soon after the first is a fool's errand. You've had your fun playing rebel. If you were smart, you'd go home and focus on finding a good husband to take over your family land. Stick to what you're good at, Raetawy. Leave the rest of it to the men."

Rae's temper flared. "Perhaps you should stick to beer and cowardice. That seems to be what *you're* good at."

"I'm protecting my family," the brewer snarled. "Which is more than I can say for you. Your poor father, after everything he's been through—"

"Don't speak about my father."

"I'll say what I want to say, not that you'll listen." He waved a hand at her dismissively. "Go ahead, call your meeting. But don't say I didn't warn you."

Rae watched him walk away, her cheeks burning with anger. The brewer had a talent for saying just the right things to get under her skin. *You've had your fun playing rebel. Leave the rest of it to the men. Your poor father…*

Steaming, she made her way to the weavers' workshop. She hoped to see Tamerit, though it was unlikely they'd have the opportunity to talk. Still, after the kiss they'd shared the last time they were together, simply seeing her would brighten Rae's day after that infuriating encounter.

It was busy as usual inside the workshop, and filled with the hum of women's talk as they bent over their looms and spindles. Rae scanned the room for Tam, but instead saw someone unexpected in the corner, talking quietly with Mamet Mut.

"You bring up the cat, and it comes jumping," Rae said as she approached. "Hello, Asim. I was just talking about you."

Asim glanced over at her. His gray-speckled beard had grown unruly, and though there were bags under his eyes, they sparkled with excitement.

"Good morning, Raetawy."

Mamet Mut looked between them, curious. "You two know each other?"

"The girl has certain skills that have recently come to my attention," Asim said wryly.

"Too young for you," Mamet Mut scolded, misunderstanding Asim's meaning. "Besides, if the young carpenter had any brains, she'd already belong to him."

Rae smirked, choosing not to mention that her heart already belonged to someone else, as the older woman was called away to fix a snag on one of the looms.

"Have you spoken to Omari this morning?" she asked Asim. "Did your friend survive the night?"

"He's alive, thanks be to Ra, though we'll have to keep an eye on that wound. But he's a lot like you, Rae. Stubborn. We'll probably have to tie him down to get him to rest."

Relieved, Rae relayed the brewer's story. Asim's eyebrows rose at the mention of the nomarch sending many of his men downriver to resupply.

"This is our chance!" He bristled with excitement. "We can wrest power from the nomarch while he's vulnerable. By the time the men return, we'll have already struck another blow."

"That's what I thought too!" Rae exclaimed. "As soon as I heard, I came to tell Mamet Mut to pass a message along to you. I thought the Horizon should meet tonight to discuss plans for our next attack."

Asim chuckled. "Perhaps I underestimated you. Not a kitten after all, but a lioness! A few lessons in military strategy and you'll be battle-ready, Raetawy."

The mention of battle reminded Rae of something she'd been wanting to ask him since the night they met. "You were a soldier in King Rahotep's army, weren't you?"

The sparkle in Asim's eyes dimmed at the mention of the dead king's name. "I was." She thought he wasn't going to say more on the subject, but then he added, "A captain, in fact. My father was a member of the royal house."

"A captain…" Rae repeated. She stood a little straighter, her perception of the rebel leader altered. If the Great War had gone the other way, Asim would probably be living in the palace, admired and respected by all, and clothed in fine linen. He wouldn't be lurking in alleys, wearing dark, ragged robes. How strange the way life can change so quickly, Rae thought, depending on the direction fate was flowing!

The river will get its way, in the end.

Rae's fingers went to the Sekhmet amulet around her neck. Its protection had served her well the previous night. But that begged another question, and it was out of her mouth before she could consider whether she should ask it.

"How did you survive?" she asked. "Didn't Sematawy's men slaughter the entire royal guard when they besieged the palace?"

Asim's expression turned to a mixture of pain and regret.

"I'm sorry," Rae blurted. "I shouldn't have—"

"I ran away," Asim replied before she could finish. His lip curled as he spoke the words, as if they were still a fresh burden in his mind. "When they attacked, I knew it was hopeless. There was no time to assemble our forces or organize a proper defense. We were outnumbered, overrun. So I…"

He stopped and took a deep, steadying breath before continuing. "I told myself I wanted to survive so I could avenge them. The king. My brothers-in-arms. My family. But I knew in my heart those were just excuses. I ran because I was *afraid*."

Rae didn't know what to say. She felt terrible for reopening an old wound. She hadn't meant to cause the man pain. Around them, the weavers' friendly chatter hummed, disguising their conversation, but some of the women glanced over, their expressions curious.

Seeing the discomfort on Rae's face, Asim's expression softened. "I'm telling you this, Raetawy, because it's the reason I created the Horizon in the first place. For years, I had been living like one of those old soldiers you see on every street corner. Then one day, I realized that if I died and my heart was weighed against the feather of Maat, it would be so heavy with shame that I'd have no chance of salvation. I had to balance the scales. It won't bring my men back, it won't undo all the mistakes I've made, but… It's all I *can* do. And I have to try."

Rae spoke solemnly. "My father worked in the palace too, as a scribe. The High Khetarans took his hand, counted him among their slain enemies, but let him live. He's always wondered why he was allowed to survive when so many others were not."

"And what does your father think of your involvement with me?" Asim asked. "Have you told him about it?"

"Not exactly." Rae shrugged a shoulder. "But I think he knows. He wants freedom as much as the next person. He's just..."

"Afraid of you getting hurt?"

Rae nodded.

"The price of freedom is high," he said gravely. "Are you sure you're willing to pay it? I cannot promise you safety, you know that."

"I know," Rae answered. "And I hate worrying my father, but I'm doing this for him. He can't keep going on like this, pushing himself so hard to keep up with the king's unreasonable demands. He deserves better."

"We all do."

"It's like you said, we need to balance the scales. I know it's dangerous, but I still want to be part of it."

Asim reached out to squeeze her shoulder. "Your father is a lucky man. I would be proud to have a daughter like you."

Rae blushed.

Asim motioned for Mamet Mut to rejoin them. "The Horizon meets again tomorrow night at the Garden of the Dead," he told her. "Spread the word."

Rae watched him go, her heart feeling even lighter than it had that morning.

Not long after Asim left, Tam arrived, carrying a basket of flax on her hip.

Just who I wanted to see, Rae thought. Without a word, she rushed over to the weaver and grabbed her by the hand, pulling her to the back of the workshop where the rest of the flax and other materials were stored, and away from all those prying eyes.

"Hi, Rae," Tam said. She set the basket down on the floor, a little breathless from the journey. Her round cheeks shone with exertion, and wisps of her dark hair framed her face. Her beauty was effortless, her voice like water over smooth stones.

"I didn't know if I'd see you today," she went on. "I heard all about the—"

Before she could finish the sentence, Rae pulled her into a kiss. She pressed Tam's back into the wall, relishing the ample softness of her, the musky smell of her skin, the taste of her lips. When she pulled away, Tam looked at her with delighted surprise.

"What was that for?" she asked.

"Because today is a gift we might not get again," Rae said, feeling so light, she might just float away.

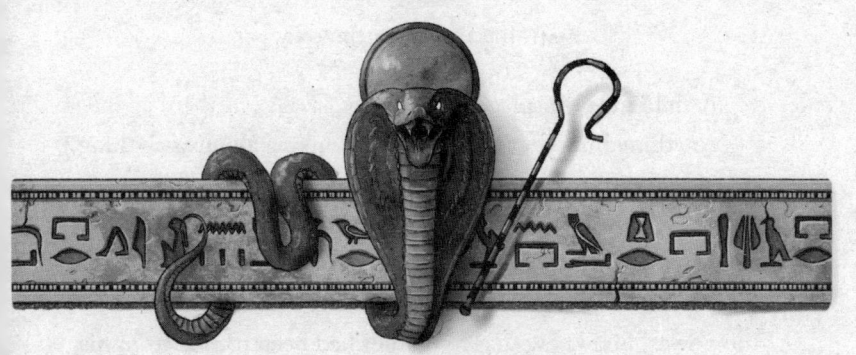

22
SITA

Sita sat on the steps of the palace swimming pool, her feet ankle-deep in the cool water. Nebet perched on a low stool behind her and brushed almond oil into Sita's hair with long, rhythmic strokes. Of all the women bathing, the middle-aged attendant was the only one clothed. The pool was cross-shaped, deep in the middle, with a shallow area for lounging on each side. It was surrounded on three sides by a shaded colonnade, and because it was situated at the back of the palace, offered a view of a desert so empty and still that one could almost forget that the city was mere steps away. The columns were painted with lush floral patterns in blue and green, and depicted images of naked women luxuriating in the water, almost identical to that afternoon's tranquil scene. Some of the king's lesser wives and concubines had gathered to spend the afternoon swimming and chatting quietly about trivial things.

New dresses.

Boat rides.

A child's toy, misplaced.

Anything but what they were all thinking about. Anything that might distract them from what was really going on.

They, like everyone else in the palace, were waiting.

After the king's collapse in the pleasure garden the night before, he'd been rushed to his chambers to be attended to by the priests. Sita knew that her father had been roused from his faint, but beyond that, there hadn't been any further news of his condition all through the night and morning.

Sita hadn't slept. She watched the other women chat but kept to herself. She was numb, exhausted, incapable of pretense.

Tadia was there, chatting amiably with one of the other, less-favored concubines. Despite putting on an air of solemnity, the girl hid a smile in the corner of her mouth. Sita got the feeling that Tadia was secretly quite eager for the opportunity to court a young, handsome new pharaoh. Sita wondered how many of the other women felt the same. Most of the lesser wives were at the pool too, with one notable exception.

Maet's mother.

Sita swallowed. Her mouth was bitter despite having eaten a whole plateful of sweet, fresh melon.

Was it worth it?

Part of her wanted to walk to the jar of wine sitting on a little table nearby and guzzle the entire thing, but ever since Maet fell sick, she'd been unable to drink another drop. The smell of it made her want to vomit. In fact, she couldn't bear the thought of pleasure anymore—carnal or otherwise.

She wanted to suffer.

She'd buried the truth, wrapping it in excuses and justifications, only to find that she'd buried an innocent child along with it. Something about her father's anguish over Maet's death, his own collapse right in front of her, all while she'd been thinking the most horrible, selfish thoughts, had given her new perspective. Her guilt was a physical presence now, a vulture that circled her. Because wherever she went—death seemed to follow close behind.

Her blood is on your hands.

Sita still believed in Mery's vision for Khetara, still believed his intentions were good—though she had started to wonder if, in fact, this had been the only way.

The sting of remorse made her wince.

"Oh, I'm sorry," Nebet said, thinking she'd caught a knot in Sita's hair. "I'll try to be gentler."

"No, no, it's nothing," Sita replied.

Misconstruing the true source of Sita's grief, Nebet laid a hand on her shoulder and squeezed. "Losing Maet so suddenly was a terrible thing. But you did everything you could to save her, Sitamun. Your actions got her home quickly, so that she was able to spend her final hours with her mother—"

"I'm going to swim for a bit," Sita said abruptly, no longer trusting herself not to cry.

"Wait, your hair!" Nebet objected.

But Sita had already risen to her feet and pushed off the step, diving into deeper water. She swam most of the length of the pool, then blew all the air out of her lungs, allowing herself to sink to the bottom. She sat there, the sun-warmed water soothing on her naked body, her hair hovering around her in a black, shimmering nimbus. The alternating blue and green tiles made her feel as if she were suspended in a multifaceted jewel, protected from the passage of time. She was tempted to stay forever in that glittering silence.

Eventually, though, her traitorous lungs cried out for air, and she had no choice but to push up from the bottom and back into the world. She tossed back her hair, sleek and shining, and wiped the water from her eyes.

Her mother strode toward her from the colonnade. One by one, the other women fell silent as they caught sight of Queen Bintanath's approach.

The queen stopped at the edge of the pool, the kohl lining her eyes unblemished by tears. "He's asking for you," she said to Sita, loud enough for all to hear.

A collective breath was released. Everyone knew what those words meant.

The pharaoh—King Amunmose III, Son of Amun, Sacred of Appearance, Lord of the Two Lands—was dying.

"Mery is gathering the viziers and will meet us there. But I must send a messenger to fetch Kenna." The queen gave Sita an appraising look and sighed. "Get dressed," she commanded, and turned on her heel.

Sita stared at her mother's retreating back until it disappeared around a corner. Then she swam to the set of steps at the other end of the pool and walked out of the water. Nebet rushed over, wrapping a linen towel around her body and placing sandals at her feet. Sita stepped into them, her chest suddenly heavy and tight.

"Shall I help you dress, Sitamun?" Nebet's voice was soft, like a caress.

"Thank you, Nebet," Sita heard herself say, "But I'd rather do it myself."

"As you wish."

Sita took the quickest route back to her quarters. The passages were eerily quiet and empty, and the few maidservants she did pass bowed their heads, not meeting her eyes. She was relieved when she finally reached her rooms. She was pushing her door covering aside, trying to remember if her simplest white kalasiris was clean, when she saw someone standing in her bedchamber. It was a short, stooped woman wearing a mottled green robe and a pair of rough leather sandals that barely contained her wide, flat feet.

Sita stopped in the doorway, blinking at the stranger's back as she stood examining the Hounds and Jackals board sitting on the table by the window. She had one of the jackal-headed pieces in her hand, and was moving it forward, one space at a time, until she finally placed it in the shen hole at the top of the board.

Sita stiffened. How had a peasant woman wandered into her rooms? She knew most of the guard were on call at the king's chambers, but this was ridiculous.

"All these games, they're much the same, aren't they?" the woman croaked without looking up from the board. Her voice was gravelly and slow, as if she had something stuck in her throat. "Snakes, hounds, jackals... a little strategy here, a little luck there, but they're all a race to the finish. I don't really like playing, myself, but I like watching. I like waiting to see who will win."

Sita cleared her throat. "Excuse me, but who are you? I don't know how you got in here, but I'm afraid you'll have to leave. I don't have time for visitors. I've been summoned." She grimaced, realizing how much she sounded like her mother.

"I'm an old friend," the woman said, unhelpfully, and looked up from the game board. Sita was shocked by the sheer unsightliness of the woman's face. Her mouth was too wide, and her eyes, which had a yellowish cast to them, bulged from her head. The worst of it, though, were the dozens of warts that covered her leathery, sun-weathered skin. She took in Sita's barely concealed dismay but didn't seem to be bothered by it. She didn't even blink.

"My two friends and I met your mother many years ago, on the night you were born. The queen was in quite a state without her nurses and priests, so we assisted her through her laboring. I came to pay my respects. And to see you."

Then, her entire face split in two—or rather, that's what it looked like, until Sita realized she was smiling. "The others wanted to come, but they were..." She paused, thinking, and at long last, blinked. "Busy."

Sita was amazed. She'd grown up hearing Nebet tell the story of her birth, and of the three strange dancers who'd appeared to help bring the triplets into the world. In the seventeen years since, no one had ever seen them again, or discovered who they'd been.

Until now.

In her stories, Nebet had described the three women in detail. There had been the fair one and the dark one, who looked like sisters. The fair one, Nebet told her, had been the first person to hold Sita after she was born. And then there was the short one with bad skin, who Sita had to assume was the same woman standing before her.

She must be ancient, Sita thought, and yet the woman moved without a hint of stiffness, and her unusual yellowish eyes were bright and lively.

The woman began examining other items in the room, arranging Sita's cosmetics palette and brushes in straight lines and tutting at an empty wine jar on the floor. Sita followed her, wanting to tell her to stop but sensing this woman couldn't be controlled. The woman found the white kalasiris Sita had been thinking of wearing and set it out, along with a pair of fresh sandals, before glancing at Sita expectantly.

Feeling as if she had little choice, she allowed the woman to help her dress.

"Does the queen know you've come?" Sita asked as the woman slipped the kalasiris over her head. "I'm sure she'd be pleased to see you after all these years."

"I came to see *you*," the woman replied, as if that was an answer. "I came to remind you during this difficult time..." She moved to smooth the strap of Sita's dress over her shoulder with small, dexterous hands. "That death is only the beginning."

Sita frowned. To say that the phrase was a timeworn Khetaran maxim would be an understatement. It was like saying, "The sun is hot." The concept of a glorious afterlife was central to Khetaran belief, beginning with the story of Osiris's resurrection and ascension to King of the Underworld. Why someone would make a special trip after nearly two decades to tell her this... well, it made no sense.

Maybe age has addled her mind, Sita thought. She'd seen it happen before. "I appreciate the message," Sita said carefully, "and I'm honored by your visit. But perhaps we could—?"

"My husband," the woman croaked on, undeterred. "He always said you were meant for great things."

"Your husband?" Sita asked. "Do I know him?"

The woman laughed, a low, wet chuckle. "Oh, everyone knows him! Or rather, he knows everyone. He's a potter—always at the wheel. He told me a story, a long, long time ago, about you and three others. Such an exciting story too! But he only told me the beginning, not the end.

"Isn't that awful? I scolded him, because I hate being teased. He said I should stop being so impatient." She snorted. "He doesn't understand. But you love stories, don't you, Sitamun? I bet you understand. I bet you want to know what happens next. Well, I have good news for you."

At that, she leaned in confidentially and said, "You get to decide how it ends."

How did she know I love stories? Sita wondered dimly. The woman spoke in riddles, yet there was an odd sort of sense in her words. Perhaps her husband was a seer of some kind?

You don't have time for this! an urgent voice reminded her.

"I'm very sorry," she said to the woman after she'd finished getting dressed, "But I really must go. My father is quite ill, and as I said before, I've been summoned to his bedside."

"Ah, yes, your father," the old woman said, nodding. "For his sake, I hope that he leaves this world with a light heart, as we all should." She smiled up at Sita meaningfully, as if she knew much more than she was letting on.

"One thing before I go," she added. "Do not forget, Sitamun, that you are She Who Knows All the Names. Your words have power. When the time comes, remember that the word is the deed."

A chill settled over Sita at the ugly woman's portents. She backed toward the door, trying to remain cordial. "Yes, I'll do that. I'm, ah, sure Nebet would love to see you... She's probably still at the swimming pool, if you're interested."

The old woman clapped her hands in delight. "Ah! I love a good swim."

"Good," Sita said, gesturing toward the door. "I can show you the way if you'd—" She started to lead the old midwife out of her chambers, but when she turned to hold back the doorway drapery, the woman was nowhere to be seen.

She must have slipped out the other door while my back was turned, Sita guessed. *Though I'm surprised she could move that fast.* Hopefully she wouldn't wander into trouble with the guards, but they had better things to do than worry about a harmless old woman roaming the halls.

And so did she.

By the time Sita made it to her father's bedchambers, both Mery and Kenna were standing by his door. They stood a distance apart—Mery bedecked in his finest scarlet schenti and blouse, cinched at the waist with an obsidian-encrusted leather belt; and Kenna, unadorned, clothed in a simple white tunic. They were like the sun and the moon, her brothers, rarely seen together, yet unable to escape each other's orbit.

"Sister," Mery murmured in greeting, his eyes shining.

"Sitamun," Kenna said curtly.

Sita stepped into the space between them. "So this is what it takes to bring the three of us together?"

"Who better to share my sorrow with than with my beloved siblings?" Mery said, in a tone so artless Sita almost believed him.

Kenna crossed his arms, but said nothing.

A moment later, Queen Bintanath emerged from the king's chambers. "Good, you're all here. He doesn't have much time." She scrutinized each of them in turn—first Mery, then Sita, then Kenna—her favor dimming as she went.

"For gods' sake, Kenna, is this the best you've got to wear? We'll have to commission something decent for the coronation."

"The king has moments to live, Mother," Kenna said mildly. "Forgive me if fashion wasn't my primary concern."

The queen looked annoyed at this rebuke, but also a little pleased.

She adjusted a pleat on Kenna's tunic. "Perhaps there's some fire in you after all, Bakenamun." Then she beckoned them all forward. "Hurry now. Your father is waiting."

Mery went first and Sita followed, pushing through the heavy curtain with Kenna trailing behind her. The air in the chamber was thick with incense, and sunlight streaked in through blousy curtains, striking the clouds of smoke and giving the room a blurry, dreamlike quality. Everything that Sita remembered cluttering the room—jars of carob tree extract and propolis resin from the palace beehives, used but not useful; plates of food, untouched and swarming with fruit flies; foul-smelling bowls strategically placed by the bedside—had been removed. All the messy remnants of life had been cleared away to make room for death.

Sita felt a great weight on her chest as she approached the bed where her father lay, gray and fleshless. They'd dressed him in the same river-blue robes he'd worn at his coronation, the ones embroidered with golden fish with malachite eyes. The robes had been made to fit his once robust frame, but now he was drowning in its folds. His thin, berry-black hair had been hidden once again beneath a striped headdress. His eyes were closed, and for an instant, Sita thought he might already be dead. But he stirred at the sound of their approach, his unfocused gaze lost before it found them.

"Well," he said hoarsely. "Whoever said the wicked live longer was grossly mistaken."

Sita put one hand over her mouth to catch the sob rising in her throat. He was a neglectful parent, a feckless king, and a lech of the highest order, but...

He's still my father.

The king beckoned them closer. Mery and Sita moved to kneel on one side of the bed, Kenna on the other. The king glanced at them each in turn, a sense of wonderment on his withered face.

"My children," he said with a chuckle. "I remember the night of your birth like it was yesterday. What a surprise that was! Not a single priest foresaw that there would be three of you. For all their visions and their Heka, it took three dancers from Amun-knows-where to predict your arrival."

Sita nodded. "One of them is here in the palace, Father. She said she came to pay her respects."

The king's eyebrows shot up. "You'll have to tell Nebet. She was convinced the women were goddesses incarnate, come to earth to usher in a new dynasty." He scoffed, then paused. "It's a nice sentiment, and believe me, I ran with it. It was a great story to tell those fools who challenged my place on the throne. Three children born to three goddesses! A triad within a triad! I couldn't have written it better myself. Still, one would think that Isis, Nephthys, and Heqet would have better things to do than attend to a squalling woman during a rainstorm."

Sita sat back on her heels, remembering. Nebet sometimes referred to the three women as dancers, but other times, she had told Sita that they were three goddesses. *Isis was the fair one, Nepthys the dark one, and Heqet was the short one with the...*

She gasped.

With the warts.

Heqet... compared to Isis and Nepthys, she was a lesser-known goddess, but Sita remembered her tutor explaining she was the frog-headed goddess of fertility and rebirth. Heqet was also the consort of Khnum, a god represented either as a ram-headed man or occasionally, a lamb, and otherwise known as the Divine Potter, who formed man out of clay on the Great Wheel.

Sita thought about the strange old woman in her bedchamber and what she'd said about her husband.

Everyone knows him! Or rather, he knows everyone.

He's a potter—always at the wheel.

The earth tilted sickeningly beneath her.

It couldn't be... could it?

"You'll need to wrangle the viziers," the king was telling Mery as Sita snapped back to attention. "They're a bunch of nags. They'd tie up this kingdom in endless bureaucracy if given the chance."

The king paused, his breath labored and shallow. "Take one of my lesser wives as your own—perhaps Tadia. She's young and ripe, she'd suit nicely for your Great Wife." He patted Mery's hand. "Rule as I have, son, and Khetara will continue to flourish."

"You have taught me much, Father," Mery replied. It sounded like a compliment, but Sita was sure he didn't mean it that way.

Then, the king turned to Kenna.

"Bakenamun, you'll oversee the embalming ritual and the completion of my tomb. I'm depending on you to get it right. Only the best of everything, understand? Sematawy's should look like a pauper's tomb compared to mine."

Kenna frowned as if he'd tasted something bitter, but he nodded. "As you wish."

Satisfied, King Amunmose licked his dry, peeling lips with a pale tongue. "You know," he muttered, his voice heavy with irony. "We spend so much of our lives thinking about death, imagining how glorious it will be when we reach the Duat, we never stop to remember that no one has returned to tell us what it's really like!"

He laughed and was seized with a horrible fit of coughing. When it finally abated, his eyes were wet and red.

"Let me tell you," he gasped, "from someone standing at the border between here and there... that dying is absolute *shit*." He grinned. Mery was the only one who smiled with him.

"What about me, Father?" Sita asked. She knew she should stay quiet, but she couldn't help herself. "What do you wish me to do?"

King Amunmose shifted his head to look at her. He lifted a skeletal hand to caress her hair, as one might admire a flower in a garden. "Marry well."

Sita waited for more, but none came. And just like that, her fragile grief was smothered before it could take its first breath.

"I'm... tired," King Amunmose murmured, his voice weaker than before.

On cue, both Mery and Kenna stood.

Kenna bowed his head. "May your heart be light, and your westward journey be swift, Father. All of Khetara will join in celebrating your ascension to the House of the Gods."

Kenna's words echoed in Sita's mind.

May your heart be light.

A light heart was free of sin. Of guilt. Of shame.

She couldn't know the weight of her father's heart, but her own felt as heavy as a stone.

Without another word, Kenna turned on his heel for the door. Mery went to follow but stopped when Sita spoke up suddenly.

"May I have one more moment with you, Father?" she asked. "Alone?"

The king made a low sound. The visit had exhausted him.

Mery shot her a look. *What are you doing?* he mouthed.

She ignored him.

"I won't be long," she assured the king.

"Neither will I, Sitamun," King Amunmose murmured. With a sigh, he waved Mery out.

Mery hesitated, eyes flitting from Sita to their father and back, before departing.

"If you aren't satisfied with the Tashan prince," her father said before she could begin, "surely your mother can find—"

"This is all my fault," Sita blurted, the words rushing out like water from a burst dam. "I could have stopped this. I could have saved you, but I didn't."

Her father's breathing had become more labored.

"It's not your fault, child," he wheezed. "Only the gods themselves could have—"

"No, you don't understand," she said.

This is your last chance. Unburden your heart before it's too late.

Sita squeezed her eyes shut, a toxic mixture of love and hatred for her brother and her father swirling inside her. She'd do it, but she was too much of a coward to meet his eyes and see her betrayal break what was left of his spirit before he died.

She listened to the sound of her father's breathing grow quiet as he waited for her to speak.

She kept her gaze trained on his hands and the golden ring he always wore.

"It was the honey cakes," she finally said, her voice flat. "Mery has been poisoning them, and I knew about it."

Her father didn't gasp, didn't cry out in horror. So she took a deep breath and told him everything.

When it was over, she felt empty. Lighter.

"I'm so sorry, Father," Sita said into the silence, her voice a little stronger. She laid her hand on his—and found it cold. She glanced up at his face. "Can you ever forgive me?"

The king stared back at her, unblinking, his pupils dilated. Sita searched his expression, desperate for a hint of shock, horror, rage—anything.

But he was dead, and her chance at forgiveness had died with him.

How much did he hear? she wondered. *All of it? None?*

She'd never know.

The reign of King Amunmose III was over.

May he live forever in the West.

Sita stepped through the curtain, still reeling. In the corridor, the crowd had grown. The viziers had arrived, as well as palace officials and a few of the lesser wives. When she appeared, they all stopped talking and turned toward her.

Sita wished with all her heart that the duty would have fallen to someone else. Anyone else. Her hands shook.

You are a princess, said a voice in her mind. *Try to act like one*. The voice was her mother's, and it was already disappointed.

Sita straightened her back, and when she finally spoke, she relayed the message as simply as she could.

"He's gone."

Her words struck the crowd like a lightning bolt. The reaction was immediate.

"Send messengers to every nomarch in every city," the queen told the viziers, while a bevy of priests pushed past Sita into the king's chamber. Guards sent unnecessary onlookers on their way and swarmed around Mery—their new charge.

Kenna stood to the side, his long hands clasped in front of him, his face settled comfortably into mourning. He caught Sita's gaze, and for an instant, she was a little girl again, crying as Kenna helped her bury a dead bird she'd found in the garden. He'd always been a strange, quiet boy, but he'd always been kind. He treated even the smallest creatures with respect—in life and in death. Mery had never understood him; the brothers were too different to relate to each other in any way. But Sita understood them both. Until Kenna left them for the priesthood.

We were close once. What happened to us?

She wanted to go to him, fall into his arms, and confess. She wanted him to tell her how to begin to fix all that she'd broken. But the last time she went to him, he had scorned her and turned her away. Perhaps she deserved that. Still, as she looked at Kenna across the bustling crowd, her own sorrow reflected in his face, she wondered if he didn't wish he could go to her too.

Suddenly, a hand was on her shoulder and lips at her ear. "Come with me."

Seeing his brother at Sita's side, Kenna grimaced and turned his back on them all, walking briskly back the way he had come.

"Wait," Sita said, but Mery's grip was firm as he pulled her away.

A sob rose in her throat, but she forced it down and allowed Mery to lead her.

They'd only gone a few steps before the head guard caught up to them.

"My prince," he said, "I must insist that you come with us. There is much to attend to, and we must ensure your safety."

Mery stopped. "You forget yourself," he said sharply.

A momentary hush fell over the gathered. Mery's normally

charming, cajoling tone was gone, replaced by something fearsome that had been waiting for its time to emerge.

"I may not yet wear the crown, but you are speaking to your future king. Our father is dead. You will give us a moment to grieve."

The guard's throat bobbed, and he bowed his head. "Of course, my prince. Please forgive me."

The guard stood pinned by the prince's imperious glare, until Mery released him with a dismissive wave.

Mery led Sita to a quiet corner and folded her into a tight embrace. It was exactly what she'd wanted from Kenna, but she didn't feel comforted. It felt like it wasn't for her benefit, but for the people watching. As soon as Mery bent to whisper in her ear, she knew her instincts were correct.

"You told him, didn't you?" His hand cupped the back of her head, his touch both tender and predatory. "You told him our secret. Before he died."

Sita's breath caught in her throat, the sound proving her guilt just as surely as words could.

"Just couldn't keep your mouth shut, could you?" Mery snapped. "Not that it matters now. But I'll remember this, Sitamun. I'll add it to the list of all your other *indiscretions*."

He smoothed the back of her hair with his hand, like one might stroke an animal. "You'll need some work before you'll make a fit queen. Lucky for you, I'm up to the task."

Sita went rigid.

"What are you talking about?" she whispered.

Mery scoffed. "Did you really think I'd let you be sold off to some foppish prince from Tash? Did you really think I loved you so little?"

What is he suggesting? He can't possibly think that I would, that we would…

"Y-you can't," she stammered. "I'm your sister, Mery. No one does that anymore, not for a thousand years!"

He pulled back to look at her, his beautiful face inches from hers. "But that's exactly why we *must*." he purred. "Khetara lost its soul when it rejected the old ways. It's up to us to bring them back, to restore our kingdom's prominence—and *you* are part of that, Sitamun. Of all the women in the land, your blood is the purest, the closest to the divine. The priests must bend their noses to papyri to learn the ways of Heka. But not us. You and me, our very flesh is godsflesh. We have magic in our veins. Don't you see? We belong together—it's our birthright. Just as Osiris had his sister-wife Isis, and Set had Nephthys, so will I have you. My twin. My mirror."

His arms around her were suffocating. He was so close that the only air she could draw came from his lungs as he narrated her fate. She had no choice but to breathe it in.

"Once I am crowned, Khetara will have a god-king once again, in name and in action. This kingdom has been crumbling while Father buried his face in cakes and concubines."

His lip curled in disgust, but only for a moment. Then he smiled, his hand moving from the back of her head around to her face, his fingers soft and fragrant. "No more. With me on the throne and you by my side, Khetara will be powerful once more. You'll see."

He let her go, then strode away, off to attend to the multitudinous duties of a king-in-waiting, to plans and decisions and fittings and ceremonies and condolences followed by pledges of allegiance. He gathered a crowd around him as he went, guards and viziers and officials swarming like moths to a flame.

Sita watched him go, and her mind traveled once more to the night of the Bast Festival. She thought of her prayer to the goddess, the one she'd made instead of asking for her father's salvation. Not that it would have mattered. Even Bast could not have saved the king.

It had become abundantly clear that Bast wasn't going to answer her prayer either.

Sita wasn't free. She never would be.

The net had snapped shut around her.

23
NEFF

Neff had never known such quiet.

Since the king's death the night before, it was as if a mourning shroud had been thrown over the Temple of Amun. Priests went about their daily tasks, speaking in whispers, their heads bowed as they moved from place to place. The Wabet had disappeared from the women's chambers in the early hours to begin the lengthy preparations for Amunmose's funeral ceremony, which would take place in exactly seventy days. Even the birds in the pleasure garden seemed to sing in muted tones.

Through her reading, Neff had learned that the time between the death of a pharaoh and the crowning of a new one was fraught with peril. The currents of time continued to flow, pulling Khetara toward an uncertain future. But until the prince's coronation, there was no man at the prow, no one to navigate the kingdom through dangers that might lie ahead.

Perhaps this was why the priests were so hesitant to raise their voices. Perhaps they feared attracting the attention of evil forces that roamed the land, emboldened by the king's death.

In the silence, Neff daydreamed about home. She imagined waking up on her mat, going upstairs, and seeing her mother sweeping the sand off the roof in the morning sun. She imagined sitting down at the breakfast table and telling her father that she'd met the king. That she'd been summoned to the palace, and he'd asked her to interpret his dream.

I knew he was going to die, she imagined saying to her father, *but I was afraid to tell him. So I lied. I lied to the king and now he's dead.*

She pictured the horror on his face. The disappointment.

Her father's words before she boarded Bast's boat echoed in her mind. His voice and the voices of the gods melded together into a great cosmic condemnation.

Nefermaat.

Perfect justice.

That's you.

You're going to make us proud.

Every word stung like vinegar in an open wound.

Master Montuhotep and the chief scribe were busy with preparations for the king's funeral and Prince Meryamun's coronation, so Neff was excused after her daily tasks were complete. With the day to herself, she found herself back in the women's quarters, alone. After washing her hands and face in the basin, she knelt on her sleeping mat and prayed, sending her plea to the goddess who had brought her to this place.

"Help me, Bast. What do I do now? How can I make it right?"

She waited for a sign, but none came.

After a while, she moved to get up and heard a couple priests coming down the hallway.

"Thank Amun the natron delivery came yesterday," one said as he passed. "The embalmers will surely need it now."

Neff blinked. She'd seen the natron delivery—the man from her vision, Karim, had snuck into the temple with the natron vendor and his donkey. News of the king's collapse and death had pushed the events in the House of Life from her mind, but now they came rushing back.

The mysterious pharaoh named Setnakht. The Oracle of the Lamb.

Ancient forces had drawn her to this place, and then had drawn Karim to her. When she'd first seen him in the courtyard, she'd felt it—like an invisible cord pulling them together. She'd felt a similar sensation when she'd seen Princess Sitamun the night of the Bast Festival but hadn't realized its importance at the time.

One wore a crown...

If she, Sitamun, Karim, and the Sakeshi farm girl he'd mentioned were the four figures in her vision, then the oracle was truly coming to pass.

A deep dread grew within her. It spoke of events beyond her knowledge, events that had already been set in motion.

It was all too much to keep inside. She needed to talk to someone, to stop feeling so alone. After giving thanks to Bast, she left her rooms to seek out the only person she could trust.

Kenna was easy to find. All Neff had to do was follow the sound of the commotion to the embalming chamber, where his voice rose above the others, its volume jarring among the overwhelming silence. Curious, she crept to the open doorway and peered around the edge, hoping to get a peek inside without being spotted.

The prince stood facing half a dozen Sem priests, his face flushed and his arms akimbo. Neff had never seen him that way before.

"Please, my prince," the oldest Sem priest said, his expression pained. "Our only desire is to assist you with the king's embalming ritual. You know as well as anyone that this isn't a one-man job, and for a *pharaoh*, it's—"

"He's not merely the pharaoh," Kenna said, his voice cutting through the other man's like a blade. "He is my father. No one shall touch him but me. Do you understand? This is my duty. I must do it alone."

The elder priest's shoulders fell. "As you wish," he said, and gestured for the others to follow him out.

Neff leaped back from the door and slid behind a pillar until all the Sem priests had gone. In the wake of their departure, silence washed back over the hall—so completely that Neff began to wonder if Kenna had gone with them. But then he spoke.

"You can come in now, Neff."

She emerged from her hiding place. "How do you always know?" she asked as she entered the chamber.

Kenna stood in the center of the room, his head bowed over a familiar form that lay across the two stone pedestals where the old woman's corpse had once been. It had been obscured by the crowd of priests when she'd first looked in, and seeing it made her heart leap into her throat.

The king.

Neff stopped, covering her mouth with one hand.

Amunmose's thin, ravaged body was naked aside from a fine linen shroud draped over his waist. The last time she'd seen his face, it had regarded her with hope, begging for a message from the gods that he felt had abandoned him. She'd offered him lies, and now he was gone.

"I'm so sorry," Neff blurted. It was both a condolence and an apology.

Kenna looked up at her, his eyes red-rimmed but dry.

"Thank you. We weren't close, my father and I," he said, his gaze drifting back down to the body. "But unlike Mother, he never objected to my decision to join the priesthood. Father thought people should do what they wanted." He paused. "*He* certainly did. Perhaps putting desire over duty made him a poor king, but… I owe him this final honor for allowing me my freedom."

He went to the table where his tools lay waiting.

"I should let you be alone," Neff said, taking a step back toward the door.

"No, wait." Kenna sighed and turned, and Neff noticed just how tired he was. He must not have slept much since the king's collapse the night before.

"The priests' company would have been burdensome. Yours would be a comfort." He pressed his lips together in a thin line. "I should warn you, though. The embalming ritual isn't for the fainthearted. Do you think you'll be all right?"

Neff bit her lip. Kenna was a prince. He could have commanded her to stay if he wished it—but he wasn't commanding. He was asking. And despite her apprehension at witnessing a harrowing process she'd only heard tales of, Neff couldn't abandon her adopted brother in his time of need.

"Of course I will," she replied.

Kenna studied her face, and seemed to reconsider. "No—I cannot ask this of you. You're just a girl, and this… it's important and necessary, yes, but it's very unpleasant if you're not comfortable with the dead."

"I want to stay," Neff assured him. She sounded more confident than she felt. In truth, she was already feeling queasy, but she was determined to be there for him. "I'll learn so much by helping you. It can be… part of my education as a priestess."

Kenna brightened. "Yes, that's very true," he said, taking to the idea. "It *is* extremely illuminating. Not simply the ritual itself, but what it can teach us about the body and how it functions. I'd be happy to explain the process as I go, if you think it would be useful."

Neff swallowed. "I do."

"Then let's begin."

Kenna seemed more relaxed as he returned to his tools and assumed the role of teacher. He plucked the long pointed metal shaft from the table and placed it on his father's chest. Neff forced herself to move closer as he tilted the king's head back and braced it with a small curved piece of wood.

"First we must extract the organ inside the skull," he said, taking the shaft in his hand. "It's essential that all moisture be removed from the body to prevent putrefaction. The dead must retain their physical bodies in the Duat, so it's our duty to make sure they are perfectly preserved."

With that, he inserted the sharp end of the shaft into the king's nostril until it could go no farther. Then, with a swift, forceful motion, he forced it through with a dull *crack*.

Neff made a small squeak as she felt her breakfast threaten to reappear.

Kenna glanced up at her. "All right?"

"Fine," Neff replied weakly.

Kenna nodded and resumed his work. He moved the shaft around in slow circles inside the skull before sliding it back out, slick with dark blood. Next, he set the tool back on the table and picked up the shaft with the spoon end.

"Now that the organ has been carved into smaller pieces," Kenna said, "we can remove it without damaging the skull."

Neff watched as he reinserted the shaft into the king's nostril and began systematically pulling out spongy globs of gray matter with the spoon, dumping it into a clay bowl with horrible wet noises.

"I thought…" she managed, swallowing the bile rising in her throat. "I thought you were supposed to preserve everything."

"Yes, everything except that." Kenna grimaced as he attempted to scoop out the last bits of flesh. "The organ inside the skull is of no use. We remove and preserve the lungs, stomach, liver, and intestines in Sons of Horus jars—only the heart remains inside, to take with him on his journey West. It's as the embalmer said in that old letter we found in the House of Life. At the moment of judgment, the heart is weighed against the feather of Maat, and if it's lighter than the feather, he is welcomed into the Duat. Without a heart, he cannot face judgment and is doomed to wander the earth for eternity."

"Is that next? Removing everything except the heart?" she asked, unable to keep the dread from her voice.

"Yes," Kenna replied, wiping a sheen of perspiration from his brow as he finished the extraction. He set the bloody tool aside and took up a clean cloth. Gently, he moved his father's head back to a resting position and began cleaning the spattered gore from his face. As he did this, Neff saw something change in Kenna's serious expression. A subtle flare of the nostril, a quiver in the corner of his lip that betrayed his grief.

He must have sensed her watching him, because he cleared his throat and tossed the soiled cloth in the bowl with the rest of the viscera. He turned away, leaning on the table with both hands for a moment before coming back to the body with a shard of obsidian.

"Now we open the abdomen and remove the vital organs. Once that's done, we pack the body with natron and wait seventy days for the preservation process to be complete." He glanced over at Neff, his emotions roiling just under the surface. "Are you still with me, little sister?"

Neff didn't want to see more. In fact, she wished she could

wipe what she'd already seen from her memory. But staying felt like the first step in making amends for what she'd done. If she was ever to find forgiveness, she'd have to be brave. She'd failed the king; the least she could do was be there for his son.

"I'm with you."

Kenna gave her a crooked smile and nodded. Then he lowered the blade to the left side of his father's belly and pierced the soft flesh. He dragged the blade down, slicing the skin open like Neff had seen fisherman do at the market. He cut all the way to where the cloth covered his father's waist.

"There," Kenna said, inspecting the incision. What little blood oozed from the cut was torpid and dark. The prince took a deep breath and pushed his left hand through the opening.

"Bring me a bowl," he grunted, indicating one of the clay vessels on the table. "The largest one, please." Neff scurried over to retrieve it and bring it to his side. A moment later, Kenna began pulling a long pink tube from the body, more and more of it, until it almost overflowed the bowl.

"Another bowl," he said, and reached in again, this time extracting a thicker curved organ, cutting it free from its bonds with the obsidian blade, and depositing it into the second vessel. Neff held her breath as she transported the viscera back to the table, trying desperately not to inspect its contents too closely.

What emerged next was a massive cone-shaped organ, nearly too large to fit through the incision. It was an angry, violent-looking thing—dark, brownish red, and unexpectedly heavy. Kenna gave it a curious look before depositing it into the bowl.

"What's wrong?" Neff asked him.

Kenna shook his head. "Probably nothing. Strange, though…" He turned back to the body, steeling himself. "One more," he murmured, and reached deeply into the body, nearly up to his shoulder.

With effort, he pulled out two more spongy organs, one identical to the other. They were surprisingly light in comparison to the one before, and marred by several odd growths on their surface. Curiosity overwhelming disgust, Neff peered closer. The growths reminded her of a fungus that sometimes grew on old food left too long in the dark—whitish and soft and edging toward rot.

"Kenna…" Neff said as the prince got up to wash his arm in a basin of clean water. "What is that?"

Kenna inspected the growths, his expression shifting from interest to suspicion.

"Let me see," he said, and brought the bowl over to the other three lined up on the table.

He examined each one in turn, growing more agitated with every passing second. Taking up his blade, he sliced the curved organ open and poured its contents onto a shallow dish. What came out was a grayish-brown mash.

The smell of it nearly made Neff swoon, but she gripped the edge of the table and forced herself to focus.

Kenna sniffed the gray pulp gingerly, and then set it down. His expression thoughtful, he put both palms flat on the table, leaned forward, and cursed.

Neff stood next to him, her earlier dread growing stronger. "What is it?"

Kenna took a deep breath. "About a year ago, a man was brought in for embalming after it was revealed that his wife had poisoned him. She'd taken her time about it, adding a little bit of the stuff to his dinner each night until he'd sickened and died. She almost got away with it, but had been betrayed by a neighbor who'd overheard her discussing her plans with her lover. The woman had hoped to run away with him after her husband's death.

"Once she was confronted with the truth, the wife confessed

and was executed, and after that, her husband's family paid for a proper embalming. It was one of the first rituals I performed myself, so I remember it very well.

"During the extraction, I noticed curious things about the man's viscera. His liver, for example"—here, Kenna indicated the heavy dark organ—"was swollen and much larger than normal. Much like my father's."

Neff became very still. *No*, she thought. *Please, don't let it be true*.

Next, Kenna pointed to the spongy organs. "I also noticed that the man's lungs were spotted with decaying growths, much like these here. And the food inside his stomach had an odd smell that didn't match what he'd eaten that day." He indicated the gray mash—the contents of the king's belly. His last meal.

"That is the half-digested remains of a honey cake," Kenna said. "But the smell is more like garlic. It's not right, Nefermaat. None of this is right."

Neff stumbled back. "Amun forgive me," she whispered.

Kenna did not seem to hear her. His long fingers, the nails still encrusted with blood, curled into fists. "I can't believe I'm saying this, but I don't think my father died from some plague or curse. I think he was murdered."

Neff closed her eyes, the sick feeling in her stomach intensifying as the words she hadn't said came tumbling from her lips. "'He is betrayed by those closest to him. He will die at the hand of one, while the other bears silent witness.'"

Kenna whirled on her. "What did you say?"

Neff felt a sudden surge of fear, but knew she had to tell him the truth. "When your father called me to the palace to interpret his dream, that was the message I received. But I was too afraid to tell him what I saw, so I told him something else. I didn't know this would happen. I didn't think anything I said would matter."

Neff sniffed, her eyes suddenly suffused with tears. "I'm so sorry."

Kenna's face went slack. "'Betrayed by those closest to him… silent witness…'" He stared at the ground; then his mournful expression turned to anger as a single word slid from his lips, as sharp as the obsidian blade.

"Mery."

He banged his fist against the table, causing the tools to rattle. Kenna moved to straighten them, his breath coming in short bursts. Neff could feel the fury radiating off him, and it frightened her.

He'll hate you for what you've done. You'll be thrown out of the temple. You'll be a disgrace to your family. You're a liar and a coward and you've ruined everything.

She suddenly recalled the conversation she'd had with Prince Meryamun that day at the palace. She'd told him about her vision! She'd promised him to keep it to herself!

I'll make sure that the king is taken care of, he'd said.

And he had.

I'm so stupid, Neff thought.

She started to cry. "I'm sorry," she said again, her head in her hands. "I'm so sorry."

Kenna touched her shoulder. She winced, but his hand was gentle.

"Dry your tears, little sister," Kenna said, his voice calm once again. "None of this is your fault. If anything, it's mine."

Neff's brow furrowed. "What do you mean? How could this be your fault?"

"Sita tried to tell me something was wrong at the palace. She practically begged for my help, hinting that there was something suspicious about Father's illness. But I didn't want to listen. I thought it was just her imagination…" He turned to look at his father's body, emptied of all its secrets. "I should have listened to her."

Neff's breath still came in halting gasps, but she was relieved he wasn't angry at her. "What are you going to do?"

Kenna shrugged. "What can I do? Mery is poised to be crowned. If I know my brother, he's already gathered support from the viziers and the other priests. Father had enemies in his own administration who would jump at the chance to swear allegiance to a bold new pharaoh. In fact, I'd wager that some of them were in on this plan. If I cast accusations at him, I'd only be endangering myself and those around me."

Neff thought of the fierce young prince she'd met in the palace, so different from his gentle brother. She thought of him seated on the throne, his radiance so dazzling that it blinded people from seeing who he truly was.

With that thought came a sudden rush of impending doom, and the doleful voice of the lamb from her dream.

Beware, for soon the Great River of Khetara will turn to blood.

"Mery has won," Kenna continued.

Take heed, Thonis, Great House of Amun! Beware of what is unseen among you!

"There's nothing I can do but move on."

Sorrow and ruin to the Children of the Two Lands!

Neff gasped.

"Are you all right?" Kenna asked.

"You must stop him," she said.

"I can't." His tone was apologetic. "The throne is his."

Numb, Neff watched Kenna move the sack of natron over to the body and begin packing salt into the king's empty torso.

It can't end this way, she thought. *But if a prince can't do anything, what can I do? Why would the gods choose someone as powerless as me for this task?*

"I'll get you some fresh water," Neff offered, taking up the basin. She needed an excuse to get some air.

She turned to leave and saw a cat sitting in the doorway, sniffing the air. It was old and striped, probably one of the palace cats that roamed freely. Its eyes narrowed as it took in the strong scents, and the fur on its back stood on end. Then it padded away, to a place where the air wasn't so heavy with death.

Or maybe it was more than that. Maybe the cat sensed the dark portents hanging over her, over the room and the body, over the young priest who believed in gods and rituals but not in himself, over the chaos that would stem from his silence.

She followed in the cat's wake, holding the basin tight to her body as if to give her the courage she didn't feel. Someone had to act. And in the absence of another option, that someone would have to be her. She still didn't understand why Bast chose to bring her to this place, chose to lay this challenge at her feet, but then again, who was she to question the will of the gods?

Show me what I must do, goddess, Neff thought, *and it will be done. I will be silent no longer.*

24
PAWS

Prey skulked nearby. She could smell it, young and tender. It would shriek when she sank her teeth into it, which always made her want to bite harder.

The striped cat slipped silently through the passageways of the palace, tracking the scent. Night had fallen, so she'd returned from her day at the temple. She'd often go there to partake in the burnt offerings meant for the gods. And why not? She too, was a kind of god. Should she not have her bit of flesh?

It had been a trying day. None of the humans were adhering to their normal routines. Everything alive smelled like tension, and everything else smelled like death.

It reminded her of a night long, long ago, when she was barely out of kittenhood, and rain had fallen from the sky in torrents. The cat hadn't seen any clouds on her way back to the palace that evening, and yet it felt as if a storm was coming once more.

She followed the scent of prey into a chamber flickering with candlelight. A young man sat at a table, studying a strange object.

It was a flat piece of wood with the image of a coiled snake carved into it, its body divided into sections. Black and red stones of various sizes were placed within the snake's coils, as well as two larger pieces of each color. The man held several short sticks that were white on one side and black on the other. He rolled the sticks in his hand and stared at the snake, deep in thought. All around him, half-curled papyri lay in messy piles, twitching and sliding across one another in the breeze.

He paid the cat no mind as she entered—few did, except those who stopped to offer worship with a scratch behind the ears. Most people simply allowed her passage wherever she wished. It had always been that way, and somehow, she knew it always would be.

The cat had seen the young man many times before. She'd seen him birthed on that stormy night long ago, and watched him grow up to be a lithe, bright-eyed creature with flashing teeth. She didn't *like* him, per se. Not the way she liked Cook and the girl who watched fish in the garden—but she respected him. He was a predator, like her.

She sensed a mouse moving along the far wall, and was stalking it when a shadow fell through the doorway.

"Greetings to you, my prince," a female voice said. "Am I disturbing you?"

The man turned to see who it was. "Hello, Tadia," he rumbled. "Not at all. Come in."

It was one of the girls she often bedded down with at night. The women's chamber had the softest blankets and the softest flesh, and the cat loved nothing better than curling up in the crook of an arm or leg, warmed by the blood thrumming beneath.

The girl came into the room and bowed, the beads in her hair tinkling softly. She never took her eyes from the man's face.

"I thought you might enjoy some company," she said, trailing a hand down her gossamer linen dress. "I often visited your father in the evenings. He liked to watch me dance."

The man raised an eyebrow. "I'm sure he did."

"I offer myself to you, Prince Meryamun," she said, reverent and coy. "As I was your father's, now I am yours to do with as you wish."

The prince rolled the wooden sticks in his hand as he regarded her. Then he pointed at a chair opposite him at the table.

"Sit."

Tadia sat, eager and erect.

"Do you know how to play Mehen?" He indicated the snake board between them.

The girl's shoulders fell slightly. "No, I don't really play games... but I can learn!"

"There is a red player—that's me," the prince explained. "And a black player—that's you. On our turns, we each throw these sticks to see how many spaces we can move our pawns." He pointed to the small stones. "When the first pawn reaches the head of the snake, it moves off the board and becomes the Jackal."

At this, he took up one of the larger pieces—carnelian carved into the shape of a dog's head—and moved it around and around the coils of the serpent. "The Jackal can move any way it wants, killing the opponent's pawns."

Having finished his explanation, he leaned back in his chair. "So tell me, Tadia, how do you think one goes about winning the Snake Game?"

Tadia blinked, clearly unprepared for a test. She looked down, studying the board as if it would provide the answer.

"Well," she began, uncertain. "Maybe it's whoever gets all their pieces to the head of the snake first?"

"You'd think so, wouldn't you?" the prince said. "After all, that's how most people see the path to victory. Start at the beginning and be the first to reach the end. Simple."

He leaned over the table conspiratorially, and Tadia leaned in to match him. "But you're wrong."

The cat's hackles rose. The energy in the room was shifting. She could feel a dark current running through it and growing stronger.

"No, Tadia," the prince continued, "one does not win the game by being the first to the goal, but by being the last left *alive*. The first player to eliminate all the other player's pawns from the board is the victor. Do you understand? This game has a very important lesson to teach us. Like life, Mehen isn't a journey. It's war."

He chuckled humorlessly, rolling the throw sticks in his hand. They rattled like bones.

"It's funny, you know, because my father was the one who first taught me to play, and yet he never learned that lesson. Because of his weakness, his sloth, his arrogance, Khetara stands at the edge of ruin."

He glanced at the scrolls piled around his feet. "Today, when I wasn't in meetings with his viziers, I was in this room, reading. Grain tax reports, letters from the nomarch in Sakesh and from the army commanders. The situation is worse than I thought— far worse than what Father let on. And Amun knows what the neighboring kingdoms think of us. Only a generation ago, they feared us! They paid homage to us in return for their survival.

"But no more. Now, my mother is forced to fawn over a delegation of sour-faced Tashans in the hopes that they'll cough up a prince for my dear sister." He scoffed. "This is the legacy my father leaves me. This *mess*. Thank the gods he died when he did, or else the damage would have been too much for even me to repair."

If the girl was shocked by the man's speech, she didn't show it. In fact, she seemed aroused by it. The cat could feel the heat pouring off her body in waves as she listened, her lips slightly parted.

"Father boasted of his peaceful reign," the prince went on, "but peace is an illusion. Men are born for war. If you keep them from it for too long, they either become useless or savage. There is only one language that all men understand, and only one path to victory over them: *power*. With the crook I will gather them under my dominion, and with the flail I will destroy all those who refuse to submit. That is my promise."

"You speak like a true king," Tadia responded, her voice sultry. "Please, allow me to serve you. Let me remain at your side as you lead us into glory. I will give you everything you want."

The man licked his lips. "Is that so?"

"Yes." She slipped off the chair and onto her knees.

The prince rolled the throw sticks in his hand as he watched her slither toward him. "And what do you desire in exchange for these offerings?"

"Only your favor, my prince," she replied, slipping her shoulders between his legs. She rubbed her cheek against his thigh in a gesture familiar to the cat, a gesture of possession, of territory claimed. "With so many burdens on your back, you will need pleasure. Release. I can give you that, and more." She reached out to touch him.

The prince's hand darted forward, catching her wrist. His expression twisted into disgust.

"Do you really think I'd want my father's half-chewed meat?" he snarled.

The girl's face went pale.

"You think you can crawl into my bed, simply because you amused him? A man who'd mate with anything with two legs?"

Tadia shrank back, staring at the prince as if seeing him for the first time.

The cat's tail twitched with nervous anticipation, the mouse all but forgotten.

The prince rose from his chair. "I am going to wipe everything he fouled with his touch from the face of the earth," he said, prowling after the girl as she tried to scurry away. "Starting with you."

He lunged and caught her by the throat.

It happened so quickly that the girl didn't have time to scream.

The cat flattened itself against the ground as Tadia tried to wrench her body away from him. Her arms batted against his chest with futile blows as her face swelled and purpled. She flailed, sweeping the snake board off the table, scattering the red and black pieces across the floor. She pried at his fingers, her mouth opening and closing.

The prince drank in the sight and continued to squeeze.

Soon, Tadia stopped struggling. The room fell to silence. The prince released his grip and she slid to the floor, her eyes open and staring.

With a sigh, the prince sat back in his chair. He pushed a loose lock of hair from his eyes, reached for the cup of wine sitting on the table, and drank deeply. When it was empty, he set it back down.

"Guard!" he called.

A tall, barrel-chested man entered from the other room. He glanced at the body on the floor but didn't seem particularly alarmed by it.

"Yes, my prince?" he said in a clipped tone.

The prince waved a hand toward the girl. "Clean up this mess."

"Yes, my prince." The guard stooped down to gather up the corpse, then draped it over his shoulder like a beast after slaughter.

The prince stopped him before he departed. "I think it's time for you and the others to take care of the king's personal guard. Don't you?" He patted the big man's arm affectionately. "Much to do tonight."

"I will take care of it, my prince. As we discussed." With a crisp bow, he was gone.

That done, the prince carefully gathered up the red and black pieces from the floor and set them on the table next to the Mehen board. When he found the red jackal piece, he placed it on the snake's head and smiled.

The cat, ever curious, slunk out from her hiding place to sniff at the black jackal piece that had landed near her. Unable to resist, she batted it across the square tiles.

The prince turned toward the sound, noticing her.

"Hello there, cat," he crooned. "Out for a hunt tonight?" He chuckled, and a primal hunger flashed in his eyes. "That makes two of us."

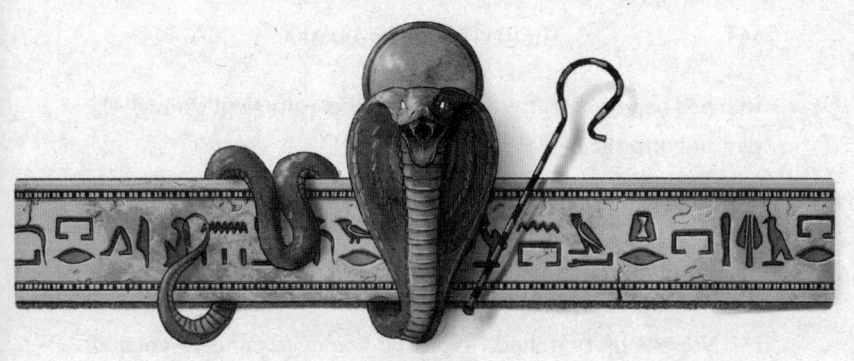

25
SITA

Sita woke to the sound of a falcon crying.

She sat up in bed with a gasp, startling Nebet. The older woman sat in a chair by her side, mending a hole in one of her fine dresses.

"It's all right, dear," she said, patting Sita's hand. "It's all right."

"What was that?" Sita asked, looking out the window into the thick darkness. There was no falcon in sight, yet it had sounded so close…

"Hmm? I didn't hear anything." Nebet's voice was strange. She fumbled her sewing needle, and picked it back up with shaking fingers. "Go back to sleep, Princess. You need your rest."

Sita rubbed her eyes. Nebet had found her wandering the palace halls after her father's death earlier in the day and escorted her back to her chambers. She'd been so distraught, she hadn't told Nebet about Mery's intention to make her his queen. She dimly remembered falling into bed and crying herself to sleep. But that had been in the afternoon… Had she really slept through the day and into the night?

Outside, she heard a distant commotion. A dull clatter of footsteps. Alarmed voices that were quickly stifled.

"What time is it?" she asked, suddenly feeling an inexplicable sense of urgency. "What's going on?"

Nebet's lip twitched. "Nothing you need concern yourself with, Sitamun. Best if you stay here with me." There was an unspoken coda to that sentence. *Where it's safe.*

Unease bloomed in the pit of her stomach. She'd assumed that since Mery told her about his plot to kill their father, he'd shared all his secrets. But he hadn't said a word about his plan to marry her. That he'd kept in the dark. What other plans would be brought into the light, now that the king was dead?

"Nebet," she said, "I command you to tell me what's happening."

The older woman stared at the dress. She clutched it so tightly that her knuckles turned white. There was a long pause before she finally spoke.

"A little while ago, one of the other attendants informed me that seven of the king's personal guard have been killed."

"Killed?" Horrified, Sita threw the covers aside and went to Nebet. *Was Femi one of them?* Her heart raced. "How?"

"All I know is that the prince himself ordered their deaths. It is… upsetting…" Nebet's face crumpled, but she quickly recovered her composure. "But I trust he had his reasons. It is not my place to question the will of a pharaoh." She reached out and gripped one of Sita's hands. "Neither is it yours."

Sita pulled her hand away. "How can you say that? What possible reason could he have for such savagery?" Her voice was high and a little hysterical. "I have to find Femi."

"Sitamun, *please*." Nebet clung to her, her face filled with terror. "Don't go. I implore you."

Sita narrowed her eyes. She'd known Nebet all her life. She could tell when the woman was keeping something more from her. "What aren't you telling me?"

The attendant pressed her lips into a thin line.

She'd commanded the woman to speak, and yet still she held back. *What could be worse than the deaths of the guards?*

"Nebet!" she cried in frustration. She was about to grab the older woman by the shoulders and shake her until she confessed, when Mery's words came back to her.

You and me… we belong together… my twin… my mirror.

Was it true? Were she and Mery so alike? In the past, such a comparison would have made her proud, but no longer. Her brother may have started out with good intentions, but he'd gone too far. He justified one murder in the name of the greater good, but clearly it hadn't ended there. Where would he stop? How could she have not seen it sooner? And what had keeping that secret done to her? She nearly assaulted her beloved Nebet for trying to keep her safe. A fresh wave of self-loathing washed over her.

If it's not true, she thought, *if you're really not like him, then prove it.*

Be the one thing Mery could never be.

Honest.

She took a deep, calming breath. "Let me bring you some water," she said to Nebet.

The attendant, who'd been watching her with apprehension, slowly relaxed. When Sita brought her a cup, she wrapped her hands around it like a talisman.

"Thank you," she said, and took a sip. Sita knelt before her, a gesture which seemed to take Nebet by surprise. "Sitamun?"

"I love you, Nebet." Sita had never said it before, though she hoped her actions had. "You have been more of a mother to me than my own, and you've given me more devotion than I deserve."

Nebet's eyes shone. "What are you talking about, child?" she said, her voice thick. "Of course you deserve my love. You've never done anything wrong."

"I haven't done many things right either. I know you're trying to protect me from whatever is happening in the palace, but you can't. You have to tell me, Nebet."

She clasped her hands together in prayer.

"You have to let me go," Sita said quietly.

Nebet let out a small sob, then nodded. "As you wish, Sitamun." She steadied her voice. "The girl who told me about the guards—she'd come looking for Tadia. Tadia hadn't returned to the women's chambers, and they'd received a message that all the king's servants, concubines, and lesser wives were to go to the Horus Room to attend a special ritual to honor the late king. She didn't want Tadia to be late, so she asked me to pass along the message if I saw her.

"I thought... I thought it was strange to call all those people together at this time of night. And the Horus Room? Why there? I just... I have a bad feeling, Sitamun."

Sita shivered.

A tear trickled down the attendant's cheek. "Your brother was always so beautiful, you know? So charming. Even as a little baby. 'He Whose Face Is the Sun,' that's what they called him. He shone *so brightly*. But now it makes me wonder. The sun shines, Sitamun, but it also *burns*." Her lip trembled. "Don't go."

Sita clambered to her feet, her heart hammering. "I'm sorry," she said, and rushed out the door.

Sita ran through the desolate halls of the palace, a place that had come to feel more like a cage than a home.

The Horus Room was a seldom used ceremonial chamber,

one of the many relics of a palace built long before her father's reign. Unlike his predecessor, Amunmose considered himself a modern king, and had done away with some of the more archaic rituals that Sematawy had been keen to restore. Growing up, the dusty Horus Room had often been a secret playground for her and Mery, where they would pretend to be king and queen and reenact ancient ceremonies using whatever was at hand. Thinking back on those once-fond memories set Sita's stomach twisting.

She didn't stop running until she reached the muggy, forgotten corridor, lit by dim torchlight. The door to the Horus Room stood at its end, covered by a red linen curtain. A woman stood before it, dressed in mourning yellow.

"Mother?"

Queen Bintanath turned, and Sita flinched at the sight of her. The heavy kohl around her mother's eyes had run down her face in black rivulets. She looked haunted, like a shell of her former self.

"Sita," she said softly. "It's so nice to see you."

"What's Mery done, Mother? What's happening in there?"

Sita tried to step past her, but Queen Bintanath refused to move aside. She seemed dazed, distracted. She laid a hand on Sita's cheek in an uncharacteristically affectionate gesture and smiled, sending a chill down Sita's spine.

"Such a beautiful girl," she said. "A face born to be carved in stone—I always thought so. And now it will be, for you will become queen of this kingdom and sit by Mery's side as he leads Khetara into a great future. Isn't that wonderful?"

Sita jerked away. "Wait, you *approve* of this? Your own children, bedding together?" Her life was spinning out of control. "Did you know he was planning this marriage? How could you possibly—"

"*Shh…*" Queen Bintanath said, putting a finger to her lips as if she were speaking to a child. "Mery only confessed his love for you this evening, before me and the viziers. Oh, we were surprised at first, but after your brother explained it to us, it made perfect sense.

"Your father, may he live forever in the West, allowed this kingdom to stray too far from the old ways. In order to bring Khetara back to the prosperity it once had, we must return to our roots. And that begins with you, Sitamun. The blood of Isis flows through your veins, my girl. Nebet always claimed that it was she who blessed you when you were born, she who named you. I never believed her, but now... now I do. The gods are speaking through your brother's lips, and like Isis and Osiris, he will soon have you as both his sister and his wife. And through your union a new nation will be born."

"How can you say these things?" Sita asked, shaking her head. "How can you not see that this is all wrong?"

Only after the accusation left her lips did Sita feel its sting in her own heart. Couldn't anyone, had they known the truth, have said the same to her? *Isn't that how I sounded when I was under Mery's spell? Didn't I nod and smile and parrot his words, because he'd poured them so sweetly into my ears?* She'd known about the poisoned cakes. Known that they were going to kill her father and an innocent child.

How can you not have seen that it was all wrong?

"Before Mery takes the throne," the queen went on, as if Sita hadn't spoken, "your brother wishes to send his beloved father to the Duat in the manner of the ancient kings. Kings who brought with them an honored retinue to serve them in the afterlife."

Sita's agonized thoughts came to a sudden halt. Her heart quickened as she turned her gaze toward the red curtain, and her ears to the ominous silence coming from beyond it. If her father's lesser wives, concubines, and servants were all inside that room, why was it so quiet?

"No," she said, her voice hoarse. She looked from her mother to the portal of the Horus Room. "He wouldn't…"

Then, before the queen could stop her, Sita plunged through the curtain.

Sita thought about that moment many times in the days and months that followed. It remained perfectly preserved, stored in the deepest, darkest corner of her mind until the day she died.

The space was much cleaner than Sita remembered. The assorted bric-a-brac that had been thrown into it over the years had been cleared away, and even the walls, painted with images of falcon-headed Horus, seemed fresh.

A luscious feast had been set on the large low table in the center of the room. Breadcrumbs, bare bones, and the skeletons of grape clusters lay abandoned on golden platters, along with three elaborately painted wine jars. It could have been the scene of any celebration, any formal ceremony meant to raise a glass to the pharaoh.

They were all there. Her father's four other wives, who'd clucked at her when she was a toddling nunu playing with wooden dolls and who'd taught her how to apply the kohl to her eyes when she'd grown.

Maet's mother was there too.

So were the concubines, young and beautiful, and the servants, his faithful litter bearers, his personal attendants, the cook and his helpers, and the courtly, gentle Ineni, who'd remained at the king's side until the very end. All of them were in attendance around that table to honor the memory of King Amunmose III.

And all of them were dead.

Some had collapsed onto the table, their heads resting on fine plates, almost as if they were sleeping. Others had fallen backward and lay splayed across the blue tiled floor, their hands clutching their throats or stomachs or each other. Ineni lay closest to the door, his slender body fixed in a contorted pose, his lips slack and blue. Maet's mother had curled into a fetal position on the floor. She looked almost peaceful.

Almost.

None of them appeared to have suffered any violence, and it would have been a wholly bloodless tableau, if it wasn't for the wine.

It spilled from toppled cups onto the table, dark and gruesome, and dripped in crimson rivulets onto the floor, seeping into the cracks between the tiles. It soaked into white linen dresses and stained cooling skin. It filled the room with a thick, sour tang that nearly made her gag.

Despite there not being a single wound on anyone in that room, Sita knew a weapon when she saw one.

And she knew her brother.

Whatever was in the wine, it took down two dozen vibrant lives in the matter of moments, as swift as a cobra's kiss.

The scene swam before Sita's eyes like a mirage, too horrible to be real. She dashed forward, falling to her knees before Maet's mother's body, dragging the woman's head into her lap.

"Wake up," she begged. "Please…"

Maet's mother was still, her eyes open and dry.

No more tears.

Only a few days ago, her father had been bouncing Maet on his knee at that banquet, while the little girl's mother looked on. *Now, all three of them are dead*.

Stifling a sob, Sita plucked the empty wine cup from the woman's hand and threw it across the room. It hit the wall and shattered into a thousand pieces. The sound was so loud it jolted her.

She was struck by a sudden, terrible clarity, like a curse finally broken.

This is just the beginning, she thought. She'd played enough games with Mery to know an opening gambit when she saw one. *Sacrifice the pawns to advance to a superior position.* In one night, Mery had eliminated everyone in the palace who'd been truly loyal to their father. Everyone except for the queen, Kenna, and her.

She had no idea what his plans were for her mother and brother, but the thought of what he meant to do with her was too sickening to contemplate.

If I don't get away now, I'll be trapped in this nightmare forever.

Just then, a man stepped through a door at the back of the room. She recognized him as one of the guards Mery was particularly fond of. His fierce expression softened when he saw Sita kneeling at the woman's side. He cleared his throat.

"Excuse me, Princess Sitamun, but you shouldn't be here," he said slowly, carefully. "Please, allow me to escort you back to your chambers."

"No, no," Sita replied, quickly stumbling to her feet. "I'll go on my own, thank you. I was merely… saying goodbye…"

The guard bowed his head but watched until she backed out of the room, until the red curtain dropped once again between her and the grisly scene.

Then, she ran.

She was nearing her chambers when Sita turned a corner and slammed into someone coming from the other direction. Instinctively, she lashed out in terror, ready to fight. Strong hands took hold of her wrists and held them.

"It's all right, Sitamun. It's me."

"Femi?" It took a moment for her to register his kind, familiar face. "Oh, praise Amun, you're alive!" After so much loss, the blessing of Femi's survival felt like a miracle. Heedless of who might see, she wrapped her arms around his chest and held him tight.

"I am," Femi said. "For now."

He looked shaken and exhausted, and there was blood staining the edge of his schenti. Sita suspected it wasn't his.

"I can't believe my brother spared you. I was certain you'd be targeted. He saw us together, after all…"

Femi scoffed. "I don't think it's mercy that stayed his hand, Sitamun. Strategy, more like. Though to what end, I've no idea." He took her hand and tugged her down the hall. "Now, please, come with me, Princess. I must get you back to your chambers before anyone sees us."

"No," Sita said, resisting him. "I'm not going back."

Femi frowned, his brow furrowed in confusion. "What do you mean?"

Sita lifted her chin. "My brother intends to take me as his queen." Femi's eyes widened. "He told me this afternoon, just after my father's death. A death, like so many others, that could have been prevented. The prince is…"

She felt a lump rising in her throat. "I knew he was ruthless, but I thought his intentions were good. I never… I never thought…"

Words kept failing her. In the end, she was left with one simple truth. "I am a fool."

"I don't understand," Femi asked. "How could you have prevented these deaths? What could you have done?"

"I could have confessed," Sita said savagely. "I could have fought. I could have died. Anything would have been better than what I did—which was nothing."

"Sitamun," Femi said in a low voice. "Are you saying that there was a plot to assassinate the king? That the prince… murdered him?"

It was too late for the truth to matter. Too late for it to save anyone—not even her. But since she was given the opportunity, she told it anyway.

"Yes."

Femi reeled from the impact of her words. She wanted to explain more, to tell him everything, but there was no time.

"I will not remain here and be Mery's prize. I've got to escape—tonight. Will you help me?"

Femi paled. "But where will you go?"

Sita shook her head. "I don't know yet," she said rapidly. "But I must leave before Mery puts me under watch. For all I know, his men are already waiting in my chambers. One of them saw me in the Horus Room."

"All right, all right," Femi said, running a hand through his short hair. "Come, there's a supply room nearby. I can get you a plain dress and robe, a waterskin, some dry provisions, and a small blade… but not much else."

"That's enough," Sita said.

Femi met her eyes, his weary expression tinged with sorrow. He'd already lost so much, and he was about to lose more. He looked as if there were a thousand things he wanted to say, but instead he bowed his head. "As you wish, my princess."

They hurried to the supply room, where Sita changed her clothes by candlelight. She stuffed her fineries into a rough pack and slung them over her shoulder. Perhaps she could trade them for more supplies later on. The robe she'd chosen was plain and black with a wide hood that would shield her face from curious eyes. Femi fitted her with a leather belt to hold her dagger and waterskin, cinching it tight around her waist. When she was ready, they emerged back into the hallway.

They hadn't gone three steps before a clatter of footsteps approached.

"Get back inside!" Femi whispered, shoving her into the supply room.

Sita pressed herself against the wall and held her breath.

The footsteps stopped just outside the door.

"Femi," a deep voice said. "Have you seen the princess?"

"Not tonight," Femi lied. "She should be asleep in her chambers. Is she not?"

The other guard grumbled. "She blundered into the Horus Room and then took off. The prince wants her found. The other men are checking the women's chambers. If you find her, bring her to the throne room immediately."

"Of course," Femi replied.

Sita listened as the footsteps faded.

Femi poked his head through the doorway. "We must be quick. The shortest path out of the palace is through the gardener's entrance in the pleasure garden. Let's go."

Pulling the hood over her face, Sita reached for Femi's hand and hurried with him toward the main hall. They were halfway through the shadowy chamber when two more guards approached. She and Femi dashed behind one of the columns, hearts hammering, and waited until they'd passed. Sita felt sick with fear, unable to breathe until they finally emerged from the palace and out into the cool, fragrant air of the pleasure garden.

The fishpond rippled with movement, reflecting a jagged moon. A stiff breeze ruffled Sita's robes, bringing with it the scent of smoke and honey and wine. It rushed through the boughs of the sycamore tree, the sound hushed and urgent.

Shhh.

The time had come for her to leave him. To leave everything.

"Come with me," Sita blurted. She hadn't thought it through—she hadn't thought *anything* through—but she was terrified of being alone. "You're not safe here. When Mery realizes I'm gone, he'll think you helped me escape."

Femi shook his head. "If I go with you, they'll know that for certain. They'll hunt us down like dogs, and I cannot protect you from that. But if I stay, I can throw them off the scent.

"As soon as you leave here, head south. Get out of the city as fast as you can. When they come for me, I'll tell them you'd mentioned wanting to travel north to the delta by riverboat, but that I had no idea you'd intended to run away. They'll spend hours searching all the boats at port, giving you time to get as far from here as possible."

The plan made sense, and Sita was impressed that Femi had devised it so quickly. There was a problem with it, though.

"Your lies may convince the guards, but when they fail to find me, my brother will come for you. He'll see right through the deception." She took a deep, steadying breath. "He'll torture you, Femi. He'll bring you to the edge of death unless you tell him where I've gone."

Femi's expression didn't change, as if he'd already reached the same conclusion. "Then you mustn't tell me where you're going, Sitamun. If I don't know, I won't have to lie to a future king."

Sita stared at Femi, suddenly seeing him in a new light. He'd been a mere plaything to her, although she'd also come to see him as a friend. Still, though, she'd failed to notice his strength, his courage, his sense of honor.

Once again, her arrogance had blinded her to the truth. Femi may have been a lowly guard, but he had the heart of a commander.

"I don't deserve your sacrifice. I have used you, been cold to you—if I'd only just left you alone, you'd never—"

"If you'd just left me alone," Femi interrupted, "I never would have known what it is to love you. Even if it was only for a short while."

The words pierced her like a knife. It was as she'd feared. "You can't love me," she protested. "Why would you love me?"

Femi smiled, a sad smile that nearly broke her. "You may not ever be queen of this kingdom, but you have always been mine. It would be an honor to die protecting you, Sitamun. I can think of no better way to leave this life."

Sita threw her arms around his neck and kissed him, long and fierce, a kiss to last. When she pulled away, her cheeks were wet with tears.

"I will return," she vowed. "I don't know how, but I will find a way."

Femi nodded and looked back toward the main hall, toward the sound of distant, shouted commands.

"We're running out of time," he said. "You have to go. Now."

Sita followed his gaze, taking one last look at the palace. "I don't even know who I am away from this place."

"Then go and find out, my princess," Femi said, his eyes roaming her face as if to memorize it.

With a solemn nod, Sita turned toward the gardener's entrance.

"Goodbye," Sita whispered, to Femi, to Nebet, to Kenna, to her mother, to the garden of her youth, to the only life she'd ever known.

She stepped across the dark threshold, and fled into the vast desert beyond.

26
RAE

That night, in the Garden of the Dead, plans grew.

Rae and Omari met Big Ears at the entrance and provided the Horizon code phrase, though he made it clear they needn't do so.

"Oh, I know you," the gruff man said, punching Omari in the shoulder. "If it weren't for the two of you, I'd be neck-deep in natron, with my guts in a jar."

"Good to see you up and about," Omari said.

"And so quickly," Rae added. Considering he'd had a knife in his belly only a day before, he seemed surprisingly hale. "You hardly look any worse for wear."

The man waggled his voluminous eyebrows. "Well, can't look much worse than I already do, can I? Just don't make me laugh, or run, or get up from a chair." He laughed, despite himself, then winced.

Rae chuckled. "You know, I'm ashamed to say it, but I don't

actually know your name." She felt bad thinking of him as "Big Ears" all that time.

"Eh, that's all right. In our business, sometimes it's safer not to know. A man's name is not to be shared lightly. Mine is Menkaura, but you can call me Menk."

Rae followed him into the grand necropolis with a smile, feeling as if she'd just been given a gift.

The Hesep-Mut was as uncanny as it had been every other time she'd visited, with its high walls and its still, stale air. Asim and some other Horizon members stood leaning against the broken stone altar at its center. It was a smaller group than it had been at their other meetings.

Asim turned to see them, relief washing over his face. "Good, you're here. We were starting to discuss next steps."

"Where is everybody?" Rae looked for the shepherd and the grumpy brewer, but neither were in attendance. "I didn't think we were late."

"You're not," Asim said. "It's possible Mamet Mut didn't get the message to everyone in time. Or they decided to lie low until things calm down a bit." He crossed his arms and sighed. "The raid certainly thrust a stick into the pharaoh's beehive, so I suppose you can't blame a man for not wishing to be stung."

"I can," Omari complained. "This is our chance to break High Khetara's hold on us before they can regroup and come back stronger. Any man who deserts us now to protect his own hide is a coward, plain and simple."

Asim's nostrils flared. "You're a very young man to speak with such authority, Omari. I'd advise you to take care with your words. There is nothing plain or simple about any of this."

Omari seemed surprised by this reaction, and cast his eyes to the ground. "I'm sorry, Asim. I don't want this crucial moment to be wasted."

Asim gave Omari's shoulder a hearty pat. "The heat of your passion is admirable, Omari. Just remember to tend that fire, lest it burn too freely." He turned back to the others. "Let us not dwell on those who haven't ventured out tonight but celebrate those of us who have."

The men nodded in agreement.

"We have much to do," Asim went on. "News of our victory has spread across Sakesh, but there are those who have yet to hear of our cause. We must ensure every man knows of the coming revolution and our plans for the future—and sees the wisdom of joining us in the fight. We cannot hope to repel the High Khetarans as a fringe group. We must do it as one people."

There was some discussion then, with a variety of questions posed and ideas shared. How could they best canvass the city without the risk of exposure? How should they divide the arms they'd amassed from the raid? And how would they prepare for the Medjay's return from the north with their reinforcements? Rae listened closely, mustering the courage to make good on her promise to Tam.

"I think we should bring the weavers into these meetings," she said. "I know for a fact that some of those women want to be involved, and not simply in carrying messages. They are capable of more."

The other rebels were skeptical.

"I doubt the men of this city would appreciate us placing their mothers and daughters in danger," one said. "The weavers have stout hearts, but what greater use could they possibly be to us?"

Rae's anger flared. "Am I also so useless? Have I done so little to further our cause?"

"You're not like other women, Raetawy. I'd have thought that was obvious," another man said.

Rae was about to educate him on the immeasurable depths

of his stupidity when Asim raised his hands in a calming gesture. "Please. Let us not bicker among ourselves. You both have valid points—perhaps we can speak to the weavers and ask how they'd propose to help. It's possible they can do more without us having to place them in harm's way. Does that suffice?"

Rae and the man grumbled their assent.

"Perhaps I'm not the only one in need of fire tending," Omari whispered in her ear.

"Shut up, oaf," Rae said and elbowed him.

"Clearly, we have plenty of ideas, so let's decide who can manage each of these tasks," Asim said. "Rae, let's start with you."

Kroo! Kroo!

The group fell silent.

Menk's signal could mean only one thing. Something was wrong.

Without a word, Asim and the others extinguished their torches in the sand and stood quietly in the ensuing darkness. A tingle of fear crept along the back of Rae's neck as she held her breath, listening for any sound. The wind whistled through the gaps in the vast stone ruin, and somewhere beyond, a fox shrieked among the dunes. Other than that, there was nothing.

After a long moment, Omari bent his head toward her and whispered, "You stay here. I'll go check on—"

Before he could finish the sentence, a whizzing sound came from above and an arrow buried itself in Omari's shoulder. He staggered back from the force of it, his hand coming up to grip the shaft.

Rae stared at him, open-mouthed.

"Oh," he said and collapsed.

In the next instant, a dozen more arrows rained down from above, humming through the air like a deadly swarm.

The silence shattered.

"Take cover!" Asim shouted, but not before another man was struck.

The rebel cried out in pain, an arrow in his back, and fell to the ground.

Panic surged in Rae's chest. *It's an ambush!*

Amid the confusion, she looked up and saw four archers perched on the crumbling walls of the necropolis, their forms silhouetted against the night sky. As they reloaded their bows, Rae dropped into a crouch and began dragging Omari by the armpits toward the remains of a low stone wall. An arrow sliced past her arm, missing her by a handsbreadth.

Across the way, another rebel fell. Then another.

Faster, go faster, Rae thought, her breath ragged as she did her best to ignore the searing pain in her back. The effort of carrying Omari's heavy body was stretching her wounds to their breaking point, and fear had sapped the strength from her limbs.

She tried not to look back, tried not to wonder which of the men she'd just been speaking to was bleeding to death, or to think of his family waking in the morning to find him gone.

Not now.

She kept moving. Even when another man went down, and when an arrow sunk into her left hip. Only when she and Omari were concealed behind the low wall did she allow herself to collapse next to him, dizzy with pain. Though the arrow had only pierced the fleshiest part of her flank, it bled freely.

Reaching out, she lay a trembling hand on her best friend's chest, relieved to find a steady thrum beneath her fingers.

Thanks be to Ra.

Then a new voice called out—a strangely familiar voice, though she couldn't place it. "Hold your fire! We're going in. I want the leader alive."

Rae scooted herself against the wall and peered around

it, squinting into the murk. Five guards filed in, two carrying torches, the others armed with khopesh. Rae recognized them immediately—the nomarch's personal guard. The one who had spoken was the same man who'd so cruelly twisted her arm behind her back when she'd gone to the shepherd's aid.

The nomarch's men, Rae thought, heat flooding her cheeks. *This is his doing.*

The remaining rebels, wild-eyed with panic, brandished their daggers as the guards advanced upon them.

Rae cursed through gritted teeth. With the arrow still lodged in her backside, she unsheathed her dagger and struggled to her feet, ready to enter the fray. But a strong grip pulled her back behind the wall.

"Get down!" Asim commanded. "Get down and be still!"

"No!" Rae said, resisting. "We can't hide here and watch them die."

"*We* aren't going to," Asim replied. "I won't be responsible for taking you away from your father! Not if I can help it!"

"That's not your decision to make!"

Asim's face was desperate as the cries of dying rebels filled the air. "Please, Raetawy, please give me this. Help me lighten my heart before it's too late."

Rae sagged back to the ground, careful not to jostle the arrow shaft as she did. She wanted so badly to fight, to loose a battle cry and wet her knife with the blood of those guards— but she could not refuse Asim.

"As you wish, Captain," she said.

Asim nodded and rose to his feet, moonlight catching his shaggy, rough-hewn face. Despite his tattered robes, she'd never seen a man look so noble. "Not a sound, no matter what happens. Understand?"

Rae nodded reluctantly.

"Good." Keeping to the shadows, Asim darted toward the guards who were converging on the last two rebels. One had already been shot in the leg, and the other stood with his fists held defensively before him, having just been disarmed.

The guards were about to strike when Asim charged, snatching up a fallen asa stick from the ground and slashing it through the air, taking out one of the guards with a savage blow to the head.

While the guards were distracted, the two rebels took the opportunity to flee. Asim thrust the tip of the asa into another guard's neck with a vicious crack. The man made a strangled, gurgling noise, but before he could do more than grasp his throat, Asim brought the stick swinging straight across the guard's temple, dropping him like a stone.

"What is wrong with you fools?" shouted the head guard. "Take him down!"

Rae watched it all, rapt. Asim turned to attack a third guard, but didn't see another one circle behind him, blade in hand. Rae wanted to cry out a warning, but she kept her promise and stayed silent.

The blade slashed across Asim's back with a spray of blood.

Asim grunted in pain, his back arching—but wasted only a moment before he whirled on his attacker with the asa. This time, though, the remaining guards were ready and fell upon him en masse, tearing the asa from his grasp and tossing it away.

"Tie his arms," the head guard commanded, wiping the perspiration from his brow.

One of the guards produced a length of rope. "What about the two who got away?" he asked.

"The archers will pick them off before they can get far," the head guard replied. He sniffed, watching as they pinned Asim's arms behind his back and forced him to his knees. "So, you're the leader of this rabble?"

Asim said nothing.

The head guard shrugged. "No matter. Your skills with the asa speak for themselves. It's obvious the rest of them were farmers' boys and old soldiers, far past their prime. You're hardly more than a beggar yourself, but perhaps you *were* something, once."

He placed the curve of his khopesh under Asim's chin and lifted it, forcing the rebel leader to look at him. "If you think I wanted you alive to squeeze you for information, you're wrong. You've conspired against the king. Your life is forfeit. I simply wanted to kill you myself."

Omari stirred, grunting softly as he regained consciousness.

The head guard turned his head. "What was that?"

Her pulse racing, Rae shifted silently and put her lips to Omari's ear. *"Shh…"*

Asim spoke up again. "Amunmose isn't worthy of Khetara's throne," he barked, loud enough to cover any sounds Omari might make. "Never has this kingdom seen a more feckless pharaoh. That is why we rise against him, not only for Sakesh, but for all—"

"King Amunmose is dead," the head guard said.

Asim fell silent.

"We received word earlier this evening, along with new orders from Crown Prince Meryamun. I've heard he's quite a different man from his father and models himself on the Great Uniter: King Sematawy himself. I've heard he wishes to return the kingdom to its former might—starting with bringing you Low Khetaran dogs to heel."

When Asim spoke again, his voice was somber. "This new king changes nothing. Kill me if you wish, but my death won't divert the people of Sakesh from their purpose. They have suffered for long enough. They will come together and take back this city, take back their dignity—"

It was at this point that Rae realized Asim was no longer talking to the guard. He was talking to her.

"—and come tomorrow, hear me, come tomorrow, the falcon will sail across the sky, and we shall meet him on the—!"

There was a sharp, wet sound, followed by a dull thud.

Then, silence.

Rae bit back a sob, her body quaking with grief.

"Pick that up and bring it with you," the head guard said, nonchalant. "The nomarch will want to see evidence of our victory. Perhaps he'll have it as a keepsake."

The other guards gave their assent, then began the business of collecting fallen weapons and comrades. It seemed an age before they made their way out of the Garden.

Rae held her breath as they walked by her. With the arrow protruding from her body and her robes soaked in blood, both she and Omari made convincing corpses. It was only after they'd safely passed that she opened her eyes to peer after them. Her blood turned to ice.

One of the guards held Asim's head by its hair, no differently than one would carry a dead goose killed in the marshes. It swung pendulously from the guard's grip, the mouth gaping open as if those final aspirational words were still caught on the tip of Asim's tongue.

Rae squeezed her eyes shut, flooding her cheeks with hot, angry tears.

Soon, the guards were gone. Rae dared not move a muscle until the sounds of their travel had long since faded.

Lying awkwardly on her side, she gazed up at the shroud of imperishable stars. Each one, her father had taught her, was the soul of a pharaoh. She wondered how many of them had been moral men, and how many had been blood-soaked tyrants like Sematawy, or greedy like Amunmose. And she wondered bitterly why they, regardless of their actions, were given the opportunity to shine.

Sometime later, an unexpected voice broke the stillness.

"Ra be merciful. No. No. Asim… *Asim!*"

Rae struggled to rise and peered around the low wall to see a man kneeling beside Asim's headless body, his back hunched in anguish.

"Menk?" Rae whispered in amazement.

Menk's head shot up, alarm quickly changing to disbelief. "Raetawy? You're alive!"

"Shot in the ass, but yes," Rae replied with a grunt. "Omari too—please, come quickly, he needs help."

Menk rushed over to her, shaking his head at their injuries. Omari was regaining consciousness, but he was fuzzy-eyed and unsteady.

"They killed them, Menk," Rae said as he struggled to get Omari to his feet and took in the destruction around them. Her voice was high, verging on hysteria. "They killed them all."

"I know. I tried to warn you, but by the time I saw them, it was too late."

"You did everything you could."

"No, I didn't. I could have fought them! I could have died with them!" He cursed and dropped his head in his hands.

Rae, too, felt the burden of guilt heavy on her shoulders. "I would have died with them too," she said softly. "But Asim wanted me to live."

Is this what it was like for him? she wondered. *To survive when so many others did not? Is this what made him the man he was?*

Omari leaned against Menk for support and gazed blankly at the corpses. "What do we do now? We can't leave them here like this."

Rae pressed her lips together, considering the fallen rebels, their blood soaking into the sand. She wouldn't have called any of them her friends, but they were good men. They'd given her a chance. They'd come that night on her suggestion and walked straight to their deaths.

"We have no choice," she finally said. "We're in no condition to carry them home, and after tonight, it will be too dangerous for any of their families to venture here to claim them. The nomarch's men will surely be watching for that. But we'll do what we can before we go."

Though each step gave her pain, Rae paid her respects to each of the dead men, crossing their arms over their bodies and laying her father's copper dagger on their chests before she prayed.

"Hear me, Ra. Maker of Hours, Lord of Days—hear me and cast your light upon this man. Burn away the fear in his heart, and watch over him as he travels West to the Field of Reeds…"

When they were done, they left the dead men resting in the dawn's light. After a thousand years, new bones had been planted in the Garden of the Dead.

Rae shivered with cold as they made the long arduous journey back to Sakesh. But even as the sun bled over the horizon and kissed their filthy, tear-streaked faces, Rae never once felt its warmth.

Her heart was just too heavy.

27
NEFF

"Where are the Wabet?" Nehshi asked, exasperated.

Neff blinked up at the young priest, her face dripping with water from the basin. She was preparing for her morning chores when Nehshi appeared in her chambers, his face shiny with sweat.

"They all left early to continue preparations for the coronation," she answered, drying her face with a clean cloth.

Nehshi moaned, a deep, lowing sound she'd heard him make so often that he might as well be a cow. "How am I supposed to perform the daily ritual without help? 'Not now, Nehshi,' they say, 'I'm too busy with *important matters* to deal with your problems, Nehshi. Ask someone else, Nehshi.' But if Amun is angered by the lateness of his offerings, who will be to blame? Nehshi!"

Neff sighed and laid the folded cloth across the edge of the basin. She still felt a little guilty for manipulating the priest the day Karim had shown up at the temple. "I'll help you, all right?"

Nehshi harrumphed. "What do you know about administering the daily ritual? Have you assisted with it before?"

"No, but I know enough," Neff replied. "Besides, do you have a better offer?"

Nehshi stared at her, then reached down to stroke the golden buckle he'd attached to his belt. "I suppose if Montuhotep trusts you to chaperone his foreign guests, I can trust you to assist with one morning's ritual."

Neff smirked and followed him out of her chambers and through the Great Temple. She was pleased that Nehshi hadn't followed up on her lie about the man from the Red Lands being a guest of Montuhotep—as she'd guessed, the priest was too worried about himself to ask questions. Her reputation was safe.

Still, she hadn't stopped thinking about Karim since his departure. She'd never met a Red Lands tribesman before, no less had a lengthy conversation with one, and although she had the feeling he wasn't being altogether honest with her, she'd liked him all the same. He'd spoken to her with respect and had a charming manner that was difficult to resist. And of course, he'd put a name to the vision that launched her on this journey: the Oracle of the Lamb. But with those answers came more questions. How were the four people—her, Karim, Princess Sitamun, and a mysterious farm girl from Low Khetara—connected? What were their roles in the days to come? And what exactly was coming?

Beware, for soon the Great River of Khetara will turn to blood.

Ever since Kenna uncovered the king's murder, she'd been convinced that Meryamun's ascension to the throne must be part of it. Not only had she seen the evidence in the embalming room when he made the discovery, but Kenna suggested that Sitamun had known that her father had been poisoned, and that her earlier visit to the temple had been a cry for help.

So, two of the four figures in the oracle were already involved in the conspiracy.

Lies will grow fruitful as wheat in the fields.

But Neff knew there was more at stake.

Karim had said that Setnakht, his missing pharaoh, was the key to unlocking the secrets of the oracle. Why else would fate have brought Karim to her? The letter they'd found in the House of Life made it clear that people had despised the heretical king—but that was a thousand years ago. Setnakht was long dead. What could he possibly have to do with what was unfolding in Khetara now? She recalled another line from her vision, and wondered at its significance.

A secret shall rise from beneath the earth.

Neff shivered.

Despite not entirely understanding how all the pieces fit together, Neff could sense them falling into place and disaster rushing toward them on swift waters. But what could she do to alter such a course? She'd prayed to Bast for answers, but so far, the goddess had been silent.

She'd wanted to talk to Kenna about it, to tell him all that she knew, but after that morning in the embalming room, Kenna had locked himself in his chambers and refused visitors, including her. So she'd been forced to spend far too much time alone with her thoughts, haunted by ill portents she was powerless to avoid.

She and Nehshi walked through the courtyard. Some other Wab priests went about their business around them, quietly completing the everyday tasks of the temple. The sky was unusually overcast, turning everything a muted gray.

At the far end of the courtyard, they climbed a few steps and entered a large columned hall. This was followed by more steps, then another, smaller hall, just like the first. Then came more steps into the Hall of Offering, a chamber only big enough to fit half a dozen people. She'd been told that the temples were designed this way, with priests ascending steps into smaller and smaller chambers, so that as they approached the holy of holies, they'd feel as if they were rising into the heavens for a private audience with the divine.

Finally, they reached the door to the sanctuary. It was sealed with a wax-encrusted cord wrapped around the doorknobs.

"I'll break the seal and bring the offerings," Nehshi said, gesturing toward the materials laid out neatly on a table next to the door. "You carry the incense."

Neff suddenly felt nervous. *It's a common ritual*, she told herself, *done three times a day. Nothing to worry about.* Still, her hand shook as she set the resin inside the bronze censer aflame. Coils of fragrant smoke began to spill lazily from the censer's head, quickly filling the small space. Through the haze, Neff watched the priest unwind the cord and open the door. She ascended the three steps first, swinging the incense before her, and found herself in the presence of Amun.

Being that he was the patron god of Thonis, the kingdom's capital city, Amun's statue was immense. Set on a tall pedestal, it was the height of three men and carved from white limestone. Not a drop of paint, nor any other stone or metal interrupted its purity save his eyes, which boasted pupils of the finest lapis, as blue as a summer sky. It made sense that he was unadorned. He was, after all, the Invisible One, God of the Unseen. He needed no embellishment. He was nothing and everything, nowhere and everywhere. In that space between ignorance and knowledge, Amun built a house called mystery and invited all to pass through its doors.

Neff lifted her eyes to his and felt a kinship there. Back at the market in Bubas, she'd often complained when people ignored her attempts to draw them to their stall. "It's like they don't even see me," she'd told her father.

He'd tutted and given her a knowing look. "Ah, but there's power in being invisible," he'd said. "Invisibility creates opportunities. To observe, to learn, to *act*. No one is listening to you? Fine. You go listen to them, to their idle conversations, to their secrets. Find out what people really think, Neff, and you can change the world from the shadows."

She stared into the deep blue eyes, unable to look away. *Amun created everything, even himself. And all while no one was watching.*

As these thoughts drifted through her mind, she felt the air in the sanctuary shift. The sensation reminded her of that moment in Bubas when Bast had revealed herself, but even more powerful. Bast's spirit had grabbed hold of her like a cat with a mouse, whereas Amun's energy insinuated itself into her like smoke, seeping in through her mouth and nostrils with each breath until it filled her completely.

She was dimly aware of Nehshi kneeling before the statue, kissing the ground and singing the morning hymns, his arms raised in worship. The priest was right beside her, yet he felt very far away. It was as if her ba—her bird spirit—had taken flight and hovered before the face of Amun, high above. It was a tranquil face, betraying nothing of the heavy weight of the tall double-plumed feather crown upon his brow.

Voices filled her mind. They were her father's voice, and Kenna's, and the voice in her mind that asked questions at night when she could not sleep. They were all and none of them at once.

You must trust that which you cannot see, the voices said. *Do not fight the currents that carry you toward your fate, lest you arrive late or not at all. Use the gifts you have been given and cause them to multiply within you, for they are borne of we who have crafted you from the earth for this purpose.*

Amun's eyes grew larger with each word, obscuring everything else in Neff's vision until her world was a smoky blue cloud, pregnant with possibility.

You may feel alone on this journey, but like the streams that flow to the great river, you are one of many, and many are but one.

Her heart swelled.

And then she was sinking—back to herself, back to Nehshi's diligent offerings of water and oil and prayer.

Much is hidden.

The voices faded to a whisper.

But much will be revealed.

Neff gasped, the arrival back in her physical body abrupt and strange. She felt heavy, her arm holding the censer blazing with the pain of holding it aloft for so long.

Nehshi looked up, having finished wrapping Amun's feet in special white cloths. "What's wrong with you? Why are you crying?"

Neff touched her face, surprised to see her fingers come away wet with tears. She shook her head. "I… I don't know."

He was about to press further when a loud, ululating cry echoed from outside the sanctuary, calling everyone in the vicinity to attention.

"What's that?" Neff asked.

Nehshi arranged the empty offering plates and bottles back on the tray and rose to his feet. "The watchman. Someone important must be coming. We should go and see if we're needed."

With one last glance up at the patron god, Neff followed Nehshi outside and waited while he resealed the door. Together, they hurried through the ever-larger halls and out into the main courtyard. The few priests who were not tending to the king's tomb or preparing for the coronation were already there, peering with interest through the front gate. Neff saw Kenna among them and rushed to his side. He stood still, his expression as inscrutable as Amun's.

"Who is it?" she asked, following his gaze.

Kenna's lip curled. "My brother."

Meryamun came through the gate on a finely carved palanquin carried by four litter bearers. He was dressed in the same translucent linen blouse and schenti that Neff had seen him wear before—but his adornments had grown more opulent. Golden cuffs ringed his wrists and ankles, and a magnificent pectoral necklace lay upon his chest, depicting two kneeling goddesses praising the prince's name. His eyes were lined with kohl, and his luxuriant black hair was dotted with golden beads.

The litter bearers sank to their knees. As soon as the palanquin was set down, Mery rose from his throne and stepped toward them.

"Bakenamun," he said with obvious distaste. "It's good to see you again so soon. And you, young Nefermaat. How serendipitous that you both should be here to meet me."

Kenna stepped in front of Neff, blocking her with one arm. "You will not touch her," he said to Mery, hardly loud enough for her to catch the words. If the litter bearers heard anything, they didn't let it show. "If you've come to kill me, then fine. But leave the girl alone."

Neff stiffened in horror. *Kill him?*

Mery smiled and patted Kenna on the shoulder. "Don't be so dramatic, brother. I haven't come to kill you. What a terrible waste of energy, given that you barely live at all. What gave you that idea?"

Kenna's jaw tensed. "You slaughtered Father's court last night."

Neff felt the blood drain from her face.

"*Tsk. Slaughter* is such a harsh word," Mery said blithely. "I prefer *sacrifice*. Those honorable men and women *sacrificed* themselves to spend eternity serving their king. You're a man of faith—you of all people should know the doctrine."

"And you of all people should know we stopped following that doctrine a thousand years ago. It's barbaric."

"Only those with weak hearts and feeble minds mistake strength for barbarism," Mery shot back. "Mark my words, if the pharaohs of old could see the kingdom today, they'd opt to wipe it from the face of the earth rather than allow it to fall further into impotence." He leaned in closer. "The blood of a few is a small price to pay to restore the glory of the kingdom."

"A small price?" Kenna spat. "You've paid with your immortal soul."

Mery shook his head. "Take a look at yourself, Kenna, then look at me."

Neff glanced between them. Next to Mery—strong, lithe, golden—Kenna looked like a pale specter.

"My heart is light. How about yours?" Mery taunted.

Kenna's face twisted with anger. "How can you say that, after you… you…"

"After I what, Brother?" Mery's eyes flashed.

Neff willed Kenna to speak. *Accuse him! Say it now, so that everyone will know he murdered the king!*

Kenna's gaze dropped. "Forget it."

Mery shrugged. "As ever, Brother, you have the tenacity of a boiled onion. But! As much as I enjoy it, I didn't come here to argue with you. I've come to collect the little priestess."

Both their faces turned to Neff. Her mind whirled.

He's come for me?

"What? No," Kenna seemed stunned by the abrupt shift in conversation. "You can't just take her."

"I can, actually," Mery said. "Don't worry, she will be quite safe."

"But she belongs here!" Kenna exclaimed.

"Not anymore. The girl is wasted at the temple, poring over scrolls in caves. She belongs in the light, with me."

"But what will Montuhotep say? She is his ward!"

"Montuhotep will say nothing, as it is no longer his concern. I've already spoken to him." Mery turned to face her. "You have proven precious to me, Nefermaat. Your prophecy saved my life out on the marshes."

Neff was surprised. She remembered her vision of the crocodile god. "Your dream. About Sobek."

The prince nodded. "If I hadn't knelt before his image on that hunt, I wouldn't be standing here now. You're not like these other pretenders, I know that now. The voice of the divine is in your ear. That's why you belong by my side."

He paused, considering. "Still, my brother has a point. I cannot force you to share your gifts. I want a companion—not a slave. So it's your choice, Nefermaat. Stay here with my brother or join me at the palace. If you join me, you will want for nothing. I will robe you in riches befitting a child of the gods. I give you my word."

She glanced from one brother to the other, uncertain.

"Neff, what is there to think about?" Kenna whispered after a long silent moment had passed. "He's giving you a choice—tell him you want to stay here!"

She closed her eyes.

Do not fight the currents that carry you toward your fate.

Neff wanted to stay. She was actually starting to feel comfortable with her life as a priestess. The idea of being whisked away to yet another place—the palace, no less!—filled her with fear. But at the same time, she knew she couldn't ignore the prince's proposal. He wasn't merely offering her a seat by his side, he was offering her his trust.

Ever since that day on the streets of Bubas, she'd tried to understand her role in the goddess's plan. She was young, invisible. Was it possible that those attributes were strengths, rather than weaknesses? Could it be that it was those very qualities, along with her gift of prophecy, that earned her the prince's faith? For who would suspect a simple merchant girl of manipulation or political subterfuge?

If I choose Meryamun, my word could bend the will of a king.

It would be dangerous. She'd have to observe, learn, and act against him while still maintaining his trust. If he ever found out she was undermining him…

She swallowed.

Did she have the courage to play such a dangerous game?

"You're going to make us proud," her father had said the last time she saw him. "They'll come to see me from all over Bubas, from all over Khetara, to hear your story."

What story do you want him to tell? she asked herself.

Neff took a deep breath, and when she released it, she knew the decision had been made.

She stepped toward the crown prince. "I will return to the palace with you, Prince Meryamun."

Kenna went rigid.

Mery smiled. "A wise choice."

Neff glanced at her adopted brother's emotionless face. Even though he didn't show it, she knew how deep she'd cut him. She desperately wanted to tell him about her plans, but she knew she couldn't. *Not now. Not yet.*

"I appreciate everything you've done for me, Prince Kenna," Neff said, bowing her head so she wouldn't have to look at him. "But my place must be with the new king."

As if he were used to being the lesser choice, he replied flatly, "As you wish."

Mery clapped his hands to punctuate the end of the conversation.

"Well! Come along, little seer, we have a busy day ahead of

us. You'll be fitted for new garments straightaway. I'll not have you walking around in those rags." He directed her to sit on the edge of the palanquin at his feet, and Neff obeyed.

"Oh!" Mery said to Kenna before ascending the palanquin. "Before I go—have you seen our dear sister today, by any chance?"

Kenna frowned. "Sitamun? No... She almost never visits here. You know that. She's not at the palace?"

A thin line appeared at the center of Mery's brow. "No," he said mildly. "The princess seems to be missing." Then the line vanished, burned away by the blaze of his smile.

"Not to worry. You know Sita. Without her attendants and her fineries and her wine, our dear sister is quite helpless. She'll turn up. In fact, she may be waiting for us upon our return. Shall we go see, Nefermaat?"

Neff nodded, folding her hands demurely in her lap.

Once the prince was resettled into his throne, the litter bearers rose to their feet, lifting them into the air. Neff's feet dangled over the ground, giving her the same weightless sensation she'd felt in the sanctuary, carried aloft by something bigger and grander than herself.

"Goodbye, Brother," Mery said. "I'll see you at the coronation."

As the litter bearers walked to the temple gates, Neff allowed herself one last look back at Kenna. The sight of him nearly broke her heart.

Fighting back tears, she turned to face the path ahead, echoing Mery's words in her mind.

Goodbye, Brother.

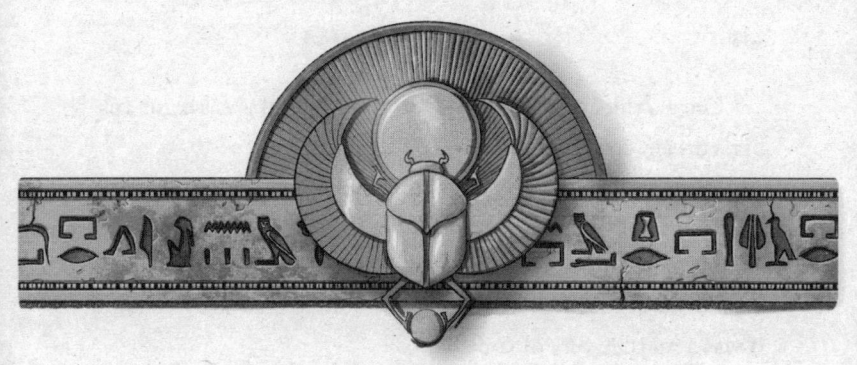

28
KARIM

If sound were food and color drink, Karim could have remained forever filled at the Thonis marketplace. Compared to the traveling traders of the Red Lands and the bazaars of Khetara's smaller towns, the market was an experience unto itself. He spent the rest of the day exploring it, trading bits and bobs from the tomb for fresh supplies, and then returning to feed Behkai. The dog had taken his job of guarding the skiff quite seriously, and seemed to enjoy many industrious hours spent by the river, dozing and catching fish. It was a welcome diversion for them both, filling Karim's senses with so many sights and smells that he had hardly any room left for dark thoughts.

Over and over, his hand drifted to the item in his tunic, where he kept his latest plunder.

He hadn't enjoyed stealing from the temple. The little priestess had stuck her neck out for him, and removing a scroll from their House of Life was no way to repay her kindness. But when he'd caught a glimpse of what it was, Karim knew he had to have it.

Once a thief, always a thief—and that scroll was a tomb robber's dream come true.

It was a rough drawing, depicting mountains, the familiar long blue finger of the river, and multiple locations marked with red stars. The locations were labeled with indecipherable Khetaran symbols, but Karim didn't need to be able to read them to know it was a map. A very old one.

And where there were ancient places—there was probably treasure too.

He recognized one particular valley on the map that was marked with a star. He'd been there. It was the location of Setnakht's tomb, where Karim had found untold treasures. Who knew what might be hidden in those other secret places?

He felt a thrill of excitement at the thought of undiscovered tombs, but it was quickly followed by shame. When he'd discovered it inside the hidden compartment, he'd convinced himself that the map was essential to his search for more information about Setnakht and the oracle, which was why he needed to take it. But was that really true? Or was he more interested in returning to his old ways to seek out buried treasure?

Well, why shouldn't I? Karim thought. *Why shouldn't I fund this journey with Khetaran spoils? I may have opened the door to that tomb, but the curse hidden inside was of their making, not mine. Leave it to the Khetarans to force a tribesman from the Red Lands to clean up their mess!*

That night, as he and Behkai bedded down on the riverbank outside the city, he made his decision. He'd spend one more day trading and gathering supplies, and then start trying to decipher the different locations on the map. He needed to figure out which one could mark Setnakht's capital city. Maybe he could copy the symbols from the scroll and find someone who could translate them for him. He was loath to actually show anyone the map itself, for fear that they couldn't be trusted. So that was the plan: he'd find the lost city, and perhaps make himself richer along the way.

That night, the little priestess's haunting eyes appeared to him as he tried to fall asleep, her final, oddly ominous words echoing in his mind. *I have a feeling we'll meet again, Karim of the Red Lands.*

I hope not, sena, he thought. *For your sake, and mine.*

The next afternoon, Karim returned to the market to seek out a midday meal. Located along a vast winding corridor that cut through the heart of the city, the marketplace consisted of hundreds of merchants—some displaying wares outside their workshops under vibrant crimson and gold canopies, others huddled inside makeshift tents, and yet more with their goods arrayed on blankets spread along the sides of the street. The air was filled with shouts advertising oils from the north, incense from the south, and everything in between. Once you added in the squawks of ducks and geese for sale, and the braying of goats being led home to new owners, it was quite a racket. All along the corridor, customers packed close together, and as Karim allowed himself to be carried along with them, he caught snippets of their conversations.

"She says demons took King Amunmose because he'd done nothing to settle the unrest in Sakesh…"

"You traded *how many* geese for that necklace?"

"Something happened at the palace last night, but no one knows exactly what…"

"I heard it's going to be the biggest coronation in a hundred years…"

"We could use a new wine jar, you know. Look at this one…"

"Prince Meryamun must soon take a queen. I wonder who it's going to be?"

Karim's ears perked up. Mention of the prince brought to mind the image of the three royal children he'd seen in the oracle.

Bakenamun was the man I met, and his brother is expected to take the throne. But it was the sister, Sitamun, who was central in the painting. And it was Sitamun who appeared in the little priestess's vision.

What's the princess's role in all this? he wondered.

He dropped out of the flow of the crowd and made his way to a food stall he'd visited the day before. A hunched elderly woman was busy turning skewers of meat over a small fire, while stirring a pot that sat bubbling over the coals. The scents in the air made his mouth water.

The woman looked up as Karim approached and grinned. "Well, hello again! Come back for more, have you?"

"How could I resist?"

"I've got duck, green onion, and stewed lentils today," she said, nodding toward the fire.

"Delicious," Karim said warmly, then added, "much like the young lady serving it."

"Oh!" the old woman squealed. "Such a rascal." Despite the scolding, she served him a double portion of everything.

Karim accepted the hot food, wrapped in layers of fig leaf, and offered a pretty bauble in exchange. The woman took it gratefully, and Karim touched his knuckle to his nose in thanks. A little charm and flattery, he'd learned, went a long way with the female vendors. Although he wore the Khetaran tunic, some of the vendors still eyed him with distrust, so he'd learned quickly where to take his business.

He was about to head back to Behkai when he spied a fruit stand with baskets overflowing with a variety of sensuous-looking fruit. There were fragrant melons in different shapes and colors, and some other items he'd never seen before. Curious, he flipped the vendor a bit of gold and picked up some deep blue grapes and a round pink fruit with a hard little bloom on one end. He was weighing it in his hand, wondering how he was supposed to eat it, when his gaze was drawn to a young woman shopping at the next stall.

Upon first glance, there was nothing extraordinary about her. She wore unremarkable black robes, her hood pulled over her head to block out the afternoon sun. She looked no different than a hundred others in the bustling crowd, but there was something about her graceful bearing, the liquid way she moved, that caught his eye.

The woman inspected the loaves of bread arranged on the table in front of her, but when the vendor offered a trade, she shook her head and moved on to the fruit stall. Unlike everyone else in the crowd—aside from Karim himself—she seemed to take in everything around her with fresh eyes. Perhaps she, too, was a stranger to this land.

A shout came from somewhere nearby.

The woman startled, and her head snapped toward the sound. In that moment, Karim caught a glimpse of her face. The first feature he noticed was her prominent, aquiline nose. On another woman it might have looked severe, but on her it was regal, elegant. Her full lips were pursed, and her eyes were wide with alarm beneath dark, arched brows.

Who is she? And why is she so scared? Karim wondered.

There was something contradictory about this woman and her plain, rough robes. She was too refined, her copper skin too unblemished and her cheeks too full, to be a peasant. And yet, she was dressed like one.

Just then, a group of three men who were dressed differently from everyone else appeared at the far end of the marketplace. Their white schentis weren't rough or rumpled, but crisply pleated and belted with fine leather. Around their necks were shining gold collars shaped like falcons with wings outstretched.

Some kind of military men, or guards, Karim guessed.

People scattered to give them a wide berth, and Karim watched as they made their way down the street, stopping to interrogate the merchants and inspect every young woman who passed by.

A tingle crept up the back of Karim's neck as he glanced at the woman in black. She was watchful, rigid—like a hunted animal on the edge of flight.

If she runs, she'll only attract their attention.

He had no idea who she was or why she appeared frightened of the approaching guards, but he felt compelled to help her. Maybe it was because she was beautiful, but he preferred to think that he was repaying Nefermaat's good deed, as she claimed to have done for him. The little priestess had risked her safety to come to his rescue at the temple, it seemed only right to do the same for this stranger.

"Greetings, sena," he said, moving to the woman's side. "You look like you could use a hot meal. Why don't you come and share mine?"

The woman turned to him with alarm and pulled the hood closer to her face. "No, thank you," she said, and started to move away.

The guards were getting close.

"Please," Karim said, reaching for her arm. "I'm just trying to help."

"Let me go!" Her tone was that of someone accustomed to being obeyed. She yanked her arm from his grasp and pinned him with an imperious glare. "I don't need your help."

Karim saw one of the guards turn toward them with a frown.

"Sena," Karim warned her, his apprehension growing. "I really think you should come with me." He reached for her arm again.

"Leave me alone, you pig!" she cried, trying to pry him off.

"Pig?" Karim huffed, offended. She was stronger than he expected. "Will you stop struggling, woman!"

It was too late. The guards were headed their way, their hands reaching for the hilts of their khopesh.

Karim broke into a cold sweat. The woman saw them too and paled.

Do something!

They drew closer.

Anything!

With a murmured apology, Karim slapped the woman across the face.

She gasped, one hand going to her reddening cheek. She ducked her head from the blow. The hood dropped back over her face, shielding it from sight.

The guards stopped in their tracks, taken aback by this new development.

"What's this about?" one asked sternly.

Karim cleared his throat and gave the three men a rueful look. "The wife... I tell her to buy bread; instead she trades all our geese for jewelry. What can you do?"

The suspicion on the guards' faces turned to amusement.

"Keeping her in line, are you?" one asked.

"I certainly am," Karim said, chuckling nervously. "She's a wild animal in need of taming!"

Next to him, the woman made a quiet, infuriated noise—but kept her head bowed.

"Come along, old girl," he said to her. "Time to go home."

"Good luck with that!" said another guard.

This time, when Karim guided the woman by the arm, she came willingly.

Behind them, Karim heard one of the guards issue a command to his companions.

"You two double back and check every woman you see. I'll finish searching this end of the market. The princess must be around here somewhere."

Karim's stomach dropped. *The princess?*

He shot the woman a sidelong glance. The image of Sitamun's face in the Temple of Khnum appeared in his mind. *Marked with a black cobra, holding a heart in her hands.*

It had been merely a painting, but much like his own likeness, the image had looked very similar to the woman in black.

Karim cursed under his breath. It seemed that no matter where he went, the oracle followed. *First Raetawy, then Nefermaat, and now this.* Events seemed to be drawing them together—but for what purpose, he still had no idea. He felt like a pawn in someone else's game, and wondered what move he should make next.

Did it even matter?

Had the gods of this accursed kingdom already decided his fate?

The two of them walked in silence until they reached the outer edges of the marketplace, where the crowd thinned. Karim pulled her out of the flow of people and under the shade of a palm, then released her arm.

He had just opened his mouth to speak, when she slapped him. Hard.

"Ow!" Karim cried, cupping a hand to his jaw.

"That's for putting your filthy hands on me!" the woman snapped. In her haste, she'd allowed the hood to fall away from her face. She was radiant with fury. Rivulets of thick shining hair, as black as a raven's wing, tumbled out from her robes.

"And that's for slapping me, and for calling me 'old girl.' I am *not* an old girl and certainly not *your* old girl…" She seemed to run out of steam. "And, well… I suppose I should thank you."

Karim raised his eyebrows. "I suppose you should."

"I just… I thought you were making a move on me. How was I to know you were trying to help me get away from those guards? If you'd *explained* yourself—"

"I tried to."

"No, you offered me a *hot meal*." She raised an eyebrow, as if such an offer was obviously obscene.

Karim scoffed. Twice.

"And then you slapped me."

"That's a very reductive way of viewing the situation, sena," Karim replied.

"Is it?"

They stared at each other, each sporting a reddened cheek.

"You enjoyed that, didn't you?" Karim said.

"What? Slapping you? No." The woman frowned. "Maybe."

"Do you want to do it again?"

Her other cheek reddened to match the first. She crossed her arms. "No! Who are you, anyway? How did you know those guards were looking for me?"

Karim shrugged. "It was obvious they were searching for a young woman, and—let's say, you don't exactly fit in." He cleared his throat. "Princess Sitamun."

The princess inhaled sharply, fear and suspicion returning to her striking face.

"I hate to disappoint you," she said in a low voice. "But I'm not carrying anything of value, only the clothes on my back. No riches to reward your… kindness."

His heart quickened at the thought of her parting with those clothes, but he quickly shook away the image.

Don't be stupid, he scolded himself. *She's a Khetaran princess. She's probably arrogant, spoiled, used to having everyone at her beck and call*. Although why such a woman would find herself on the run from the royal guard gave him pause.

"I need no riches," he replied. "I ask only two simple favors—both of which I believe you can easily provide."

The princess narrowed her eyes.

"It's nothing to provoke another slap, I promise," Karim added.

"Fine," she said.

"Good," Karim said with a nod. "One, perhaps you'd like to apologize for calling me a pig, hey? Considering my recent heroics?"

The princess pressed her lips into a thin line. She lifted her chin. "Very well. I am sorry. You're not a pig. Does 'dog' work better for you?"

"It does," Karim replied blithely. "Much more fitting, I would say."

Sitamun suppressed a smile. "What's the second request?"

Karim gestured toward the river. "Join me for that hot meal. Duck and lentils, nothing sinister, I promise you. We'll have to share some with Behkai, I'm afraid, but it should be enough for all of us."

"Behkai?"

"My dog." The words came naturally, and Karim was surprised at the warmth that flooded his chest when he said them. The damned beast had grown on him.

Sitamun nodded. "So now that I know your dog's name—what's yours?"

Karim hesitated, always wary of sharing his name with strangers—especially Khetarans. But then again, if the oracle had brought them together, had he any choice but to trust her?

Perhaps if he shared his food and his name, she might share something useful with him too.

"Karim," he blurted, before he could reconsider.

"Karim," Sitamun repeated, her lips forming the name as if she were tasting it.

"Now that we're properly acquainted... what do you say? Will you come?"

"I suppose I am a little hungry," she admitted.

Karim grinned. "Well then." He gestured toward the riverbank. "Two dogs eagerly await your company."

It annoyed him—though he couldn't quite explain why—that Behkai took to Sitamun so readily. When he and the princess arrived at the skiff, the dog leaped to his feet. Karim expected him to start barking at the stranger, but instead, he trotted over to Sitamun like an enormous puppy and began drooling over her. Literally.

"Oh," she crooned, taking his face in her hands and rubbing him, with no regard for the drool. "What a sweet boy. What a good boy."

"Traitor," Karim muttered to the dog as he passed.

Behkai ignored him—that is, until he smelled the food. Karim sat on a rock, and as soon as he began unwrapping it, the dog trotted over to investigate.

"Have a seat," Karim told Sitamun, gesturing to a boulder opposite him.

She perched on the boulder with as much decorum as she could muster.

Decorum went by the wayside, however, once Karim handed her the food. The princess fell upon the duck and lentils with zeal, devouring everything she'd been given in minutes, and then doing the same with the second serving he offered. He watched with amusement as she sucked all the grease from her fingers, one by one. When she caught him looking, she dropped her hands to her lap and sat up very straight.

"Good?" he asked.

"Yes," she replied primly. "Thank you."

Karim stuck the last onion in his mouth, letting its burnt greens hang out the side, and munched on it while he tossed the last of the meat to Behkai.

"There's fruit too," he said, pulling out the grapes and the round pink thing. "Not sure what this is, but I thought I'd give it a try." He was about to take a bite out of it, but the princess snatched it out of his hand.

"It's a pomegranate, you fool. You don't bite into it. You have to cut it open." She produced a fine dagger from inside her robes and made four long slits around the stem of the fruit before opening it like a flower. She handed it back to him, the insides gleaming with jewellike red clusters.

"Look at that, hey?" Karim said, amazed at the fruit's surprising beauty. "Like a bunch of little rubies." He took an experimental bite. The little clusters burst inside his mouth, filling it with a magnificent sweetness. "It's good!"

Sitamun watched him with interest. "Where are you from, Karim? Your accent... I don't recognize it."

Karim licked the crimson juice from his lips. He'd been prepared to tell her his name, but everything else? Not yet.

"I'm a traveler," he replied vaguely. "No one of consequence, unlike yourself. Speaking of which," he went on, "why is a princess on the run from the royal guard? Isn't your brother about to take the throne? I'd have thought you'd be needed at the palace."

The princess narrowed her eyes. She'd noted the deliberate change of subject—and Karim had the feeling that she wasn't going to let the matter go.

"Well, Karim the mysterious traveler. It's a long story, and not one I'm likely tell someone I just met. No matter how charming their company might be."

Karim flushed.

Sitamun tilted her head to Behkai, who sat worshipfully at her feet. "I meant the dog."

Karim crossed his arms. *This woman is really something else.*

Seeing him, Sitamun relented. "Let's simply say I wasn't safe there, all right?" Her gaze drifted over Karim's shoulder, to the river. "And I'm not safe here either."

Following her gaze, Karim turned to see a fine ship coming down the river toward them, sporting a black and red ram's head on its sail. A host of guards, dressed similarly to the ones in the marketplace, stood on the deck, scanning the riverbank as they went. They were distracted by some women washing clothes a little farther up, but the ship had only to come a little closer before they'd notice Karim and Sitamun sitting by the skiff.

The princess leaped to her feet, pulling the hood back over her head. "Thank you for everything you've done," she said, "But I must go."

Karim shook his head. "I don't understand. Your brother is going to be king—who could you possibly be running from?"

The princess's face crumpled with sudden anguish. "Him. I'm running away from *him*."

Shocked, Karim thought of the image of Meryamun in the oracle—a handsome young man with bronze skin and a red cobra over his head. What had he done to send his own sister running for her life?

Run from the palace and straight into my path.

"Where are you planning to go?" he asked.

"I thought I'd travel south to Bubas. It's the closest village large enough to hide in. I'll have to go by foot, though. The guards are searching every vessel that leaves Thonis."

Karim scoffed. "A woman like you, all alone, on *foot*? You'd never make it, sena! Between the heat, the lions, the wandering brigands..."

"I appreciate the encouragement," Sitamun replied drily, and started to walk away.

"Hey now, wait a minute!" Karim went after her, Behkai trotting at his heels. He glanced back at the approaching boat, his thoughts racing.

I'd have to abandon the skiff, and I barely have enough food for the dog and me, no less a ravenous woman with no survival skills. And if the prince's men find me with her, they'll probably slit my throat on the spot.

If I was smart, I'd let her go, he reasoned. *I've already got one stray to take care of. I don't need another.*

Djet's puppy-dog face appeared in his mind, his eyes full of admiration.

You wouldn't abandon a princess to the dangers of the desert, would you Karim-sen? he imagined the boy saying. *Especially a princess so clever and so beautiful?*

For some unknown reason, Djet had believed he was a hero.

He wasn't. Far from it.

And yet... Karim couldn't help but sense the boy still beside him, watching his every move.

He cursed under his breath as he tossed his pack over his shoulder and grabbed Sitamun's hand.

"W-what are you doing?" she stammered, stumbling along after him as he began running toward the open desert.

Behkai, thinking it was all great fun, galloped after them.

"I'm helping you, woman!" Karim replied, glancing back to make sure the guards on the boat hadn't seen them. "Now run a little faster!"

Sitamun picked up her robes so she wouldn't trip over them and increased her pace. "But being with me is dangerous!"

Karim laughed with heavy irony, the wind rippling the dark curls of his hair.

"Don't worry, sena, you'll find out soon enough that it's even more dangerous being with me!"

29
RAE

Rae stood barefoot at the river's edge, watching the boats sail by as the sun set. She would have preferred to sit, but the fresh arrow wound in her hip made that somewhat difficult.

With the cool breeze blowing across her skin and the sound of the river rushing past, it should have been peaceful. But inside Rae's mind, she was still in the Garden of the Dead. Still running for her life, still hiding and bleeding in the dark as men fell like reaped wheat around her. She saw it all—the bodies, the open, staring eyes, Asim's severed head—every time she closed her eyes.

In a way, she never left that place.

She wondered if she ever would.

A sudden noise made her jump—but it was only the *clack* of the cattle gate closing. Her father had finished taking care of the zebu for the night.

"Come inside, Raetawy," he said, approaching. "You need rest."

When she got home from the Horizon meeting the night before, despite the ungodly hour, her father had been awake. He'd been sitting at their eating table when she'd stumbled in, dirty, tearstained, with an arrow sticking out of her rear end. Upon seeing her, he had simply gotten up and started gathering ointment and bandages.

Luckily, the healer had left enough supplies behind after her encounter with the nomarch to take care of this injury too. Ankhu hadn't said more than a handful of words the entire time and didn't question what had happened. When he was done patching her up, he'd helped her down onto her sleeping mat, and then settled onto his own. Sleepless, she'd watched him doze fitfully in the moonlight, his good hand reaching toward something in a dream.

The arrow wound hurt very badly—but the despair on her father's face that night hurt more.

When he reached the riverbank, Ankhu stopped to lean against the wooden staff he used to encourage the zebu to go into their pen. His bare chest was leathery from work in the sun and his rough schenti was speckled with mud. There was something about him that reminded her of Asim—two hard-bitten men, relics of another time, protecting what little was left to them. It was no wonder she'd taken to the rebel leader so quickly.

A fresh wave of grief washed over her.

It was better not to think of Asim.

Her father spoke quietly. "I know what happened last night. One of the fishermen told me. His son…" He was silent for a long moment before finishing. "Many are mourning today. I'm grateful not to be one of them."

Rae wanted him to be angry. To shout at her and punish her for sneaking out and nearly getting herself killed.

Again.

But he just sounded tired.

"I'm sorry," she whispered.

Ankhu flinched as if from a blow and shook his head. "What are you going to do now?" The apology dangled in the air between them, unacknowledged.

Rae looked back at the river and the sun melting onto the horizon. "I don't know. I'm not sure how the rebellion will survive without Asim. But it has to! Especially after the news I overheard last night. The nomarch's men said that the pharaoh is dead."

Ankhu's eyes widened. "Dead?"

Rae nodded. "His son Meryamun will soon be crowned—and he sounds even worse than Amunmose himself. He's not yet on the throne, and already he sends word to slaughter us. Last night was only the beginning. The new king means to quash any hint at rebellion in Sakesh. Unless we do something, the small freedoms we still enjoy here may soon be gone."

Ankhu dropped his head and sighed. "You mustn't take this burden onto yourself, Rae. We have survived hardship before, and we'll do it again—as long as we stay together."

"I don't know if I can let this go, Yati," Rae murmured, her voice unsteady. "You weren't there. You didn't see what happened."

"I've seen *plenty*, Raetawy," Ankhu said harshly. "Plenty and enough to know that if you continue on this path, the person you are now will be lost. War changes you. Do you understand? Violence changes you. Once you've visited that bleak country, there's no coming back." He leaned the staff against his chest so he could grasp her shoulder with his hand. "Please, we can talk about this more inside. It's getting dark."

"Not yet."

Her father sighed but didn't argue. She turned back to the river and listened to his slow footsteps recede.

The light on the horizon was almost gone.

She stood there for a little longer, lost in thought, her fingers tangled in the Sekhmet amulet still hanging around her neck. She might have stayed until nightfall, except for another sound snapping her out of her reverie: the sudden bleat of a sheep.

Rae turned toward it. A ram stood by the riverbank, watching her with its strange rectangular pupils.

"What are you doing here?" she asked the sheep.

Not surprisingly, the ram didn't provide an answer.

Probably one of Baki's, Rae guessed as she stepped toward it. It wasn't uncommon for the shepherd to lose one of his flock when he put them in their pen for the night, but they never strayed far.

"Come on, now," she said. "Time to go home."

The ram didn't put up a fight. He allowed her to lead him by the horn back toward Baki's land, and the shepherd intercepted them halfway. Apparently, he'd already noticed the ram's disappearance and had come searching for him.

"Rae?" Baki exclaimed when he saw her. He looked haunted, unwashed, unshaven. "Oh, thanks be to Ra, I thought you were dead! I heard what happened when I went to town this morning. I couldn't believe it. I still can't believe it! Asim, and the others..."

Rae blinked, and in that instant, she was transported back.

The blood.

The screams.

The whizz of arrows sailing past her head.

She inhaled sharply and felt a pain in her chest, but quickly shoved the memories back into the dark.

"Yes," she managed.

"I can't believe it," Baki repeated, as if he'd forgotten there were other words to say.

"Where were you last night?" Rae said. "So many men were missing from the meeting." She tried to keep the resentment and suspicion from her voice, but she needed to know the truth. At the time, the absence of so many of the Horizon members at the meeting seemed reasonable—it had been short notice, they hadn't gotten the message, or they hadn't come out of an abundance of caution. But in light of the ambush, she wondered if there was more to it than that.

"I received the message, and I was planning to come," Baki told her. "But then I ran into the brewer later in the day, and he told me not to go. He said it was too dangerous to meet again so soon after the raid, and that we should all lie low until things settled down."

"What?" Rae said sharply. "He did?"

Baki nodded. "It sounded sensible enough, so I stayed home. He must have spoken to some of the other men as well, because I bumped into a few of them in town last evening. Knowing what I know now, I'm glad I listened to him." The shepherd dropped his eyes, abashed. "But at the same time, I can't help but feel guilty for surviving when so many died. I'll hold my son a little tighter tonight."

Rae didn't answer. She'd gone rigid, her body thrumming with an emotion whose presence felt like a comfort, burning through her shame and sorrow like a raging fire.

Fury.

"Maybe we survived to avenge them," she said, slipping on her sandals.

Baki frowned as she handed over the horns of the sheep and started to walk past him.

"Rae, wait!" he said. "Where are you going? It's not safe to be out this late!"

"I'm going to pay the brewer a visit," she replied, leaving Baki and his sheep staring after her in the gloaming.

She kept to the shadows when she reached the city, slipping between buildings and through the alley where the fights took place each day. The streets were empty and filled with a heavy, mournful silence. She passed the darkened bakery, its workers gone home to get a few hours of sleep before returning to shape loaves for the new day.

Next door was the brewery.

Thin reed mats covered the windows, but through them Rae could see flickering lamplight and a figure moving inside. The front door was ajar.

She pushed through it without knocking.

An unpleasant, sour-sweet smell assaulted her senses as she stepped into the long, dimly lit room. The brewer stood with his back to her next to a line of tall vats nestled in piles of embers, each one filled to the brim with a bubbling brew. Shelves built into the back wall were filled with sealed jars of finished beer, waiting to be sold.

"We're closed," the brewer said, not turning to see who it was. He dipped a cup into one of the steaming vats. "Come back tomorrow."

Rae stepped past the grain-sifting trays and ceramic sieves and into the lamplight. The brewer was a squat man, shaped not unlike one of the beer jars, and Rae towered over him.

"It was you," she said.

The cup stopped halfway to the brewer's fleshy lips and hovered there for a moment. Then he slowly set it down on a table.

"When I saw you coming out of the nomarch's house that day," Rae went on, still speaking to his back, "you weren't delivering beer, were you? You were delivering *information*. How long have you been working for him? Days? Weeks? Or were you with the High Khetarans from the very beginning?"

The brewer turned. "Raetawy, how disappointing that you aren't dead."

"I should have guessed you were a traitor," she said, ignoring the comment. "You were always the loudest voice at those meetings, preaching cowardice disguised as reason, trying your best to keep the men from fighting for their freedom—"

"*I was keeping them safe!* And doing a mighty good job of it until you showed up, you stupid, *stupid* girl."

"Safe?" Rae asked in disbelief. "You told the nomarch about the meeting! We walked straight into an ambush because of you! All those men are dead because of you!"

"Their deaths are on *your* hands, Raetawy, not mine!" the brewer countered. "I tried to warn them. I even tried to warn you! Those that listened to me are still alive. And those that didn't?" He threw up his hands. "What can I say? You reap what you sow."

With a roar, Rae lunged for him, grabbing his tunic and shaking him roughly. "What did the nomarch pay you in exchange for the lives of those men? For the old soldiers? For the fishermen's son? For Asim? What did he give you?"

The brewer shoved her away, and Rae stumbled back into one of the vats, sloshing some of the hot beer onto the dirt floor.

"I would have done it for free," he sneered, spittle flying from his mouth. "Asim was a damned fool. He had it coming!"

Rae's vision narrowed as rage overtook her. She wanted to hit him and keep hitting him and never stop. She went to reach for him again, but then there was movement at the door. She whirled to see who it was.

Three hooded men, their faces shrouded in shadow, had slipped inside the brewery.

"Rae?" the biggest one said. "What are you doing?"

She squinted at him. "Omari?"

"Baki came to get me and Menk. He told us you were coming here but didn't know why. Did something happen?"

She pointed at the brewer. "He betrayed us! He's been working for the nomarch this whole time. That's how they knew we'd be at the Garden of the Dead last night. He told them everything!"

The three men were silent.

"Is this true?" Baki finally asked the brewer. "You knew about the attack?"

The brewer straightened his tunic. "You know, Baki," he said mildly, "I've always liked you. You're not very smart, but you mean well. That's why I told you not to go to that godforsaken meeting."

Baki shook his head in horror. "How could you do this?" he asked. "How could you stand with us all this time and then betray us? I thought you were my friend."

"I *am* your friend!" the brewer said, slamming his fist against the table. "I saved you, didn't I? And the others!

"It was all under control until the attack on the Medjay. I'd managed to convince the nomarch that the Horizon was harmless—just a bunch of grumbling malcontents. But then, you had to go and rob their armory…

"After that, well, he was out for blood. So I made my choice—sacrifice a few to save the rest. The men who showed up to that meeting were too foolish and stubborn to be saved. They got what they deserved." He turned to the shepherd. "You see now, Baki? I did you a favor. It's time to put all this behind us and move on."

"And what about us?" Omari asked. "What about the stubborn fools that survived your butchery?"

The brewer shrugged and gestured toward the bubbling beer vat. "All it takes is a few bad seeds to ruin the whole batch. Since you didn't have the courtesy to die, I'll be forced to pass along your names to the nomarch as traitors to the crown. You managed to evade execution last night, but it won't happen again."

He stepped close to Rae, his lip curling into a sneer.

"I'm sure the nomarch will take his time with you. He's a man who likes to savor his pleasures. Maybe he'll even let you watch when his guards collect your father and finally put him out of his misery."

At the mention of her father, something inside Rae—already bent to its breaking point—snapped.

In a flash, her dagger was in her hand. With the other hand, she gripped the brewer's shoulder, pulled him toward her, and thrust the blade into his ribs.

The brewer's eyes widened. A surprised, strangled noise erupted from his throat.

"Rae!" Baki exclaimed.

She held firm, pressed close against the little man. She had always thought it would be difficult to stab someone. That it would take a lot of effort to plunge a knife through all that muscle and sinew. But it wasn't. It was actually very, very easy.

Really, it took no effort at all.

After what seemed like a long moment, Rae released her grip on the brewer and jerked the dagger free. The man staggered back, his legs tottering under him like a drunkard's. Rae and the others watched, silent, as he crashed into the table, knocking the beer cup to the floor. His tunic was already soaked with blood. He pressed a hand to his wound, but the blood poured over his fingers. There was no stanching the flow. No one moved to help him.

The brewer looked up at them, his face bright with hatred. His mouth opened to say something, but no words came out. Instead, he collapsed onto the dirt floor.

Nobody moved.

Finally, Rae nudged the brewer's body with her foot. No response. She looked down at the dagger in her hand, stained crimson up to the hilt, the wedjat eye engraved on its handle staring up at her from between her fingers.

She waited for the horror. For the regret. For the self-loathing she'd felt when she'd killed that man at the House of the Medjay. But none of it came. Whatever part of her that had once held remorse for the deaths of the wicked was gone.

If you continue on this path, the person you are now will be lost.

A rustling came from the back room, where the brewer had his living quarters.

"We have to go, Rae." Omari's voice was soft but urgent. "We have to go *now*."

"Ra forgive us," Baki muttered, his stare locked on the corpse.

Menk spat. "Son of a dog deserved it."

"Father?"

A young woman emerged from the shadows. Her hair and clothing were rumpled, as if she'd just woken from a deep sleep. Her eyes went first to the bloody dagger in Rae's hand, then to the body on the floor.

Rae recognized the brewer's daughter. His wife had left him years ago, but the girl was about Rae's age, and she'd often bumped into her at the market.

Without her own hood to shield her face from view, the brewer's daughter recognized Rae too.

The girl raised her palms in submission. Rae expected to see hatred or despair in the girl's eyes—but all she saw was fear. "Please don't hurt me," the girl said.

Rae's heart roiled with a thousand different emotions, and suddenly she felt dizzy. She backed away from the girl to Omari's side.

"Take me home," Rae said.

"You can't go home, Rae," Omari said, leading her to the door. "Not tonight…"

"Then when?"

Omari didn't reply. Grabbing a robe hanging by the door, he threw it over Rae's shoulders and pulled the hood over her head as they stepped out into the dark.

Once you've visited that bleak country, there's no coming back.

Out on the street, they passed an old man who sat slumped in the doorway of an abandoned house, humming to himself and chanting orisons to whatever gods or goddesses would listen.

"The lamb," he intoned. "The lamb, the lamb, the lamb…"

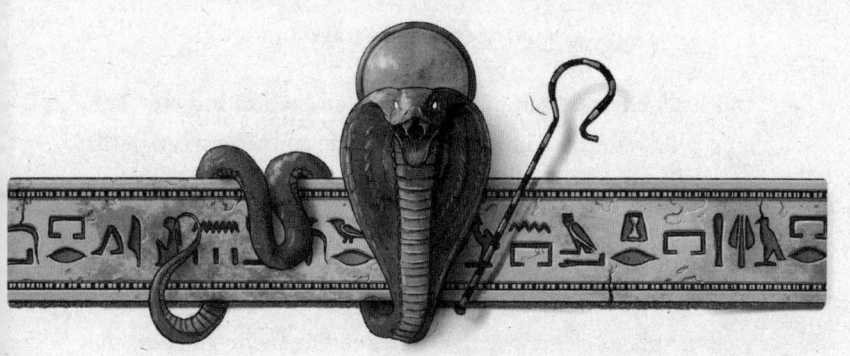

30
SITA

Sita saw many wonderful things during her journey out of Thonis—farms of golden wheat, herds of humpbacked gray zebu, pyramids piercing the horizon like sharp teeth. But what enchanted her most were the flowers.

Her pleasure garden was home to many lovely blooms, some brought from distant lands as gifts to the king, others so delicate they could only survive in the rarified soil nurtured by the royal gardeners. Everything grew within its allotted space, and any rebellious sprouts that dared venture beyond those limits were quickly rooted out. Sita had always thought it was the most glorious place in the world, but that changed after only a few hours of walking through the Khetaran landscape with Karim.

He'd led her away from the river to avoid being spotted by Meryamun's ships, but they remained within the fertile strip of land that surrounded the Iteru on both banks, following its general direction south. Along their path, flowers flowed in torrents over the earth: deep-purple cornflowers, golden river hemp blossoms, and frilly chrysanthemums in orange and white and red. They grew wild, intermingling with nightshade and bitterweed until it was difficult to tell the flowers from the weeds.

How different are they, anyway? Sita wondered. They were all beautiful, and the weeds deserved respect for having the strength to thrive even in the harshest terrain. She was amazed at how well the plants all grew with no one tending them, and how they tangled up in each other to survive the capricious winds. The wildflowers may not have been the faultless blossoms of the pleasure garden, but in a lot of ways, she preferred the freedom of the natural landscape. On a whim, she picked a yellow chrysanthemum bloom and tucked it into her hair.

They'd been walking in silence since leaving the city—Sita, Karim, and the black dog. It was easier to make headway in the afternoon heat without the effort of conversation, and besides, Sita needed the time to think.

The past few days felt like a violent storm that had brought devastation with surprising speed. The thing was—she'd seen it coming. She'd seen it rolling in from the horizon ever since the Festival of Bast. But she'd done nothing to avoid it. Nothing at all.

Now, they're all dead.

Maet.

Father.

The pharaoh's entire court.

All at the hands of a brother she had trusted and loved—a brother who was about to take the throne for himself. A brother who had planned—for days, weeks, years?—to take her into his bed.

It was unthinkable.

How could someone she'd grown up with, someone she thought she knew as well as her own heart, turn out to be such a monster? The revelation threw everything she believed into chaos. She combed over her memories during that walk, viewing them with new eyes, and was shocked to see evidence of Mery's intent everywhere among them.

The way he liked to pick out dresses for her to wear to the banquets, and how he'd linger to chat while she changed into them.

The way he'd brush his hand against hers across the table whenever they played Mehen or Hounds and Jackals.

The way his eyes had flashed when he'd caught her with Femi in the ship's cabin the night of the festival.

In retrospect, his objective hadn't been hidden. Not really. But how could she have anticipated what was to come? How could anyone?

Not that it mattered, because as far as she was concerned, the blame rested fully on her shoulders. She wasn't stupid. She always got through her lessons quickly and frequently beat Mery in their games. She was as sharp as her brother, despite what members of the court—and her own family—might think.

But Mery knew all her weaknesses, her blind spots, her naivete.

Sitamun, Sitamun, you look at the board, but somehow you don't see it.

She turned back toward the huge white pylons of the palace, now barely visible on the horizon.

Mery never truly cared about winning the little games we played, Sita thought. *He only cared about winning this one.*

With a heavy sigh, she lifted her robes again and trotted quickly after Karim and Behkai, who hadn't noticed her slowed pace.

"Wait for me!" she called out. Her feet throbbed. She wasn't used to walking in the heat for so long, and her sandals were made for looks, not travel.

Karim halted and squinted back at her, his rugged yet boyish face peering out from his dark hood.

"Tired, princess?" he asked—a little flippantly, she thought.

"Not at all," she replied, raising her chin. She made an effort to catch up, then surpass him. In response, Karim accelerated his own stride until they were both out of breath. Finally, they fell into an easy rhythm, side by side.

Sita studied him from the corner of her eye. Earlier, he'd removed his white tunic and slipped into a set of dark voluminous robes that he'd taken from the skiff before they'd fled, robes that were similar to her own. He was lean, and a little taller than her, and hairy. *Is that what all men would look like if they didn't shave?* she wondered. Despite her initial disapproval at his lack of hygiene, she had to admit she didn't mind it so much. There was an audaciousness about his look and manner that she almost found appealing.

But there was a secrecy about him too. His manner was light and breezy, but an undercurrent of tension lay beneath it, and she wondered at its source. She'd noticed that he glanced over his shoulder as they walked and startled at sounds in the brush.

What's he so scared of?

The most obvious answer was the royal guard. It was unlikely that Mery would have sent soldiers out this far, but it made sense that Karim would keep a lookout. Though she deeply feared being caught and taken back to the palace, she'd surely be taken alive. Karim, however, was a different story. She had no doubt that if they were found together, he'd be executed right then and there.

The black dog, much like his master, also seemed to be on alert. He'd often scout ahead, sniffing around and then bounding back to them, pink tongue lolling. He'd been doing just that when he ran up to her, dropping a dead shrew at her feet with obvious pride.

"Ugh, why?" Karim kicked the mangled creature off the path. "At least find us something we can eat."

But Sita was pleased at the gift and patted the dog on his big head. "Thank you, Behkai," she said with a smile.

Karim grumbled and walked on.

Clearly, she owed the man a debt for his help getting her out of Thonis, but after having plenty of time to think, she'd started to wonder if his actions were purely altruistic. He was, after all, leading her farther and farther from civilization, and if there happened to be a band of desert thieves waiting at the end of this journey, a runaway princess would be quite the bounty. For all his charm, he could be nefarious as the rest of them.

If she'd learned anything from her recent experiences, it was to stop being so trusting. She felt for the dagger at her waist. If it came to that, she'd do what she had to do.

"We'll stop here, sena," Karim announced, his arms akimbo. They'd crested a small hill and came upon an irrigation canal at the edge of a farm, with a stand of willow trees surrounding it. "We should rest and refill our waterskins."

Sita nodded—she was parched. Mimicking Karim's movements, she bent to dip her waterskin into the canal and held it there until it was full. Then she took a long drink. It was cold and fresh, and she guzzled the whole thing. It was easily the best-tasting water she'd ever had—probably because she'd never been so thirsty before. She hurried to refill her waterskin so she could have more.

"Take it easy," Karim scolded her. "If you drink too fast, you'll throw it all up again."

She pouted but slowed down.

Pulling off his hood, Karim ducked under the drooping branches of one of the trees and sat in the shade. He took a deep, slow swig of water, letting the excess drip down his throat and onto his bare chest beneath. Then he poured the remainder over his head, closing his eyes as the water soaked into his dark curls and caught in shining droplets in the stubble on his cheeks. She watched him, her lips still resting on the mouth of her waterskin.

He opened his eyes. He must have sensed her watching.

Sita looked away. "We only have a few more hours until nightfall. Is it safe to stay this close to the river?"

"We'll venture farther out to set up camp," Karim answered. "But you needed a break."

"I told you, I'm *fine*." Annoyed, she bent at the edge of the canal and splashed cool water on her face. She blinked at her reflection. Her hair was messy, her face sunburned, and her lips chapped. She should have been mortified but couldn't bring herself to care.

Behkai ran up next to her, bending to noisily lap at the water before shaking his head, spraying slobber everywhere.

"Eugh!" Karim exclaimed, swatting at the dog.

Behkai capered around him, mistaking it for a game.

Sita couldn't help but laugh. She couldn't remember the last time she'd done that. It felt really freeing at first, but then it felt wrong. *How can you laugh after all this tragedy? How can you even smile?*

She stopped. With one wet hand, she tried to smooth the wild strands of her hair. Only when she'd managed to tame it did she turn to face Karim again.

He sat gazing at a browned translucent papyrus spread out on a rock in front of him. It was covered in rough sketches of mountains, valleys, and little red stars.

"What's that?" she asked.

Karim glanced at her, and for a moment, Sita thought he might reroll the document and give her some vague answer—like when she'd asked where he was from. But he set his jaw and replied.

"It's a map."

Interested, Sita sat next to him where she could see the

papyrus for herself. It was a partial map of Khetara, showing lands south of Thonis. Some of the town and city names were familiar, others less so—and many places that should have been marked on the map were missing.

"This is old," Sita remarked, her interest piqued. "Really old. Where did you get it?"

Karim tensed beside her. Then he asked, "Can I trust you?"

Sita frowned. It was the most unexpected question she could imagine. "Can *you*"—she pointed to him, with his bristly face and coarse robes, and then back at herself—"trust *me*? I'm Khetaran royalty, for Amun's sake."

"Yes, exactly," he said with slight distaste. "So, can I trust you?"

Sita raised her eyebrows. "Um, yes?"

"You don't sound so sure."

She sighed in frustration. "Yes, Karim. You can trust me."

"Sena, I pray to your gods and to mine that your word is good."

"The word is the deed," Sita intoned.

"What?"

"You've never heard that before? It's a common Khetaran phrase, something you'd say at the end of a prayer. It means that words have great power. When you speak something out loud, it goes from your lips to the gods' ears, and by doing so, you make it happen—you make it true." She cocked her head. "You really aren't from around here, are you?"

Karim shook his head. "I hail… from the Red Lands."

Sita's eyebrows shot up. *The Red Lands! Of course!* She'd heard of the desert tribesmen, but had never met one herself. Her father had considered them little more than bands of godless, unscrupulous ruffians who spent most of their time fighting among themselves. Someone like Karim would never have been invited within a mile of the palace.

"You don't seem like a warrior."

"I'm not. Most of my tribe are shepherds, not warriors. But I'm not one of those either. I'm a... a..."

"A what?"

Karim hesitated.

"Spit it out, will you?" Sita said impatiently.

His cheeks flushed. "I'm a tomb robber, all right?" he said, a little too loudly.

Behkai whined, his tall ears flattening against his head.

"I was part of a group called the Jackals. We'd find Khetaran tombs in the desert, strip them of valuables, and sell the spoils. Now, the map—that I stole that from the Temple of Amun—but strictly speaking, that's an outlier. Usually I steal from the dead, not the living. So there. Now you know."

Sita rocked back. Karim had given the whole speech in a fast, angry rush, and then fallen silent. She'd heard of men—Khetaran and otherwise—looting tombs, but somehow Karim didn't fit the image in her head of what such a man would look like.

"Your disgust means nothing to me, sena," Karim said, his voice harsh. "If your people agreed to formal trade with mine and didn't treat us like heathens, perhaps we wouldn't have to resort to such activities, hey? You all think you're superior, with your fertile river and your hundreds of gods and—"

"I'm not disgusted!" Sita broke in. "I'm... surprised."

Karim folded his arms over his chest.

"I have no right to pass judgment over you and the things you've done in the name of survival," Sita said. The tribesman's confession, though shocking, was refreshing in its honesty. It made her want to be honest too. "You've stolen baubles from the dead. But I..." Guilt nearly took her breath away. "I've stolen life from the innocent."

Karim's anger melted into astonishment. "You *killed* someone? That's why you're running?"

"No, not exactly," Sita replied, and suddenly, she found herself telling him truth. "My brother poisoned the king, our father, so that he could take the throne for himself."

Once she started, the secret poured out of her like water. "He did it slowly, over a long period, so it would seem like an illness. No one suspected—although he inadvertently killed a child in the process. Then as soon as the king was dead, my brother slaughtered the entire court so he could replace it with his own."

Karim puffed out his cheeks. "And here I thought you Khetarans were supposed to be civilized!"

Sita shot him a withering look.

They sat in silence for a moment before Karim said, "I don't understand what you meant about stealing life from the innocent. Your brother killed those people—not you."

"But I knew about the poisoning," Sita argued. "I found out when there was still time to save my father and Maet. Yet I was too afraid to speak. I wanted to believe Mery was doing the right thing, even though deep in my heart, I knew it was wrong. My brother may have dealt the killing blows, but my silence was just as deadly."

She wrapped her arms around herself and spoke more softly. "The same day my father died, Mery told me that I would be his queen. It was an ancient royal custom, marrying your sister—much like killing a king's court so a pharaoh could bring them to the afterlife—but it hasn't been done in a thousand years. It's all part of Mery's plan to return Khetara to its former glory. He's fanatical about it—he believes it's his destiny. I know he will be pharaoh, and a pharaoh is like a god, and yet… I fear what he'll do, how far he's willing to go to achieve the greatness he seeks." She swallowed. "Not all gods are good gods."

"So… you ran away?"

"One of the guards helped me escape," Sita replied, her voice breaking as she thought of Femi. "I can only pray that Mery hasn't killed him too. I can't bear another death on my conscience."

"Well, sena," Karim said, running a hand through his hair. "That, at least, is something we have in common."

"What do you mean?"

"I've made some questionable choices of my own lately. Do you see this?" Karim pointed a red star on the map, located deep in a mountain valley. "That star marks an ancient tomb. I found it, untouched and full of treasure. I had a young boy with me, Djet—and he and I were in the middle of ransacking the place when it happened."

"When what happened?"

A haunted look came into Karim's eyes.

"Something… awoke. It rose from the grave and killed Djet."

Sita was incredulous. "You must be mistaken. It could have been an animal, or—"

"No. I thought that too, at first, but no. I saw it with my own eyes, sena. You're the first person I've told. I… I can't keep the secret any longer."

Sita had read papyri about Heka magic and the existence of powerful spells of reincarnation. Though how a tribesman from the Red Lands could trigger one, she wasn't sure.

"So you're telling me a mummy killed your friend—what happened next?"

"I tried to stop it from escaping the tomb. But it followed me and killed again—an old priest in a Temple of Khnum."

"Khnum?" Sita suddenly felt dizzy, remembering her strange interaction with the old woman who visited her at the palace before her father's death. The woman spoke as if she was the goddess Heqet, consort of Khnum, the ram-headed creator god who sometimes appeared as a lamb.

Karim explained how the old priest had helped him discover

the name of the man who'd been buried in the tomb: a forgotten king named Setnakht. And how he'd traveled to the Temple of Amun seeking more information about the old pharaoh, where he stole the map from the House of Life.

"You met Bakenamun?" Sita asked when his tale was finished. "And that young priestess you described... I think I know who she is." She recalled the strange girl who'd stared at her with intensity at the Bast Festival, and who Mery claimed had saved his life with a premonition. Could it be the same person? "What an odd coincidence."

"That's the thing," Karim said. "I don't think it's a coincidence at all. I saw something else in that Temple of Khnum. The old priest explained that this painting on the wall was an ancient oracle. He called it the Oracle of the Lamb."

Sita felt a chill up her spine.

"There were four figures depicted," Karim continued. "They all surrounded this image of a bloody lamb. One of them was me."

"You? In a Khetaran oracle?"

Karim nodded. "The second was a warrior, the third a priestess..." He swallowed, his eyes meeting hers. "And the last was you."

"What?" Sita shivered as a cool wind blew through the willows, bringing with it a strange scent—sweet and smoky and intoxicating. Behkai raised his quivering nose to the air, but as soon as it had come, it was gone. "How can you be sure?" she asked.

"There were three royal children," Karim explained. "Your two brothers and you. Your face. Your eyes. It could be no one else."

As an afterthought, he added, "You held a heart in your hands."

Sita shook her head. It was all too much to believe. Still, she was shaken by the thought of her image holding a heart, weighing it as the gods did at judgment. She and Mery had taken lives into their own hands—what punishments might they face for usurping the gods' will? "What did it foretell, this oracle?" she asked.

Karim's expression darkened. "Nothing good. Ruin. Betrayal. War. A river turned to blood."

A hysterical laugh bubbled up Sita's throat. She put one hand on Behkai's head, and the dog leaned against her leg, as if to comfort her. The hysteria subsided.

"Naturally," she said bleakly when she regained her composure. "Since both you and your siblings are pictured, maybe your brother's rise to the throne has something to do with the oracle. And this business with Setnakht—that's part of it too. The painting showed me opening his tomb."

Karim cast another glance over his shoulder. "I thought I'd killed the monster—the 'mummy,' as you call it—but ever since we left the city and its crowds and distractions, I can't shake the feeling that I'm being watched. It is as if these events are connected... like streams converging into one river."

So that's why he's been startled by every little noise, Sita thought. Still, she was skeptical. Without seeing this so-called oracle for herself, she had only a few coincidences and Karim's word to go on.

"So what are we supposed to do about it, us four? Did the lamb happen to mention that?"

Karim shook his head.

"No, of course not," Sita said.

"You don't believe me."

Sita gave him an apologetic look and shrugged.

"Now, listen, princess—these are *your* gods who dragged me into this, not mine! That young priestess knew all about it already. She'd had visions of all this. *That's* why she helped me at the temple. I didn't want to believe it either! I only came to Thonis because I made a promise to that old priest before he died. And just when I thought things couldn't get any stranger—*you* show up. When I found out who you were, I knew our meeting couldn't be a coincidence."

Sita dropped her head onto her hands and stared at the map lying between them. Evading Mery and figuring out how she was going to stop him was hard enough—now this? The very idea that she was wrapped up in some kind of ancient prophecy was simply too much for her mind to handle.

Her eyes focused on a block of text written next to the red star marking the location Karim had indicated as the mummy's tomb.

"'Here lies Setnakht,'" she read aloud. "'His spirit indestructible, as powerful as a god. If he commands you to die, you will die. If he commands you to live, you will live. The word is the deed.'"

Karim stared at her.

"You can read it?" he asked, and then smacked himself in the forehead. "Of course you can read it. You're probably the most educated woman in the kingdom. Is there more?"

Sita squinted at the next words, which were faded and harder to decipher. "'He shall not travel West, for his work is unfinished. Through the...'" She paused. "I'm not sure about this symbol. Blood? Flesh? 'Through the... flesh of an acolyte, he will live again.'"

Silence fell between them.

Karim had gone pale. "His work is unfinished... What work?"

"Unless you found more information about him at the temple, I guess we'll never know," Sita said.

"There was a letter," Karim went on, "From an embalmer who'd been involved in the king's burial. It didn't say much, but it did mention that Setnakht abandoned Thonis and built his own capital city in the desert, away from the rest of the kingdom. Do you know where it is?"

Sita shook her head. "I've never heard of such a place. But that's not surprising. If Setnakht's very existence was erased from the history books, his city was probably abandoned too. It's been a thousand years—it's probably been retaken by the sands."

Karim grew excited. "Maybe, or maybe not. Do you think you could find it on this map?"

Sita studied the other marked locations. Ignoring the ones she already knew, she went through the unfamiliar names one by one. Most were too close to the Iteru to have been overlooked, and others seemed to simply be old names for new towns. There were a few burial sites marked as well. However, one outlier caught her eye, located midway between High and Low Khetara, deep in the eastern desert. The symbols written beside the star were an open square—the symbol for house—and the Set animal. Sita pointed to the name. "Perset, The House of Set."

Karim gazed up at her, his eyes wide. "That's got to be it, princess. Perset. That's where we have to go next!"

Sita pushed the map away, her momentary fascination with the story of Setnakht soured by the certainty in Karim's voice.

"No, no, no. There is no 'we.' If you want to head into the desert to find this ruin, be my guest—but I'm not going with you."

"But the oracle, sena!" Karim protested. "If it's true, then we were meant to face this together."

"And if it's not true?" Sita argued. "I could waste weeks chasing ghosts while my brother tightens his grip on the kingdom. If he kills more innocent people in his quest for power"—her voice broke—"more people that I love, then I could never forgive myself for being diverted by some tribesman from the marketplace."

Karim's face fell.

Sita felt a tug in her heart but didn't allow it to take hold. She'd just met Karim, and despite how easy it was to talk to him, and how so much of what he said rang true—she couldn't allow herself to fully trust him. She wasn't sure she could trust anyone ever again.

"This 'oracle' of yours makes it seem like every encounter has a greater purpose, is part of a larger plan," she went on, her voice harsh. "But real life isn't like that, all right? We each make our own decisions. Real life isn't a story, Karim."

She stood, her whole body trembling. "I believed in stories once. I won't make that mistake again. We'll stay together for the night, but when morning comes, we part. I'll find my way to Bubas alone."

Karim stood too. "As you wish, sena."

He went to gather up his things, and she tried to overlook the disappointment on his face. Even the dog seemed subdued.

As they left the canal, Behkai trotted beside her with his tail between his legs. They walked in silence for a few minutes before Karim spoke again.

"For what it's worth, before today I would have agreed with you. My life before all of this was arduous and sometimes felt devoid of meaning. This oracle has brought terrible things into my life, but it also brought experiences I never would have had without it. I took a journey down the river. I ate a pomegranate. I inherited Behkai." The dog cocked his head at the sound of his name.

Karim gave her a sidelong glance. "I found you."

Sita could not meet his eyes.

"These past few days, I've started to wonder if my life would be different if I stopped running away from things, and started running toward them. Do you know what I mean?" When Sita didn't respond, Karim cleared his throat. "All I'm trying to say, sena, is that even if we never meet again—to me, none of this has been meaningless. And for what it's worth, I hope your story gets a happy ending."

His words touched her—Sita couldn't deny that. And regardless of how outrageous it all sounded, she couldn't deny that something in his story of the oracle seemed genuine. But Sita knew better than to let herself be carried away by some fantasy, by a romantic notion that she was singled out, with the others, to save the kingdom from destruction. The most she could hope for was to somehow repair the damage she herself had done, and even that seemed insurmountable. Still, she had to try.

Though she knew she must, she didn't look forward to parting ways with her new companions, the hound and the jackal. They were so strange, and yet so familiar—two pawns moving across the landscape, hoping to reach journey's end in one piece.

Sita hoped that, for once, she was seeing the board clearly. That she wasn't making another mistake.

They walked the rest of the way in silence.

31
RAE

Rae floated through the next few hours in a blur of activity. After leaving the brewery, Omari, Menk, and Baki ushered her to the shepherd's farm, careful to stick to the narrow darkened streets until they got out of the city. She argued at first, telling them that her presence put Baki's family at risk, but the shepherd wouldn't hear of it.

"I owe you a debt, Raetawy. The least you can do is allow me to repay it."

After that, she let them pull her along without further protest. Everything seemed to move too slowly, as if she were underwater. Even the voices of her companions were oddly muted to her ears.

When they reached the farm, Baki steered her into the stable, promising to remain on watch outside, while Omari and Menk went back into town on reconnaissance.

"There will be consequences for what happened tonight," Menk told her before they left. "Better for us to know what they are before they arrive on our doorstep."

And then, she was alone with her thoughts.

Or at least, she thought she was alone.

An oil lamp burned on a table just inside the stable, sending flickering shadows against the walls. In the near dark, she saw a dozen sheep gathered inside. They watched her with distrust but made no move toward or away from her as she settled herself against a bale of straw. The arrow wound was painful, but she was too tired to stand any longer.

The stable was stuffy and pungent with the musky, earthy smell of the animals, but it wasn't unpleasant. Soon, the sheep seemed to lose interest in her and retreated to the corners to sleep.

It was only by watching the progress of the moon that Rae had any concept of time passing. Night had only begun to fall when she'd first set out for town, and now the moon had traveled halfway across the sky.

She tried not to think of her father.

She thought of her father.

Eventually, she must have nodded off. One moment, she was in the stable, and the next she was back in the brewery.

The dagger in her hand—

The blade slicing through skin and muscle and viscera—

The warm gush running over her fingers—

The surprise in the brewer's eyes—

It was so vivid, so real, that when she woke, she couldn't remember where she was or how she'd gotten there.

Disoriented, her breathing heavy, she sat up and tried to regain her bearings. The flame on the oil lamp was guttering wildly, casting bizarre shadows across the walls. One appeared to be the silhouette of what looked like a ram with four heads, each one pointed in a different direction. But as she blinked the last dregs of dreaming from her eyes, she saw it was simply the shadows of four sheep standing close together, keeping watch for predators.

Stumbling to her feet, Rae walked to the trough and splashed cold water on her face, trying to get her thoughts under control. She hadn't killed the brewer merely to avenge the men who'd died in the attack, but to protect herself and the ones she loved. But had she actually done that? Or had she made the situation worse?

She was drying herself on her robes when she heard footsteps approaching. Quickly, she retreated to the shadows, pressing her back to the wall beside the stable door. A moment later, the door opened slowly. She held her breath.

"Rae?" Omari whispered.

She exhaled and moved back into the light. "I'm here."

Omari came in and closed the door behind him. He moved gingerly—she could tell his injured shoulder had been bandaged beneath his tunic. His expression was grave.

"I relieved Baki so he can attend to his family," Omari said, his eyes downcast.

Rae's body went stiff. "Something's happened, hasn't it?"

Omari frowned.

"What is it, Omari? Tell me."

Still, Omari said nothing.

A surge of anger welled inside her. "Tell me, damn you!" Rae cried, shoving him back, "What happened? What did they do?"

It was then that she smelled the smoke wafting in through the window.

"The nomarch's men burned your farm," Omari said hoarsely. "The land, the house... everything. Most of the zebu got away when the fence burned, and some of the men are trying to gather them, but—"

Rae cried out and made for the door, but Omari grabbed her by the waist and held her back.

"There's nothing to be done!" he grunted. "If you go out there now, the Medjay will catch you—and what good would that do?"

"No!" she cried and fought against his grip. "Let me go!"

But Omari held firm.

With a wail, she stopped struggling. She focused on the stable window, where a dim red glow flickered in the distance. She could hear men shouting, and the panicked cries of cattle.

"Omari," Rae whispered.

"I'm so sorry, Ay," he replied. "The brewer's daughter recognized you, and she must have told the nomarch's men what happened. They came right away with torches. I got into the house before they did, though, and I managed to salvage these." From his pack, he produced her robes, with the winged golden armor and stone scepter they'd stolen during the raid wrapped inside. The golden ring the Jackal had given her was in there too, and she put it on her finger to ensure it wouldn't get lost.

"Omari," she said again, holding the armor and scepter in her hands.

"They're looking for you," he continued. "But it won't be long before they start looking for me too. Everyone knows we're friends. I already evacuated my family—they're going to stay with some relatives in Per-Abu until the danger passes. *If* it passes..."

He began to pace, disturbing the sheep. "What are we going to do, Rae? What are we—"

"*Omari!*"

The harshness of her voice quieted him. He stilled.

"Where...?" she began, hardly able to get out the words. "Where is my father?"

Omari sighed, and it was like someone stole the sun from the sky. Rae's entire world went black.

A sob rose from her throat as she recalled the last time she saw her father, his kind, sun-weathered face aglow in the dying sunlight.

What was it that he'd said to her?

"Please, come inside. It's getting dark."

If only she'd listened.

She'd promised to keep him safe. She'd promised nothing bad would happen to him. And now, and now—

She couldn't breathe. She swayed and was about to fall to her knees when Omari caught her and said, "He's alive, Rae. He's alive. But... they've taken him."

Rae gripped Omari's arms, holding on to him and his words for support.

"Taken him where?"

Omari licked his lips. "The nomarch's men handed him over to the Medjay. Their reinforcements arrived from Thonis only hours ago, and they're planning to return to the capital with Ankhu and some other Low Khetaran prisoners. We should count ourselves lucky to not be among them."

Rae released her hold on him and leaned heavily against the wall. This news—it was better, and yet worse.

"Why would they take them to Thonis?" she asked.

Omari shrugged. "Not sure. But we know Prince Meryamun plans to crack down on insurgent factions in the south, so he'll probably try to pump the captives for information... or make a public example of them."

Rae dropped her head into her hands. *Execution.*

Her father was still alive, but he probably wouldn't be for long.

"We can avenge him, Rae," Omari went on. "We can avenge them all. We have the weapons we took from the Medjay. If we arm ourselves and fight back, we can take the city by storm."

"And lose how many more in the process?" Rae asked. "That's exactly what the Medjay are expecting. That's exactly what they want. What makes you think they won't destroy Sakesh, just as they've done with my farm?" She shook her head. "We can't endanger everyone in the city with this crusade, not until they've agreed to be part of it."

"How could they not agree?" Omari fumed, gesturing toward the fire in the distance. "How could they not see that this fight concerns us all?"

"Not every mind works as yours does. We cannot speak for every man, woman, and child. If we do, then are we any different from the High Khetarans?"

Omari huffed in frustration. "Then what do you propose, Ay? We do nothing?"

"No!" Rae shot back, her own temper rising. "That's not what I'm saying at all. Aren't you the one always telling me to think before I act? I let my anger overtake me tonight, and look what happened! Do you really want to repeat that on a grand scale all over the city? I can't be responsible for the deaths of any more innocent people."

As soon as she spoke the words, she realized how true they were. The brewer's accusation had struck its target and buried itself in her mind.

Their deaths are on your hands, Raetawy, not mine.

"That dog deserved to die," Omari growled. "I would have killed him myself if you hadn't."

Rae's brow furrowed. It was true, the brewer gave her little choice but to silence him, and his wickedness had brought vengeance to his doorstep. But there was more than that in Omari's tone. She'd never heard him speak with such venom.

"Everything of value has a cost, Rae," he went on. "And freedom demands the highest price of all. We cannot be afraid to pay it."

They were almost the same words Asim had said to her back at the weavers' workshop. But when Asim had said it, she'd thought he meant sacrificing his own life for the cause—not the lives of others. What Omari seemed to be suggesting sent a shiver down her spine. She was about to reply when there was a noise outside the stable.

Omari put a finger to his lips and then pointed to the door. Someone was coming.

The sheep stirred, bleating.

Rae clamped her lips shut and stood, her hand going to the dagger in her belt.

Then came a low voice.

"The falcon sails across the sky."

Both Rae and Omari nearly collapsed with relief. She opened the door a crack and whispered, "We shall meet him on the…"

The last word stuck in her throat when she saw who stood outside, silhouetted by the fiery glow.

"Horizon?" she finished.

"Hello in peace, Raetawy," said Tamerit. The weaver was wrapped in a robe not unlike the one Rae wore, a hood covering her dark curls. Menk stood next to her, wearing something between a smile and a grimace.

"Room in there for more?" he asked gruffly.

Rae nodded and made way for them both to enter the stable. Except they weren't alone. Behind them came nearly a dozen others, among them Mamet Mut and several other weavers, a few of the surviving Horizon members, and an old soldier who Rae often saw begging in the street. There were some young men that Rae recognized from the street fights too, including—most surprisingly—Buto.

The brawler nodded at Rae as he entered, a penitent expression on his face. She'd never noticed how crooked his nose was. Others must have broken it before she'd gotten a chance to.

"Hi, Rae," he said.

"Buto," Rae replied, utterly confused. "What's all this about, Menk? I thought it was too dangerous to congregate."

"It's all right," Menk assured her. "The Medjay and the nomarch's men are all at the riverbank, readying for their journey back north. I've also left a lookout. He'll send up the alarm if anyone approaches."

Rae exchanged glances with Omari, but he appeared as bewildered as she was by the people assembling around them amid the sheep.

"The thing is, Rae," Menk went on, "As I was gathering information, I seemed to gather people too. People who wanted to see you after they heard what happened tonight. They wouldn't take no for an answer. More wanted to join me, but I managed to convince them to stay home so we wouldn't attract too much attention. Most of these folks lost kin in the ambush at the Garden of the Dead."

The assembled murmured their agreement.

"My father," said a man.

"My son," said another.

"My uncle," said Buto. "When I found out that he'd had been killed by the Medjay, I vowed to avenge him. I went to the brewer for advice—after all, he had his hands in everything, knew everyone. I had no idea he was a traitor! If you hadn't figured it out and stopped him, Rae… well, he probably would have turned me in too." Buto cleared his throat. "So I suppose I owe you a debt."

"You owe me more than one," Rae grumbled.

"Fine," Buto said, the usual playful smirk back on his face. "Two."

"Menk said you spoke up for the weavers too," Tam broke in, moving to Rae's side. "That's why he came to see us. We've tried to tell the men we want to help many times, but no one's ever been able to get through to them. Except you."

Tam's hand found hers and squeezed it.

"I–I still don't understand," Rae stammered. "Why have you all come?"

"It's never been clearer that the Horizon must endure," Menk replied. "What had once been a group with ideas has become a group of action, and Sakesh needs action now more than ever." He paused. "It's what Asim would have wanted."

The lump returned to Rae's throat at his name.

I would be proud to have a daughter like you, he'd said.

But now he was gone, and her own father too. Would Asim still be proud, if he knew what she'd done? Would Ankhu?

Menk said, "I brought these people because I wanted you to see that despite the blow to our number, there are still many who wish to dedicate their lives to the cause."

"Wanted *me* to see?" Rae echoed. Her gaze flicked to Omari. An inscrutable expression passed over his face, one she couldn't identify.

"Yes, you," Menk insisted. "Now that Asim is gone, we need a new leader. He believed in you, Rae. You were the catalyst that helped him start this fight. And with any luck, you'll be the one to end it." He tipped his chin to the stone weapon in her hand. "Besides, you carry the Sekhem scepter."

Rae hefted the weapon. "I stole it from the Medjay. It's not really mine."

"It wasn't really theirs either," Menk told her. "The lion goddess works in mysterious ways. She made sure it got into the right hands."

Rae felt a prickle at the back of her neck as she touched the Sekhmet amulet hanging from her neck, the one she'd chosen from the Jackal's bag of treasures. *Maybe it wasn't so random after all.*

"So?" Menk asked. "What do you say?"

The crowd turned to her, expectant.

Rae felt her stomach twist. "But Menk," she whispered, pulling him close and turning her back to the others. "I'm no soldier.

I know how to cultivate wheat, tend cattle, and wrestle for some extra income. How could I possibly lead a rebellion?"

Menk shook his head. "Raetawy, what we need is someone who can help us grow in number, shepherd us to greener pastures, and have courage in the face of adversity. Think about it, about what you just said. You can do all those things. Whatever you don't know, you will learn on the way." He put a thick hand on her shoulder. "No one is ever ready to lead, Rae. They only need to be willing. Are you willing?"

Rae scoffed. *This is madness*, she thought. She should refuse Menk's offer and tell him to lead, or someone else—someone older and more experienced. After all, the rebellion's survival didn't depend on her leadership.

She scanned the shadowy faces around her, all of them waiting to hear what she would say.

She had a sudden jarring sense that everything she'd done, every choice she'd made, had led her to that moment. The choice to defend Baki against the nomarch. The choice to ask Omari to take her to that first Horizon meeting. The choice to speak up. The choice to fight back. If she had done any one of those things differently, nothing would have turned out the same way.

She looked down at the four sides of the golden ring—the snake, the feather, the eye, and the scarab—and remembered once more what the Jackal had said about the inexorable pull of fate, how it carried you to your destiny. Rae wondered if it was true. Was her fate drawn in the stars long before she was even born? Or did she truly have agency over her own path?

Perhaps it was a bit of both.

Maybe the gods offer us opportunities to choose our fate, she thought, *but it's ultimately up to us whether or not we take them.*

The river's current tugged at her, willing her to speak.

"Well?" Menk asked, nudging her with his elbow.

Rae closed her eyes, took a deep breath, and let the current take her.

Turning to the gathered flock, she said, "If you'll have me, I promise to do my best."

Menk clapped her on the back and many others followed suit. Some of the men still looked uncertain, but Rae had eyes for only one person. Tam stood in the center of the throng, her hands clasped at her breast, her eyes glittering with pride.

"So we fight!" Omari said. "We bring the battle to the Medjay and show them we will not submit!"

The men began to murmur their agreement when Rae spoke up. "No!"

The room fell silent once again, all eyes turned to her.

"The raid on the Medjay was successful because Asim had a clever plan. His plan minimized violence and focused on a specific objective. If we're going to take back Sakesh, we must do the same—but on a much larger scale. We cannot do it with a dozen fighters. The Horizon must encompass all that the light touches."

Rae glanced uncertainly around the stable, but no one protested.

She went on. "First, we must spread the word far and wide. The weavers will help expand our outreach to every corner of the city, but we must do it quietly. We cannot afford to be betrayed again."

She turned to Menk. "Work with them to gather our forces and begin to strategize next steps. If blood must be shed, so be it—but let's try not to spill any more than necessary."

Menk nodded, but his brow furrowed. "It's a good plan, Rae, but why me? Shouldn't you be the one leading the charge?"

Rae shook her head. "Omari and I, and a few others—if they're willing, of course—will be busy with another mission."

Omari had been standing with his arms crossed, looking aggrieved, but he perked up at this. "What mission?"

Rae gripped the scepter in her hand, the weight of it keeping her rooted to the earth. Her eyes drifted to the window, to the smoldering ruin of her old life, her old self.

"If we want to win this," she said, "we can't limit our fight to Sakesh alone. Every city and village is affected by High Khetaran rule, not just us. If the king wants to send a message by abducting and executing our people—well, we need to send a message too." She paused, thrilled and terrified by what she was going to say next.

"We must take our fight to the pharaoh himself."

The stable went still. Even the sheep seemed to recognize something momentous was happening, and all turned their unsettling eyes upon her.

"Menk, Tam—we'll need all the information we can get, and quickly. Building a resistance in Sakesh will help us win the battle, but we need to strike at the heart of the kingdom if we want to win the war." She gripped the scepter tightly in her hand. "As soon as we can make ourselves ready, we sail for Thonis."

A moment passed, and Rae was afraid she'd gone too far. Asked too much.

Then, a voice spoke up. It was Buto.

"I'm with you."

"And me," Tam said.

"And me," said the old soldier.

Others spoke until every voice in the room had joined the chorus, was heeding the call. And with each offering, Rae's heart lifted a little more.

A meaty hand clamped onto her shoulder. Omari's. "To Thonis," he said to her with a nod.

Rae nodded back, and the others began speaking together at once, all the recent tragedies transformed, alchemically, into action. Rae closed her eyes and sent a message out into the midnight heavens, hoping that somehow, it would be delivered to its recipient.

Father, I'm coming.

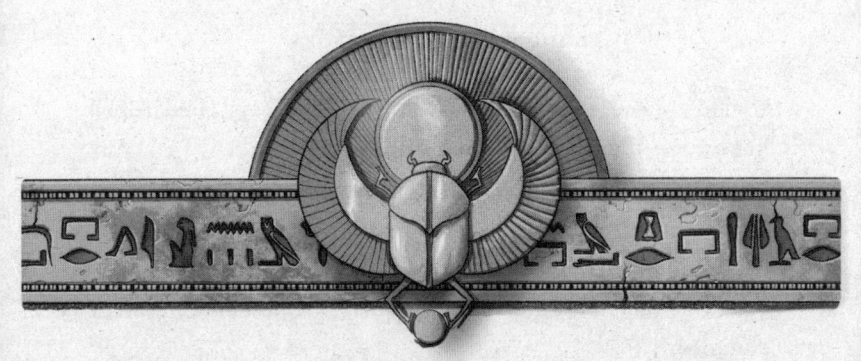

32
KARIM

He kept watch while the princess slept.

They'd reached a shallow valley at dusk and decided it was a good place to stop for the night. The rocky walls on either side shielded them from the river, so that anyone passing wouldn't see the fire. They'd eaten a meager meal, and he offered to stay awake for the first half of the night so she could rest. The princess had agreed without complaint, bedding down on the sandy ground and falling asleep, curled like a cat into the blanket he'd purchased back at the Thonis market. For a girl who'd probably only slept on a plush bed, she didn't seem to mind rough living.

Behkai dozed next to her, his great black head resting on her legs. It was as if the dog knew their time together was limited, so he was soaking up as much of Sitamun's presence as he could.

Karim poked the small campfire they'd built from his supply of dung cakes until the embers flared.

Come tomorrow, I'll be on my own again, he thought. He

couldn't blame the princess for wanting to part ways. He'd helped her escape Thonis, but he was still a stranger to her. He'd surprised himself with how much he'd wanted her to join him on his journey to Perset. Maybe he'd been alone too long and was merely desperate for a companion who wouldn't lick his face.

Although if Sitamun did such a thing, he probably wouldn't complain.

A darkling beetle crawled onto Sitamun's shoulder and Karim reached over to brush it away. She twitched and snorted softly but did not wake. Leaning over, he pulled the edge of the blanket closer around her and tucked it under her chin, making sure not to dislodge the yellow chrysanthemum from her hair as he did.

He hadn't intended to be so candid when they'd stopped by the canal. After all, they just met, and she was Khetaran—one of the most powerful women in the land. Like the pharaoh himself, royals like Princess Sitamun represented everything he hated about the river kingdom.

And yet, he'd been drawn to her. It was as if the same invisible rope that pulled him toward buried treasure pulled him to Sitamun. It was why he'd opened up to her. Why he'd pulled out the map to study, knowing she'd notice, knowing she'd want to see it for herself.

Sitamun was headstrong and imperious—but she was also witty and intelligent. Whatever her life might have been like in the palace, she still had the ability to appreciate the simpler things. A hot meal. Wildflowers. And it must have taken no small amount of courage to leave the palace behind and set out on her own with nothing but a waterskin and a dagger to her name.

She'd been awfully candid with him too. They had both made mistakes that led to the deaths of innocent people. And they were both searching for a way to make it right. Karim had thought that maybe they were supposed to conduct that search together, but perhaps that was wishful thinking. His path led to Perset, and hers to Bubas and beyond. Perhaps the oracle only intended for them to meet and give each other aid—as he had done with Raetawy and Nefermaat—before parting ways once more.

He sighed, annoyed that in the end, he wasn't all that different from the dog. He liked the princess, and selfishly, he didn't want her to go.

"Well," he murmured to Behkai, giving him a gentle pat on the rump. "At least I'll still have you, boy."

Behkai opened his eyes, then sat up with a start. At first, Karim thought that his touch had startled the dog out of sleep, but Behkai saw Karim sitting beside him and still didn't relax. His eyes were fixed on the ridge above them, ears perked, body rigid.

"What is it?" Karim squinted at the ridge but saw only darkness. "What do you see?"

A growl bubbled up from deep in Behkai's throat. Karim held his breath, listening over the crackling fire.

There was nothing.

Karim closed his eyes, shutting out every sense except sound.

Still, nothing.

And then—

A soft rustle. The shifting of rough fabric. Feet moving through sand.

Moving quickly, Karim kicked sand over the fire until there was nothing left but embers. Shushing Behkai, he crouched over Sita, shaking her gently by the shoulders.

She woke with a violent snort and blinked up at him, bleary-eyed.

"Is it my turn already?"

Karim put a finger to his lips. He pointed to the top of the ridge and then tilted his head toward a shallow cave dug out of the wall of the valley. He hoped his message was clear. *Keep quiet and go hide*.

Sitamun understood. With a frightened look, she rose from her makeshift bed and slipped into the cave.

Karim rubbed the black dog's sleek neck and bent to whisper in his ear. "You too, boy. Keep her safe, hey?"

The dog hesitated, seemingly unwilling to leave his master's side—but Karim gave him a pat and a nudge, and Behkai followed Sitamun, disappearing into the shadows.

Karim turned back to the ridge, wondering what could be coming their way. Surely the crown prince's men wouldn't be searching at this time of night—but he supposed it was possible. Maybe they were travelers or tribesmen like him, looking for a place to make camp for the night. His hand went to the dagger in his belt.

Karim watched and waited. The valley was cloaked in a darker shadow than the desert above it. Perhaps the traveler would pass by without even noticing him.

The shuffling footsteps drew closer.

A prickle of dread crept up Karim's spine. Instinct warned him there was something wrong with the sound. It was too quiet. Such a strenuous march through the desert would cause anyone to breathe heavily, to falter, to struggle.

But there was no breath, no faltering. There were only the footsteps, as steady as a heartbeat and as persistent as a curse.

No, Karim thought as the possibility arose in his mind. *It can't be.*

The crown of a head appeared over the ridge. It was hairless and glowed white in the moonlight.

Karim stood transfixed as the figure revealed itself, little by little, one step at a time.

The flashing eyes.

The tattered wrappings.

The places where bone showed through sinew.

Then, like the return of a nightmare, the jagged hole where a broken tree had dealt what should have been a fatal blow.

Karim's entire body began to tremble as he willed the apparition to vanish or reduce itself to a figment of his weary mind. But it remained.

It's alive, he thought, his terror rising.

Setnakht is alive.

Behkai barked once—a high, frightened cry—and Karim glanced toward the cave, afraid that Sitamun and the dog might emerge. They didn't. But when he turned back and looked up at the ridge, Setnakht was gone.

His brow furrowed. Had he imagined the whole thing? *Was it some kind of illusion?*

He heard another footstep, and his gaze dropped to find the monster just ahead, down in the valley with him and still advancing.

Karim gasped and stumbled back, nearly tripping over the smoking ruin of their campfire. How had the creature moved so quickly, so silently? He had touched it back on the riverbank, so he knew it had weight and form, so how could it move like smoke on the wind?

"Don't come any closer," he said, pointlessly.

Setnakht didn't respond. The monster took another step toward him. And another.

It was near enough now that Karim could see the holes in its time-stained skin. The lips had worn away to nothing, leaving behind a permanent snarl of brown gums and teeth. It reached a hand toward Karim, some fingers still covered in paper-thin flesh, others only bone. The movement caused some of its desiccated skin to crack and flake away.

Every instinct told Karim to run. If he stayed, he and Sitamun would end up like Djet and Pasenhor. And did he really want to empower the creature further by returning the scarab amulet that was his heart?

If I do that, or if I keep running, who else will die? he thought. *I started this the day I opened that tomb. Maybe I need to listen to my own advice. Maybe I need to stop running away from things, and start running toward them.*

Setnakht was nearly upon him. Its pace neither increased nor slackened. It moved toward him like it had all the time in the world.

Gritting his teeth, Karim went to pull his dagger from its sheath but reconsidered. No, his blade was useless. Even being impaled on a tree hadn't stopped the creature. He needed something else. Something that would destroy Setnakht for good.

Karim's eyes dropped to the smoking coals. A few of them were still aglow. He'd burned the creature before. This time, he needed to be sure to finish the job.

He wrapped a bit of his robe around one hand and waited until Setnakht's bony fingers were close enough to touch. The monster's body crackled softly as it moved, its scent a mixture of salt and wine, dust and myrrh.

Then, in a flash, Karim dropped down, scooped up a handful of red-hot embers from the fire, and shot forward, thrusting them deep into the creature's chest.

The response was immediate.

Setnakht howled, the ear-shattering screech ricocheting off the walls of the valley. Its mouth opened wide, so wide that Karim thought the thin strands of sinew holding its jaw to its skull might snap. It recoiled violently, trying to wrench itself away, but Karim grabbed its shoulder and held on tight.

"You want me?" he grunted, "Here I am, sen. Here I am!"

In seconds the embers burned straight through his robe and set his skin aflame. The pain was searing, but Karim held on. The embers flared as they met the dry wrappings and resin covering the creature's body, and within seconds, bright flames had bloomed and spread along the tatters, turning them black.

Setnakht was ablaze.

Unable to stand the pain any longer, Karim let go of the embers and tried to pull away. But the creature grabbed him by the shoulder, mirroring him. Karim cried out as the flames licked him too. Smoke filled his lungs, and he began to cough, his eyes streaming. Everything was heat and fear and pain, with he and the monster holding one another in a macabre version of a lover's embrace.

Karim battered his burned hands against the creature, but it only made the flames spread. They consumed the sleeve of his robe, searching for the flesh beneath. As the fire reached the skin of his arm, the pain was a thousand hissing snakes, a thousand bee stings—sharp and hot and biting. Karim bit back a scream, not wanting to inhale more smoke.

He couldn't breathe. Darkness began to creep in from the edges of his eyes.

He thought about the oracle.

Maybe this is how my story is supposed to end, he thought.

As he began to lose consciousness, a sense of peace washed over him. At least he'd finished what he'd started, and the curse would be broken.

He spared a thought for his mother, his brother, his sisters, and wished he'd been able to do better by them.

Then again, they probably already thought he was dead, so he wouldn't be missed.

Over Setnakht's shoulder, behind the flames, Karim swore he saw Djet watching them in the moonlight. He looked just as Karim had remembered him, bright-eyed and round-cheeked, his smile undimmed by so much tragedy.

I'm so sorry for what happened, Karim told the specter of his friend. *I'm sorry I couldn't protect you. But at least it's over now. At least it's done.*

Suddenly Karim felt the creature's hand press against his

chest, as if Setnakht were trying to feel his heartbeat. But then, the bony fingers began to dig in.

Karim recoiled, but couldn't escape. What was it doing? Couldn't the monster just die? It must know the end is coming, and it was furiously trying to tear Karim apart before it burned to ash.

Except why was it smiling?

The monster's half-rotted mouth twisted into a skeletal grin as it pushed its fingers deeper into Karim's chest.

Karim had expected fury, hatred, despair—but all he saw on the creature's face was triumph.

It didn't make sense. Unless—

The truth hit Karim like a lightning bolt.

The blood he'd spilled on Setnakht's coffin.

The words in the letter: *Isn't it just what he deserves? To travel all the way West, only to be turned away at the moment of judgment? To have his miserable ka wander the earth for eternity?*

Heartless in life, heartless in death.

The prayer on the map: *He shall not travel West, for his work is unfinished.*

It was Karim's blood that woke the creature, connecting them, but blood hadn't been enough to bring him back. Not completely.

Setnakht needed more. Not the amulet, but something else.

Through the flesh of an acolyte, he will live again.

Sitamun hadn't been certain of her translation. He was now. The word wasn't *flesh* or *blood*.

Karim finally screamed as the monster's fingers pierced his chest.

It was *heart*.

The creature ripped away skin, then muscle and rib. Blood poured from Karim's wound and sizzled in the flames, but the creature did not stop.

Karim screamed and screamed, consumed by agony. There was no fire, no moon, no ground beneath him. There was only pain.

Dimly, he was aware of Behkai charging out of the cave to attack the creature. He lunged and snarled like a demon, but Setnakht reached down and laid his hand on the dog's face. Karim heard Behkai yelp.

Then he was silent.

Stupid dog, Karim thought, tears streaming down his face.

Deep inside him, he felt Setnakht's fingers close like a trap. With each harsh breath, blood spilled from Karim's chest and mouth. He was choking on it, gurgling, no longer able to scream.

Had the fire stopped burning?

Karim's head lolled back, his eyes wide open. His despair was as black and vast as the night sky. He could have stopped this. If he had thrown himself into the river or slit his own throat, the creature wouldn't have been able to achieve its goal. But instead, he'd given it exactly what it wanted.

If Karim had never found that tomb, the creature never would have woken—all Setnakht's true acolytes were long dead. If Karim hadn't shed blood onto the coffin, the ritual never would have begun. And if Karim had killed himself, the monster would never have been able to harvest his beating heart.

All the small streams, the strong current, they had been carrying Karim toward this moment. Except the destination wasn't what he'd expected at all. He'd expected to die a hero.

Instead he was the sacrificial lamb, slaughtered in the name of a god he didn't believe in. He'd been wrong. Nothing was finished. The oracle's prophecy had only just begun.

Images flashed through his mind as his heartbeat slowed.

Behkai sleeping on his lap on the skiff.

Sitamun bending to smell flowers along the path.

Djet smiling at him as they stood by a valley, far away. *I'm coming with you!*

I'm sorry, he thought. *I'm sorry, I'm so—*

There was a sickening lurch, and Setnakht wrenched his heart from his chest.

Karim didn't see what happened next.

He didn't see the creature press the dripping, glistening heart into the ruin of its own chest. Didn't see the reddish glow that erupted from the creature's body, surrounding it, knitting together bones and ligaments and skin and infusing it with the blush of life.

Soon the wounds and burns and missing pieces were filled in, patched up, made new. Loose threads of sinew wove back into place as if guided by an unseen hand.

Karim felt nothing when Setnakht dropped his body to the ground and stood, not a flesh-and-blood man, but much closer to one than he'd been before. He couldn't hear the ancient king's voice when he finally spoke, with a throat made whole and a tongue that had been stilled for a thousand years.

Perhaps that was for the best.

To hear such a sound, a sound not unlike the eerie vibrations of the wind over the desert hills, was to hear doom itself.

"You made a poor acolyte," Setnakht said, gazing down at Karim's wide, unseeing eyes. "But your heart is strong." He looked up at the stars, seeming to take note of their position in the sky. "It has been many years, but it is never too late to start again."

The last embers died as Setnakht left the valley. In his wake, the desert was silent except for the distant sound of a woman weeping.

33
NEFF

Neff studied her reflection in the polished bronze disk. For the second time since she'd arrived in Thonis, she'd been transformed.

From the moment she'd woken that morning in a grand chamber at the palace, Neff hadn't had a single minute to herself. She hadn't even gotten out of bed when four female attendants arrived with trays of sumptuous food and a jar of freshly pressed grape juice. They'd sat by impatiently as she ate the best meal of her life, and then whisked her straight into a deliciously warm, jasmine-scented bath. After that, they dried and rubbed her all over with fragrant oils and began to dress her. It was, in every way, more enjoyable than her initiation into the temple with the Wabet, but it felt equally strange. Instead of being purged of her old life, it felt like a new one was being grafted on, using fine linens and makeup and jewelry.

Back at home in Bubas, it took the space of a minute for her to get dressed for the day. She'd smooth out her kalasiris dress, comb her fingers through her hair, and that was that. Her ablutions at the temple had taken somewhat longer, but still not a lot of time.

At the palace, despite the fact that there were four other people helping her, dressing took hours.

When they finally finished, the attendants left in a flurry, off to complete the next task on their list for the prince's coronation ceremony at the temple. Alone in her chambers, Neff sat in a daze on an acacia-wood stool by her dressing table, staring at herself in the handheld mirror.

She could hardly believe her eyes.

Is that really me?

Her lips and cheeks were rosy with rouge, her large round eyes lined with black kohl. Over her bald head, they'd affixed a black wig cut in a chin-length style, its tresses woven through shiny gold tubes in a complex pattern. It was nothing like her natural hair, which had been curly and mouse brown. The wig was bold and rich and alluring.

The rest of her costume was no less impressive. Golden cuffs clasped her ankles and wrists, and they'd placed a jeweled collar with an image of Bast around her neck, a tribute to the goddess who'd brought her to Thonis. Finally, they'd wrapped her in a pleated sky-blue dress, its hem decorated with lotus flowers stitched in gold.

I'm moving up in the world, she thought, recalling her father's words, *and I need to look the part. If I want people to respect me, I must command respect!*

The first step in her plan was complete. She'd hidden herself and her true intentions beneath a cover of jewels and kohl and featherlight gowns. That was the easy part. The next step was to use the position Meryamun had offered her in his court to influence him in the days to come. Her lifesaving prophecy had proved to the prince that she was an important asset, and at least for now, he trusted her. But his belief wasn't enough. The whole palace needed to accept her if she was going to exert influence over anything. To do that, she needed to believe in the product. She needed to believe in herself.

Neff stood up straighter, squared her shoulders, and tried on a few confident expressions for size while running through her father's list of rules for success.

Always look the customer in the eye, so they know you mean business.

Tell them what they want to hear.

Speak clearly, and don't overexplain.

Don't take no for an answer.

It was almost as if she could hear Pepi's voice in her ear, like a mischievous god imparting wisdom of his own. She missed him and her mother more than ever, maybe because they'd never felt so far away. She thought of how simple her life had been, spending her days selling spell scrolls at the Bubas market, and wondered what her father would think of the kind of magic she'd witnessed. She'd never forget the sight of the serpent staff in the Heka priest's hand, changing from wood to flesh before her eyes. Forbidden powers, accessible only to a choice few people in all the kingdom, those most trusted by the pharaoh.

Neff gasped as an idea struck her.

No, I couldn't, she murmured.

The mouth says no, her father's voice whispered, *but the heart shouts yes!*

Well, she thought, *why not?*

Setting the hand mirror down on the table among the cosmetic palettes, hairbrushes, and bottles of oil, Neff slipped into the sandals the attendants had left for her. After a lifetime of woven reed sandals that blistered her feet, the fine leather shoes felt like a comforting embrace. With one final look at her white dress from the temple, discarded in the corner like an old snakeskin, she left the room, making her way through the palace toward the royal chambers.

The halls were crowded with servants and courtiers preparing themselves for the coronation ceremony, which was set to begin in two hours' time. She wound around them, relieved to go unnoticed. There was an air of excitement among the crowd, but Neff sensed tension too. Some of the smiles seemed forced, and conversations muted. Neff strained to overhear them as she passed by.

"I called out for Tadia when I woke this morning," one middle-aged woman said to another. "She wasn't there... or the other wives either. And Ineni! The king's favorite. And so young! I can't wrap my mind around it, Nebet. The prince says they all chose to join their king in the Duat, to serve him in the afterlife, but I *spoke* to Tadia before she left that night. She didn't say anything out of the ordinary. She didn't even say goodbye..."

The other woman reached for her friend's hand and squeezed it. "You must keep these thoughts to yourself, do you hear? Lest they be used as weapons against you. Come on, we shouldn't linger here." And with that, she pulled her friend away.

Neff watched them go, a fresh chill crawling up her spine. She'd already known about the slaughter of the king's court, but hearing it again was a stark reminder of to whom she'd sworn allegiance.

A cold-blooded killer.

She shivered. *If Meryamun ever finds out what I'm doing, if he ever realizes that I've lied to him, he'll kill me.*

All right, then, she told herself. *Then make sure he doesn't find out.*

She raised her chin at an imperious angle, as if her importance should be obvious to everyone, and kept walking.

She moved past a host of guards into an empty corridor, sumptuously arrayed with green tiled floors and walls painted in black and gold. Two braziers burned on either side of a portal covered by a sheer curtain. She tried her best to walk with purpose, as if she belonged there.

Sure enough, no one stopped her, nor asked her a single question. They simply nodded at her as she passed. The prince, it seemed, had made it clear that she was under his protection, and was free to move about as she pleased.

She stopped at the sheer curtain, hearing voices beyond.

"The ships from Sakesh are due back any time now," a gruff voice said. "If all has gone to plan, they'll be carrying some high-value Low Khetaran prisoners who may offer information about the insurgency."

The prince's voice was impatient. "Never mind about that. Where is she?"

"I'm sorry, my prince?" The man sounded flustered.

"My sister, you ass! *Where is she?*" There was a bang, like a fist crashing upon a table.

"I-I sent my best men after her, I swear it. They've scoured every fingerbreadth of Thonis. The princess may have had help getting out of the city, I'm afraid."

Meryamun growled with irritation. "How about that guard—Femi? Has he told you anything?"

"Unfortunately no, my prince. He claims to know nothing about Princess Sitamun's flight, other than some talk about her traveling north. But all the ships heading downriver were thoroughly searched."

"And you've offered him plenty of... encouragement, I assume?"

"If we *encourage* him any further, he won't live to see another sunrise." There was a pause. "But we haven't given up the search. She will be found, my prince. I give you my word."

"Don't give me your word, damn you," Meryamun sneered. "Keep it."

Neff sidestepped from the door as the guard burst through the curtain, so preoccupied with his thoughts that he didn't notice her.

Neff stared at the shadowy figures moving behind the curtain and took a deep breath before pushing it aside.

"Prince Meryamun, may I—" she began. The next words stuck in her throat.

Meryamun turned his head toward her. He was lounging on a polished wooden couch, wearing a loincloth and nothing else. Two servant girls, whose clothing consisted of little more than what the prince himself wore, knelt beside him, massaging his hands and feet. His body was long and lithe, his skin a warm golden brown. Her eyes followed the V-shaped curve of his pelvis down to the edge of the loincloth, and she blushed.

"Oh, I-I'm sorry," she stammered, and had started to back away when he called to her.

"Nefermaat," he purred. "Don't go. You're welcome here."

With effort, Neff turned back to face him. He waved the girls away and they left without a word, moving soundlessly into a side chamber.

Neff and the prince were alone.

Her pulse quickened, and she started to drop her gaze to the floor.

Look him in the eye, so he knows you mean business.

She looked up.

Meryamun smiled and stood, padding toward her on bare feet. "You look extraordinary. Did you come to show yourself to me?"

Neff considered this as he came closer, bringing with him a fragrance of balsam wood and spice.

Tell them what they want to hear.

"Yes, my prince," she answered. "You honor me with this gown and this jewelry."

Meryamun chuckled with pleasure. "And these?" He reached out to shift the straps of her gown, revealing tattoos of small wedjat eyes on either side of her chest. The skin around them was still a little pink. "Did it hurt?"

As soon as she'd arrived at the palace, Meryamun had ordered a priest to apply the tattoos, which marked her as a high priestess, sacred to the crown. She'd lain on a table while the man dipped a sharp needle in a bowl of soot mixed with water, then used it to carve the ink into her flesh. He'd put one on each side of her chest, and two more on the small of her back—identical to the ones the high priestess of Bubas had. The process had been excruciating.

"It was fine, my prince," she said.

Meryamun laughed. "You're a terrible liar."

Am I, though? Neff thought.

Meryamun brushed his thumb against the outline of the eye on her right shoulder, and Neff resisted the urge to wince.

"Now everyone will know that you are under the gods' protection, as well as mine," he said. "Whatever action they take in your presence will have a divine witness. These marks are made from the ash of sacred flames. Did you know that?" He leaned in close. "You see? You don't need the temple anymore, my girl. You *are* a temple."

Neff swallowed. *This is your chance. Speak clearly, and don't overexplain.*

"Speaking of the temple," she began. "Since I cannot continue my lessons with Master Montuhotep—"

Meryamun scoffed. "You don't need him. And frankly, neither do I. He was useful to me for a while, but now that I have you... he's become quite unnecessary."

He was useful... Neff mused. Perhaps Montuhotep really had known about the prince's plans, and had lied to the king in hopes of securing his position in Meryamun's favor. He must be very displeased with Neff for taking his place, but that was a problem for another day. "As you say, my prince," Neff said with a dip of her head. "However, I do wish to continue my education."

The prince looked at her with interest. "You already have an open channel to the gods. What else could you need to learn?"

"I wish to learn the ways of Heka."

Meryamun's eyes narrowed. "Magic?"

Neff nodded. "What good is knowing the future if I don't have the power to change it?"

The prince's expression was inscrutable. "Indeed," he murmured.

As the seconds passed, Neff began to sweat. Had she asked too much, too quickly?

Don't take no for an answer.

"I ask because I wish to serve you as best I can," she said, filling the silence. "Not only as the voice of the gods, but as their hand as well. With the power of prophecy and Heka combined, there is nothing we could not achieve." She paused deliberately. "But if the knowledge is forbidden…"

"Nothing is forbidden! Not from me!" Meryamun exclaimed, just as she'd hoped he would.

He regarded her, his eyes intense, the heat from his body radiating like an aura around him. "If I allow you this knowledge, you will use it to bring glory to my reign?"

Neff's thoughts turned to "The Forty-Two Ideals of Maat," the scroll she'd recited over and over again in the House of Life. They were vows made to a goddess whose name she shared, and whose essence was truth.

She'd vowed that she wasn't guilty of sin, nor of wicked magic against the pharaoh.

Neff took a deep breath and sent a message to the heavens.

Forgive me, goddess.

"Everything I do," she said, "I do in your service, my prince."

The prince licked his lips. "Then there is nothing beyond your grasp, little priestess. All you desire, consider it yours."

"Thank you, my prince." Neff bowed, deeply enough that the prince could not see the emotional battle on her face. It was the struggle of a truth-teller who'd uttered a lie that would seed itself in her soul, be fruitful there, and multiply.

"I'm sorry to interrupt, Prince Meryamun," said a voice from behind her.

Neff was surprised to see two figures standing in the portal behind her. One wore a falcon mask, and the other the mask of a long-beaked ibis. Each of them carried a large ceramic jug in his arms.

The Heka priests, she thought with alarm, *you bring up the cat and it comes jumping.*

"Not to worry, Nefermaat," Meryamun said, mistaking her alarm for a childish fear of the strange-looking men. "The Heka priests are here to perform my ritual purification before the ceremony." He gestured for them to enter.

"Fresh water from the Iteru, my prince," said the one wearing the falcon mask, raising the jug for inspection. His gaze flicked to Neff, but only for a second. Either he didn't remember her or knew better than to question a girl under the prince's protection.

"Very good," the prince replied, and made his way to the gleaming copper basin sitting by a window. Stepping inside, the prince knelt while the two priests poured the contents of the jars over him, speaking sacred words. Neff watched the water roll over his shoulders, down his back and chest, cleansing him body and soul.

Is it really so easy to erase your sins? she wondered. Her lie was the first of many, that she knew. She scolded herself. *You must do whatever it takes to stop him. For Kenna. For Bubas. For Khetara.*

Still, she couldn't help but think that she would never feel clean again.

It felt strange being back at the Temple of Amun that afternoon. It had only been a day since Neff had left, and yet so much had changed. The atmosphere was akin to that of the Bast Festival, but multiplied a hundredfold. Festivals happen every year, but the coronation of a pharaoh? For most, that was a once-in-a-lifetime event.

Upon arrival, she was led through a throng of priests and priestesses making frantic last-minute preparations. Some of the Wabet passed by, dressed in translucent skirts and bead-net dresses. She waved to them, but they only turned to each other, whispered, and hurried on.

Nehshi crossed her path, and the young priest at least had the courtesy to acknowledge her.

"Nefermaat?" he said, his eyes wide. "Is that you?"

Is it? she thought.

She nodded.

A host of emotions passed over Nehshi's round face. Finally, he broke eye contact and bowed, keeping his head low until she'd passed by.

Neff's cheeks flushed. *I think I prefer being ignored.*

The attendants led her toward the side of the temple, where a wide platform had been prepared as the site for the ceremony. While Meryamun received blessings from Amun in the sanctuary and was anointed with sacred oils, she and the rest of the royal assembly gathered in the alcove adjacent to the platform, shielded from view by curtains hung from the roof high above. Beyond the curtains, Neff could hear the sound of a massive crowd, abuzz with anticipation.

Once the attendants touched up her face and hair, they dispersed to tend to other courtiers. Left on her own, Neff scanned the area. The tension she'd felt in the palace halls persisted in the crowd—if anything, it had increased. The concubines and servants that had been spared, newer additions or people close to Meryamun himself, huddled in groups, smiling nervously. The courtiers' moods, near and distant relations of the king and queen, seemed uncertain, as if they were waiting to see how things would play out. On the other hand, several of the palace officials and viziers seemed more at ease, drinking their wine with what looked like a sense of satisfaction, discreetly raising their cups to each other as if in congratulations for a job well done. Neff wondered how many of them had known all along what was going to happen.

Among the gathered flock, in the emptiness between one group and the next, Neff sensed the ghosts of the missing. She wondered how long it would take Meryamun to fill them with new acolytes. She thought of him in his chambers, the blessed waters pouring over his shining body, and thought:

Not long. Not long at all.

Queen Bintanath stood nearby with one of the two middle-aged attendants Neff had seen earlier. The queen's saffron-colored gown, accented with an amethyst-studded vulture-wing collar, was gorgeous. But her face, lovely as it was, was devoid of emotion. Her attendant offered her a painted goblet, which she took and drank, but her expression didn't change.

The queen had been much the same when the prince had presented Neff to her upon their arrival at the palace. It wasn't surprising, really. Within days, she'd lost her husband, her daughter had vanished, and her son—who'd had most of the king's court massacred—was preparing to take the throne.

Looking at her, Neff thought the queen was no different from the goblet in her hand. They were both beautiful, and both empty.

There was really only one person Neff wanted to see, and she found him on the outskirts of the crowd.

Despite being a prince, Kenna's costume was more austere than everyone else's. He had exchanged his priest's tunic for a robe that was fine but still white, and his only nod to the magnitude of the occasion was some kohl around his eyes and a gold pectoral featuring Anubis, the god of the dead. All around him, courtiers chatted quietly together, yet Kenna stood apart, silent and grave. When he noticed Neff looking at him, she glimpsed the hurt in his eyes before he turned away.

Considering the manner in which she'd left the temple, Kenna probably thought she'd seen the prince's offer as a step up from the monastic life of a priestess, as if the friendship between them had meant nothing at all.

Neff had anticipated this moment and taken a side trip to the temple gardens to retrieve something before rejoining the rest of the group in the courtyard. She held it in her palm as she slowly made her way toward Kenna. She could feel his eyes on her as she approached, but she kept her gaze elsewhere, like she was intending to retrieve a goblet of juice from a table behind him. She didn't want to be seen speaking to Kenna, or even standing too close to him, for fear of raising suspicions. But as she passed him, she reached out and slipped the little object from her hand to his.

Only after she'd picked up a drink from the table and moved back across the room did she chance a look in Kenna's direction. Sure enough, he was studying the object with a puzzled expression.

It was a tiny pomegranate, still green and unripe.

He looked back at her, and she clasped her hands together,

hoping he would understand her message. *Trust me, Brother*, she thought. *I am still with you.*

Kenna's confusion cleared, like sunlight breaking through the clouds. Almost imperceptibly, he smiled.

Just then, a ripple of excitement rolled through the crowd.

Meryamun was coming.

The courtiers parted to reveal the three Heka priests walking toward the platform. They were all bare-chested, their skin shining with oil, and they wore elegant, elaborately pleated schentis. A hush fell over the crowd as they processed, each carrying a sacred item in their hands—

The ibis-masked priest, carrying the royal crook.

The falcon-masked priest, carrying the royal flail.

And finally, the priest Herihor, wearing the mask of a horned ram, carrying the double crown of Khetara.

Behind them, resplendent in a blue and red schenti shot through with gold, a lion skin thrown over his shoulder, came the crown prince.

He was magnificent. The cuffs on his wrists and ankles, as well as his winged golden collar, were studded with rubies and sapphires that glinted in the sunlight. His already striking face had been expertly painted with rouge, kohl, and green malachite powder that brought out the color of his eyes. His nose was strong, his lips inviting. No longer simply a man, he seemed to descend from the heavens to walk among them, radiating his own golden light.

The sight of him seemed to clear much of the tension from the air. The men looked upon him with admiration, the women, desire. There was one sentiment they seemed to share, though—a heady mix of wonder, veneration, and dread.

Awe.

Neff felt it too. It would be so easy to fall at his feet, to explain away all the horrible things he'd said and done, and worship him. It was temptation of the highest order. It was the lure of a serpent's intoxicating, undulating dance.

Armor your heart, she told herself, fists clenched at her sides. *Remember why you're here.*

But when he stopped beside her, bending so that his luminous face was level with hers, and said, "Are you ready, little goddess?" Neff feared for her soul.

Lips trembling, she replied, "Yes, my prince."

The crowd shifted as a flustered, disheveled man pushed through them.

"Prince Meryamun!" he exclaimed. Neff could hardly believe it when she saw the man was Master Montuhotep.

What in the world has happened to him? she wondered.

"I've brought the ceremonial mace," he said quickly, lifting a weapon with a richly engraved pear-shaped head. "I would have been here sooner, but I was not summoned. There must have been a misunderstanding. Did your messengers not know where to find me? I've been managing the completion of your father's tomb."

"You were not summoned because you are not needed, High Priest," Meryamun said mildly. "I thought I made that clear during our last meeting. Although I appreciate you bringing the mace. We will need it for the unification ritual." He plucked the weapon from Montuhotep's hand.

Montuhotep blinked several times, as if he'd been slapped.

"Not needed?" he repeated. "But my prince, as high priest, it is my duty to participate in the coronation. Your father—"

"My father," the prince broke in, "is dead. As are his conventions. Today the sun sets on Amunmose's Khetara." He turned from the Master and toward Neff, placing the mace in her hands. "And rises on mine."

Montuhotep stared at her, speechless.

As Neff followed the Heka priests and the prince toward the platform, her last glimpse of the high priest was of the big man standing alone, his face reddened with indignation.

Meryamun gestured for Neff to stand next to him behind the priests.

"It's time," he said to the waiting attendants, and with bowed heads, they pulled the curtains aside.

Neff gasped.

After her experience at the Bast Festival, she thought she'd seen it all. But nothing could have prepared her for the great roar that met her ears or the teeming multitude that flowed over the land in every direction.

Neff's gaze flitted like a butterfly, unable to remain anywhere for more than an instant.

A sea of faces—men, women, children riding their fathers' shoulders—their mouths open and hands outstretched.

Garlands of purple cornflower and creamy jasmine draped over every statue in sight.

Potted palms and huge burning braziers decorated the platform, where a group of musicians and the Wabet began to play and dance, their bodies sinuous and full of grace.

It was as if the entire kingdom had gathered there to celebrate, all of them crying out for their glorious godling to lead them into a shining tomorrow.

Neff's attention was drawn to a face in the crowd. It seemed impossible to pick out a single person in the blurred masses, but she did. Maybe it was because everyone else was looking at the prince—but he was staring at her. Her breath caught in her throat.

"Yati?" she whispered.

When he caught her gaze, her father waved vigorously and shook Neff's mother by the shoulder. "Ahura!" Neff saw him say. "She sees us!"

Neff watched her mother's face light up as she began to wave too.

Shyly, Neff raised a hand and waved back, a swirl of emotions erupting within her. On one hand, the pride bursting from her father's face was everything she'd ever wanted. She watched him elbow those standing nearby in the crowd, pointing her out to them. She watched his lips form the words over and over again.

"That's my daughter! Do you see? That's my girl!"

Her mother, however, didn't look so well. She was gaunt, like a woman who had not eaten in weeks. She looked like she'd been deprived of the very thing that gave her life.

"Mamet," Neff whispered, suddenly feeling like a child who wanted nothing more than to fall into her mother's arms.

Armor your heart, she thought once more, smiling at her parents as she fought back tears. *Remember why you're here.*

Then Herihor, the ram-headed priest, stepped forward and raised his arms to the sky. The people fell silent.

"Praise to Amun, King of the Air, Mysterious of Form, God of All That Is Seen and Unseen. Today we rejoice in the ascension of your humble servant and messenger to the throne of Khetara."

Meryamun stepped forward, chin high, his body glistening with sacred oils.

"I name you," said the falcon-masked priest, "Horus of Gold, Divine of Appearance, Lord of the Two Lands." He handed him the crook.

"I name you," said the ibis-masked priest, "Mighty Bull, Arising in Thonis, He of the Two Ladies, Enduring in Kingship." He handed him the flail.

Neff had been watching this exchange when she was distracted by a flicker of light in the crowd, just below the platform. Three women stood together, three very strange women. They were dressed in ornate, extravagant gowns, one in white, one in black, and one in green. The woman in white was sand-skinned and pale eyed, and when she saw Neff look at her, she bowed her head. The woman in black was a somber reflection of the first woman, with eyes like deep pools and hair black as midnight. When she saw Neff's eyes meet hers, she put a finger to her lips. Both women's hair was dyed deep blue. The one in green was a mottled, stout old woman who gave Neff a too-wide smile and a knowing wink.

Are they performers? Dancers? If so, why aren't they up on the platform with the others?

She'd never seen the three women before, and yet something about them felt familiar. Neff felt her mind drift to that middle place between heaven and earth, to the center of the flame where her visions were born.

Her mind swimming, as if in a waking dream, she turned back to the coronation ritual, which was nearly complete.

"I name you," declared the ram-masked priest, who loomed larger than before, "Meryamun, Son of Amun, He Whose Face Is the Sun."

At this, the prince dipped his head, and the priest placed the double crown on his brow.

Neff watched the face of the priest change from a painted mask to a real ram's head, with long twisting horns and strange, horizontal eyes. Amun—or was it Khnum? They were both rams, after all. Perhaps one had led to the other, or perhaps they were one and the same: gods hidden within gods, streams all flowing to the same river.

Much is hidden.

"Arise, King of Khetara," boomed the priest.

But much will be revealed.

King Meryamun stepped up to her. Still in that surreal dreaming place, Neff flinched. The king blazed so brightly that her eyes hurt to look at him.

The sun shines, said a voice within her, *but it also burns*.

Had she heard that voice before? Those words? She couldn't be sure.

Meryamun took the ceremonial mace from her hands and turned to Kenna, who had advanced to the middle of the platform. Despite the brightness of the day, he stood in shadow. His was a soft inner glow, like moonlight. Two brothers—one dazzlingly bright, the other shrouded in darkness. They were incomplete, Neff realized. Without the princess, they were out of balance.

Where is she? Neff wondered, her mind drifting to the oracle. *Where is Sitamun?*

"As is tradition," Herihor announced, "the king and his brother will now conduct the unification ceremony. With this ritual, we honor our ancestors with a reenactment of the creation of our kingdom, when the first great pharaoh smote his enemy and united our two lands. With this ritual, may Khetara be victorious over her enemies forevermore!"

Kenna came forward and knelt before the new king. He placed his hands behind his back, like a prisoner awaiting execution. With relish, Meryamun took a handful of his brother's hair in his hand and pulled, forcing Kenna to look up at him. Then he raised the heavy mace above his head.

Kenna closed his eyes as if in prayer.

Neff's heart began to race. *It's pretend*, she told herself. *He won't hurt him.*

But she saw the pleasure in Meryamun's face, and she was afraid, and nearly cried out as the mace crashed down—

Before it could crush Kenna's skull, the mace stilled, harmlessly touching the top of Kenna's head like a kiss.

Meryamun released his grip on his brother's hair, and Kenna's head dropped in a pretense of death.

The crowd roared with approval.

Neff slumped with relief.

Meryamun set down the mace and took up his crook and flail. He raised his arms to the masses, drinking up their adulation. When he lowered them, the people quieted.

"People of Khetara," Meryamun boomed. "I come to you today not only as Pharaoh, but as a bearer of the truth. Beware! The truth has long been a stranger to this land, so your ears may not be accustomed to hearing it. But I believe in you. I believe you are strong enough to be tempered, not destroyed, in the heat of the truth. Am I correct, Khetara? Are you strong enough to hear my words?"

The people cheered.

Neff leaned forward, wondering what it was the king was about to say.

"Then here it is. Here is the truth," Meryamun said dramatically. "My father, may he live forever in the West, was a good man, and I feel his loss keenly. But people of Khetara, a good man does not always make a good king!"

A shocked murmur rippled through the crowd.

"He was, as I am now, a holy vessel," Meryamun went on. "However, I believe that in his later years, he turned a deaf ear to the word of the gods. Ruled by weakness and sloth, he allowed this once great kingdom to run fallow. Why do you think the land does not grow as it once did? Why does the river not flow as swiftly as it has in the past? Why do you suffer where once you thrived?

"Because when you offer nothing to the gods, you receive nothing in return. We have forgotten that only through strength and sacrifice can this kingdom reach its potential. Khetara has suffered in this drought for too long. But tomorrow, that drought will be over. Tomorrow, the season of inundation begins."

Neff felt that strange, otherworldly feeling intensify. Suddenly she was back in Bubas, standing before Bast's palanquin, visions of blood saturating her mind's eye.

Beware, for soon the Great River of Khetara will turn to blood.

"Tomorrow, the forgotten floodgates of power will be thrown wide, so the true might of this kingdom will once again flow free!"

The crowd cheered once more.

"Tomorrow, whosoever dares to oppose our great purpose will drown in the currents of war!"

Over the thundering masses, Neff heard the doleful words of the lamb.

Where once there was order, chaos will reign.

"Tomorrow," Mery thundered, "is the birth of a new Khetara!"

Neff staggered, feeling as if she were back in her vision, drowning in words and in blood.

Take heed, Thonis, Great House of Amun!
Take heed, Sakesh, Great House of Ra!
Beware! Sorrow and ruin to the Children of the Two Lands!

Neff gasped, and the dream shattered. She blinked, overwhelmed by noise and color and motion. The crowd was beginning to disperse. She looked to where the three strange women had been standing, but they were gone.

The coronation was over.

Meryamun turned to her, laying a bejeweled hand on her shoulder. "Are you all right, Nefermaat? You look pale."

She nodded. "Just overheated, my king."

"Too long in the sun?" Meryamun said, his radiance blinding.

"I think so."

"Then come. There is much still to do." He gestured for her to walk with the others back into the temple. "Feasts and celebrations long into the night, food like you've never eaten before, dance, music…"

Neff followed his lead, dazed and frightened. Already the people of Khetara, desperate for salvation, adored their brilliant young king. The truth of his wickedness sat heavy in her heart, like a stone she was meant to throw.

She thought about what he might mean when he spoke of sacrifice—and she shivered.

"We must have our fun now, little seer," Meryamun whispered in her ear. "In the morning, the work begins."

Neff squeezed her eyes shut and held fast to the truth. For it was not only a weapon—it was an anchor.

Yes, my king, Neff thought grimly, *in the morning the work begins.*

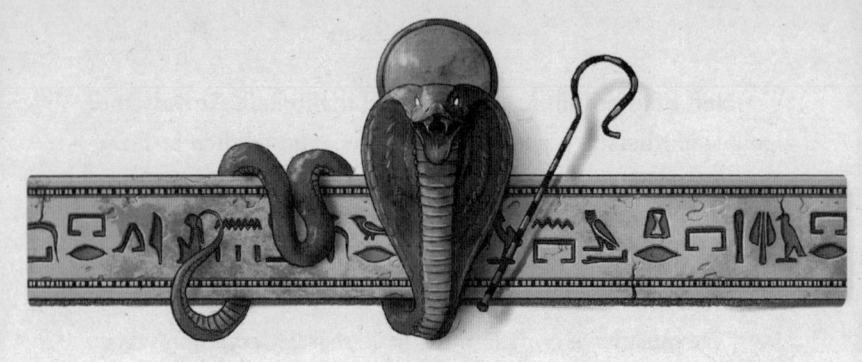

34
SITA

S ita saw it all.

When Karim sent her into the cave, she'd expected a pair of palace guards to descend into the valley, or maybe a band of robbers who'd smelled the smoke of their campfire on the wind. She'd huddled in the dark, her arms around Behkai, praying that Karim had been wrong about the noise, that it was an animal or his imagination running wild.

But her prayer must have fallen on deaf ears.

The creature seemed to appear out of nowhere, as if throwing off a cloak made of the night itself. It was a shambling, grotesque figure, crafted of nothing more than cloth and skin and bone. And yet, somehow it was moving toward Karim with slow, relentless steps.

Was this the mummy Karim had claimed to have woken from his tomb? Was this Setnakht?

Amun forgive me, she thought. *I should have believed him.*

Behkai struggled against her grip, but Sita held him fast. "No, boy," she whispered softly. "Please, you can't go out there…"

She saw Karim lunge toward the creature. She lost control of Behkai, and he raced out of the cave toward them. She nearly cried out when she heard the dog's terrified yelp a moment later.

Everything else happened very quickly.

The fire.

The blood.

The screams.

The crimson light.

She wondered if she'd imagined what came after that. How else could she explain it? The way the creature's desiccated flesh knit itself back together around Karim's bloody, still-pumping heart? The way the creature stretched its restored limbs once the light faded, like a man waking from a long sleep? How could such a thing be real?

Sita watched as the man, clothed in nothing but tatters, knelt by Karim's side. She heard him murmur something, but the words were too quiet for her to comprehend.

Then the man stood, and she could have sworn he sensed her presence. His flashing eyes lingered on the shadowy cave long enough for her legs to turn to water. She pressed herself against the cold stone wall, not daring to breathe.

Then he turned away and didn't look back as he climbed the ridge and left the valley.

Sita waited a long time, there in the dark. Her body was stiff with terror, and she worried that if she moved a single muscle, the monstrous man would reappear and find her.

Dawn broke on the horizon. She squinted into the light and thought, *I can't hide here forever. I have to go out there. I have to see.* So she struggled to her feet and slowly emerged from the shadows.

Sita staggered toward the gruesome tableau. In the campfire, a few embers still glowed orange among the ash.

Something black lay nearby, curled into a tight ball.

"Behkai?"

One of the dog's ears quirked at the sound of her voice. Slowly, he lifted his head.

Sita gasped. A mark had been burned into the left side of Behkai's face, leaving his fur the color of bone and his eye cloudy and pale. It was the exact size and shape of a man's hand.

Sita squatted in front of the dog and took his head in her hands. "What did that creature do to you?" she asked, her voice unsteady.

Behkai sniffed her and gave her face a slow, laborious lick, as if trying to comfort her even though he was the one who was hurt.

She watched the dog's eyes—one black, one white—shift from her face to the corpse behind her. His nose quivered. Then, with effort, Behkai rose to his feet, and made his way over to his master. From the corner of her vision, she saw the dog settle on his haunches near Karim's body, until he finally laid his great head on one booted foot and was still.

Sita didn't want to look. She didn't think she could bear to see him up close.

It's like Maet all over again, she thought. *But worse. So much worse.*

Sunlight spilled over the valley, illuminating every rock, every leaf, every thread of the blanket under which she'd been curled. Soon, there was no darkness left to hide what had happened there.

Sita squeezed her eyes shut.

I'll go mad. I can't do it. I can't. I can't!

But she did.

She looked.

Karim lay on his back, his arms splayed out on either side.

His stubbled, blood-spattered face was tilted to the sky, his lips slightly parted, his eyes open and sightless.

Hours ago, that same face had been lit by firelight and so alive.

"You can sleep now," he'd told her. "Don't worry, I'll keep watch through the night."

Her gaze drifted down. His robe and tunic had been ripped away, exposing his naked chest beneath.

Her stomach twisted and she put her hands on her knees to keep from falling.

She gagged and raised a hand to her mouth to stifle the scream.

There was so much blood.

It covered Karim's entire torso, spilling in dark rivulets down his belly and the curves of his hips. It flowed down his collarbones, pooling in the hollow of his throat. And within that wet burrow, beyond jagged, broken ribs and shredded pink flesh, there was—a void.

That monster, that man… had plucked out Karim's heart and discarded his body like a hollow shell.

Suddenly, Sita remembered the text she'd translated from Karim's stolen map.

Here lies Setnakht, his spirit indestructible, as powerful as a god. He shall not travel West, for his work is unfinished.

Sita paled as she recalled the final line. "'Flesh of an acolyte,'" she murmured, "Or maybe, 'heart?'"

Her eyes followed Setnakht's footsteps in the sand, leading off into the desert. If the ancient, fearsome king had gotten what he wanted, if he was truly alive once more, what would he do next?

Sita thought of what Karim had told her about the Oracle of the Lamb, and its grim portents of ruin, betrayal, and war. Of a river turned to blood. Looking back on her final days at the palace, leading to the events of that very night, she sensed that grisly river had already begun to flow.

It was so cruel. She'd finally confided in someone, and he'd confided in her. And even after she refused to help him with his quest, he'd still been kind.

I hope your story gets a happy ending.

Sita approached him on bare feet. Overwhelmed with grief and shame and despair, she fell to her knees beside Karim's ruined body and began to cry.

She tore at her hair—her beauty, her pride, but what did it matter now? The pain was good. She needed her body to suffer with her spirit. She rocked back and forth, the rhythm counting the seconds, the minutes, the eternity of her mourning. Not only for Karim, but for all who had been lost.

As she rocked, her two amulets swung in time with her movement, reminding her of Nebet's prayer.

The blood of Isis.
The spells of Isis.
The magic words of Isis.

Nebet, Nebet—where was she now? Was she safe? Was Kenna? Would she see any of them ever again?

She cursed the amulets. All this time, the scarab and Isis knot were supposed to protect her from harm. But what is suffering, if not harm? What good is a strong body with a broken heart?

Queen of the throne. Goddess of magic, Sita prayed. *Why have you forsaken me?*

Sita thought of the girl she'd been—lying by the fishpond, staring into the water and dreaming of love. Sita mourned her too. She was as dead as all the rest.

After a long while, the torrent of her tears slowed to a trickle. Her breathing evened. She had no idea what to do next, but she had to do something. Behkai needed her. The kingdom needed her. The problem, of course, was that she had no idea what to do. She was a princess, but what did that count for, alone there in the desert? What good was her royal blood without the power of the crown?

One thing at a time. The least I can do is give him a decent burial, she thought.

Sita wiped her eyes and sniffed. Gingerly, she grabbed the edge of Karim's singed, blood-soaked robe to cover his body when something slipped out of its folds and onto the ground beside her.

A large lapis amulet, carved in the shape of a scarab.

She picked it up. *Another one of his spoils,* she guessed, *stolen from some long-forgotten tomb.*

Brushing the sand from its surface, she saw that a shenu—the elongated oval that encircled names of pharaohs—was carved into one side. She'd seen its symbols before. Quite recently, in fact.

"Setnakht," she whispered.

The amulet wasn't from *some* tomb. It was from *his* tomb.

With trembling hands, she turned over the amulet and found more faint symbols engraved on the back.

It said: *This is the heart of a king.*

Sita stared at the blue stone in her hand, like a piece of the heavens come loose from the firmament. Suddenly, words and images began to flash through her mind, memories that, at the time, hadn't meant very much, but now joined together and gathered strength, like streams converging into a fast-flowing river.

Her father, sickly but alive: *When you're in* really *deep shit, you must seek something unexpected inside you.*

Mery, his hand on her cheek: *The priests must bend their noses to papyri to learn the ways of Heka. But not us. You and me, our very flesh is godsflesh. We have magic in our veins.*

Karim, telling her about some oracle in a dusty, forgotten temple: *You held a heart in your hands.*

And that mottled old woman, a too-wide smile stretching

across her face in the afternoon light: *Your words have power. When the time comes, remember that the word is the deed.*

The word is the deed.

Sita's skin prickled, up her spine and belly and into her chest, like a storm riding the western winds, filling her with a sensation that was both delicious and overwhelming.

Sita gasped as the sensation grew more and more powerful, and when she thought she could not take any more, it grew stronger still.

Was her skin glowing? Or was it simply the dawn's light?

She cried out, arching her back, but never letting go of the stone.

The light grew brighter. Like white fire that warmed but didn't burn.

She loved and hated this feeling. She wanted it to stop, and she never wanted it to stop.

And then—

The energy inside her body stilled. There was no sound anywhere, not a bird, not a hum over the dunes.

An unimaginable peace filled her. She felt light, both in weight and in radiance. She was herself, but something more too.

She looked down at Karim, at his defiled, empty body, and her peace was broken. Seeing him there, she was filled with displeasure. A piece of him had been stolen and spirited away. Such an insult must be remedied. Such an emptiness demanded to be filled.

She looked at the valley before her, and a voice called out to her from the earth and from the sky. A mother's voice. Not her own mother, but the mother of all. The first voice she ever heard, the voice of the one who named her.

The lamb.
The lamb.

The lamb.

The—

"I am tired of death," she said, the words strange to her ears. Her gaze drifted to the blue stone, which pulsed in her hand as if it were alive.

She turned back to Karim. "You can't die, tomb robber. I told you, I can't bear another death on my conscience." She spoke with an almost supernatural calm. "I can't do this alone, Karim of the Red Lands. Your story is not finished. This kingdom needs you."

The stone throbbed in time with her own heartbeat.

Thrum. Thrum. Thrum.

"I need you."

Sita pressed the amulet into the dark chasm of Karim's open chest.

"Come back to me!" she commanded.

There was a flash as sunlight lanced over the horizon. Behkai yelped in fright as a ring of force burst from the center of the valley, throwing waves of sand up into the air. Sita cried out as she was thrown backward. As she fell back to earth, her head struck the edge of a rock.

She knew nothing more.

Sita blinked and groaned. She lay on her back on the valley floor, her head aching. How much time had passed? It couldn't have been long. The position of the sun looked the same.

She tried to remember what happened, but her memory was foggy. She remembered an overwhelming sensation, words and images, the amulet…

The amulet!

With a gasp, she struggled up to her elbows.

Karim was sitting up in front of her, staring off into the growing daylight. His body was still soaked in blood, but the gaping wound in his chest had knit back together beneath a scarab-shaped scar.

At her movement, Karim turned to her, and his eyes flashed with an otherworldly light.

"Sitamun," he said, his voice low and frightened. "What have you done?"

EPILOGUE
PAWS

The palace had become very noisy of late, and the cat did not like it. She was accustomed to the regular rhythms of days past, but recently, her sleep, appetite, and even her morning ablutions had all been thrown off course. Voices rang out all day and night, and heavy-footed men paraded everywhere with no regard for paws or tails. What was worse, no one spared a single moment for a back scratch.

It was terribly inconsiderate, really. Of everyone.

She missed the company of the young women who used to sleep in the ladies' chambers, and the little girl who'd sneak plates of meat to her after evening meals. They'd all gone, leaving her to sleep alone in cold, empty beds.

After a particularly fitful night in her old rooms, the cat decided to find a new place to call home. The palace was large; surely there was somewhere worth her time.

The throne room wouldn't work. It was constantly full of people yammering on about war and trade and a princess mislaid. Besides, the bright-eyed man with flashing teeth was there. Predators knew well enough not to tread on each other's territories.

The rooms below were equally unsuited for her needs. One of them smelled too much like death, even for her taste, and others were full of filthy men and women, guarded and hobbled like cattle. One of them actually smelled like cattle and soil. She liked that one. He was missing a hand, but used the other to give her a scratch behind the ears. Still, that place was dark and dirty and smelled like fear—no place for a cat, surely.

The pleasure garden was too hot.

The main hall had no soft places on which to sleep.

She had almost given up hope entirely when she came upon a bedchamber newly inhabited. Poking her head past the curtain, the cat peered in. A girl sat upon a floor cushion. She'd seen her before at the temple. The girl was surrounded by all manner of curiosities. There were stacks of rolled papyri, tiny alabaster jars and pink limestone bottles, amulets in red and blue and green, bits of wax, an oil lamp, a hippopotamus tusk...

The cat's nose prickled. Here it smelled like power. It smelled of smoke and honey and wine.

The girl held a scroll, but she wasn't looking at it. Instead, her eyes were on the open window, her gaze toward the golden horizon. In front of her, perhaps the only homely object in the room, was a small crooked twig.

It was only after the cat entered, and her paw crinkled one of the scrolls, that the girl's reverie was broken.

"Oh!" she said to her visitor. "Well, hello again. Aren't you a pretty kitty?"

Why yes, thought the cat. *As a matter of fact, I am.*

"Would you like to stay with me a while?" the girl asked. "I don't really know anyone here yet, and I could use a friend."

The cat considered the girl. She was hairless, which was odd, but not unpleasant. Perhaps, like a newborn kit, she needed tending. She gave the girl a tentative sniff. Despite her baldness, there was something strangely feline about her. All cats were touched by the goddess, and it smelled as if this girl had been too.

After some hesitation, the cat flicked her tail in assent, and rubbed her face against the girl's outstretched hand.

"Can I tell you something?" the girl asked, stroking the cat's back just the way she liked it.

It was natural, of course, to tell cats secrets. They were very good at keeping them. The cat suspected that the girl, in her own way, was also a keeper of secrets.

"I had the strangest dream last night," the girl went on. "There was a lion with wings, a snake shedding its skin, and a blue beetle shining with light… What do you think it means?"

The cat merely purred.

The girl shook her head, as if shrugging off a chill, and returned her attention to the scroll in her hand. "Well, I can't worry about that now. I have work to do."

And so, she lit the oil lamp, took up the hippopotamus tusk, and began to read.

"'Amun,'" she recited, "'Open to me your hidden places. Bast, open to me your power and your secrets. Maat, open to me the truth of all things. Isis, open to me the names of all things. Heka, open to me the words and ways of magic. Open my eyes, bless me with your wisdom, and I shall be your humble vessel on this earth.'"

The girl read on, moving the tusk over the twig in complex gestures, pausing, then continuing.

The cat's ears prickled with interest. *This is a good place*. The girl in white was comfortable, warm, and most of all—curious. And that curiosity, well, that was irresistible.

Finally, the girl spat on the twig and waited.

After a long, tense moment, the twig began to twitch, sinuous, serpentine.

Then, it stopped.

The girl beamed, her eyes bright with excitement, and began again.

The cat sauntered over to a cushion and turned her body round and round before settling herself down to watch. She couldn't wait to see what happened next.

SERIES GUIDE

SETTING

KHETARA: The united kingdom of two lands, High Khetara in the north and Low Khetara in the south. High Khetara consists of the delta region, and Low Khetara the more mountainous, arid region.

THE RIVER ITERU: The lifeblood of Khetara that runs south to north in the middle of the kingdom, feeding the crops on either side of its banks and acting as a trade route to other kingdoms.

THONIS: The capital of High Khetara and location of the royal palace.

BUBAS: A village southeast of Thonis, sacred home of the goddess Bast and her temple.

SAKESH: A city in Low Khetara, still crippled by the impact of Unification.

THE RED LANDS: The western desert outside of the borders of Khetara, where nomadic tribes live.

CHARACTERS
(IN ORDER OF APPEARANCE)

FROM THONIS:

QUEEN BINTANATH: Great Wife to Amunmose and mother of the triplets Sita, Mery, and Kenna.

NEBET: Attendant to the queen—and later, to the princess.

PRINCESS SITAMUN A.K.A. "SITA": Seventeen-year-old daughter of Amunmose and Bintanath, sister to Mery and Kenna.

FEMI: A young palace guard.

KING AMUNMOSE: Pharaoh of Khetara, husband to Bintanath (among many other lesser wives), father of the triplets.

MAET: Six-year-old daughter of one of Amunmose's lesser wives and half sister to the triplets.

PRINCE MERYAMUN A.K.A. "MERY": Seventeen-year-old son of Amunmose and Bintanath, brother to Sita and Kenna.

MASTER MONTUHOTEP: High priest of Amun and Hour priest.

HERIHOR: Head Heka priest at the Temple of Amun.

PRINCE BAKENAMUN A.K.A. "KENNA": Seventeen-year-old son of Amunmose and Bintanath, brother to Sita and Mery, and a Sem priest in the House of Amun.

TADIA: Amunmose's favorite concubine.

KING SEMATAWY (DECEASED): The Great Uniter—the High Khetaran king who preceded Amunmose. Went to war with Low Khetara during his reign and slaughtered the southern king, King Rahotep, in order to unite the Two Lands under the double crown.

NEHSHI: A young novice priest.

############################ **FROM BUBAS:** ############################

NEFERMAAT A.K.A. "NEFF": A thirteen-year-old common girl.
AHURA: Neff's mother.
PEPI: Neff's father, a spell vendor.
HENHEN AND ISTARA: Neff's friends.
MISTRESS KARO: The powerful high priestess in charge of the Temple of Bast.

############################ **FROM SAKESH:** ############################

RAETAWY A.K.A. "RAE": Nineteen-year-old farm girl, daughter of Ankhu, and occasional street fighter.
BUTO: A street fighter.
OMARI: Rae's best friend, a nineteen-year-old carpenter, and part-time rebel.
TAMERIT A.K.A. "TAM": A twenty-year-old weaver.
MAMET MUT: Head of the weavers and town gossip.
ANKHU: Rae's father, ex-scribe, and wheat and cattle farmer.

THE NOMARCH: Sakesh's governor, elected by King Amunmose.
BAKI: A local shepherd with a young family.
ASIM: Leader of the Horizon rebels.
MENK: Asim's right-hand man.
KING RAHOTEP (DECEASED): The last king of Low Khetara before the war of Unification. Slaughtered by King Sematawy along with most of his court.

FROM THE RED LANDS:

KARIM: A nineteen-year-old tomb robber—one of the group that call themselves the Jackals.
HAGER: One of the Jackals.
BABU: Twenty-one-year-old leader of the Jackals.
DJET: A thirteen-year-old boy, the newest member of the Jackals.
PASENHOR A.K.A. "PA": An old priest of Khnum.
BEHKAI: Pa's dog—then Karim's dog.
SETNAKHT: An ancient pharaoh whose name was erased from history—only to be rediscovered a thousand years after his death.

GODS

AMUN: The blue-skinned invisible creator god of air and mystery—also known as the Hidden One. Like Khnum, he is sometimes seen with a ram's head.

ANUBIS: The jackal-headed god of funerary rites and guide to the underworld.

BAST/SEKHMET: The cat-headed goddess of pleasure and women's secrets. She can also appear with a lioness head as Sekhmet, goddess of war, to represent her more savage aspect as a defender and protector from evil.

HEQET: The frog-headed goddess of fertility and the final stages of childbirth, and the wife of Khnum.

HORUS: The falcon-headed son of Isis and Osiris, who avenged his father's death by defeating Set in battle. The Eye of Horus (the wedjat) is considered to be a protective symbol.

ISIS: The Great Mother, goddess of magic and kingship, protector of the kingdom. She is sister to Nephthys and wife of Osiris.

KHEPRA: The scarab-headed god of creation and renewal, as in the progression of the sun across the sky each day.

KHNUM: The ram-headed Divine Potter god who is said to have molded man from clay on the Great Wheel. He can sometimes be represented as a lamb.

NEPHTHYS: Protector goddess of darkness, childbirth, and magic. Sister to Isis, wife of Set.

OSIRIS: The green-skinned god of the dead, Judge and Lord of the Underworld. Husband to Isis, who resurrected him after he was killed by his brother, Set.

RA: God of the noonday sun, order, and kings, and thought to be Khetara's first pharaoh. He is portrayed in many different forms, including a falcon, a scarab, a man, and, while in the underworld, a ram.

SET: The god of chaos, storms, the desert, and the color red. Portrayed with the head of a strange canine-like black animal. Seen as a villain among gods but worshipped by certain sects.

SOBEK: Fierce crocodile-headed god of the Iteru River.

TERMINOLOGY

HEKAT: A Khetaran measurement, as in for crops.
KALASIRIS: A type of simple, close-fitting dress.
KHAMSIN: A hot, dry desert wind.
MAMET AND YATI: Mama and Papa.
MEDJAY: The police force in Khetara.
MUTU: A spirit who does not move on to the afterlife and is left to wander the earth.
NUNU: A very young child or toddler.
SCHENTI: A short pleated skirt worn by Khetaran men.
SEN/SENA: Brother/sister.
SHEDEH: Fermented pomegranate juice.
SHEMSU HOR: An event during which the pharaoh travels throughout Khetara to visit the people and assess the kingdom.
SISTRUM: A rattle-like instrument used for sacred ceremonies and rituals.
WEDJAT: The protective Eye of Horus.
ZEBU: Humpbacked Khetaran cattle.

TYPES OF PRIESTS:

HOUR: Those who interpret dreams and make predictions about the future.
HEKA: Those who utilize spells, wands, and rituals for magical purposes.
SEM: Those who conduct funerary rites and embalming for the dead—otherwise known as "Men of Anubis."
WAB (WABAU/WABET): Lower-rank novice priests/priestesses, sometimes healers.

AUTHOR'S NOTE

This book is the result of a lifelong passion for ancient Egypt. Both of my parents and three of my grandparents were born in Egypt, so I grew up surrounded by sepia-toned images of my family in Cairo and Heliopolis, eating Egyptian food and hearing stories of their lives there. From a young age, I began learning as much as I could about Egypt's ancient history, an epic filled with brilliance, mystery, incredible achievements, and magic. Through the creation of this book, I have learned a lot—but what I know now is still only a tiny fraction of the history of a kingdom that spanned five millennia, a single pinprick of light in a constellation of marvels. I am so grateful that this series has allowed me the time and space to continue my education.

The kingdom of Khetara is a fantasy world, but its religion, culture, geography, and history are closely based on ancient Egypt itself. I was deeply inspired by many primary and secondary sources, including stories from the Westcar Papyrus, the Papyrus of Ani (currently the finest example of *The Book of the Dead*); the Amarna period and Akhenaten, the "Heretic King"; worshippers of Set in Avaris; and most of all, the Oracle of the Lamb, an ancient prophetic text from AD 4. Thank you to all the amazing Egyptologists whose work over the centuries made these texts available for the modern reader. I used many different books and digital sources for research, but I want to pay particular homage to Bob Brier—both for his lecture series on the history of ancient Egypt and his book *Ancient Egyptian Magic*, and to the late great

Barbara Mertz (a.k.a. Elizabeth Peters) for her book *Red Land, Black Land: Daily Life in Ancient Egypt*. Those three sources were instrumental in the development of this novel and were truly the sparks that lit the fire of my imagination.

They say you should write the book you want to read, and I certainly did that with *His Face Is the Sun*. As a humble student of Egyptology, I also wrote it in hopes that readers would find within its pages their own passion for ancient Egyptian history and be inspired to learn more about one of the greatest kingdoms ever to exist on this earth.

Because reading and writing were reserved for the holy and the powerful, the ancient Egyptians viewed writers as magicians. Like the gods, they created life out of nothing—and not just any kind of life, because unlike people, words lived forever. I am incredibly grateful to have had the opportunity to send these words of mine out into the world, and it is my greatest hope that they will continue to reach readers for many years to come so that they too can smell the smoke-and-honey-and-wine-scented wind and—even just for a little while—believe in magic.

Michelle Jabès Corpora
May 2025

ACKNOWLEDGMENTS

Talk about a dream come true! Although it is the tenth novel I've published, and although I love each and every one of those books, *His Face Is the Sun* is the most ambitious and most personal story I've ever written. There are so many people to thank for giving me both the opportunity and the courage to write this book. The first of those, the person who was with me the moment this idea was conceived is my incredible agent, Allison Hellegers. Alli, without your constant faith and expertise, none of this would have been possible. Thanks so much to you and to everyone at Stimola Literary Studio for your unwavering support. Next, I want to thank Annette Pollert-Morgan, Jenny Lopez, Karen Masnica, Lia Ferrone, Delaney Heisterkamp, and the entire team at Sourcebooks for believing in Throne of Khetara from day one. Annette, your editorial brilliance and infectious exuberance made me smile through the toughest writing days and taught me so much about how to be a better novelist. Huge thanks as well to Lizzie Clifford and everyone at Hachette UK for their passionate dedication to the series, and to all the other publishers across the world who took the plunge on Khetara and on me. In the same vein, massive thanks to Clementine Ahearne, Elizabeth Guess, and everyone at the Intercontinental Literary Agency, as well as Friedericke Belder and the whole team at Schlueck Agency, for doing an amazing job representing Khetara to the international market. And to Jason Dravis, thank you for seeing something great in this series and for taking me under your exceptional wing.

To Tom Roberts and Micaela Alcaino, thank you both for giving this book such beautiful, shining faces—your cover designs bring tears of joy to my eyes every time I see them. I will be admiring your artwork for the rest of my life. And to artists Gerralt Landman and Bassel Elkadi, thank you for illustrating the world and the characters of Khetara so brilliantly! To my dedicated beta reader, Heather Allen, thank you for your astute observations and suggestions and for being one of the first people to read the rough draft of this book and tell me that it was something special. To my jiu jitsu teammates and coaches at Crazy 88 MMA, especially my great friend and coach Nathan Allen, thank you for convincing me that I could do impossible things, for making me strong, and for teaching me what it feels like to be thrown on the ground repeatedly. (They say to write what you know!) To my sister, Nikki, thank you for being both a beta reader and a cheerleader for this series and for me, always. I love you, big sis. And to the rest of my wonderful family on both sides—all the Jabèses, Stones, Finkelsteins, Corporas, Mszanskis, and Rihns—and to my lifelong friends, thank you for always being there to support my writing career over the years. To my mom and dad, thank you for your ever-present, unconditional love and for being the inspiration for this series. I hope you know that your touch is on every page. And Ma—I'll never forget that lunch we shared at Memories, the day I got "the call." Thanks for being with me every step of the way. To my beautiful daughters, Gwen and Ellie, thank you for your hugs and kisses, for the cups of tea, and for always bringing me my stuffed alligator when I needed it most. I hope one day you'll look back on all this and remember that when it comes to dreams, anything is possible. And finally, to my husband, Adam, thank you for the pep talks, the brainstorms, the celebrations; thank you for bragging about me to strangers in the mall; thank you for always finding my books in the bookstores and sending me videos of you pointing at them; thank you for vacuuming and doing the laundry and cleaning the bathrooms and taking the girls to their appointments when I was too busy or too tired; thank you for being the best business and life partner anyone could wish for and for giving me the space I needed to create a world in our little loft upstairs. Elk loves you, dear. We did it!

Photo © Adam Corpora

Michelle Jabès Corpora is the author of many novels for middle grade and young adult readers. A lifelong bibliophile, Michelle has worked as an editor and concept creator in children's fiction for eighteen years. Michelle's parents and three of her grandparents were born in Egypt, and her family's stories about their lives there sparked an interest in ancient Egyptian history from a very young age. That enduring passion was the inspiration for this series. In her spare time, Michelle trains as a blue belt in Brazilian jiu jitsu at Crazy 88 MMA and plays Dungeons & Dragons with her friends. She lives in Maryland, USA with her husband and two daughters.

Follow Michelle on Instagram @michellejcorpora or visit her at michellejcorpora.com.